NO

Mother

of Mine

A Novel by

P.J. HOWELL

No Mother of Mine

Copyright © 2012 Paula J. Howell

All rights reserved.

This is a work of fiction. Names, characters, businesses, places, events and incidents are either the products of the author's imagination or used in a fictitious manner. Any resemblance to actual persons, living or dead, or actual events is purely coincidental.

ISBN: 1479170747
ISBN-13: 978-1479170746

DEDICATION

To my family, the best anyone could ask for:

To my husband, Carl, who has believed in me from the very beginning and who has never faltered in his own dedication towards me, and to my sons, Jordan and Conner, who have shown nothing but love and support...the three of you mean more to me than words could ever express. And to the rest of my family, who have helped me in one way or another, big or small, through thick and thin, with support, thoughts and prayers...thank you from the bottom of my heart. I love and appreciate every single one of you.

NO
Mother
of Mine

A
Jorja Matthews
Mystery

~Prologue~

She awkwardly carried the bundles wrapped in the sheet as she left the house by the back door. She partially stumbled down the stone steps before walking down the garden path. It began to drizzle but she felt nothing; not the rain, not the pain and no compassion for what she held in her arms. She was no longer any resemblance to the person she had been just a few days before. She was lost, both in mind and in spirit, and had no strength to stop the manic identity that had taken over her. She reached the back of the rose garden and knelt down on the ground, laying the bundles down as she rested her knees in the dirt. Her thin white cotton gown began to sag from the rain and her wet hair hung limp around her face. The sheet was now soiled from the garden dirt along with the blood she had earlier wiped from her legs. She used her bare hands to begin digging a hole between the red rose and the yellow rose bush, her favorite. Once the hole seemed big enough, she reached into the sheet to grab a tin filled with items she no longer wished to keep. She threw the tin into the freshly dug hole and reached for the sheet. A tiny hand suddenly sprang from one half of the bundled sheet and then a small cry rang out. It startled her. She thought her sins had been forced on the little ones and that they had not drawn any breath at all. The second bundle began to kick at the sheet and also began to cry. She felt confused but as insane thoughts rushed through her head, she understood from those thoughts that she would have to take responsibility for her sins. To take responsibility would mean to give back that which she should never have had in the first place. She reached down to pick up one of the bundles, never for a moment thinking a rational thought regarding what she was about to do. She wrapped the sheet more snugly and then held the bundle tightly against her chest. She could feel movement only slightly but as she held the bundle even tighter, the movement soon stopped.

"What are you doing?!" The rain muffled the sound of footsteps so that she was startled to hear the voice yelling at her from behind.

She turned to face her intruders, but in her state of mind she was barely able to recognize who they were. "I am taking responsibility for my sins," she said to her father.

"Is that the baby? What do you think you are doing?" Her father reached down and forcibly took the baby from her arms.

Standing next to her father, her mother shrieked, "What did she do?!" Her mother began to cry as she turned to her and said, "My God, what have you done?"

She did not believe her mother's question deserved a response, so she did not reply.

Her father grabbed her arm and pulled her up off the ground. She looked away from him as he questioned her. "*What* have you *done*?" Having already disassociated herself from what had been hers, she pulled her arm from his grasp and walked away to sit on a nearby bench.

Her father quickly opened the sheet to get a look at the baby wrapped inside. "Oh, please, God, let the baby be okay." As he attempted to determine the fate of the one he held in his arms, he heard a cry from the other half of the bundled sheet still on the ground.

Her mother bent down to open the sheet. "There's another one? She had twins?" Her father then spotted the freshly dug hole near the yellow rose bush. As his wife picked up the second baby, he held the first baby in a protective hug and quietly wept as he began to understand the horror of what his daughter had been about to do.

CHAPTER 1

Jorja Matthews choked back sobs as she briskly walked down the sidewalk from her office towards a nearby coffee shop. She tried to regain her composure before other pedestrians saw her distress. As she wiped away the tears and ran her coat sleeve under her nose, she kept up her quick gait towards the coffee shop two blocks away. Her best friend, Taylor Bishop, was a barista at the coffee house and Jorja desperately needed to see Taylor after receiving distressing news. She knew Taylor would have some comforting words to say about her recent predicament.

"Nate told you what?!" Taylor looked around the coffee shop to see if she had startled anyone with her outburst after hearing what Jorja had to say. There were a few patrons but they only gave her a quick glance. Taylor turned back to Jorja and fiercely said, "I *cannot believe* they are letting you go! You've been there for what? Six years? I thought Nate said you were the best legal assistant he's ever had. What possible reason does he have to let you go?"

Jorja wiped at a tear as it escaped down her cheek. "He said he had to let me go because the firm isn't doing well. The lease at the office was just renewed at a higher amount and they are earning less revenue while incurring additional expenses. He offered me severance pay for the rest of this month and also for next month while I look for another job. Really, there's nothing I can do about it." As Jorja spoke she felt her face begin to flush again and she worried she might begin sobbing at the table. "Can you just go make me a cinnamon latte so I can sit here and lick my wounds in comfort for awhile?"

Taylor got up from the table but as she walked behind the counter she said, "Okay, no problem on the latte but don't be too sure I won't leave here on my break to egg Nate's car."

Jorja was not surprised at Taylor's statement. She might have laughed at Taylor's reaction and apparent need to protect her, but not today. "Don't you dare, Taylor. I'd be embarrassed to think you would do that. Don't even think about it." Jorja had to stop herself from shaking a finger at Taylor's mischievous thoughts. She wondered why her anger did not match Taylor's but as she thought more about her current dilemma, she knew Nate was only doing what he thought was right for the firm. If she were in his shoes, she would probably do the same. She came to the decision to accept what hand she had been dealt. She just had to figure out what to do next.

As she watched Taylor skillfully fix her a latte, Jorja asked, "Hey, are they hiring here?"

Taylor looked at Jorja with a grin and replied, "What? You think because you went to school to learn how to expertly draft up legal pleadings you can just waltz in here and make a great cup of Joe?" Taylor then winked and said, "At least you have one thing in your favor...you know how to deal with difficult and impatient people."

Jorja could not help but return Taylor's smile as she teased, "That's a good point, Taylor. I've been putting up with you for quite a few years and that alone should make me qualified for the job."

Taylor's mouth pouted as she pretended to be wounded by the statement, causing Jorja to chuckle. Although the loss of her job was still distressing, Jorja accepted the latte from Taylor with a lighter heart.

~ ~ ~

After cleaning out her desk and saying her goodbyes at the office, Jorja drove the short distance home and was welcomed with quick barks and a happy whine from Piper. Piper was a lab mix but what the mix was, Jorja wasn't quite sure. After finding Piper on the side of the road more than a year ago, she would never forget how angry she felt after discovering someone had struck Piper with a car and left her for dead. Her anger had changed to relief after a vet informed her Piper was weak and dehydrated but that her injuries were not life threatening. When no one stepped forward to claim Piper, Jorja decided to adopt her. She never regretted the impulse to adopt Piper, who never failed to make her day, regardless of how badly the day went.

As Jorja entered the house, she placed her bag, jacket and office mementoes on the living room couch before moving into the kitchen to make a cup of tea. She decided against dinner, having no appetite after such a difficult day but Piper's stare clearly demonstrated her appetite was in full force. The phone rang just as Jorja began to gather what she needed to feed Piper.

"Hello?" Not bothering to look at the caller I.D., Jorja knew it was her mother who never failed to call just about every evening after work.

"Hi honey, how was your day?" Jorja had forgotten how emotions could erupt upon hearing the voice of a parent after the occurrence of a stressful situation. She tried her best to stop the tears and choke back a sob as she told her mother about losing her job. Helen Matthews had always been good at listening and Jorja was thankful for her mother's ability to hold back motherly advice when it wasn't needed.

"Oh, honey, I'm so sorry about your job. I cannot believe they had to let you go, especially after all the time you've been with the firm. What are you going to do? Are there any other firms hiring?"

"I don't know, Mom. I doubt there are any other local firms hiring right now because many of them are in the same situation. I'm sure if there are any possible jobs, I will get a great reference from the firm."

Jorja heard her mother sigh heavily over the phone. "You know I'm here for you and I wish I could be there to give you a big hug rather than try to comfort you over the phone. What will you do the rest of the week? Do you want to come up and stay with your dad and me?"

Her first thought was that it sounded like a good idea but she quickly decided she needed to face what had happened rather than run to her parents to be consoled. "No, that's okay. I'll stay here. I have some chores around the house I've been putting off so I will tackle those while I look for another job."

"Okay, honey, but you make sure to call me if you need to talk. On the other hand, I could drive down tomorrow and stay with you for the week. How does that sound?"

Oh boy, she thought, *Mom to the rescue.* She loved her mother but right now she did not want to be smothered with mother-pity. Her mom meant well but there were times she treated Jorja like fragile glass.

"No, Mom, I'm okay. I have plenty to keep me busy around the house while I look for another job. I'll be okay and maybe I'll drive up to see you and Daddy next weekend."

As she hung up the phone after saying goodbye, Jorja wondered if she had just lied to her mother. She now had doubts about how she was going to hold herself together as she adjusted to this unexpected turn of events.

CHAPTER 2

Jorja was very frustrated with the limited number of jobs available in the area, especially those even closely related to her field. Two weeks had already passed since the firm let her go and she realized she was up against a very daunting task. She spent yet another morning scanning the paper and online job listings before moving on to her to-do list. The quaint two-story two-bedroom rental house was small but it was the perfect size for her and Piper. Jorja eventually wanted to own her own home and she had been saving money towards a down payment but now, without a secure job, she wondered if she'd ever be able to save enough.

Things will get better and eventually it will happen, she thought as she tried to think positive. She was unwilling to give into the desire to just lie on the couch and sleep off the depression she feared she could be headed towards. Pulling her chin length auburn hair back into a small ponytail, she thought about what she could do around the house. Her hair wasn't long enough to make a decent pony but while working at home, she didn't care how her hair looked, only that it stayed out of her face while she was working. For good measure she grabbed her favorite Seattle Mariners baseball cap and put it on to completely hold her hair in place. Jorja thought back to when she bought the baseball cap and realized it had been too long since she and her dad had gone to a Mariner's game.

Jorja turned her attention to her to-do list, noting some of the items had been there for a few months. It struck her how much of a procrastinator she had become.

She peeked down at Piper lying on the floor with her muzzle resting on her paws. "Okay, Piper, what should we start with first?" At the sound of her name, Piper's head popped up.

Taking one more look at the list, she said, "Let's get the windows over with before it gets warm outside." Once the comment slipped out, a question suddenly struck her. *I wonder if other people speak to their pets the way I speak to my dog?*

She dug the Windex out from under the sink, grabbed a role of paper towels and got to work on the larger windows in the living room. After cleaning the second window, she was thrilled to be interrupted as she heard a knock at the door before Taylor yelled, "Knock knock, you decent?" Jorja barely had time to climb off the back of the couch before Taylor burst into the room.

"Hey, how are you doing? I see you're keeping busy." Taylor said as she gave Jorja a hug. Dressed in jeans and a t-shirt with *Twilight* characters on the front, Taylor demonstrated her love for any type of vampire movie, although *Twilight* was by far Taylor's favorite series.

"Yeah, I'm keeping busy. I'm doing okay." Jorja wasn't surprised Taylor stopped by to check on her and she was glad for the distraction.

Taylor placed her hands on her hips as she looked around the room and said, "What do you need done? Whatever it is, I'm here to help."

Jorja found Taylor's offer tempting. "Well, the windows need to be cleaned, I need to replace the screen door on the back door, I have some outside plants I'd like to repot and then I need to start digging through the old garden shed to see what I should keep and what I just need to throw away."

Taylor pretended to look at a non-existent watch on her wrist and said, "Gee, look at the time, I forgot I have to donate blood." Taylor giggled and then winked at Jorja before saying, "No problem, I'll help you. Just offer up a cold drink, your ice tea would be great if you have any, and then maybe you can also make me lunch."

Jorja did not hesitate to accept Taylor's offer. She was thankful not only for the help but for the company. Taylor was a true friend who knew when Jorja needed her.

After the windows, screen door and plants were taken care of they decided to take a break to eat before tackling the garden shed. As they ate lunch Taylor could no longer resist asking, "So what do you think you will do about a job?"

Jorja shrugged. "I don't know yet. There really aren't many jobs available, especially in my field or for the pay I earned. The severance pay Nate gave me won't go very far so I may have to dip into my house savings just to get by."

Taylor patted Jorja's hand as she said, "It will all work out. This is just a hiccup in life you have to deal with, that's all."

"Thanks, Taylor. I'm sure you're right." Jorja finished the last of her tea, stood up and then with a smile she asked, "Okay, are you ready to tackle the dirt and spiders to see what's hidden in the back of that garden shed?"

Taylor's *least* favorite thing in the world was any chore dealing with "tackling spiders" but she had agreed to help. "I'm as ready as I'll ever be but you get to go in first!"

~ ~ ~

Jorja and Taylor were placing items from the garden shed into separate piles in the yard when they heard the phone ringing in the kitchen.

"Whew! Break time!" Taylor uttered with excitement, glad to escape from the cobweb-infested shed.

"I'll be right back." Jorja said before she ran into the house and grabbed the receiver. "Hello?"

"Jorja, its Mom."

"Oh, hi Mom. You should see what Taylor and I are doing. I'm finally cleaning out the old garden shed. You won't believe all the stuff I have in that shed. I think I should have a yard sale to get rid of a bunch of stuff. Maybe you could come down and help me? I can schedule a date--"

"Jorja. I need to tell you something."

"What? Is everything okay?" She waited for her mother's response but Helen remained silent.

A sense of dread came over Jorja as she hesitantly asked, "What's wrong? Is it Dad?" She felt her chest tighten at the possibility that something had happened to her father.

Helen finally answered, "No, it's not your father. It's your Aunt Gloria." Jorja heard her mother choke back a sob. Gloria was her mother's younger sister.

"What about Aunt Gloria? Is she all right?"

"I'm afraid not, Jorja. She's had an accident. I don't have all the details yet but it appears she may have had some sort of attack while she was driving, a stroke possibly. Her car left the road and struck a tree."

Jorja's hand tightened on the receiver. "Oh my God, Mom, is she okay? Where is she?"

She could hear her mother crying softly as she said, "She's gone, Jorja. Whether from a stroke or the accident, I don't know but she's...gone." Helen then broke down sobbing and Jorja, who had been holding back tears herself, also began to cry.

"Mom, I am so, so sorry. I will drive up tomorrow to stay with you and help with the funeral arrangements, okay?" Having no tissue nearby, Jorja grabbed a hand towel to wipe the tears from her cheeks.

"Honey, if you can come up, I would appreciate it. I didn't want to ask but I really do need help with everything that will need to be done."

"That's okay. I will drive up first thing in the morning. Do you mind if I bring Piper with me?"

"First thing tomorrow is fine and yes, bring Piper with you since I'm not sure how long it will take to make all the arrangements. I will see you tomorrow. Love you and drive safe."

"I love you too, Mom. I will see you tomorrow but if you need to talk, call me, okay? I don't care what time it is, you call me."

As she hung up the phone and wiped again at the tears on her cheeks, she thought about what her mom must be going through. Her mom had already had to bury her own parents, who had both died within a year of each other when Jorja was in high school.

"So who was that? Someone finally offering you a job?" Taylor said as she walked into the kitchen. Taylor then noticed Jorja's tear-streaked cheeks and watery eyes. "What happened? Why are you crying?"

Jorja found it difficult to speak. "That was Mom. She said that...my Aunt Gloria had an accident and she's...she died." Once the words were out, she could no longer hold back the tears. She began to cry as Taylor rushed over to give her a hug. Taylor continued to hug her while she cried until Jorja eventually pushed away to wipe at her cheeks and her eyes. "I need to get a Kleenex. I must look like a mess."

Taylor tried to smile at her friend. "It's okay if you look like a mess. Besides, I've seen you look worse." Jorja knew Taylor was trying to lighten her mood and she felt fortunate Taylor stopped by because she would not have wanted to be alone at this moment.

Taylor grabbed Jorja's shoulders to look her in the eyes. "Go blow your nose and wash your face. I'll be waiting out back and once you're done, come outside so we can sit and talk for awhile, okay?" Taylor then gave her another hug before heading out the back door to the patio. Jorja did as she was told, thinking that while she had lost a dear family member, she was lucky to have such a dear friend.

CHAPTER 3

Jorja checked the house one last time before heading out to her jeep. She had hoped to get an earlier start but she slept in after tossing and turning all night. After making a strong pot of coffee and drinking twice as much as she normally would, she was fully caffeinated and ready for the long drive. The three-hour drive to her parents' house in Edmonds was long enough without having to deal with heavy traffic on her way through Seattle so she was hoping for a smooth drive. She let out a quick whistle at Piper as she grabbed her purse and car keys. She then had to side step to avoid being tripped by Piper as she rushed out the door in her excitement at the prospect of going for a ride. Jorja was still amazed at how Piper equated a car ride with a good experience even after having been struck by a vehicle.

During the drive north on I-5, she thought about her mother and her Aunt Gloria. Her aunt had been six years younger than her mother and while they seemed to get along well enough, Jorja had always sensed there was a gap between them. She assumed it could have been a generation gap but she also knew it might have something to do with the fact that Aunt Gloria had spent a number of years in a mental institution. She felt cheated from having such a short amount of time with her aunt, having formed a relationship only after Gloria was released from the hospital when Jorja was in her early twenties. She never fully understood why her aunt had been in the institution or even at what age she had been institutionalized, but she knew her aunt had been in the hospital for quite some time. Helen would not speak about why Gloria had been sent away, even though Jorja had asked. While she knew her mother had some concern about her relationship with Gloria, Jorja had remained persistent and was finally able to form a friendship with her aunt. Choking back a sob, she thought about how much she would miss Aunt Gloria.

Jorja passed the exit she would have taken to visit Aunt Gloria about an hour and a half into the drive. She was thankful now that she had been able to regularly visit with her aunt on her way up to or back from her parents' place. Aunt Gloria had been living in the house where Jorja grew up and also where Gloria and Helen had lived with their parents. The small, quaint town of Tenino was a nice, safe place for her aunt to reside and Jorja thought it likely she herself would still be living there if she had not moved to Vancouver to attend college. Now, she wondered what her parents were going to do with the old Victorian house. It had been in the family ever since her grandfather's parents built it so she hoped it would remain in the family. Losing Aunt Gloria in such a terrible fashion was painful and it would be further distressing if her childhood home had to be sold off to some stranger.

~ ~ ~

Jorja remained quiet during the car ride to the attorney's office, spending most of the drive deep in thought as she stared out the back passenger window. She wished she could have stayed behind at her parents' condo to take Piper for a walk instead. It was a much better alternative to tagging along with her parents while they met with the attorney who handled her aunt's estate. She was thankful her parents weren't in the mood to talk during the drive because she desperately needed some peace and quiet. The house had been full of visitors all week and Jorja hadn't realized how emotionally and physically exhausting the whole process would be. Now they had been summoned for the reading of the Will, which she would have opted out of if given the choice. She did not anticipate receiving much from her aunt other than some trinkets and small pieces of furniture from the house she had always told her aunt she adored.

Once they arrived at the attorney's office, Jorja's curiosity began to get the better of her. She didn't know what to expect when they walked into the Seattle law firm but she wasn't surprised at how plush the office looked as they were instructed by the very polished and manicured receptionist to sit and wait on the leather chairs in the lobby. The law firm where she had been employed was what some might consider "comfortable" or "homey" but certainly not posh-looking like many of the law firms in Seattle.

It wasn't long before a legal assistant escorted Jorja and her parents back to a conference room. They all took a seat at the large conference table and waited a few more minutes until a stately, older man entered the room and introduced himself as Mr. Zimmerman. The associate beside him was casually introduced as Ms. Pike. Ms. Pike was quite a bit younger than Mr. Zimmerman and Jorja assumed she was a new associate still learning the ropes. She watched as both Mr. Zimmerman and Ms. Pike took a place at the table and then Ms. Pike began pulling papers from a large file.

Mr. Zimmerman grabbed the document from the top of the pile. "Here we have the Will of Gloria Lorraine Paige. You have all been asked to be present during this meeting because you all have an interest in items held as part of Ms. Paige's estate. I will read to you the Last Will and Testament of Ms. Paige and afterwards you can indicate to me whether or not you have any questions or concerns."

As Mr. Zimmerman began to read her aunt's Will, Jorja listened with mild interest but her attention sharpened as she heard Mr. Zimmerman say her name.

"And to my niece, Jorja Anne Matthews, I leave Hillcrest, to include all furniture and personal belongings not otherwise gifted to my sister, Helen Matthews." Jorja listened in stunned silence as Mr. Zimmerman continued on with the remainder of the Will before finally asking if they had any questions. She looked at her mother to see if she was as surprised about the reading but it did not appear her mother was surprised or even upset about it. Jorja knew this was not the time or place to speak to her parents about her confusion so she remained silent as her parents finished meeting with the attorney.

After they left the attorney's office and Jorja was climbing back into her parents' car, she could not contain herself any longer, "What the heck just happened? Why would Aunt Gloria leave *me* the house rather than leave it to you? I don't understand. I expected a few pieces of furniture but not the whole house!"

Helen turned in her seat to look at her, "It's okay, Jorja, I'm glad she left the house to you. It's not like your father and I want to move back into that house and leave our condo. If we had the house we'd just have to rent it out and you know how awful it is to find good renters. Not everyone is a great renter like you are." Helen gave her daughter a wink and turned back to face the windshield.

"Yeah, but, what am I going to do with the house? And all that furniture? I certainly don't want to sell the house but I also don't want to rent it out either."

Her father's bright blue eyes stared back at her in the rearview mirror as he said, "Maybe you should think about living in it?"

Jorja was about to say more when her father's comment finally sunk in. She sat back against the seat, stunned at her father's proposal. "Live in it? You mean move?"

"Well, you'd be an hour and a half closer to your mother and I and it's a nice big place where you could raise children when you get married. We've kept up on the maintenance so there isn't much you need to worry about. Since you are between jobs it would be the perfect time to move, wouldn't it? It would be nice to have you closer to us, I'll admit but there are other good reasons for you to move into the house."

Jorja reluctantly took in what her father was saying. All his points were good ones. The only negative she could come up with was that she would be leaving Taylor behind.

"I'll have to think about it, Dad. It's a big change and there are a lot of factors to consider but I will think about it, okay?"

Rick Matthews knew his daughter well and he knew he had planted an idea that would soon grow to great heights. He felt comfort in knowing that possibly something good was going to come from Gloria's death after all.

CHAPTER 4

It did not take much thought before Jorja realized the idea of moving back into her childhood home might not be a bad idea. She had no job, no prospects of a job, she was renting month to month with no lease requiring her to remain where she was and she even liked the idea of moving back into a smaller town while she got back on her feet. The concept of taking care of a large home was a bit daunting but it was also a challenge and she liked a good challenge. She also thought of how much Piper would love the back yard, walks around town and visits to the nearby park. Her only regret would be leaving Taylor behind. She knew how easy it would be to lose touch with each other.

As Jorja packed up the few remaining items to be placed in the moving van, she heard a knock at the door.

"Knock knock!" Taylor yelled as she pulled open the screen door. "I see you have the moving truck here. The guys are cute. Think either of them is available?"

Taylor's grin was infectious and Jorja laughed as she gave Taylor a once-over, noting the skinny jeans, tank top and sandals. "I don't know if they are available or not...relationships were not discussed between the subject of boxes and furniture. Either way, I'm sure they were already checking you out as you sauntered up to the house."

"Oh? You think so?" Taylor failed at her attempt to portray ignorance. "I guess I'll have to hang out for awhile in case one of them wants to ask me out. Besides, you probably need more help, right? Sorry I couldn't come by earlier but they needed me to stay an extra hour at work."

"That's okay. You did a lot to help last night and I was able to get the rest finished this morning."

Taylor's grin faded as she said, "I know you really aren't moving that far away but I'm really going to miss you, Jorja. I don't have my schedule yet but do you want me to come up and stay with you the next time I have two days off? I would love to help you clean up the old house."

Jorja did not want to get sentimental because she knew she would cry if she did. "I would love it if you came up for a couple of days. Other than airing out the house and doing light house cleaning, there's a lot I can use help with. And maybe you can give me some pointers about decorating."

Taylor's mood brightened again at Jorja's request for help. "I would love to give you some ideas. I'll let you know when I can come up once I get my schedule. So, not to change the subject, but have you decided what you're going to do about a job?"

Jorja shook her head as she said, "I think I'm going to wait to get settled in before I start job hunting again. At least now the issue of money isn't such a headache because I have my savings to fall back on. I'm not going to stress about it until I can give job hunting my full attention."

Although Taylor was concerned for her friend, she tried to hide her worry by smiling as she said, "It'll be good if you can take some time off so you can get the house in order. It's like a vacation, except it's also work...but at least it's work you can enjoy."

Jorja smiled in return. She knew it was going to be work but it was exciting to think of the move and the prospects of a new life and a new job someplace else. She also believed her aunt would be very happy she was taking over the house with such anticipation and zeal.

~ ~ ~

Taking a nice long sip of coffee as she sat at her new dining room table, Jorja tried her best to enjoy the flavor while attempting to ignore her anxiety. After two weeks in Hillcrest, she was just starting to feel settled in. With both her mother's help and also Taylor's, Jorja felt the old house was finally beginning to take on a new personality. When she wasn't cleaning or moving furniture, she was seriously considering what she was going to do with her life. She had kept an eye on the local paper for any job prospects but Tenino was a small town with few job openings at any given time. She also consistently looked at job listings in Olympia, which was less than a half hour away, but it appeared the economy had affected a number of businesses there as well.

She was anxiously waiting for Taylor to arrive, who had asked for time off so she could spend a week with her. Taylor thought she was coming to visit in order to help Jorja with more decorating but she had other ideas.

Piper let out a few short barks and Jorja realized Taylor had pulled into the driveway. She took a quick sip from her coffee cup to help steady her nerves. *Okay, here we go.*

She set her coffee cup down and quickly moved to the front of the house. With Piper on her heels, Jorja opened the front door to step out on to the long front porch, one of the best attributes of the house. "Hello! How was the drive?"

Taylor let out a yawn and stretched her back as she stood beside her car. "It's only an hour and a half but sometimes it sure can feel a lot longer than that. I didn't sleep well last night and the drive here was difficult because I'm already ready for a nap."

Jorja had to avoid tripping over Piper, who was excited to see Taylor. She gingerly stepped around Piper as she moved down the porch steps and grabbed two bags from Taylor's trunk.

"Wow. Three bags? You planning on staying for a week or a month?"

Taylor laughed and said, "You know me. I dress according to my mood. I had to bring just about everything I like to wear because I won't know what I want to wear until I wake up each day."

Jorja lugged two suitcases up the front porch as Taylor followed behind with her purse and the remaining suitcase. Taylor also had to avoid tripping over Piper who was excitedly trying to get her attention.

"Ok, Piper. Just give me a minute." Taylor set her suitcase down in the foyer and bent down to give Piper the attention she was craving. Piper immediately lay down on her back with all four feet up in the air, giving Taylor full access to rubbing her belly.

"She's so cute and happy. How has she been doing? Is she used to the house yet?"

Jorja nodded as she smiled at Piper on the floor. "Oh, she's completely used to the change and she seems to love all the room she has to move around. I put a doggy door on the back door so she can enjoy the back yard whenever she wants. She seems very content here."

Taylor gave Piper one last pat on the belly and stood up. "Well, that's good. You always have to wonder how an animal will deal with a major move so I'm glad she's accepting it well. I'm sure she's just happy because she's with you. She'd probably live on the moon with you if she had to."

Jorja laughed. "You're right about that. Now, let's get you settled into your room and then we can sit down and talk while we have some coffee and scones. I have one of the spare rooms ready for you."

Jorja helped Taylor take her bags to a spare room on the second floor. Jorja enjoyed how big the house was but she was still getting used to all the extra space. She used the master bedroom on the second floor which included an on suite bathroom and walk-in closet but the house also included three other bedrooms on the second floor and a fifth bedroom on the third floor, which also had its own on suite bathroom.

After placing the luggage on the floor in the spare room, Taylor waved Jorja back out into the hallway.

"Let's worry about this later. I can put it all away after we visit for awhile. I'm dying for a good cup of coffee after I take a much needed bathroom break. I'll meet you downstairs in a minute."

Jorja went back downstairs to the kitchen where she prepared two cups of coffee and placed them on the table in the small dining area off the kitchen along with some scones. This was the country kitchen she had always wanted. The house also had a formal dining room, which Jorja doubted she would ever use, a large living room and a smaller family room she used as a den. The two-car garage was a treat, having only had a carport for the past six years, and the garage itself had a large storage area with a work bench where she could work on projects. Also off the garage was a laundry room where Jorja had been relieved to see her aunt had replaced the washer and dryer with a fairly brand new set.

Jorja sipped her coffee while waiting for Taylor. She began to feel nervous again but she brushed the thought aside, knowing Taylor would support her no matter what idiotic idea came to her head.

"Ok, now I feel refreshed and ready to give you my undivided attention until Piper demands more of it than you do." Taylor had already changed into a pair of sweats and a t-shirt. "Sorry I'm so dressed down but I don't plan on doing anything requiring me to be all decked out. I'm sure you were already planning to put me to work anyway, weren't you?"

Jorja hesitated to answer as Taylor sat down and took a sip from her coffee cup. "Oh, this tastes so good. What kind of coffee are you using?"

Jorja found her voice and said, "It's a new French roast I got at the local coffee shop. It has a good flavor, doesn't it?"

"It sure does." Taylor took another sip and sat back in her chair. "So, how have you been since I was here last?"

"Oh, you know...I've finished up with most of the unpacking and I've also taken some time to look for a job but so far I haven't been able to find anything."

"That's the way it seems to be for a lot of people right now. Even if you do find a good job, you'll be interviewing for it along with a ton of other people also desperate for a new job."

Jorja took another sip of coffee before saying, "Well, I don't think I'm really that desperate any longer. In fact, I don't think I need to look for a job any longer."

Taylor gave her a curious look. "What do you mean you don't need a job? How are you going to live? You can't plan on using up all your savings while living here. This house will eat that up and besides, you're too young to just quit working."

"I'm not saying I don't have a plan, Taylor. Rather than work for someone else, I think I would rather work for myself. I have decided to open my own business, or rather, businesses. And the best part? I want you to work with me."

Jorja's last comment caused Taylor to hesitate a beat before asking, "Doing what? What kind of businesses are you planning? *Where* do you plan to have these businesses located? That takes a lot of money, you know that don't you?"

"I know, I know. The startup costs will be a strain on my savings but I'm willing to take the risk. I have made up my mind and what I'm hoping is that you'll support me and be a part of it."

It only took Taylor a moment to see the determination in her face. Taylor finally smiled and said, "Jorja, you *know* I'll support you. There's no question there. So tell me, what's this idea of yours and how do I fit into the equation?"

CHAPTER 5

Jorja took a deep breath before she said, "I want to open a book store and coffee shop. I got a lucky break and found out a local shop owner wants to sell and it would be the perfect spot for a small book store. The owner wants to retire and he's willing to give me a good deal on the property and his inventory, which already includes some books. I'd need to remodel, make room for the coffee stand and some tables…"

Taylor held up her hand, halting Jorja's next words. "Hold up, hold up. What the heck got you thinking in this direction?"

Jorja knew she'd have questions to answer and she was ready for them. "I've always wanted to own a book store. Not that I thought I ever would, but if I could ever own a business, a book store would be it. I know I won't make money selling books so that's why I also want to include a coffee stand with a seating area. We can hold book readings, students can hang out and do their homework because I'd like to set up WiFi at the store, mothers can enjoy coffee while their kids read a book, friends can talk over coffee in a comfortable atmosphere and I thought it would be fun if we could start a book club too."

Taylor could hear the excitement in Jorja's voice and knew there was no stopping Jorja once she got an idea into her head. "Well, it all sounds like a great plan but where are you going to get all the money for this new venture? You're not going to use all your house money you've saved, are you? And, wait, you haven't said what I have to do with this? What do you mean by 'we' can start a book club?"

Jorja's smile broadened, reminding Taylor of the Cheshire cat in *Alice in Wonderland*. "I'd like you to be a part of this with me. You don't plan on staying at your job forever do you? You could move here, live in the bedroom on the third floor where you'd have your own space and your own bathroom. Your rent here would be part of your pay and on top of that I'd pay you a certain amount every month to help me with the coffee stand and whatever else you want to take on. Don't you think it would be exciting? And don't worry about the money. I saved up for a house but now I have one and I don't plan on moving. After moving in, I found out from Mom that more than enough money has been set aside in an account to cover the expenses that might come up with the house. So I have money to take care of the house and I can use my own savings to put towards the business. If I don't have quite enough, I'll get a loan. And if a bank won't loan me money due to the fact that I'm not working, I'm sure I can get a loan from my parents."

Taylor was now certain Jorja's mind was made up about opening a business. "Wow, you really are serious, aren't you?"

"You bet I am. I don't want to work for anyone else anymore. I want to open my own business and be my own boss. I know it won't be a bed of roses but at least I won't have to answer to anyone but myself. What do you say, Taylor? Would you want to move here and work with me?"

Taylor was already affected by Jorja's excitement and she knew Jorja's determination would win over any obstacles they might come across along the way. She was also ready for a change, having been at the same job for much too long. Taylor was pushing thirty and she wanted something more meaningful than a job living paycheck to paycheck. At this point, Taylor couldn't think of anything else more meaningful than helping her best friend make a dream come true.

"Okay, I'll do it. I'll give my two-weeks' notice and move here at the end of this month if I can get out of my lease."

Jorja jumped up from her chair and leaned over to give Taylor a hug. "Thank you, thank you, thank you! I will feel so much better about going into this if you are with me to help me out along the way. Oh, I can't wait! I have a meeting with the store owner tomorrow afternoon to discuss the details. I'm hoping we can hash everything out and make an agreement on the amount he will take for the building and the inventory. Then I have to get my business name set up, my license with the city, the utilities switched over...oh, there's just so much to be done but that's where I'm hoping my parents will help out. Mom was a bookkeeper for years and I'm going to ask if she'll work for me part time doing all the necessary paperwork and keep up the books for me."

Jorja finally took a breath so Taylor took the opportunity to reply. "Asking your mom to help out is a great idea. Will she be able to do most of the work from her own place so she doesn't have to travel too often?"

"Yes, I've thought about it and with computers and scanning documents and all the technology available to us, she could easily manage most of the paperwork from her house and just come down here a couple of times a month. I plan on leaving that up to her."

Taylor took a sip of coffee and grimaced when she realized it had gotten cold. As she got up to top it off with fresh coffee, Taylor had a thought and turned back towards Jorja.

"Hey, did you ever figure out why your aunt left you this house? Why didn't it go to your Mom?"

Jorja shrugged. "I really don't know why. When I've asked Mom about it, she assures me it was what Aunt Gloria wanted and that she has no hard feelings about it at all. She keeps telling me she wouldn't know what to do with this place anyway. From her perspective, it would seem this was the best result all around and really, now that I have a place to stay, money to live and the possibilities of running my own business, I have to agree."

Taylor refilled her cup and sat back down. "I'm so happy everything seems to be working out for you, Jorja. I'm also very excited about this idea of opening a book store and coffee shop. Where is the building located? Is it nearby?"

"It is. It's two blocks from the center of town and right on the corner so I'll have more options of sprucing the place up to catch the eye of anyone driving by."

"I can't wait to see it. Can I come with you tomorrow when you meet with the owner?"

"I'd love for you to come with me and look around the place while I talk to the owner. Then you can also give me your ideas about how we should remodel and decorate the place. That is my ulterior motive for having you here, you know. I need your advice on how to make the place look warm and inviting but also organized."

"So what do you plan to call your bookstore?" Taylor asked before taking a big bite of her scone.

Jorja had already thought about what might be catchy and also easy to say whenever she had to answer the phone. "Well, I was thinking 'Books 'N Brew' for the name. What do you think?"

Taylor rolled it around on her tongue and after a few tries she said, "I really like it. It's easy to say, it's catchy and it is what it says."

Jorja breathed a sigh of relief after hearing Taylor's reaction.

"I'm so glad you like it. Really, if you said you didn't like it, I was at a loss for any other names."

Jorja stood up and set her cup by the sink. "I guess I should go call my parents and fill them in on my plans. I also want some advice before my meeting with the owner tomorrow. Go ahead and make yourself at home, Taylor, and when I'm done with my phone call, we'll go through the cupboards and figure out what we can make for dinner."

"Sounds good, take your time. I think I'll take a walk out back and check out your back yard." Taylor felt she really had no choice. As Jorja got up to use the phone, Taylor realized Piper had been expectantly waiting for anyone willing and able to take her outside to play catch. Piper sat in front of Taylor's feet and gently placed her muzzle on Taylor's knee while holding a chew toy. Taylor's heart melted as she looked down at Piper's big brown eyes.

"Okay, okay. You win, I give up. Let's go outside."

That's all it took and Piper quickly ran out the back door through the doggy door, causing Taylor to laugh. As she followed Piper out the door, Taylor began to wonder how well Piper and her cat, Bella, were going to get along if they were soon going to be roommates.

CHAPTER 6

"Hey, Jorja, where do you want this last chair placed?" Taylor yelled from the back of the store where she was attempting to finish with decorating.

Jorja looked around the store to find the perfect spot. She was amazed at all the changes that had taken place during the past few months. She lost her job, lost her aunt, and inherited a house and some money to help live in the house. Now she was the proud new owner of a small corner building near the center of her hometown where she would soon open the newest business in town. They were only two weeks away from the open house and Jorja was pleased they were on track to have everything done in time.

Finally finding the ideal spot, she pointed as she said, "How about over there against the end of that bookcase?"

The football players Jorja had hired to help move furniture picked up the chair and moved it to its new location. She adjusted the chair slightly, looked around the store once again and breathed a heavy sigh of relief. "Wow, never thought we'd get it done but that's pretty much it. Thank you, boys, so much for helping out. I really appreciate it. Make sure you finish up the rest of that pizza if you're still hungry, okay?"

Bruce, the tallest of the group and apparent leader of the boys waved his hand in dismissal. "Hey, no problem Miss Matthews, we don't mind helping at all. And thanks again for the pizza, it was great. If you ever need anything else, just tell Coach and he'll send us over after practice." The other boys nodded and also chimed in at how much they enjoyed the food and did not mind the work.

"Well, thanks, Bruce, I really appreciate that. And you don't have to call me Miss Matthews. You can call me Jorja, okay?"

"Sure, if that's what you'd like Miss Matt...er, Jorja. Are you sure you don't need anything else?"

Jorja shook her head. "No, that's it for now but I will definitely let you know if I need anything else."

Bruce and his friends each grabbed more pizza and a can of pop before heading out the door. Piper, who had been with Jorja every day while the store was being remodeled, had been sitting nearby the table where the pizza had been placed, hoping for just one morsel to drop to her level. As the boys left the store, Piper watched them with hopeful eyes only to turn her stare towards Jorja once the boys left.

"Oh, stop it. You get enough to eat as it is." Jorja could not contain her grin and then she laughed as she grabbed a storage container she had placed behind the front counter. "Here, you can have this nice healthy dog treat. No pizza for you." She threw the treat at Piper, expecting her to catch it but instead Piper let the treat hit her on the nose before it dropped to the floor. Piper then turned her head away. "Suit yourself," Jorja said as she walked towards the back of the store to find Taylor but after a few steps she peeked over her shoulder to watch Piper sniff at the treat before obediently, and unenthusiastically, eating it.

Jorja found Taylor in the break room, storing cleaning supplies under the sink. Taylor looked up as Jorja came into the room. "So will you be contacting the coach to get the boys to help us out some more?" Taylor knew she was hitting a nerve with the question but she thought she'd have a bit of fun.

Jorja raised one eyebrow before responding. "I don't know. It depends on whether we have any more lifting we can't do on our own. Why, do you think we still need their help?"

"Well, I thought you might not mind having a few conversations with the coach, whether about the boys or anything else."

Taylor's eyes sparkled with a devilish gleam and Jorja realized what Taylor was up to.

"All right, knock it off. There is nothing between us other than an old friendship. Don't get your hopes up."

She hoped she sounded convincing but when she thought about the coach of the football team, Brad Dawson, she could not deny he stirred up some of the old feelings she had for him. After forming a good friendship during high school, Jorja and Brad dated until he moved away his senior year. She later learned Brad moved back to town when the coaching position had been up for grabs. While she knew Taylor hoped she and Brad might rekindle their high school romance, Jorja did not think a relationship during high school was enough to ignite a real adult relationship after ten-plus years. So what if Brad looked even better than he did in high school? Jorja had discovered this fact when she first contacted him about the boys helping her out but she wasn't about to make a fool of herself by assuming anything when it came to his interest in her.

Taylor grinned at Jorja and then decided it was best to move on to another subject. "Hey, I'm not trying to fix you up; I'm too busy working here. So, what do you think? How does everything look?"

"Taylor, you outdid yourself. I think it looks great and I am so happy with how the whole store *feels*. I just know customers are going to enjoy coming here. We'll have everything, books, coffee, baked treats, WiFi, a great children's section and comfortable seating areas. What more could they ask for?"

Jorja was still slightly fearful about whether or not the business would do well but hers was the only bookstore in town and she felt sure she would be able to draw in the customers.

"After we open we'll have to work on what types of gatherings we can schedule here to bring in regular and new customers. We will need to start a book club and offer a few of the self-employed locals a chance to hold parties here. I thought we'd also check with the City to see if they'd like to hold small business meetings here, as well. We could make money on either renting the place or selling coffee and other treats."

Taylor was nodding her head as Jorja went on about the possibilities. "That all sounds great, Jorja. I'm sure once the word gets out, we'll have even more groups wanting to hold meetings here."

"Hello? Is anyone here?" Jorja and Taylor looked curiously at each other as they heard the voice from the front of the store. Taylor followed Jorja as they left the break room to see who their new guest might be.

Standing just inside the door was a woman Jorja thought looked familiar.

"We're not open for business yet but what can I do for you?"

The curious guest gave Jorja a penetrating look, as if Jorja should already know the answer to her question. *Ok, I'll bite*, Jorja thought to herself.

"Do I know you?"

The guest nodded her head of brown curls and gave Jorja a bright smile. It was then that Jorja realized who her guest was. "Ruth! How are you?" Jorja gave Ruth a welcoming hug and then pulled back to look her over. "Wow, I thought you moved out of the country, in South Africa or someplace like that. Do you live here?"

Ruth did not lose her grin as she said, "I do live here. I moved back about a year ago after my husband, Peter, and I became pregnant with our first child. We both decided that the constant travel related to our missionary work would just be too difficult with the baby. When Peter was appointed to take over as the Pastor at a church in Olympia, he took the job so that we could live here near my parents. When did you move back here?"

Jorja was pleased to think Ruth was living in the area. She had always liked Ruth and how solid a friend she was, even when they were young.

"I moved back here only a few months ago. I'm living back at Hillcrest."

Ruth excitedly waved her hands as she said, "I wondered who was moving in and fixing up the place! I was worried your parents had sold the place. I am so glad you are living there instead." Ruth's smile faded and she grabbed Jorja's hand as she continued, "I heard about your aunt passing away. I'm so sorry to hear what happened and how tragic her death must have been. I hope it gives you comfort to know she is in a better place."

Jorja gave Ruth's hand a squeeze in reply. "Thanks, Ruth."

Ruth quickly changed the subject. "How are your parents? It's been so long since I've seen them."

"Oh, they are both doing great. They moved up north and are living in a condo in Edmonds. Mom is actually helping me out here as my bookkeeper though so you might be able to catch her for a visit if you stop by when she's working. She would love to see you."

Ruth smiled as she said, "That would be wonderful. I would love to see her."

Ruth's gaze shifted towards Taylor and Jorja realized she had rudely forgotten her dear friend who stood nearby listening while trying not to intrude.

"Oh, Taylor, I'm so sorry. Taylor, this is Ruth, a friend of mine from way back. Ruth and I attended high school together. Ruth, this is Taylor. She and I met and became fast friends when I moved down to Vancouver. When I moved here I was able to talk her into moving with me to help me with the bookstore."

"It's nice to meet you, Taylor."

"Ruth! Where the hell are you?" Jorja's brows creased at the sound of the voice coming from outside the store. *Oh boy, I hope that's not who I think it is.*

Ruth quickly peeked outside and called out, "I'm in here, Lydia."

Before Jorja could adjust to the onset of unease she was feeling, Lydia flew into the store and lit into Ruth. "I was looking all over for you! We need to get on our way. I don't want to be late for the baby shower."

Lydia then noticed Jorja and Taylor standing nearby. As she looked at Jorja, Lydia frowned and just as quickly attempted to smile as she said, "Hello Jorja. I'd heard you moved back to town. What brought you back?"

Jorja forced herself not to react to Lydia's failed attempt at civil conversation. "I decided to move back into Hillcrest. How are you?"

"I'm fine. But I don't have time to chat. Ruth, we really need to go. I don't want to be late."

"Fine, Lydia. I'm ready." Ruth gave Jorja an apologetic look. "Jorja, it was great seeing you. I see by the poster in the window that you plan to open the store in two weeks. I'll be sure to come back by to see you and I'll bring my baby with me so you can see her too. She's adorable if I do say so myself." Ruth gave Jorja a quick hug.

Jorja returned the hug and said, "I would love for you to stop by again and I would love to see your baby. Bye Lydia, see you around."

"Yeah, see you." Lydia said as she grabbed Ruth's arm to pull her from the store. After the two had left, Taylor gave Jorja a look that required no verbal question.

"Uh, Ruth is great and you'll really like her. Lydia, on the other hand, was always a pain when we were kids and it would appear she hasn't changed very much since then. Of all the people who still live here, I was kind of hoping she had left the state. I really don't understand how Ruth and Lydia can be friends. They are two totally different types of people."

"What do you and Lydia have between you? Why doesn't she like you? Why don't you like her?"

Jorja wasn't sure there was enough time to discuss all the reasons why she and Lydia did not get along. But it had been so long, she would have thought they could act like grownups and get along just fine. Now, just seeing Lydia made Jorja realize their relationship had only been frozen in time and was just thawing out to what it had been before.

"It's not that I don't like her. I don't like how she treats people. She always used people. If they didn't do something for her, she would not give them the time of day. The fact that she's with Ruth makes me worry she's using Ruth for some reason because they certainly don't have anything in common."

Taylor thought there was more to the story than what Jorja wanted to say. "Okay, then, why doesn't she like you?"

Jorja rolled her eyes before finally admitting, "It's stupid. She shouldn't be holding a grudge after all this time."

Taylor stared at Jorja and waited for her to continue.

"It was over a boy, okay? She liked someone and so did I. It just so happened he asked me out instead of her and she just never wanted to forgive me for it. She told everyone I *stole* him from her but he wasn't even hers in the first place."

"And who was the boy? Anyone I know?" Taylor asked because she had a sneaking suspicion she knew exactly what boy Jorja was talking about.

Jorja hesitated and finally gave in. "It was Brad, okay? Brad, who just happened to move back here and now I've moved back here and with Lydia still here it's going to be a fun time heading down memory lane with both of them. Boy, this is just great. Here's hoping I don't end up bumping into both of them at the same time. I just don't need the drama right now and believe me Lydia knows how to bring on the drama."

Taylor smiled. "I can tell. But that's okay; you have me by your side to protect you. Or at least I'll be there to cheer for you when the two of you go at it and fight over Brad." Taylor laughed at Jorja's look of dread at the thought of having any type of confrontation with Lydia.

CHAPTER 7

The grand opening for the bookstore was only two days away as Jorja and Taylor finished organizing the office. Jorja was thankful her mother had stopped by earlier in the week to give them advice on how to organize the files needed for accurate bookkeeping.

Taylor slumped down in one of the chairs they had placed in the office as additional seating. "Whew! I can't believe we cut it so close. Now with all the paperwork organized and the office all put together, you should be able to run this business like a well-oiled machine."

Jorja was sitting in front of her new desk top computer, loading it with the software she purchased to help with the business records. "We did cut it close, didn't we? But I had faith we'd get it done."

Jorja hit one last key on the computer and got up from the desk to look over the loft railing down at the bookstore. From Jorja's perspective, it had all turned out perfectly and she could not wait to see how the town welcomed her new business. She had to push away the negative thoughts that crept into the back of her mind when she thought about how difficult opening a new business could be.

Jorja's attention was drawn to movement outside the store front window and then what appeared to be someone's hands as they tried to look inside the store. Certain it was just another curious local trying to get a sneak peek, she was about to turn away when she heard a tentative knock at the door. Jorja looked at Taylor and said, "Looks like we have company. I'll go down and see who it is."

Taylor got up to look over the railing as Jorja walked downstairs and unlocked the front door. Standing before Jorja was what appeared to be a young high school student.

"Hi, can I help you?" Jorja assumed the girl was another high school kid hitting up the local businesses for an upcoming fundraiser.

"Are you Jorja? Jorja Matthews?"

"I am. What can I do for you?" Jorja watched as the young girl twirled a ring on her finger and moved nervously from side-to-side. The girl seemed to realize she was moving too much when she suddenly stopped and dropped her hands to her side. She then thought better of it and held her hand out to Jorja instead.

"My name is Kathleen, or Kat, as most people call me. I was talking to a friend of mine who knows a friend of yours, Ruth Newman."

Jorja shook Kat's hand as she said, "Ruth Newman? I'm not sure…wait, do you mean Ruth Brown?"

Kat nodded her head. "Yes, Ruth Newman is her married name."

Jorja realized they were still standing in the doorway talking. "Hey, come on in and sit down if you'd like. Would you like a drink?"

Kat followed Jorja into the store and sat down at a table near the coffee stand. Jorja sat across the table from her and as Kat was about to speak, her focus was drawn to the staircase as Taylor walked down the stairs towards them. Kat seemed hesitant to speak as she again turned her attention to Jorja, leaving Jorja to wonder exactly what the girl had on her mind.

"No, I'm okay. I don't need anything to drink. I just wanted to ask you a question but if this is a bad time, I can come back." Kat quickly glanced at Taylor again.

Jorja shook her head. "No, it's not a bad time. This is my friend, Taylor. She helps me out here at the store and we had just finished with our last project so I have some time to spare. Do you mind if she joins us?"

Kat looked unsure but then said. "Yeah, I guess that's okay. Um, so I was talking to your friend Ruth and she told me that you worked at a law firm."

"Well, I used to work at a law firm but I don't any longer."

Kat's brows creased. "Oh. But you worked there for a long time, right? You know things from working there?"

Jorja wasn't sure where Kat was going with her questioning. "I worked at the firm for six years, yes, if you consider that a long time. What do you expect that I would know from working there?"

Kat began to twirl the ring on her finger again. "Well, you know how to look for things, records and stuff, maybe track down people and get information. That kind of stuff, you know?"

Jorja was getting curious and as she peeked at Taylor, she saw that Taylor was also.

"Well, sure, part of my job as a legal assistant was to track down records and help locate possible witnesses. Why? Do you need help finding someone?"

Kat's nervous look changed to sadness. "I was hoping you could try to find someone for me. I have no idea where to start and I thought maybe you could help."

Jorja wasn't sure what to say other than, "Who is it you are hoping to find?"

Kat paused as she looked from Jorja to Taylor and back to Jorja again. "It's my mom. I was hoping you could find her for me."

Jorja glanced at Taylor, whose gaze reflected her own surprise. "Your mom? You don't know where your mom is? Why, what happened?"

Kat took a deep breath. "When I was five years old my mom ran away. My dad said she just up and left, leaving only a note saying she could not 'deal with it anymore' and that he had no idea where she might have gone. My mom's parents had already died and she has no brothers or sisters that I'm aware of and I haven't heard from her since the night she took off. I just want to find her. I don't know if I actually want to speak to her but if you find her, I'd like you to ask her why. Why did she leave? Why has she never contacted me? What did I do to make her leave? Or did my dad do something to make her leave? What did she mean when she said she couldn't deal with 'it' anymore? I just have so many questions and I'd really like to know some answers!"

After her outburst, Kat sat back in her chair, seemingly deflated by the words she had apparently been so anxious to speak.

Jorja took a moment to get over the shock and sadness she felt for this girl. Jorja could not understand how any mother could leave a child and never have contact with them again. She wasn't sure if she should agree to help Kat but it was in her nature to help people and she had a hard time saying no. Jorja glanced at Taylor, who was watching her closely. She could tell Taylor knew exactly where her thoughts were headed.

Taylor jumped in before Jorja could speak, "Didn't your dad try to find her?"

Kat shrugged her shoulders and replied, "He said that when she first took off, he contacted the police and had flyers made up. He posted them around town but since he had no idea where or how far she might have traveled, he didn't know where to begin looking for her. He later told me he was so upset with her for leaving both of us that he finally just gave up because he wasn't going to force her back if she really didn't want to be a part of our family."

Jorja could not imagine how this young girl turned into what appeared to be such a nice young woman after all the turmoil she must have felt if she believed her mother did not want her.

Jorja knew she was acting with her heart rather than her head when she said, "Okay, Kat, I'll help you. I'll do some research for you and see what I can come up with but I am not going to promise anything, okay? I don't want you to get your hopes up. If your mother does not want to be found, I may not be able to come up with anything useful for you."

Kat's eyes lit up and her smile was enough to make Jorja realize even what little she could do for this girl would be enough.

"Thank you so much! Ruth said you were really nice and she thought you could help me. I wish I could pay you but I'm between jobs because my summer job just ended and I haven't found a new job since school started."

In a flash, Jorja had a thought. She was going on instinct and she hoped her first impression of Kat did not let her down. "Do you need a job? I could use someone here at the bookstore. It would be a part time job so I could easily work around your school hours. Are you a senior this year?"

Taylor gave Jorja a sidelong questioning glance. She too hoped Jorja knew what she was doing.

Kat's excitement at the proposition was immediate. "Oh, I'd *love* to work here! I'm starting my senior year and I could work part time after school or on the weekends. I'm not in any sports so you wouldn't have to work around a practice schedule but I do have my senior project I need to complete and if you could let me count my hours here at the bookstore, that could be used towards my senior project. Would that be okay?"

As Kat began to open up with her more, Jorja felt Kat was someone she would enjoy working with. She was thankful Kat came by to ask for her help, as Kat would soon be helping her in return.

"I think that would be okay. Anything to help you with school is a good idea so just let me know what I need to do to make sure your hours count towards your senior project. We open in two days. Do you think you could start tomorrow so I can show you the ropes?"

Kat's grin and excitement was infectious. "I could start today if you want me to!"

Jorja laughed. "No, tomorrow is okay. Just come by around ten in the morning and we'll get you started. Do you need to ask your dad if it's okay to work for me?"

Kat lost her enthusiasm as she said, "No. My dad died last year. That's why I finally decided to look for my mom. Whenever I talked to him about looking for her, he would just get upset about it so I finally stopped asking. Now that he's gone, I decided I should go ahead and look for her."

"I'm sorry, Kat. Who do you live with now?"

Kat made a face and said, "I have been living with my Aunt Lydia ever since my dad died. It's okay but I try to stay out of her hair."

Jorja heard Taylor try to muffle a giggle.

Jorja was almost afraid to ask Kat the question. "Lydia? You mean Lydia Myers?"

Kat nodded and asked, "Why do you know her?"

"Oh, I know her. We went to school together." *Yikes!* Jorja could not believe her luck. She had just hired the niece of the one person she preferred to have the least contact with.

CHAPTER 8

The first day of business for Books 'N Brew was a success as far as Jorja was concerned. The town had already been buzzing with the news of a new business and it didn't hurt that the owner was a prior resident who had decided to move back to town. Those who attended the grand opening were either old acquaintances who wanted to see Jorja after all the time that had passed or the small town busy-bodies who couldn't resist checking out the competition. Jorja didn't believe her business was any sort of competition, since it was the only bookstore in town, but she was aware she was competing with a couple of the local coffee stands who had settled in a few years before.

"Jorja, will you be getting a copy of the latest book by Mary Higgins Clark?" Jorja turned to find Sandra Bennett, the owner of the local hair salon. Sandra was Jorja's mother's age and had been a friend of her mother's while they attended high school together.

"Hello, Sandra, it's nice to see you. Yes, I am working on getting copies of some recent best sellers but they have not all arrived yet. Do you want me to call you when the books arrive?"

Sandra shook her head. "No, I'll just stop by again another time to see what you have. I'm sure I'll be here often for a cup of coffee and a chat with your mom when she's here working."

"Oh, so you've seen Mom already?" Jorja guessed her mother either stopped to see Sandra or the gossip chain was still working fairly well.

Sandra nodded. "She stopped by the salon the other day and bought some hair products from me. She told me she'd be working here for you once a week and she said she'd like to get together to catch up. Your mom sure looks good. The years have been kind to her and it sounds like your parents still have a wonderful relationship."

Jorja heard a slight amount of jealously in Sandra's voice. From what Jorja recalled her mother telling her, Sandra had inherited quite a fortune from her grandfather but it was Sandra's husband who delighted in spending the money whether Sandra agreed with the expenditures or not. Jorja felt sorry for Sandra if she was in an unhappy marriage but it seemed apparent the situation would never change because it was not in Sandra's nature to directly confront anyone.

"Well, thank you. Mom and Dad have both been doing well. Mom's actually working here today so make sure you find her to say hello. Would you excuse me, Sandra? I see Taylor motioning that she needs something."

Jorja said goodbye to Sandra to move towards the coffee stand, but she was quickly ambushed by Lydia. "So just what is it you think you are doing?"

Jorja stopped short, caught off guard by the question. "What? What do you mean?"

Lydia stood with her hands on her hips as she replied, "What do I mean? Why did you agree to help Kat? Nothing good can come from you digging up the past, Jorja. That woman caused my brother real grief when she walked out on him and Kat. I don't see how tracking her down now will help Kat at all. If Vera hasn't had the decency to explain her actions before this, how will it make it any better if someone like you forces her to come forward?"

Jorja took a deep breath as she thought about how she would hold her ground without saying something she might regret. Finally, she said, "I understand how you feel, Lydia, but Kat asked me to do this for her and I'm going to do what I can. I think Kat is more than capable of dealing with whatever comes from making contact with her mom if we find her."

Lydia's cheeks became bright red as she glared at Jorja. "Nothing good can come from this, Jorja. *Nothing.* Why can't you just tell Kat you can't find her and leave it at that?"

Jorja shook her head. "No, Lydia, I won't do that. Kat wants to know the truth about why her mom left and she's old enough to hear it."

Lydia continued to stare at Jorja and as Jorja waited for the onslaught of harsh words she was surprised when Lydia finally threw her hands down to her side in a huff and stormed off. Jorja shook her head in disbelief at the altercation but she was relieved it did not go any further. She drew another deep breath and then turned to continue her way towards the coffee stand where Taylor was continuously brewing lattes and mochas.

Jorja watched as Taylor finished making a Cinnamon Spice latte. Once Taylor handed the latte to the customer, she jerked her head towards Lydia's direction and asked Jorja, "What the heck was going on between you and Lydia? She didn't look too happy while the two of you were chatting."

Jorja grimaced as she shrugged her shoulders in a helpless gesture. "Her nose is bent out of joint because I'm helping Kat. For whatever reason, she'd rather I not find Vera at all. She actually asked me to pretend not to find her and I told her I wouldn't do that."

Taylor's brows rose in question but she was not able to ask anything further when another customer moved forward to ask for a mocha. Jorja figured it would be a good time to change the subject. "So the orders are keeping you pretty busy?"

Taylor grinned at Jorja as she handed the mocha to the customer. "Are you kidding? I haven't had time to even take a bathroom break. It was a great idea putting the coffee stand in here. You might not sell a lot of books but *everyone* likes a good latte."

Taylor quickly wiped her hands and walked around the coffee stand in order to speak to Jorja.

"So, the reason I needed you over here is to let you know that the cookies and muffins have also been a big hit. If you can have those and the muffins on hand every day, it would be a bonus."

Jorja had asked the owner of the local bakery, Dylan Rhoades, if he would be willing to sell some of his baked goods during her open house.

"So they're good? Everyone likes them?"

"You haven't tried them? Oh, they are good, I can guarantee that. I couldn't help but try one of the peanut butter cookies and then your mom let me try one of the blueberry muffins she had with her coffee. They taste terrific and they are very moist."

Jorja knew using a local bakery was something her customers would appreciate. The bakery, called "Dylan's Sweet Delights," was only a block from the bookstore which made access to the treats fairly convenient.

"Okay, I'll talk to Dylan and see what he's willing to do for us. Not sure when but I'll try to set something up with him next week."

"Well, if you're going to be too busy, I could go by and speak to him on your behalf." Taylor quickly turned to wipe the counter but not before Jorja saw her cheeks turn color.

Jorja smiled and knew there was more to this offer than Taylor was willing to say. "Is there another reason you'd like to go see Dylan?"

Taylor busied herself at the counter and avoided eye contact with Jorja while saying, "No, no reason. I just know I might be able to work out a good deal for you, that's all."

Jorja's smile widened and she thought about how Taylor and Dylan would look together as a couple. Dylan was tall, blond and muscular. He looked more like a baseball player than a baker but from what Taylor and the customers thought about his food, it was to his credit he followed his dream of owning a bakery. Jorja thought Taylor's tall frame, dark brown eyes and brunette hair would be a great contrast to Dylan's light coloring. She began to wonder what color hair and eyes their kids would have when Taylor forced Jorja out of her imaginary world of setting the two up.

"Do you want me to talk to him?"

Jorja forced herself to focus on Taylor's question. "Uh, yeah, if you have the time and want to go see him for me, that would be great. Make sure he knows we're closed Sundays and Mondays. Maybe we can work out a Tuesday and Friday morning delivery arrangement."

Taylor did her best to look serious and professional as she said, "Ok, I can do that for you. I'll stop by there tomorrow."

"And Taylor? Make sure you let me know when you two decide to go out on your first date."

Jorja winked at Taylor.

Taylor's eyes narrowed and she was about to say something less than lady-like when a customer approached them. Jorja laughed and said, "I better go mingle some more. These are future customers and we need to keep them happy."

CHAPTER 9

Jorja was happy to have been able to get in a decent Saturday afternoon walk with Piper before heading back to the bookstore to do some research. Piper had become accustomed to going to the bookstore with Jorja, where she could sleep off a good walk while Jorja worked. This afternoon was no exception as Piper snored under Jorja's desk while she attempted to track down information on the Internet. Friday afternoon she had met with Kat to gain as much background as she could about Kat's mother and her disappearance. The only information Kat could confirm was what her father had told her; her mother had left when Kat was only five years old, her father found a note left behind by her mother and because there was a note, the police did not view the case as a missing person's case and did not investigate further. Kat was also able to provide an old photograph of her mother, taken shortly before she disappeared, along with her mother's birth certificate and a single article from the local paper. From her review of the article, Jorja thought the newspaper only wrote the article to appease Kat's father. It did not appear that the news reporter expected the article to turn up results in any way. Her guess was that town gossip had traveled quickly and everyone believed Kat's mother had left Kat's father.

Jorja was happy to make use of the skills she learned while working at the law firm along with the tips she learned from the private investigator the firm used. She was now very thankful she kept a notebook with all the useful tips, insight and various websites where certain information could be researched. She opened the top desk drawer to remove the notebook and as she browsed through her notes, she began to put together a to-do list. One phone call she knew she had to make was to the local Chief of Police. Jorja hoped he would be able to verify whether copies of any archived reports on the case would be available. She also wanted to know who the investigating officer had been when Kat's mother disappeared. Kat was too little to remember any useful details and did not recall her father even speaking of the police investigation other than to say they 'didn't do squat.'

Grabbing the local phone book as she reached for the phone, Jorja decided she would try to make contact with the Chief first but after four rings she was disappointed when a message informed her office hours were only Monday through Friday. She left a message asking the

Chief to call her and then turned her attention back to her computer. Jorja ran a couple of searches using Kat's mother name and waited to see what might pop up. Jorja had already set up accounts with a couple of information brokers with the understanding that her access to certain information might be limited since she no longer worked at the law firm and did not hold a private investigator's license. Jorja thought about the fact that she might have to seriously look into getting licensed.

"What are you up to?" Jorja jumped in her chair. She hadn't heard Taylor come up the staircase to the office.

Jorja put a hand to her chest, trying to settle down the quick beating of her heart. She quickly looked under her desk and saw that Piper was still sound asleep and snoring. Jorja rolled her eyes and said, "I guess I might need to look into getting another dog. One that actually guards the place and makes me aware when someone enters the store."

"Sorry, didn't mean to scare you." Taylor grinned at Jorja but Jorja did not return the smile. Taylor may have verbally apologized but Jorja could tell Taylor wasn't *really* sorry. Taylor loved to scare Jorja, or anyone else for that matter. She got a kick out of it and Jorja could never understand Taylor's delight at causing someone else to panic.

Taylor could tell from Jorja's hard stare that the apology fell flat. "No, really, I am sorry. I did not purposely sneak up here. You were just so engrossed in what you were doing you didn't hear me. What's got you so entranced?"

Jorja took a deep breath to further control her heart beat before finally answering. "I'm trying to get some information for Kat. I'm running her mom's name through a couple of search engines and information brokers, hoping to come up with any address listing after the date of her disappearance."

"Well, good luck with that. I hope that kid doesn't get her hopes up. If her mom didn't want her then, what makes her think her mom will want anything to do with her now?"

Jorja didn't want to believe that was possible. "If I am able to find her, at least Kat can try to find out what happened and why her mother left. If nothing else, I hope her mother can at least confirm it wasn't because of Kat. The idea of your own mom not wanting you has got to be the worst feeling a child could ever have."

Taylor didn't seem convinced but she knew there was no putting Jorja off course. "Well, here's hoping for the best. Let me know if I can help in any way, okay?"

"Thanks. I appreciate that. Oh, I just received my first results." Jorja looked at the screen and the results she received. It was discouraging. The results of her search requests showed no information related to Kat's mother. No addresses, no property information, no hits on her social security number and date of birth, no verification that she even existed at this point. Jorja ran a couple more searches using Kat's mother's maiden name instead.

"Nothing so far. She must have changed her name. But her social security number would still be the same so I don't understand why that didn't bring up any hits. I wonder if there's something more to this story and she actually obtained a new name and somehow a new social security number? Nah, that's like something out of a movie. Besides, she'd have to illegally obtain a new social security number. It doesn't appear she'd have any reason to do that." Jorja's mind was full of ideas and she saw this as a real puzzle. Whether or not she would be able to solve it was the question.

Taylor sat down on the floor and crossed her legs. Piper, now alert to the fact that there was company, crawled out from under the desk to lie beside Taylor. Taylor absently rubbed the top of Piper's head as she said, "Maybe Kat's father was abusive and she had to run away to get away from him. Don't know why she'd leave Kat behind but maybe she knew he would look for her if she took Kat with her. Maybe Kat's mother got lucky and found a rich guy who married her, no questions asked and took care of her so that she never had to work. She'd have a new name and she could have hidden behind her new husband's name when it came to spending money."

Jorja frowned. "No, then that would make her guilty of bigamy. Why would she leave her husband and child only to marry again? I guess it could happen, if Kat's dad really was the violent type but from the conversations I've had with Kat, I just don't see that he was. Besides, if he had been violent, I'm sure at least someone would have known and the police would have looked into the possibility that he had something to do with his wife's disappearance. Maybe there's more to their relationship than Kat is aware of and maybe he did have something to do with it but that would be just awful for Kat." Jorja shook her head and sighed, "Oh, I don't know what to think. If Kat's mother left on her own, I just can't get past the fact that she left *her child*. What is bad enough to make a mother run away and leave a child behind?"

Taylor patted Piper on the head and stood up. "Those are all relevant questions, Jorja. But it sounds like you have an uphill battle because Kat has no answers, Kat's father is dead and the mother has no relatives who you can talk to. Have you thought about asking Lydia?"

Jorja sighed. "Yes, I've thought about it. But first I'll wait to see if any of my searches bring up any useful information." Jorja knew at some point she might have to speak to Lydia but she decided she would put it off until it became necessary. Jorja validated her reluctance by telling herself that if Lydia had any useful information with regard to Kat's mother, it would have already come to light.

"Well, I'm sure Lydia is just waiting for you to call her. You and she can talk over coffee and I'll stand by in case you need back up." Taylor giggled at the lack of enthusiasm on Jorja's face. "It's okay, Jorja, I'm sure the two of you can act like grownups, at least for Kat's sake anyway."

"Me? I can act like a grownup but I'm not too sure about Lydia. From the way she reacted the first day we saw each other, I'm not too sure she's changed at all." Jorja felt the early stirrings of frustration at the thought of a possible conflict. She would rather avoid it altogether.

The flush to Jorja's cheeks made Taylor realize how upset Jorja was getting. "I'm sure it'll be fine. Lydia was probably just surprised when she saw you and distracted because she thought she was going to be late for the baby shower. The next time you see her, I'm sure it'll be different, if she's not still upset about you helping Kat."

Jorja could only shrug, unwilling to fully agree with what Taylor was saying. "Yeah, maybe. We'll see. For now, I'll just do some more research and see what I can find."

"Well, don't forget to let me know if I can help. I actually came up to let you know that I placed an order for the supplies we'll need for our first book club meeting. I spoke to Dylan and he's willing to make up some special treats for the meetings and he agreed to the pricing you and I wanted. I also told him the meetings will be twice a month and he was okay with that."

"Great. I'm glad he's willing to work with us on the pricing. I'm excited for the book club meetings. I hope it will be a great way to get people here on a regular basis."

Taylor agreed with Jorja but was beginning to wonder if Jorja wasn't taking on too much too soon.

CHAPTER 10

Jorja left the bookstore feeling useless. After working on Kat's case for a couple of hours, she was not able to uncover any useful information with regard to Kat's mother. She finally decided to check into Kat's father's background but the information she was able to dig up on him did not raise any red flags. Jorja finally decided she needed to take a break and go home. She and Piper walked back to the house using the shortest route, passing a couple of local businesses on the way. While the route was the shortest way to walk home, it wasn't always the quickest if she became sidetracked by the owner of a local business or a child who wanted to pet Piper. During the walk, Jorja felt peace about her decision to move back to her home town. It was small, quaint, contained a friendly community and there was less crime than many of the surrounding cities. She truly felt she could be happy here.

As they reached Hillcrest and walked up the front porch, Piper ran ahead of her to wait at the front door. Piper instinctively knew it was close to dinner time so she was anxious to get inside. Jorja could hear the phone ringing inside the house so she quickly unlocked the front door and tried not to trip over Piper as she hurried towards the kitchen.

"Hello?" Jorja answered while setting her bag on the kitchen counter.

"Hello, is this Jorja Matthews?"

"Yes, can I help you?" Jorja glanced at Piper who began to whine for her evening meal.

"This is Chief Douglas. You called me about an old case you were looking in to. A woman who disappeared a few years back?"

"Oh, yes! Thanks for calling me back. I don't know how long you keep records like this but I'm hoping you have reports relating to the disappearance of Vera Myers. She was married to Robert Myers and was Kathleen Myer's mother. All I know is that Vera allegedly left her husband and child. Do you know if any investigation was conducted and if the reports would still be available?"

There was silence on the other end and then the Chief replied, "Allegedly? Why do you say that? Have you come across information that would suggest she did not leave on her own accord?"

"Well, no, nothing like that. There just appears to be some question as to where Vera actually might have gone. No one has heard from her in all this time and that seems odd to me. She hasn't even made any attempts to contact her daughter."

The Chief was no-nonsense. "Maybe she doesn't *wish* to have contact with her daughter. I wasn't the lead detective but I do recall there didn't seem to be any indication of foul play and I believe there was even a note left behind by Mrs. Myers. Chief Nelson was in charge then and I'm sure he did everything by the book. I don't know how you can determine anything other than that the lady ran off and left her husband and child."

Jorja realized she wasn't making any friends with the Chief. She wished she had a better rapport with him but her last memory of him was when he was a patrol officer while she was still in high school.

"I understand that might be the case, Chief, but I was just hoping I could get a look at any reports the investigating officer might have produced when she first disappeared, or left, as the case may be. Would you be able to find those records for me? Do you need me to fill out a public records request form?"

"We do have a public records request form you can fill out. Just come by the office anytime during business hours and fill one out. We'll have to check the files in archives to see what, if anything, is available. I don't know for a fact there is a report but if there is one, we can get you a copy. Will that do?"

Jorja could tell from his gruff manner that as far as he was concerned, the conversation was over. "Yes, Chief, that will do just fine. I'll stop by on Monday to fill out the form and I'll wait to hear from you with regard to what records you're able to locate. I really appreciate it."

"Don't thank me. You can thank Betsy, our front desk clerk, who will contact you once she's able to process your request. You have a good day now." Chief Douglas then hung up before Jorja could even reply with a goodbye.

Jorja hung up the phone. "Well, he's quite the bear, and I don't mean a cuddly one either." Piper, who had resorted to lying on the kitchen floor while waiting for Jorja to feed her, lifted her head and then her ears as she listened to Jorja. Not hearing any words corresponding to 'food' or 'treat,' Piper put her head back down on her paws. Piper then gave Jorja a sad look she could no longer ignore. "Oh, look at you just wasting away while I take my time on the phone. Come on, you big baby, let's go eat." Piper needed no further instruction as she leapt up off the floor and headed to her dinner bowl.

As Jorja fed Piper, she thought about her conversation with Chief Douglas. She could not understand why he was so grumpy with her about her request. Maybe he did not want to take the time to look for old records he thought would be useless but she wondered if there was another reason. Jorja shook the idea out of her head, certain there wasn't anything behind his response other than a man in a foul mood. She just hoped the records were still available so that she would be able to help Kat find some answers with regard to what happened to her mother.

~ ~ ~

Jorja had just finished taking lasagna out of the oven when she heard Taylor enter the house. *Boy, does she have a nose for food!* Taylor always had a knack for timing but when it came to food, it was almost uncanny.

Taylor entered the kitchen from the hall as she said, "That smells good, Jorja. I'm starving."

"You're just in time for dinner. I was beginning to wonder where you went. Weren't you able to close the bookstore on time or did you make a stop somewhere along the way?"

Taylor removed her coat and boots, leaving everything in the laundry room off the kitchen before heading back to the dining table. "Yes, I closed the store on time and yes, I decided to stop by to see Dylan. He is so talented. He wanted to show me the types of pastries he was planning to bake for our first book club meeting next week. He also taught me how to decorate some of those cute cupcakes he has in his bakery. They are adorable and also fun to make."

Jorja noticed the excitement in Taylor's voice as well as a sparkle in her eye. Jorja wasn't sure if Taylor would admit it but she seemed hooked not only on the pastries in the bakery but on the hunk of a baker.

"So you were with him making cupcakes? Not quite dinner and a movie, is it?"

Taylor laughed. "Yeah, but it wasn't a date. He's just fun to be around and I really enjoy hanging out with him."

"When is he going to take you on a real date? I mean, playing with pastries isn't really what it's all about, is it?"

"Jorja, we're not at that point yet. We're just friends. We have a good time together. That's it."

Jorja gave Taylor a look of disbelief and wondered why Taylor was denying her attraction to Dylan. "Okay, whatever you say. He's cute and he has his own business. At least he's a good catch from the little bit we know. There's no harm in thinking about the possibility of going on a date with him, is there?"

"I'm not saying I won't go on a date with him," Taylor replied. "I'm just saying we aren't at that point yet. When he's ready, he'll ask me and I'll say yes. Now, let's drop the subject and eat."

Taylor sat down at the table and began to dish up while Jorja poured two glasses of milk.

"So were you able to get anywhere with the search for Kat's mother?" Taylor asked.

Jorja told Taylor about not getting any hits with her computer searches and her conversation with Chief Douglas. "So, not the results I hoped for but at least I may get some records to look at and maybe have another starting point."

Taylor finished chewing and took a sip of milk. "Wow, the lasagna is great. Well, you can't always get what you want right away but if I know you, you won't stop digging until you find some answers. Here's hoping they are the answers you're looking for."

"Yeah, here's hoping. So, do you have any plans tomorrow?"

Taylor had her mouth full so Jorja waited. Finally, Taylor said, "No, I have no plans to speak of. Why?"

"Well, I thought I would take advantage of the weather to work on a few projects outside. I thought if you had no plans, you could give me a hand."

"You're not going to work on paperwork or Kat's case tomorrow?"

Jorja shook her head. "No, I'll have time to do that on Monday. I figured I'd leave Sundays to get work done around the house and since we're also closed on Mondays, those are the days I'll catch up on paperwork."

"Sounds good to me. You can't let this old house get the best of you so we better keep up on the chores. Just don't tell me we're going into any basement or attic full of cobwebs, okay?"

Jorja laughed. "No, nothing creepy like that. We'll just be working outside in the dirt, I promise."

CHAPTER 11

Sunday morning Jorja was up early after a fitful night's sleep. By the time Taylor woke up, Jorja had finished three cups of coffee and was wired and ready to go.

Jorja heard Taylor come down the stairs before finally entering the kitchen. Taylor moved slowly around the kitchen as she grabbed a coffee cup and filled it to the brim with coffee.

"Good morning, Taylor. How did you sleep?"

"I'm trying to get myself going. I didn't sleep too well last night. For some reason I kept having weird dreams and I woke up sweating a couple of times. I really need a full night's rest and I *hate* having bad dreams."

Taylor was still wearing her flannel pajamas as she stood by the counter and took a sip of her coffee. Jorja marveled at how good Taylor could look first thing in the morning while still dressed in something as simple as flannel.

"I'm sorry you had bad dreams. I didn't sleep very well either. Maybe we're both working too hard."

Taylor's eyes were closed as she enjoyed another sip of coffee. She opened them as she replied, "No, I don't think it's the work. You know I love to keep busy. I don't know what it is but I feel restless and the dreams do not help."

Jorja poured herself another cup of coffee as she asked, "How about your new friend? Maybe you're feeling restless because you don't know where the relationship is going? It's been awhile since you've met such a nice guy."

Taylor grimaced. "I don't know. Maybe the thought of getting into a relationship is a bit scary for me. I don't want to think about that right now. So what are your plans for today?"

Jorja sat down to put on her tennis shoes. As she laced them up she replied, "I thought we could work on the gardens outside, winterize the gardens and the yard and also plant some bulbs for the spring. There are a few trees that need pruning and some rose bushes I think I'd like to move as well."

"Sounds good. It will be nice to spend some time outdoors. I'll go get changed and meet you outside."

Taylor left the kitchen to head upstairs to her room. Jorja finished lacing up her shoes and then went out to the backyard with Piper right on her heels. While waiting for Taylor, Jorja took the time to gather some tools and a wheelbarrow from the storage shed. After placing all the items on the back patio, Jorja sat down on the lounge chair to wait for Taylor while she finished her coffee. She looked over the back yard with appreciation. She had never really admired or even cared about the back yard or gardens when she had been living at the house with her parents. As a kid, yard work or spending time in the back yard was not on her priority list. Now, she could appreciate the decent-sized back yard, the established rose garden and raised beds just waiting for the next vegetable garden to be planted. The yard was big enough for Piper to run around and play but it wasn't too large so that it would take forever to mow. Jorja also loved the rose garden and was thankful her aunt had been able to keep up with the pruning and other work necessary to keep the garden looking healthy. With fall just beginning, Jorja knew the roses and other areas of the yard needed some care before winter set in.

The screen door slammed shut as Taylor came out of the house. "It looks like we're going to have a beautiful day today. I feel like I haven't been outside much since we've been putting so much work into the bookstore."

Jorja gulped down the rest of her coffee and got up from the lounge chair. Piper thought it was time to play and happily dropped a ball at Jorja's feet.

"What a pill. Always expecting to play when it's time to work." Jorja picked up the ball and threw it across the lawn and Piper took off after the ball at a sprint.

"You know she's going to keep expecting you to play while we're out here. If you'd like, I'll play with Piper while you work on the yard." Taylor gave Jorja a sly grin and winked. "I'm just kidding, of course. So, what do you want me to do first?"

Jorja pointed towards the fence. "Can you help me out by pruning those bushes over there along the fence? And both trees in the corners need to be cut back. Just cut back any low hanging branches or any branches that stick out too much into the walkway. I'll get started with the bulbs I want to plant and then mow the lawn."

Jorja moved to the back area of the yard where the rose garden was located alongside the back fence. The raised garden beds had been placed between the rose garden and the fence located to the right of the yard. Jorja noticed her aunt had planted some herbs and it appeared there were still some potatoes and carrots in the ground. The tomatoes had all ripened and fallen off the plants, leaving nothing but rotten tomatoes on the ground. Jorja decided she would dig up the remaining vegetables and clean the garden area up before she planted the spring bulbs. Using a spade, she dug up the potatoes and carrots and was delighted to find a healthy supply of both that were still edible.

"Hey, I found some red potatoes and some carrots here. Maybe we can make a stew for dinner this week?"

Taylor yelled back from under the tree she was trying to prune, "That's great! If you cook it, I'll eat it!"

Jorja went back to digging up the rest of the vegetables and then thought she should set aside an area for a compost pile. As she walked around the yard to find a suitable location for the compost pile, she realized Piper was not at her side. If Piper wasn't whining to play ball or demanding attention, she would usually lie somewhere near Jorja if she was busy on a project. Jorja looked around and finally spotted Piper.

"Piper! You stop that!"

Piper guiltily looked back at Jorja as she stopped the frantic digging. When Jorja walked to the rose garden, she discovered that Piper had already dug quite a large hole between two rose bushes. Jorja's attention had been so occupied by the vegetable garden she had not noticed what Piper had been up to the whole time.

"Just because I'm digging a hole doesn't mean you get to dig too, Piper."

Piper lay down on the ground and then rolled over onto her back. With her legs up, her belly exposed and her tongue hanging out as she panted, it was difficult for Jorja to continue to scold Piper.

Jorja bent down and gave Piper's belly a quick rub. "Oh, you are a pain but you're my pain and you're too cute to hold a grudge against."

Once Jorja stood up, Piper rolled back over and jumped on her feet with the apparent understanding that she was no longer in trouble.

"Okay, let's see how much damage you've done." Before using her spade to move the dirt back into the hole, Jorja bent down by the rose bushes to make sure Piper had not damaged them. Seeing no obvious damage to the roots, Jorja moved the dirt around with her hand and was surprised when her fingers hit a solid object. Thinking it was just a rock, she moved the dirt to see more. Instead of a rock, Jorja saw something with color but as she moved the dirt around she realized that only a portion of the object was sticking out of the ground. She used her spade to dig more dirt away so as to loosen the object from its hiding place. It was then that Jorja realized the object appeared to be some sort of tin box.

CHAPTER 12

Jorja continued to dig around the box, curious now about what it was and what might be inside.

"Hey, I thought you were going to work on the rose bushes later?" Taylor said as she snuck up behind Jorja.

"I found something here. Actually, Piper found it when she decided to dig a hole."

"Found something? What?" Taylor peeked over Jorja's shoulder in an attempt to see what she was digging for.

"I don't know yet. Hold on." Jorja continued to dig until she was able to grab the box and finally pull it free. Jorja looked at the box in her hands. It was a tin box with some type of picture on the lid but it was so rusted, Jorja couldn't quite make out anything other than what might have been a rabbit. Jorja wondered if it wasn't a Beatrix Potter tin because the drawing looked similar to those she'd seen in Beatrix Potter books.

"Who the heck buried a tin out here? Is it yours?"

Jorja shook her head. "No, I didn't have anything like this. I'll have to show Mom, maybe she can tell me. But first I need to open it. Maybe whatever is inside will tell us who it belonged to."

Jorja tried to pry the lid off the tin but it was rusted shut.

"I need to go to the shed. I'll have to use a screwdriver or something to try to get the lid off."

Taylor followed Jorja to the shed where Jorja used a screwdriver to finally loosen the lid from the tin box. Jorja removed the lid and looked inside. Taylor watched as Jorja removed the items. Jorja first set aside what appeared to be folded paper. Under the paper Jorja found an old gold band. It had no stones so Jorja couldn't guess whether it was a friendship ring, engagement ring or something else. Jorja used her finger to remove the ring in order to look at it in the sunlight.

"What kind of ring is it?" Taylor curiously asked as she tried to get a good look.

"It just seems to be a simple band." Jorja placed the ring on her pinky finger and inspected the remaining items in the box. She found a rock in the shape of a heart, an old pin Jorja thought might be a high school pin and a good amount of loose material which Jorja thought may have once been dried flowers.

Taylor had to restrain herself from grabbing the paper Jorja had set to the side. Instead, she asked, "So what's the paper? Is it a note?"

Jorja looked at the folded paper. She was curious but she also felt a sense of dread. She wondered why anyone would bury all these keepsake items in the garden. She couldn't believe they were put in the ground for safekeeping. She could believe they were put in the ground to be hidden but then she had to wonder why. None of the items were of any real value or appeared to be anything that could cause trouble if someone else were to find them. Jorja knew she would have to open the note to see if there were any clues as to who had buried the tin box.

"Let's take this inside before we open the letter." Jorja placed all the items back in the box. "Will you grab a newspaper from the pile in the laundry room?" Jorja carefully held the box as she left the shed and walked back to the house with Taylor and Piper right on her heels.

Once they were both in the house, Taylor opened the newspaper and placed it on the kitchen table. Jorja then placed the tin box on the paper and removed all the items. She held the folded paper and looked at it closely. The paper had some coloring but it appeared to Jorja that the lid on the tin box had kept most of the moisture out. She wondered how long the tin box had actually been buried. Jorja carefully unfolded the letter, having difficulty as the paper tore where the letter had been folded. When Jorja was finally able to completely open the letter, it had torn into three pieces. Jorja placed each ripped portion onto the newspaper where she could see that it was a handwritten letter.

"What's it say?" Taylor asked as she moved closer to Jorja in an attempt to read the handwriting.

It had faded over the years but Jorja could make out most of the words as she read the letter out loud to Taylor.

"*To my lost love: I will never understand why you abandoned me. I cannot understand why you have forgotten all the promises we made to each other. I have kept my promise to love you forever and to keep our secret about being together. You promised we would one day be together forever. You lied to me. Instead, you have left with no word about when I would see you again. I am carrying your child. What am I to do with a baby? Have you lost your love for me? What have I done? How can I go on without you? My heart is broken and I will never be able to love another ever again. I can never trust anyone again. You have hurt me too deeply. If I knew where you were, I would send you this letter but for now it is written so that I may attempt to mend my shattered heart. Forever broken-hearted, Gloria.*"

Jorja looked at Taylor and said, "Oh my God. Aunt Gloria? If this is from my Aunt Gloria, she had a *baby*? No one ever told me that. Mom never told me that. That would mean I have a cousin no one ever told me about!"

Taylor was also shocked by the implications of the letter.

"Well, maybe there was a reason they never told you. Maybe the baby was adopted out. Maybe the baby didn't make it. Your aunt was sent to the mental hospital when she was what…about sixteen? Your parents never told you why? Maybe your aunt was sent to the hospital because it had something to do with the baby or her feelings of betrayal concerning the father. There could be any number of reasons why they didn't tell you about the baby."

Jorja wiped at tears that began to form. "I don't care what the reasons were, they should have told me. Aunt Gloria had a child, or at least was pregnant and I have to find something buried in the back yard before I find out about it. I'm going to talk to Mom. I need to know what happened."

Taylor felt sympathy for her friend so she reached over to give her a hug. "I'm sorry Jorja. I know you want answers. Let me know if you want me to go with you if you go up to your parents. Either way, I'm here for you."

Jorja folded each piece of the letter and returned it and the other items to the tin box. "Thanks, Taylor, I appreciate it. I'll find out from Mom what day she's coming down and if it's soon, I'll wait to speak to her when she's here. If not, I'll have to take a day trip to see her."

"I completely understand. You do what you have to do, okay?"

Jorja placed the tin box on the kitchen counter and picked up the phone to call her mother. She wasn't sure she could get through the phone conversation without asking multiple questions but she believed it was probably best to wait until she was face-to-face with her mother before asking her about the tin box and its contents. As she dialed her parents' phone number, Jorja hoped her mother would have all the answers to her questions but she also felt anxious about whether the answers were something she really wanted to hear.

CHAPTER 13

Jorja had to put off speaking to her mom in person until Wednesday so to keep her mind off her aunt and the tin box, Jorja kept busy with Kat's case. After visiting the police station Monday morning to fill out the public records request Chief Douglas had asked for, Jorja spent the rest of the day conducting more research and getting prepared for the first book club meeting. After submitting her request to the police department, Jorja began to worry about what she might do if no report was available so she was surprised when she received a phone call at the store Tuesday morning.

"Miss Matthews? This is Betsy over at the police department. Chief Douglas wanted me to give you a call. I was able to locate that report for you and wanted to let you know in case you had time to pick it up before we close the office for the day."

Jorja was amazed at how quickly the report had been found. "Well, that was quick. I didn't think I'd hear back from you for at least a week or longer."

Jorja heard Betsy give a small laugh before saying, "Oh, you know how it is in a small town, Miss Matthews. There's not much to my day other than answering the phone, going through the mail and filing paperwork. You were just lucky that we hold the archived reports down in the basement rather than another location."

"Well, thank you very much, Betsy. I appreciate you getting right to my request. I will definitely stop by this afternoon. What time do you close?"

"We close the business office at five o'clock sharp. A copy of the report will be in an envelope with your name on it so you can stop by anytime to pick it up."

Jorja thanked Betsy again before hanging up. She could not get past how quickly Betsy had found the report. Jorja was used to dealing with larger departments, where it could take quite awhile to obtain requested documents due to the high number of requests received each day.

Jorja left her office and walked down the stairs to the main floor of the store. Taylor was busy with a customer who had ordered a cinnamon latte so Jorja sat behind the register to review the most recent inventory list while waiting for Taylor to finish.

Taylor handed the latte to the customer after ringing up the sale and joined Jorja at one of the tables.

"So what's up? Is your morning a productive one so far?" Taylor asked.

Jorja nodded. "Can you believe that the police department already found the report relating to Kat's mom? That was who I just got off the phone with."

"Wow, that was quick. Are you going to get it today?"

"Yeah, they close at 5 p.m. and I thought I'd get a few more things done here but now I am too curious. I need to go get the report now. I want to see how much, or how little, information is in the report. Do you mind if I run over there right now?"

Taylor looked around the store. Other than the woman who had just ordered the latte, there were only two other customers perusing the book shelves.

"Go ahead, I can handle it. Are you going to tell Kat about the report when she gets here this afternoon?"

"No, I think I should review it and then attempt to verify what's in the report. I'll talk to her about it when I know I have something specific to tell her."

Taylor got up from the table as another customer entered the bookstore.

"Okay, go ahead and go. I've got it covered here."

Jorja watched as Taylor straightened her blouse and ran her fingers through her hair. Curious, Jorja looked to see who had caught

Taylor's attention and the reason for adjusting her blouse and hair. Jorja smiled when she saw Dylan standing just inside the store. He seemed unwilling to intrude and waited until Taylor walked up to him.

"Hi, Dylan. What a surprise to see you here."

Dylan gave Jorja a glance before saying hello and then turned his attention back to Taylor.

Jorja knew she was no longer needed so she said her goodbyes and left the store. Betsy was at the police department when Jorja arrived to pick up the report.

"You let me know if you have any questions, okay? That's the only report I was able to find on that case and you'll see there wasn't much to go on. But if you need anything else, you let me know. I was just starting out here at the office when Vera went missing but I might be able to recall some things if you have any questions."

Jorja opened the envelope to briefly look at the report.

"It says here that the investigating officer was an Officer Cooper? Is he still working here?"

Betsy shook her head. "No, he was here less than a year after Kat's mother's disappearance and then he took a job with another city department."

Jorja frowned as she looked at the report again. "Cooper? Is he related to Sandra Bennett? Her maiden name Cooper."

Betsy smiled at the memory. "Why yes! That's right. I forget Sandra had a brother.

Although he still lives nearby I very rarely run
into him. You'd have to ask Sandra how to reach
him if you have any questions about the case. I'm
sure he won't mind discussing it with you."

Jorja thanked Betsy for the report and left
the station. She wanted to get back to the
bookstore to finish up her day so she could go
home to review the report in detail. Jorja knew she
was hoping for a miracle but she wanted to
believe there might be something in the report that
would give her a clue as to what happened to
Kat's mother.

~ ~ ~

Jorja and Taylor finished out the day at the
bookstore and then went home to have a quick
dinner so that Jorja could begin working again on
Kat's case. Taylor finished cleaning up the kitchen
and said, "I know you want to get to work on that
report, Jorja. Do you want me to take Piper for a
walk so you don't have to?"

Although the fresh air would have been
good, Jorja was happy to let Taylor take Piper out
for her evening walk. Piper, having heard the
word 'walk' was running back and forth between
Jorja and Taylor, waiting to see who was going to
grab her leash.

"That would be great, Taylor. I would
really appreciate it."

Taylor grabbed Piper's leash and the two
left while Jorja sat down at her computer to begin

reviewing the police report. Jorja noted that the date of the report was twelve years ago, when Kat would have only been five years old. The report was limited, verifying a brief timeline and information obtained after the officer's first contact with Kat's father, Robert, and an interview with a neighbor.

Jorja dug out a handwritten statement made by Robert. Based on his statement to the police, Robert had been at a business meeting and when he returned to the house, neither mother nor daughter were home. He was able to track down Kat at a neighbor's house, where he learned his wife, Vera, had asked the neighbor to babysit Kat while she ran some errands. The neighbor was not able to give Robert any additional information because Vera had not informed the neighbor where she was going. Robert finally decided to make contact with the police when his wife had still not returned home by midnight. Robert's statement also included a brief description of his wife's height, weight, eye and hair color. Although he wasn't sure what she had been wearing, he was certain she'd been wearing her black rain jacket as well as her red leather gloves.

Jorja reviewed Officer Cooper's report again, which verified he spoke to the neighbor after taking Robert's statement but he ended his report with the conclusion that, while the case was still pending, there was nothing to suggest foul play. Jorja turned the page to discover a supplemental report completed by Officer Cooper on the following day. The second report stated that Kat's father contacted Officer Cooper again to report Vera had still not come home and had not made any attempt to contact him. The report then stated that Robert admitted he found a note from his wife in their master bathroom. According to the report, Officer Cooper asked Robert why he was only now finding the note and Robert's reply was that he had not noticed the note because he had slept on the couch while waiting for his wife to return. Officer Cooper further stated that he met with Robert in order to obtain the note, which was placed into evidence.

She looked through the paperwork to find a copy of an evidence sheet and was grateful when she found a copy of the note attached. She read the handwritten note:

"Dear Bob, I am sorry but I cannot pretend any longer. This life is not for me. I do not mean to hurt you or Kat but I have to make a life for myself someplace else. I am truly sorry. Please forgive me. Vera."

Reading the note again, Jorja was unable to believe that a mother could leave her 5-year old daughter. Leaving her husband was one thing but leaving a child was another matter. Jorja guessed Vera must have been battling some terrible demons.

Jorja read through the supplemental report. According to Officer Cooper, Robert said he was not able to find Vera's purse and although most of her clothing appeared to be hanging in her closet, a small suitcase was also missing. Robert also informed Officer Cooper that his wife's Bible appeared to be missing from her bedside table. Jorja read through the remainder of Officer Cooper's supplemental report, where he stated that Vera's vehicle had not been located and was presumably with her, Robert's alibi had been verified for the time of his wife's disappearance and that based on the evidence, it seemed likely Vera left on her own accord. Officer Cooper's final conclusion was that, while the investigation would be considered still pending, there would be no further follow up unless new information came to light.

Jorja sat back and thought for a minute. What made a woman leave to start a new life? She wondered if Vera hid money so that she could leave when she did. It didn't appear Vera could have made much money, as Jorja remembered Kat saying her mother only worked part-time at the local library. But Jorja was having a difficult time understanding how Vera could leave and then *never* have contact with her daughter again. What was it about being a mother or a wife that drove Vera away? Jorja felt even more determined to figure out how Vera dropped off the grid to start a new life. Either Vera had help changing her name in order to move to a new location or she was missing something.

Turning on her laptop to do some more research, Jorja could not push away the thought that she was missing something. She was determined to find out what it was.

CHAPTER 14

Helen had been on pins and needles ever since Jorja asked to speak with her without any hint as to why. Jorja had asked to meet at the house rather than the bookstore, which only added to Helen's anxiety. Helen pulled her car into the driveway and gathered her purse along with some paperwork for the bookstore she wanted to review with Jorja. Helen walked up the porch to the front door, opened the screen door and then rapped on the front door as she opened it.

Helen called out as she walked through the family room into the dining room and kitchen.

"Jorja? It's Mom."

Helen could smell the fresh pot of coffee so she put her purse and other items down in order to grab a cup from the cupboard. She heard Jorja yell from upstairs, "I'll be right down Mom!"

Helen heard a noise and jumped in surprise as Piper came rushing in through the dog door. Piper's excitement at having company was evident based on her happy gait as she bounced towards Helen but Helen was quick to hold out her hand before Piper could get any closer.

"Stop right there, Piper! Don't you dare come any closer."

Piper slid to a stop and reluctantly sat her bottom on the kitchen floor. Helen was wearing cream-colored slacks and heels and she did not want Piper's dark hair anywhere near her clothing. Helen quickly patted Piper on the top of her head and went back to pouring herself a cup of coffee.

"Now, you go lay down. That's a good girl."

Helen heard Jorja running down the stairs just before she rushed into the kitchen through the hallway. Piper stood up and trotted towards Jorja, expecting more attention than what she'd received from Helen.

"Now, Piper, I can't play right now. Here, go play with your toy." Jorja picked up a stuffed dog toy and threw it down the hall. Piper gleefully ran after it and was soon gnawing on the toy while lying near the front door.

"Hi Mom, how was the drive down?" Jorja gave her mom a hug.

"Oh, it was good. There's more construction going on up north so it is noticeably affecting traffic but it's just par for the course right now."

Jorja took creamer out of the fridge and made herself a cup of coffee.

"Do you want some creamer?"

"No, black is fine with me, thanks."

Jorja grimaced. "Ugh. I don't know how you can enjoy black coffee. It tastes so much better with flavor."

Helen took a sip of her coffee and said, "At my age, I need to watch my weight and those extra pounds would certainly sneak up on me if I doused my coffee with creamer like you do."

With only a hint of guilt on her face, Jorja put the creamer back in the fridge and carried her coffee cup to the table. "Thanks for coming by the house, Mom. I thought it would be better to talk here rather than at the store."

Helen raised her eyebrows at Jorja. "Well, what do we have to talk about that needs to be kept private? Has something happened? Is everything okay?"

Jorja wasn't really sure how to start the conversation. "Everything is okay. Well, I'm okay but I'm upset, I guess. I found something this weekend and I want to ask you about it."

Helen frowned. "What did you find? What is making you upset?"

Jorja got up and went to the laundry room where she had placed the tin box. She grabbed the box and brought it back to the kitchen table where she set it in front of her mother.

"What's this? This is what you found? Why would this make you upset?"

Jorja saw the look of confusion on her mother's face. She realized then that her mother may not have any idea where the tin box came from.

"It's not the box, Mom, but what's inside that upset me. Here, let me show you." Jorja reached over and grabbed the box. She lifted the lid off the box and removed the note. She then removed the smaller items and poured them onto the lid so Helen could see them.

"Do you recognize any of these items, Mom?"

Helen stared at the ring, the pin and the rock. She looked back at Jorja and said, "Well, no, I don't recognize them. Should I?"

Jorja handed her mother the note. "Here, this was with the items and it is honestly what upset me the most. Read it."

Helen hesitantly took the note. Jorja watched as Helen carefully opened the letter and placed the individual ripped pieces together on the table. She then watched as her mother read the note. Jorja watched her mother's face for any reaction and she realized quickly that her mother knew exactly who had written the note.

Helen's face paled as she placed a hand on her chest. "Oh, dear, where did you find this?"

"I found it in the tin buried in the rose garden. What is this, Mom? Did Aunt Gloria really have a child? What happened to it?"

Helen took her time answering. She gingerly refolded the letter, careful not to rip it any further. She then placed the letter back into the tin box and stared at it, lost in thought.

"Mom? Can you tell me what happened?"

Helen looked at Jorja. Jorja could see tears in her mother's eyes. She hadn't realized how upsetting this might be for her mother and was glad she had asked her to come to the house rather than the store.

"Mom?"

Helen covered her face with her hands and let out a sob. Jorja felt awful at her mom's reaction as she got up to grab a tissue from the bathroom. She handed the tissue to her mother as she sat back down at the table.

"Mom, please tell me what happened. When did Aunt Gloria get pregnant? What happened to the baby? And why was Aunt Gloria sent to a mental hospital?"

Helen wiped her eyes and blew her nose. She would not make eye contact with Jorja. Jorja watched as her mother appeared to deal with conflicting emotions and Jorja became concerned that her mother might not actually answer her questions.

"Oh, Jorja, I knew this day would come but I hoped it wouldn't."

Jorja waited but her mother seemed reluctant to speak any further.

"Mom, just tell me what happened. Did Aunt Gloria get pregnant?"

Helen took a deep breath and said, "Yes, she did."

When her mother seemed to hesitate, Jorja prodded some more. "When did it happen?"

"When she was sixteen years old. Or she was probably pregnant when she was still fifteen, I guess. I was not living at home at the time. I had been married to your father for three years by then and we were living in Spokane, only coming home to visit a few times a year."

"So she had the baby? What happened to it?"

Helen let out a sigh. "It died, Jorja. I wasn't here but all I know is that it died. My parents weren't able to save the baby and Gloria suffered a breakdown after the baby died. I guess she never told my parents who the father was but he had apparently left her and she felt abandoned. She was extremely upset about the fact that he left her and even more so after the baby died. That's why my parents placed her in the mental hospital. She was very distraught and they were afraid she was going to hurt herself."

Helen let out another heavy sigh and her shoulders slumped as she finished speaking. Suddenly, Helen stood up and said, "I need to use the restroom. I'll be right back."

Jorja was surprised at her mother's sudden exit but she remained at the table and patiently waited. She could hear her mother in the bathroom, blowing her nose again. After a few more moments, Helen finally came back to the dining table and sat down. Helen remained quiet, leaving the decision up to Jorja whether the conversation would continue.

Jorja knew her mother would prefer to close the subject but she stubbornly decided to move on. "Okay, I guess I can understand why grandma and grandpa felt they had to commit Aunt Gloria but why was she committed at the hospital for such a long time? She was institutionalized for what, something like twenty years? That seems excessive to me." Jorja could not begin to imagine how terrible it must have been for her aunt to go through losing a child but to be sent from her home for such a long time seemed even worse.

"Your aunt just never seemed to get better after that, Jorja. After quite a few years she seemed content at the hospital so my parents did not attempt to bring her home. When Mother and Daddy passed away, there was no reason to try to remove Gloria from the hospital because I thought she would do better where she was comfortable. When the doctor finally released her it was a surprise to me but I guess she was well enough. Honestly, I was glad to let her move back into the house so that we could finally buy the condo in Edmonds. The change seemed good for her and Gloria did very well on her own until the accident."

Jorja thought about what her mother said. Then another thought occurred to her.

"Wait a minute. Aunt Gloria was pregnant or had the baby when she was sixteen years old?"

Helen nodded and waited for Jorja to continue.

"And you had me when you were twenty-two years old? That means you and Gloria were pregnant at the same time? My cousin and I would have been the same age?"

Helen thought a moment and then said, "Yes, that's true. You would have been the same age."

"Did Aunt Gloria have a boy or a girl?"

Helen's eyes glistened with tears as she looked at Jorja. "She had a boy."

"What was his name? What hospital was he born in? Is he buried here in town at the cemetery?"

Helen put her hand against her forehead. "Oh, Jorja, do we really have to talk about this? I'm starting to get a headache. It's been so long since I've had to think about it. It's over and done with and there's nothing we can do to change it!"

Jorja was surprised at her mother's outburst. "I'm sorry Mom. I'm just curious. I would just like to know if the baby is buried someplace where I can visit his grave. I didn't mean to upset you."

Helen put her fingers to her temples and rubbed them. "That's all right, Jorja. I'm sorry. His name was Jacob and I don't know where he was buried. Honestly, don't look at me like that. Your grandparents only told me about the baby and that he had died after the fact. He wasn't born in a hospital because he was born here at the house and your grandparents called in their doctor to help out. I don't know where he was buried and when I found out what had happened, I didn't ask for the details."

"Okay, I didn't mean to upset you. Thank you for telling me." Jorja reached over to give her mother a hug. Helen hugged her back with a tight squeeze, reluctant at first to let go when Jorja tried to pull away.

Jorja looked at her mother and gave her another quick hug. "I love you, Mom. Thanks for talking to me about this. Do you think you'll be ready to go to the store in about a half hour?"

Helen wiped her nose with the tissue again and nodded her head. "Yes, just give me a little time to compose myself and then we can take off. I'll drive if you'd like."

Jorja got up from the table to head back upstairs to finish getting ready. As she brushed her hair in her bathroom, Jorja became lost in thought as she recalled the details her mother divulged to her. Jorja wished she could rid herself of the nagging feeling that there was more to the story than her mother was willing to share.

CHAPTER 15

By the end of the week Jorja had completed most of the online searching she could think of in an attempt to locate the whereabouts of Kat's mother. Considering how long ago Vera had disappeared, it was more than likely some records would not be accessible on the Internet for the time period when Vera had last been seen. After the searches revealed no hits Jorja began to wonder if there was another possibility. What if Vera was actually dead? What if she died shortly after disappearing? Any number of things could have happened. Jorja thought about the possibility that Vera might have gotten into an accident of some kind shortly after she left her husband and child. If Vera had no identification on her, she would have been listed as a "Jane Doe." Or it was possible Vera had been using a different name so that the authorities might not have known Vera had relatives to contact at the time of her death. The missing vehicle gave Jorja more to think about, as any accident in the vehicle would have allowed the police to identify her. She had to wonder whatever happened to Vera's vehicle.

Rolling her head around in wide circles, Jorja attempted to stretch the muscles in her neck. Feeling a little better, she turned to her computer to get back to work. Although she did not wish to discover Vera had actually been dead all this time, she hoped if something did happen it occurred close to home. If Vera had been able to leave the state and then died under a false name, Jorja knew her chances of finding that information were slim. To start the search, she decided to investigate local records relating to the death of any "Jane Doe" or the body of any "Jane Doe" discovered around the time Vera had disappeared.

Beginning first with the State Patrol, Jorja was forwarded to the National Missing and Unidentified Persons Systems. Using a basic search for unidentified Caucasian women in the State of Washington no matter the timeframe, she received just over half a dozen hits. She reviewed the data provided for each case to discover that five of the victims' bodies were found before Vera had even disappeared, one had an estimated age of a grandmother and the last, a more recent discovery, was thought to have also died very recently. Jorja decided to advance her search to various local police departments within a sixty-mile radius of town. She used the rest of the afternoon to contact various city and county officials by phone and email in order to establish how she could request the information. She then spent a good amount of time filling out requests online, providing what little information she had with the knowledge that some departments would have a difficult time processing her request.

"Jorja? Do you have a minute?" Jorja looked up from her computer to discover Kat had snuck up the staircase and was now looking at her expectantly.

"Sure, Kat, have a seat. Is everything going okay downstairs?"

Kat's ponytail bobbed up and down as she nodded her head at Jorja. "Yes, everything is fine. We've had quite a few customers today and Mrs. Pritchard's second grade class came in today for their book reading. It was so cute watching them all and I'm glad I only had a half day at school so I was here to help out. They enjoyed the book reading and they especially enjoyed the cookies."

Jorja smiled. "I'm glad to see the school classes make use of the children's book section. We'll be sure to tell Dylan how much the kids liked his treats. So, are you taking off for the night?"

"Yes, I'm done for the night but I wanted to ask you...well...I hate to bother you because I know you have a lot going on but I was just wondering if you've found anything out about my mom yet?"

"Oh, hey, you're not bothering me, Kat. I know you want to get answers and I understand you've waited a very long time for them. I have been running various searches and I'm now attempting to locate some additional records. Whether I find anything or not, I won't be able to tell you until I finish what I am currently working on."

"So the report you got from the Chief wasn't very helpful?"

Jorja shook her head and sighed. "No, not really. And it appears the police didn't investigate any further into your mom's case once the initial reports were filed because it was their conclusion she left on her own. I'm sorry nothing has come up yet but I'll keep working at it, okay?"

Kat smiled at Jorja and stood up. "Oh, I know you're working on it, Jorja, and I really appreciate all your help with this. I better get going. I promised to show up early for the game to help with concessions. Do you need me to come in tomorrow?"

"Mom will be back down again tomorrow morning to help out but Taylor needs to leave early because she and Dylan are going out on a date. Since tomorrow is Saturday, how about you sleep in and just come in around one o'clock to help me out for the rest of the afternoon until we close. Does that sound okay with you?"

Kat nodded and said, "That would be great. I'll see you tomorrow!"

As Jorja listened to Kat bounce down the stairs, her thoughts were pulled back to the records she had requested and what, if anything, they might offer. She truly hoped that the news surrounding Kat's mother's disappearance did not end as she now feared it might. Jorja could not decide what was worse; believing a mother no longer wanted her child or discovering that the mother had been dead the whole time others thought she had run away.

~ ~ ~

A week went by before Jorja began receiving emails and letters by mail regarding her requests for records from various police departments. Most of the replies informed her no such records were located or that she needed to narrow down her search request. When she finally received an email from a nearby police department indicating there might be some records relevant to her request, she did not hesitate to comply with the request to call to make an appointment to review the records. Once she learned from the records clerk that business hours did not include the weekend, she agreed to schedule her appointment for the following Monday at ten o'clock in the morning. After hanging up with the records clerk, Jorja received a phone call from a clerk at the local sheriff's office.

"Is this Ms. Jorja Matthews?"

"Yes, it is. Can I help you?"

"Oh, I think I can help you. This is Cheryl Dunham with the County Sheriff's Office. I'm the records clerk and I'm responding to your request for records. It took me a couple of days but I have some records here for you to review."

"You do? That's great." Jorja looked at her watch and saw the time was just past four o'clock. "I know it's probably too late to come in today. Could I make an appointment for sometime this weekend?"

"I'm actually not working this weekend so we'll have to set up a time to meet on Monday."

Jorja sighed. She really wanted to see those records *now*. "Okay, Monday is fine. Would one o'clock work?"

"How about one-thirty because that's when I'll be back from lunch."

Jorja agreed and hung up the phone. It looked like Monday would be a busy day for her and although she hoped the records provided her with information she also hoped that they didn't.

"Okay, Piper, I think we can go for that walk now."

Piper had been snoring under Jorja's desk and at the mention of her name and her most favorite word, *walk*, Piper's head popped up, hitting the bottom of the desk. Jorja laughed at Piper's klutziness but then feeling guilty, she bent down to make sure Piper hadn't actually hurt herself. Piper showed no pain as she finally got up off the floor and headed towards the stairs.

"You are a klutz and there is no denying it, Piper." Jorja smiled as she grabbed Piper's leash and followed Piper down the stairs.

"Hey, Taylor, will you be okay while I take Piper out for a quick walk?"

Taylor was sitting near the cash register, going through a box of new books that had just arrived. "Yeah, I'll be fine. It's quieted down. I think everyone is getting ready for the football game tonight. Do you want to head over after we close up shop to watch the game?"

Taylor noticed Jorja hesitate before answering. "Well, if you want to go, I'll go with you. Is Dylan going to meet you there?"

Taylor smiled. "Yes, Dylan will be there. But more importantly, Brad will be there. You haven't watched him coach a game yet, have you?"

"Why would I need to watch him coach a game? Why does it matter that he'll be there anyway?" Jorja turned her head from Taylor as she realized her cheeks were feeling hot.

"Oh, come on! I know you still like him! At least you are *interested* in him, aren't you?"

Jorja rolled her eyes and hooked Piper's leash onto her collar. "Look, I'll agree to watch the game with you but stop trying to set me up. Brad and I are friends and nothing more at this point, okay?"

Taylor shrugged and held a hand up as if to ward off Jorja's annoyance. "Okay, okay, I get it. I'll drop the subject...for now.."

Jorja held her tongue as she led Piper out of the store for a walk. Taylor loved to argue or at least find a way to prove her point and Jorja was not in the mood to let her complete either when it came to the subject of Brad.

CHAPTER 16

The weather was thankfully mild Sunday afternoon as Jorja drove the hour and a half it took to reach the mental hospital where her aunt had resided for almost twenty years. The sudden day trip to the hospital was scheduled after she received an odd phone call on Saturday from a woman claiming to be a nurse at the hospital. She had quickly become frustrated with the woman who would only say her name was Edna and that it was necessary to meet with Jorja in person regarding some information she wanted to share.

By the time Jorja drove into the parking lot at the hospital, her mind was racing with ideas about why Edna had contacted her. She parked her car and walked to the main entrance where a receptionist paged the nurse for her. As Jorja heard the receptionist page 'Nurse Willows to the front desk please,' she thought, *Well, now I have a full name*. Her curiosity was getting the better of her as she waited ten minutes for Edna to finally arrive in the lobby area. She curiously watched the nurse as she entered the lobby and approached her. Edna Willows looked the part of a nurse who had been employed at a hospital for quite some time. Or, at least what Jorja thought a nurse might look like. Nurse Willows' chunky frame was covered with a white nurse's uniform over white shoes, her salt and pepper hair was cut severely short and her reading glasses were hanging from a beaded chain around her neck. She was certain Edna's job was no picnic, and she could only imagine the types of people and behaviors Edna dealt with on a daily basis, but Jorja was quick to notice Edna had kind eyes and the corners of her eyes crinkled as she smiled.

Edna offered a hand. "Are you Jorja?"

Jorja took Edna's hand. "Yes and you are Edna? Edna Willows?"

Edna grinned slightly at the question. "Yes, my name is Edna Willows. Guess the front desk spilled the beans, did they? Well, that's quite all right. I didn't mean to come across all cloak and dagger on you over the phone. We have a lounge area towards the back of the building. Do you want to follow me?"

Edna's look was questioning but also assuming. She did not wait for Jorja to answer but instead turned and began to walk down a long hallway.

Jorja hesitated for only a second and then followed Edna's lead. She curiously looked around the hallway and was surprised that the inside of the building looked more like an old bed and breakfast rather than a sterile hospital. She wondered if this might be one of the reasons her aunt remained at the hospital for so long. It had a comfortable atmosphere, which was not something Jorja had expected.

Edna disappeared around the next corner where Jorja quickly caught up to discover a sitting room. No one else was present in the room as Jorja looked around. The room held two couches and various comfortable-looking chairs. A fireplace was located on the farthest wall with a few logs burning and Jorja could immediately feel the warmth. Even though it was a large room, Jorja found it to be surprisingly cozy.

"Would you care for some coffee or tea? We also have some cold beverages if you would prefer." Edna moved to a corner of the room where a counter was located and which held a microwave and a small fridge.

"No, I'm fine, thank you." Jorja was too nervous to drink anything. She wanted to hear what Nurse Willows had to say.

"Well, do you mind if I make myself a cup of tea? You can have a seat anywhere you feel comfortable. I'll only take a minute."

"That's okay, I don't mind." Jorja walked towards the fireplace and chose to sit in an overstuffed chair near the fire after removing her jacket. The chair was comfortable and Jorja took pleasure in the warmth of the fire while Edna made her tea. Edna soon joined her, choosing a chair across from Jorja. After carefully sitting down to avoid spilling her tea, Edna took a sip before placing the cup on a nearby table.

"Well, I'm sure you are terribly curious about why I called you and why I wanted to meet with you."

Jorja waited, not knowing exactly how to respond. Of course she was curious. She was so anxious she was about to scream at the nurse to just get on with it already.

Edna took another sip of her tea as she watched Jorja. When Jorja's only response was to continue to stare back at her, Edna gave a quick nod. "Of course, you are curious but you also appear to be a patient person and that is good."

Jorja finally spoke. "I'm not feeling entirely patient but you've given me no choice, really. I'm just curious about what you have to tell me in person that you could not tell me over the phone."

Edna sat her cup back down on the table and leaned back in her chair.

"I felt it was better I see you in person. First, I wanted to meet you and second, I believe some things need to be done in person and not over the phone."

"Okay, so why was it so important to meet me? You said you had some information you wanted to share and I assume you knew my Aunt Gloria but what is this all about?"

Edna folded her hands together and laid them in her lap. Jorja noticed Edna was not wearing a wedding band and she wondered if the hospital had been Edna's life.

"Yes, I did know your Aunt Gloria. I was twenty-five years old and had been working at the hospital for almost a year when your aunt came to stay with us. I remember thinking how young she was and how terribly sad she was. I worked in another area of the hospital at that time so I did not closely deal with your aunt until I was promoted the following year. I did not know the details about why your aunt was even brought here until I spent more time working with her and even then it was difficult to speak to her. She was such a lost soul. She was one patient I really tried to work with because I wanted to see her get better so that she could go home."

Jorja listened intently as Edna described her first encounter with her aunt. She tried to imagine her Aunt Gloria as a sixteen year old being forced to live in a mental hospital. She thought about how difficult it must have been for her to leave the house she grew up in after her own parents decided to place her in the hospital. Jorja now understood the reasoning for it after learning her aunt's difficulty in dealing with the loss of the baby and the baby's father but she felt sadness at how lonely her aunt must have been.

"So you were able to get to know my aunt? Talk to her more about what had happened?"

Edna smiled. "Oh, you're aunt and I became very good friends. At first, our relationship was strictly clinical, as I was her nurse and I did not want to cross the line with her. After Gloria was here for about two years, I was again moved to another section of the hospital so I was not directly involved with your aunt's care. She and I had always gotten along, even if she found it hard to speak to me about why she was here, but I enjoyed her company and she seemed to enjoy mine. We began to get together during my lunch hour to play card games and chat. Your aunt seemed to look forward to my visits. Anyway, after years of small talk and card games, your aunt was doing better, the medication she was on seemed to be working and she was well enough so that her doctor said she could go home. I was distressed to learn that she'd only been home a week when they had to bring her back to the hospital."

Jorja was lost in Edna's recounting of the past when she was suddenly struck by what Edna had just said. "Wait, what do you mean only a week? The only time Aunt Gloria came home was after my grandparents passed away and she was never sent back here. You're saying she came home before that? When was the first time?"

Edna pursed her lips. "Well, it's possible you were too young to remember or even be told about what was going on with your aunt. Your aunt was doing well and the doctor allowed her to go home after she'd been treated here for about…oh, I'd say she'd been here for eight years the first time. I was happy for her because she was finally going home, which is why I was so upset when a week later I learned she was back in the hospital."

Jorja frowned. Her aunt actually came home for a week and then was sent back to the hospital? She did not recall her mother saying her grandparents attempted to bring Aunt Gloria home. "Do you know why they had to bring her back to the hospital?"

Edna leaned forward as she explained, "Your aunt was home only a week when something happened to cause her to have a relapse. I don't know what happened but when I saw her again after she was readmitted to the hospital I was shocked at how the visit home had affected her. She was a mess and did not resemble the person I had said goodbye to the week before."

Edna paused and looked towards the window, staring off as she recalled that sad day her friend was brought back to the hospital. Even to this day her heart ached at the suffering her friend seemed to be going through.

"But why? What the heck could have happened to cause her to relapse and be brought back here?"

Edna was brought away from her memories and she looked at Jorja. "I can't say for sure what happened to cause your aunt to return to the hospital. All I can say is that something caused her great anguish and at one point made her want to take her own life. Something was terribly upsetting to her and it was too much for her to deal with but I was never able to find out from her exactly what that was. She would completely shut down if I even tried to speak to her about it. I always felt like I let her down in some way. I was her only friend and yet I never could get her to open up and tell me what really bothered her. She had been seeing a psychiatrist and I don't think she ever told him either."

Jorja thought about what Edna was telling her. Her Aunt Gloria had not just one but basically two breakdowns. She could understand the first involving the death of her baby. She wondered if her aunt had the second breakdown because she couldn't handle returning to the place where the baby had died.

"Do you think her second breakdown had anything to do with the baby?"

Edna gave a slight nod. "Yes, I'm sure it may have had something to do with that. But I could never understand why the second visit would cause her to relapse. Her treatment and the doctor's diagnosis and decision to send her home was based on the fact that she *knew* her baby had died. I don't think it was the death of the baby that caused her to relapse. I believe it was something else based on something she said to me one day. I have never forgotten it."

Jorja's eyes widened as she questioned Edna. "What did she say?"

Edna sighed and leaned back in the chair again. "You know...I have wrestled with the knowledge of this for quite some time. Your aunt let something slip I'm sure she did not mean to say. Once she made it clear she did not wish to discuss it further, we never talked about it again. I felt she needed a friend and in turn she was a good friend to me."

Edna stood up from the chair and walked to a nearby table where a box had been sitting. She picked up the box and placed it on the table next to Jorja's chair.

"This is a box of items your aunt asked me to hold for her. I don't know what is in this box but when I asked your aunt, she said they were personal items she didn't want to keep at the hospital. She was afraid someone would get into her things. She was a very secretive person but she was also mentally ill so the items in this box may or may not be anything important. The fact was that they were important to her and she asked me to keep them safe at my house for her, which I did. I have had this box since before your aunt was released from the hospital and other than Gloria asking me every once in awhile if the box was still safe, she never asked to have the box returned to her. She only told me that if anything should happen to her, she wanted the box to go to you."

Jorja glanced at the box, very curious about what was inside. Jorja wondered if the contents inside would help her understand the person her aunt had been.

"You asked me here so you could give me this box? Why wouldn't Aunt Gloria want the box to go to my mom instead? I would think she'd want her personal items to go to her sister."

"Oh, I know about your mom and no, for whatever reason your aunt told me the box should go to you. The box is for you. Whatever is inside is for you."

"But why? What did Aunt Gloria say to you?"

Edna sat down in her chair and picked up her cup to take another sip of tea, realizing too late it was now cold. She sat the cup back down and straightened her shoulders as she looked at Jorja. Jorja saw a look in Edna's eyes she couldn't quite understand…she appeared to be looking at her with compassion.

"What have you been told about the night your aunt had her first breakdown?"

Jorja replied, "All I know is that my aunt had a baby and the baby died, the baby's father left my aunt and it was all too much for her so she ended up in the hospital. I just found all this out, actually. I never knew my aunt was even pregnant and my parents had never explained why she was placed in a mental institution. Why are you asking? Is there something more?"

Edna frowned. "You didn't know until recently that your aunt had even been pregnant?"

"No, I just found a tin box my aunt had buried and inside was a letter to the baby's father. When I asked my mom about it, she finally admitted that Aunt Gloria had a child but that it had died."

"Oh, Jorja, I'm sorry you only recently found out. I'm not sure if what I have to say will be too much considering what you only recently learned from your mother."

Jorja shook her head. "No, it's okay. You can tell me. I'm not upset that my aunt was pregnant. I'm upset my parents never told me I had a cousin, even though he died. I'm sure they thought it wasn't necessary to tell me but it was sure better than the way I found out."

"That is very understandable." Edna hesitated and then finally said, "Well, okay. You're aunt was pregnant and from what I understand, there was a child that passed away. However, there was something else. You're aunt didn't have just one child, she had two."

Jorja stared at Edna as she let the words sink in. She then decided she must not have heard Edna correctly.

"Two? What do you mean, she got pregnant again?"

"No, she was not pregnant again after returning to the hospital or during the time she lived here so the only other explanation is that she had two babies at the same time. She had twins. Apparently, one died but I believe the other did not."

Jorja was stunned. "What are you saying? If my aunt had a baby and it was still living, why wouldn't my parents have told me? What happened to the baby?"

Edna hesitated again. "Well…I can't say for a fact what happened to the baby. Like I said, Gloria let something slip once when she was talking to me. She said something about losing 'both her babies' and she was so emotional it was difficult to understand exactly what she was saying. I had been told that she lost a child at birth but this was the first time anything was mentioned about another baby. When I tried to ask her what happened to the other baby, Gloria told me I had misunderstood her and we never spoke of it again. I don't know if the second baby lived or not. I'm afraid you're going to have to ask your mother about the baby because I can't tell you."

Jorja could not move. She could not breathe. How could her parents keep this information from her? Did the baby die? Did the baby live? Was the baby adopted out? Did they know where the baby was placed? Did they know where it was now? Jorja finally gathered her wits as she began to doubt what Edna was saying.

"I don't believe you. How could my aunt have another baby and no one mention it? I just can't believe my parents wouldn't say anything."

"Jorja, I know how upsetting this might be. I'm truly sorry because I did not want to upset you. I'm sure your mother will feel terrible for keeping this from you but at least she can answer your questions, where I cannot."

Jorja suddenly needed to stand and she moved towards the window to look outside. Edna patiently waited while Jorja remained quiet, lost in thought.

Finally, Jorja turned around and asked, "Why are you just now calling me and giving me my aunt's items? Aunt Gloria has been gone for a couple of months. Why did you wait to call?"

Edna stood up from her chair as well. "I would have called sooner but I didn't know your aunt had passed away. I left the country for a two-month vacation in Europe to visit with family. While I was gone your aunt passed away but I didn't hear about it until I returned to work. I'd honestly forgotten about the box until I decided to organize my spare bedroom closet and when I found the box, I realized I had to get it to you. What I wasn't certain about was whether I should tell you what your aunt said about the second baby. I hope I did the right thing. What you do with your aunt's belongings and the information I have provided is up to you."

Jorja gave Edna a faint smile. She thought her aunt was very lucky to have had a friend like Edna. "Thank you. What you've told me is upsetting but I do appreciate your honesty. I'm sure you must also miss her very much and this is probably hard for you as well."

Edna's look of relief at Jorja's response was immediate. "Yes, I do miss your aunt very much. And I do feel terrible for upsetting you but I'm glad if you understand my reasons are not to purposefully hurt you in any way."

"Did my aunt happen to mention who the father was? I guess she never told my grandparents or my mom."

Edna shook her head. "No, that subject would illicit great sadness from your aunt. She was very hurt by whatever that young man did, whether he left her or made a promise and then broke it, I don't know. She told me she'd only known love once and that it ended with him trampling her heart. She never wanted to discuss him beyond that."

Jorja gave Edna her hand to say goodbye. "Well, it was very nice meeting you, Edna. Thanks again for the box of items and telling me what you know about my aunt. I should get going because I have a long drive back home." Jorja put on her jacket and then reached down to pick up the box.

"You are welcome, Jorja. You be sure to let me know if you need anything. I hope your mother can shed some more light on exactly what happened with your aunt. I'm sure your aunt would like you to know the truth."

Jorja thought Edna's statement was odd but then decided Edna was right. Her aunt probably would want someone to know the truth, especially if Jorja had a cousin who didn't even know she and her parents existed.

CHAPTER 17

After Jorja left the hospital, she decided to stop at a diner on the way home to grab something to eat.

As she reviewed her menu, a spunky waitress approached the table. "Hello, my name is Martha and I'll be your server this evening. Can I get you something to drink?"

Jorja looked up from her menu. Martha was a short, older woman with jet black hair peeking out of the hat she was apparently required to wear as a part of her uniform. Jorja quickly noticed how bright Martha's smile was compared to her black hair and dark brown eyes.

"I'd just like a cup of hot tea, thank you. Chai tea if you have it."

"Well sure, we have Chai tea. You take a few more minutes to review your menu and I will be right back with your tea."

As Martha left to get the tea, Jorja glanced at the box lying beside her on the seat. She could not resist opening the flaps of the box to take a peek inside. At a quick glance she saw smaller boxes inside along with some items of clothing.

Jorja was slightly startled as Martha came back to set her tea cup on the table. "Here are two tea bags for you and some sugar if you need it. Do you know what you would like to order for dinner or do you need more time to look at the menu?"

"No, I think I can order now." As she laid the menu on the table she said, "Could I just have a BLT?"

"You sure can. Would you like a side salad or a cup of our soup of the day?"

Jorja shook her head. "No, the sandwich will do fine, thank you."

Martha nodded and picked the menu up off the table. "All right, I'll be back soon with your sandwich."

Jorja watched Martha walk away and then looked back down at the box. She gingerly grabbed the top item from inside the box and pulled it out to look at it more closely. It was a scarf in a beautiful dark green color and appeared to be handmade. She wondered if Gloria made it or if she received it as a gift. Reaching inside the box, she grabbed the next item. It was a small wooden jewelry box with a carving of a hummingbird on top. She opened the box to discover a few rings, a brooch, earrings and necklaces. Jorja grabbed each ring and found that her aunt had what appeared to be a diamond, a pearl and also an emerald ring. She couldn't tell if they were all real but the rings were beautiful to her either way. She thought the brooch looked like an antique but whether it was an antique or not, she realized it might be an item her mother would wish to have. Although some of the earrings appeared to match the rings, Jorja didn't think they were anything spectacular. She then turned her attention to the necklaces. One had the letter "G" attached to it, another appeared to be a pearl in a nice setting of diamonds and the third was some kind of heart symbol. She held it closer to get a better look. It was simple but beautiful. The heart was broken in half with a curved line and it reminded her of the Yin Yang circle symbols she had seen. She had never seen it in the form of a heart.

"Here you go, Miss." Jorja was so deep in thought that Martha again startled her. She dropped the necklace on the table as she caught her breath in a quick gasp.

"Oh, dear, I'm sorry! I didn't mean to startle you. Here is your sandwich. Would you like anything else?"

Placing a hand to her chest, she took a deep breath and replied, "Thank you, no. I'm fine."

As Jorja picked the necklace up from the table, Martha took notice of it.

"Well, that's a pretty little necklace. It's a Yin Yang Heart, isn't it?"

Jorja looked at the necklace again. "Yin Yang Heart? So it is similar to the Yin Yang symbol?"

"Oh, I'm not an expert but the balance of all things seems to be the general idea and the heart symbol is to remind us that love is one of the truest and dearest things. It's just always been one of my favorite symbols because of what it represents and how beautiful it can look when it comes to jewelry. Is it your necklace?"

"No, it's not mine. Well, I guess now it is. It used to belong to my aunt who passed away recently."

"Oh, I'm sorry to hear that, dear. Well, I'm sure it's nice to have something of your aunt's. You can't take it with you but you can let those you leave behind enjoy it for you. Isn't that right?" Martha smiled and winked at Jorja.

Jorja wasn't quite sure what to say so she gave Martha a quick nod and said, "Yes, I guess that's one way to look at it."

"Good. Now, you enjoy your meal and you let me know right away if there's anything else I can get you, okay?"

Jorja promised to tell Martha if she needed anything else and then she took a quick bite of her sandwich before taking another look at the necklace. It was a cute heart, half black and half white, outlined in red, with dots of the opposite color on each side of the heart. She turned the necklace over to discover an engraving. Holding it closer she was able to read, "*Two together, Two apart, Two a part of me, Forever.*" Jorja frowned. Could this poem be referring to her aunt's twins? She took another bite of her sandwich as she thought about her aunt and the life she had apparently led.

How must it have been for her aunt to get pregnant at such a young age? How was she treated by her parents? By the community? How awful it must have been when the one person who she must have relied on, the father of the babies, just left Gloria to deal with it herself. And then to lose both babies. She could not imagine the pain of losing a child. But did Gloria lose one? Did she lose both? If just one, what happened to the other?

There were so many questions running through Jorja's head, she decided she really could not wait to speak to her parents. Instead, she took one last bite as she decided she would drive to her parents' condo where she would confront them with the questions now plaguing her.

CHAPTER 18

As Jorja pulled into her parents' driveway she realized she should give Taylor a call to tell her she wouldn't be coming home. After she thought about making the long trip back home, Jorja decided it would be better to sleep over at her parents' house and drive back home the following morning. Considering the long drive, she was thankful her appointment at the police department wasn't until ten o'clock.

Jorja quickly filled Taylor in on what she learned while visiting with Edna at the hospital and why she was staying overnight at her parents' house.

"Will you take Piper for a walk and make sure to feed her tonight and in the morning?" Jorja asked.

"Don't worry about Piper. I'll take care of her. Will you be home first thing in the morning? I can't wait to hear what you learn from your parents."

She knew Taylor's curiosity would get the best of her and it would be difficult for her to sit tight until Jorja returned home.

"Well, I won't be home first thing, Taylor. I have a ten o'clock appointment at one police department and then an appointment at one-thirty at the sheriff's office to review some records on Kat's case. Do you want to meet me for lunch between appointments? We could meet at the café for lunch at noon if that works for you?"

"That would be great, Jorja. I'll see you tomorrow at noon. Drive safe!"

Jorja promised to drive safely and said goodbye as she walked to the front door of her parents' condo. Her mother was waiting with the door open after hearing her jeep pull into the driveway.

"Well, what a surprise. What brings you here?" Helen gave Jorja a hug before moving aside to let her enter the condo.

Jorja took off her jacket and hung it in the coat closet. "I just wanted to stop by to visit. I had to see someone and since I was nearby, I thought I would stop by to visit and stay overnight before heading back home. Is that okay? Do you have plans?"

Helen laughed and shook her head. "No, honey, no plans and even if I did have any, I would just cancel them. We don't get you up here often enough so it's nice that you stopped by. Your father will be thrilled to see you."

"Where is Dad? Is he here?"

"No, he's golfing but he should be home soon. I can't believe he is still golfing this time of year but once he knew today would be a decent day, he decided to get out and play. You know him; he'll golf as long as he's not wading in puddles."

Jorja smiled at that. She was glad her father was enjoying his retirement. He deserved it after all the years he worked and struggled through hard times as a business owner.

"Well, I can't wait to see him. But maybe it's good that he's not here. There's something I need to speak to you about and I'm not sure he really needs to be here."

Helen gave Jorja a curious look and said, "Well, sure, we can talk if you'd like. I need to get dinner started though so let's talk in the kitchen." Helen then led the way into the kitchen where she began to gather the items necessary for dinner. "Are you hungry? I had already planned on making chicken enchiladas for dinner and I know how you like them."

"That sounds great, Mom." Jorja loved her mother's cooking and would enjoy anything her mother made.

As Helen searched for the ingredients she would need for the chicken enchiladas, she said, "Okay, honey, tell me what's on your mind."

Jorja was sitting at the bar so that she was facing her mother while she worked in the kitchen. It reminded her of her childhood days when she would sit in the kitchen at Hillcrest and watch her mother bake cookies or make bread. Even as an adult it had a calming effect on her but today she didn't quite get that effect.

"Well, I had a very interesting meeting today with someone who knew Aunt Gloria."

Helen looked up at Jorja. "Oh?" Her expression was a mixture of curiosity and confusion. "Who was it?"

Jorja felt nervous as she tried to find the words to tell her mother about Edna. For whatever reason, she felt like she'd done something behind her parents' back but then she had to remember it was her parents who had been keeping a secret from her.

"I actually had a meeting with a nurse who works at the hospital where Aunt Gloria had been staying."

Jorja watched as her mother's movements suddenly stopped. Helen again looked up at her daughter but this time her eyes revealed apprehension.

"Why would you go talk to a nurse at the hospital? What reason did you have to even go there?"

"She called me, Mom. She had something she wanted to give me. While I was there, she told me about her friendship with Aunt Gloria but she also told me something else, which is why I wanted to speak to you."

Helen had completely forgotten about dinner. She absently wiped her hands on a towel and asked, "Who called you? What did she give you? What did she tell you?"

"Her name is Edna, she was working at the hospital when Aunt Gloria was first brought in and over the years they apparently became friends. Before Aunt Gloria left the hospital she gave Edna a box of items to hold on to and said that if anything happened to her, the box should be given to me. She also said that…"

"What do you mean she gave you a box? A box containing what? Why didn't she contact me? Where is the box? Have you gone through it?"

Jorja was surprised at her mother's rapid firing of questions and how her voice rose to a screech by the time she asked the last question. Jorja began to wonder if her mother's response was based on some sort of fear and although Jorja was curious about this fact, it also caused her concern. Jorja had to wonder what would frighten her mother so much.

"It's a box with some of Aunt's Gloria's personal items and no, I haven't gone through the whole box yet."

"I want to see the box, Jorja. Where is it?"

Jorja took a moment before answering as she looked at her mother. She had never seen her mother this upset before. "It's in my jeep. Why do you want to see it?"

"Because I want to go through the box. Gloria was my sister and I have the right to see the items. Now go get the box for me."

"But Mom, there's more than just the box. Edna told me some things that I want to talk to you about."

Helen shook her head. "No, we can talk about that later. First, I want to see the box and what Gloria left behind. Please, Jorja, go get the box."

Jorja was frustrated but did as her mother asked. She didn't understand why her mother was so upset but she didn't want to upset her further by not doing as she'd been asked.

Jorja retrieved the box from her jeep and went back inside the house. Jorja caught her mother pacing in the kitchen when she entered the room to place the box on the table.

"Here it is, Mom. So far I know the box contains a scarf, a jewelry box and some jewelry. I haven't had a chance to go through the rest of the items yet."

Helen walked over to the table and carefully opened the box. She looked inside but seemed hesitant to reach inside to grab an item. Finally, Jorja watched as her mother removed the scarf from the box. Helen held the scarf up to her nose to smell it and with tears in her eyes she said, "This was your grandmother's scarf, Jorja. She knitted it for herself when we were young and it was one of her favorites. She let Gloria take it with her when she was taken to the hospital so that she'd have something of our mother to hold on to and that smelled like her."

Helen set the scarf on the table and reached inside for the jewelry box. As she opened the jewelry box to look inside, she pointed at the brooch. "That was also your grandmother's but she did not give it to Gloria. I remember Mother asking me if I had borrowed the brooch because she couldn't find it. I had no idea where it was and I remember hoping at the time she didn't think I had stolen it. It appears Gloria took it without Mother's knowledge and was able to take it to the hospital with her."

Helen set the jewelry box down on the table so that she could withdraw another item from the box as Jorja reached inside her pants pocket to remove the heart-shaped necklace.

"Mom, take a look at this. Do you remember seeing this before?"

Jorja held the necklace up for her mother to see. Helen carefully looked at the necklace and then slowly began to shake her head. "No, I don't remember that one. Was it in the box too?"

"Yes, and look, there's an engraving on the back." Jorja held the necklace closer to her mother. Helen held out her hand so that Jorja could lay the necklace in the palm of her hand. Jorja watched as her mother slipped on her reading glasses to read the short poem. Although her mother had said she had never seen the necklace before, it appeared to Jorja that the poem caused her some kind of distress. Helen's hand moved up to her neck and she took a deep breath before finally looking at Jorja. Jorja could see real apprehension in her mother's eyes and she could no longer hold back the questions.

"Mom, do you know what this means? Do you know what the nurse told me today?"

Helen quickly shook her head and stammered, "I, uh, how would I know what that means? What…what did the nurse tell you?"

Jorja didn't understand why her mother wouldn't just admit her aunt had twins. She also did not understand what was upsetting her mother so much.

"Mom, the nurse told me that Aunt Gloria had twins! Is that true? Why didn't you tell me? Why did you lie and tell me she just had one baby that died? What happened to the other one?"

Helen was visibly stunned and sank slowly into a nearby chair. "Oh dear. She told you that?"

"Yes. And she also told me Aunt Gloria actually came home once before but something caused her to relapse so that she had to be returned to the hospital. Do you know about that? What happened?"

Helen was silent. Her face paled and Jorja was afraid she might actually pass out. "Mom, are you okay? I don't mean to upset you but I can't believe I had to hear from a stranger that I might have a cousin somewhere. What happened to that other child?"

Helen could only look at Jorja. Tears that had formed were now sliding down her cheeks.

"Mom? Why are you so upset? I'm sorry. I didn't mean to upset you so much. Are you okay?"

Jorja was beginning to panic as she realized just how distressed this conversation had made her mother. She didn't know what to do to make things right because she also wanted her mother to answer her questions.

"Honey, I'm home!" The front door slammed as Jorja heard her father enter the house. "Boy, I did great today. Beat Henry by 4 strokes and he is fuming because this is the first time he's lost to me. Oh, it's great to finally get a win. I see Jorja's jeep is outside. She surprised us with a visit?"

As Rick entered the kitchen he saw Jorja sitting at the table with Helen. "Hello, Jorja, I didn't know you'd be here today. To what do we owe the pleasure?"

Jorja stood up to give her father a hug. "Hello Dad. Glad you won a game against Henry. I just stopped by because I had to come up this way to meet with someone. I decided to stay overnight and go home in the morning."

"Great! It's always nice to have you here." Rick then looked at his wife and said, "So what are we having for dinner? Honey? Are you okay? You look like you've been crying."

Helen used a kitchen towel to gently wipe her cheeks and then she attempted to smile. "I'm okay, Rick. Jorja and I were just talking."

Helen stood up and grabbed a tissue to blow her nose. She then washed her hands and went back to preparing dinner.

"Well, what are you two talking about that has you all upset? What's going on?" Rick looked first at Helen, then at Jorja, but he did not get a response from either of them. "Okay, okay, if it's between the two of you, fine. I'm going to take a shower before dinner is ready."

Jorja watched her father leave the room and head upstairs. She wondered if she shouldn't ask him to stay and be a part of the conversation. Maybe he would shed more light on the matter than her mother would.

"Mom?" Jorja stared at her mother and waited. Finally, Helen raised her eyes to meet Jorja's. "Can we talk about this? Can you answer my questions or are you going to leave me in the dark about what happened to Aunt Gloria and her children?"

Helen broke eye contact with Jorja and looked down at her hands. Jorja patiently waited until her mother finally said, "I guess. This isn't something I really wish to talk about but I understand why you'd like to know. Will you let me finish making the enchiladas and then we can sit and talk while they are baking?"

Jorja shrugged and said, "Sure, mom. Finish with that and I'll wait. Is there anything you need me to do?"

"Actually, yes, you can do me a favor and walk down to the store for me. I need a half gallon of milk."

"Uh, okay, if you really need it. Don't bother on my account because I'm okay with water for dinner."

"No, I need milk. I'd like to make some pudding for dessert. Just grab some money there in my purse." Helen pointed to her purse sitting on a computer desk off the kitchen and then she quietly continued with making dinner.

"Alright, I'll be right back." Although Jorja was reluctant to agree to walk to the store, she felt she had no other choice. She decided her mother just wanted some time to herself before divulging the information Jorja so adamantly wanted to hear.

The store was only three blocks from her parents' condo so it didn't take much time to walk the distance. When Jorja returned to the condo she entered through the front door without knocking. She then headed towards the kitchen to put the milk in the fridge but as she walked by her father's study, she heard a noise. Turning towards the sound, she saw her mother standing in the study with her back towards Jorja. She was about to say hello when she realized her mother was going through the box belonging to Aunt Gloria. She was then shocked to see her mother remove an envelope from the box and place it in a desk drawer. Jorja felt the stirrings of anger as she walked into the study while her mother closed the drawer.

"Mom, what are you doing?" Helen jumped and her eyes widened as she turned to look at Jorja.

"Nothing honey. I just thought I would finish going through the rest of Aunt Gloria's things."

Jorja saw the color in her mother's cheeks. She was hiding something. Not just the envelope, but something Jorja guessed her mother did not want her to know.

"Mom, I saw you put an envelope from the box in your desk. Why? What is it?"

"It's nothing. It's a letter to me. I'll read it later."

Jorja couldn't understand why her mother was acting this way. She felt like she was dealing with a child. "Mom, why would Aunt Gloria leave a letter addressed to you in a box she wanted me to have? She could have just sent you the letter. Let me see it."

Jorja could not believe it when her mother shook her head. "No, Jorja, there's nothing for you to see. It's addressed to me and I don't have to let you see it."

"Mom, what are you hiding? Why are you acting this way? I want to see what you took!"

"What the heck is going on here?" Rick was standing in the hallway, freshly dressed after his shower. He gaped at both Jorja and Helen with clear puzzlement. "Jorja? Why are you yelling at your mother?"

She suddenly felt guilty. What the heck was going on? She had never yelled at her mother. But her mother had never kept secrets from her before either.

"I didn't mean to yell, Dad. I just don't understand why Mom won't show me what she took from the box. Aunt Gloria gave me that box of items and Mom took a letter and won't let me see it."

Rick looked curiously at the box. Then he looked at Helen. Jorja watched as their eyes met and her father's expression changed from curiosity to concern. "Helen, what's going on? Where did the box come from?"

"I got it, Dad. A nurse who worked at the hospital where Aunt Gloria was staying gave it to me today. She was holding on to it for Aunt Gloria and was told to give it to me if anything were to happen to her. She also told me Aunt Gloria actually had twins and I'm trying to understand what happened when Aunt Gloria had her babies."

Jorja saw the shock on her father's face as she finished speaking. He then walked into the room to stand beside Helen and as he did, he put his arm around her. Helen suddenly began to cry. Her mother's tears made Jorja so upset she too was about to break into tears.

"Will you both *please* tell me what's going on? What has Mom so upset?"

Rick looked at his wife and then at Jorja. "Let's go in the living room and talk. First, let me speak to your mom for a few minutes, okay?"

Jorja could only agree to do as they asked. She left her parents in the study and went to the living room to wait for both of them after placing the milk in the fridge. The anxiety Jorja felt was like nothing she could recall ever feeling before.

"Okay, honey, we're ready to talk to you now." Jorja's father said as her parents entered the room. Helen was quiet as she sat down on the couch next to Rick. Rick looked at his wife and asked, "Helen? Do you want to tell her now?"

Helen looked at Jorja as tears welled up in her eyes again. She took a deep breath and finally said, "Your aunt did have twins. I'm sorry for not telling you but it was such a long time ago and I just didn't see the need to tell you."

"What happened to them? Did they both survive?"

Helen shook her head. "No, one of them did die. That's what my parents told me after the fact so I never saw him. I wasn't living at home at the time. The other baby, a little girl, was healthy and adopted out because Gloria could not care for her and my parents did not have the ability to take on the care of a baby."

Jorja looked at her mother and then at her father. Neither of them seemed to wish to offer any additional information. So she asked, "Well, what about the fact that the nurse said Aunt Gloria came home once before but ended up back at the hospital? What happened then? What made Aunt Gloria have to go back?"

Jorja saw her mother give her father a look. She could not tell what the look meant but her mother said, "Yes, your aunt did come home once. She tried. She tried to live with our parents and live a normal life but something was different with her. She just couldn't seem to live at Hillcrest any longer and I expect it just brought back too many painful memories with regard to the pregnancy, losing one of the babies, and also the fact that the father left her before the babies were even born. She didn't handle that very well and never did forgive him for it."

"Do you know who the father was?"

Helen shook her head and said, "No, we never did find out who the father was. I know my mother had asked Gloria but she wouldn't say and once it was apparent that the babies' father had left, it didn't appear Gloria ever wished to speak of him again. She was very, very upset about him leaving her. Even if my parents had known who the father was, I doubt it would have made a difference in the outcome. Gloria couldn't care for a child and I certainly doubt a young man of the same age would also be able or willing to do so. The father's name is a mystery we will probably never solve."

Jorja thought about what her mother said. Her parents watched her, holding hands, as they waited for her to say something in response to the information they had just provided to her.

"So, I have a cousin out there but you have no idea where she is?"

Jorja saw another look cross between her parents. "No, honey, we have no idea. I don't even know what agency my parents used to place the baby up for adoption."

Jorja wanted to believe her parents but she could not get past the feeling that there was something they weren't sharing with her. If they knew where the child was, why wouldn't they tell her? She felt exhausted and decided to let the matter go for now. She was just glad her parents finally opened up to her about what happened with Aunt Gloria.

CHAPTER 19

Jorja did not know where her head was when she had the bright idea of driving home after staying the night with her parents. By the time she managed to make it through all the Monday morning Seattle work traffic in order to travel south on I-5 towards home, she was fighting a headache. She'd make sure never to do that again. After fighting more work traffic as she passed through Tacoma and the Lewis-McChord military base, she was thankful to make it to her first appointment with ten minutes to spare.

As she took one last sip from her coffee and placed a piece of gum in her mouth, she checked herself in the rearview mirror. She saw the hint of dark circles under her eyes after a terrible nights' sleep, most likely due to all the nagging questions she felt had yet to be answered. Jorja was feeling only slightly guilty about the fact that before leaving her parents' condo, she snuck into the study to look at the envelope in the desk drawer. There, she found an envelope, not with her mother's name on it, but her own name instead. She was shocked and then hurt by her mother's betrayal. Her mother obviously thought she had the right to take the envelope but Jorja decided it was her right to take it back. She did not give herself a chance for second thoughts as she quickly grabbed the envelope and placed it in her purse before saying a final farewell to her parents. She knew she would later have to explain her actions to her parents when her mother discovered it was missing but for the time being, Jorja was more concerned with learning the full truth and not just what her parents wanted her to hear.

Giving herself one final look in the mirror as she wished the dark circles away, she finally got out of the jeep. It had begun to rain so she quickly ran towards the building and entered the police department. A young man with dark hair who looked to be college-age sat at a reception desk off to the right. He finished his phone conversation and turned to Jorja.

"May I help you?"

"Yes, my name is Jorja Matthews. I have an appointment to view some records."

"One second. I'll get the records clerk for you. Sign your name here on the sign-in sheet and then have a seat over there until she arrives." The young man pointed to a handful of chairs in the corner where Jorja sat down to wait after the records clerk had been paged.

Jorja was grateful she didn't have to wait long before the records clerk exited the employees' only door and asked her to come inside. Jorja followed the clerk to a conference room where multiple files had been placed in a pile.

The clerk pointed to the pile on the table. "Ok, these are what I was able to pull and which are currently for public inspection. Your request was broad so I can't promise that all possible records are being provided for your inspection but this is what I found on our "Jane Does" for the twelve-year time period you gave me. Do you have any questions?"

Jorja glanced at the files. "No, no questions. Do I have a time limit here or can I stay as long as I need?"

The clerk looked up at the clock on the wall, which read '10:03.'

"You have an hour and a half or no later than quarter to noon. We need this room for a meeting currently scheduled at noon. Is that sufficient enough time for you?"

Jorja nodded her head and said, "Yes, I think that will do. If I need more time, I guess I could come back later, correct?"

The clerk tried to hide the look of annoyance that quickly crossed her face but not before Jorja noticed.

"I'll try to finish my review today." Jorja said. Based on the clerk's reaction, Jorja knew she better make good use of the time she had.

"Good. I'll check on you but if you complete your review before I come back, just leave the files here on the table and let the receptionist know when you are leaving."

With that, the clerk stepped out of the room and closed the door behind her.

Jorja sat down at the table and slowly began to separate the files that had been piled on top of each other. The files were individually labeled with the name 'Jane Doe', the case number and the year. She began with the years closest to the time period Kat's mom disappeared. There were only a handful of cases during the first five-year span. The "Jane Does" included the unidentified body of a woman found in a nearby lake, a woman who had been beaten, robbed of her belongings and left for dead in an alley, a young girl who jumped from a city building rooftop and an elderly woman who checked into a hotel room using a fake name before committing suicide. Carefully reviewing the rest of the files, she was saddened by each story. A few had committed suicide and left no information to help with their identification but most had been killed and left like a pile of garbage so that some unsuspecting soul would later find them. While she wasn't sure exactly what she was looking for, she hoped that if a case did involve Vera, some piece of information would jump out at her. Most of the files included sketches of the women found but none of them appeared to match Kat's mother. By the time the records clerk checked in with her, Jorja was just finishing with the last file.

"How are you doing on time? We'll need to clear out this room for the meeting."

Jorja looked up at the clerk and said, "Perfect timing. I'm going through the last file now."

"Did you find anything useful? Any of those women the one you're looking for?"

Jorja shook her head. "No, I'm afraid none of them appear to be my missing person. I really appreciate you getting these files together for me."

"Sure, not a problem. Don't worry about the files. I'll take care of them. Can you find your way out?"

Jorja informed the clerk she would find her way out and after signing out with the receptionist, she walked out to her jeep and called Taylor.

"Are we still on for lunch?"

It wasn't likely Taylor would actually forget their lunch date but Jorja knew how distracted Taylor had been since she began dating Dylan.

"Oh, yes! I'm on my way. I was just running a few errands. Dylan wanted me to pick up a few things he needed for the bakery so once I drop those off I'll run over to the café." Taylor sounded out of breath.

"That's okay, Taylor. I'm just now leaving the police department and will be at the café in about twenty minutes. I'll see you there."

Jorja fought lunch traffic on her way to meet Taylor, causing her to be ten minutes late by the time she finally reached the café. Days like this made Jorja thankful her small town was not yet bombarded with street lights, state workers and heavy work traffic.

Jorja spotted Taylor's Mini Cooper parked in front of the café and she was glad Taylor had already been able to snag a table. After she parked and locked her jeep Jorja walked towards the café but she did not get far.

"Hey there, beautiful."

She turned towards the voice and saw Brad on the sidewalk by the café.

"Uh, hello yourself. How are you doing, Brad?" Jorja felt flustered when she realized her cheeks felt hot.

Brad grinned. "I'm great. Got my weight-lifting class out for a run around town so I thought I'd enjoy a walk while they sweat it out. What are you up to?"

Trying to remain composed, she also wished it was still raining so she'd have an excuse to run for it. "I'm just here to meet Taylor for lunch. I need to go, actually, because I don't have much time to eat before I have to take off for an appointment."

Brad's grin only seemed to widen. "Well, have a nice lunch with Taylor. Maybe I'll see you at the auction the football team is holding next Saturday? It'll be fun. We'll have plenty of food and there will be quite a few items up for bid."

"Are you up for bid?" Jorja was startled at the question and turned to see Taylor grinning at her. Taylor went on, "You know, in case a single female needs help with some extra chores around the house?"

"Taylor!" Jorja could only forcibly whisper an admonishment before turning back to face Brad.

Brad laughed and said, "No, I'm not auctioning myself off but the boys are being auctioned off in groups of four for anyone who needs help with outside chores. You know, yard work, splitting wood, that kind of thing. You'll have until the end of the school year to take them up on the help. You should come, maybe bid on them and get some extra help around the house."

Jorja nodded at Brad and said, "Okay, I'll think about it. Maybe I'll see you there."

"Great! Well, I better go check on the boys. Make sure they're not goofing off. See you Jorja. Bye Taylor."

Both Jorja and Taylor said goodbye to Brad and then headed into the café.

"I got us a table over there by the window. I already ordered you an iced tea."

Jorja followed Taylor and sat down at the table. She unwrapped a straw, placed it in her glass and took a sip. Her face grimaced when she realized no sugar had yet been added to the tea. Jorja then grabbed the sugar and slowly began to add some to her drink.

"Hey? Are you mad at me?"

"Huh?" Jorja looked up at Taylor. She hadn't realized she had gotten lost in thought. "Oh, sorry. No, I was just thinking."

"About Brad?" Taylor raised her eyebrows and smiled.

"No, not Brad! I'm telling you, there's nothing between us so stop getting your hopes up." Jorja didn't care to admit to herself that her cheeks still felt warm.

"Whatever you say, Jorja, whatever you say." Taylor tried to hide her grin as she looked down at her menu.

Jorja knew Taylor meant well but she just couldn't think of getting into a relationship right now.

"I was thinking about Kat and her mother. I spent over an hour going through some records and I didn't realize how daunting it was going to be. Do you realize how many women end up as 'Jane Does'? It's so sad. All these women who get killed or commit suicide but are never identified."

"Did you find anything that might involve Kat's mom?"

"No, nothing so far. I'm going to the county sheriff's office after lunch but I doubt I'll have any more luck."

As Jorja finally picked up her menu to decide on lunch, the waitress sauntered over to their table to take their order.

"Hi, my name is Julie and I'll be taking care of you today. Have you two ladies decided on what you want for lunch?" Julie held her pencil directly over her pad, patiently waiting.

Taylor answered first. "I'll just have an egg salad sandwich."

"All right. Would you like a side with that?"

"Maybe some pickles?"

"Okay, and for you?" Julie asked Jorja.

Jorja made her decision and said, "I'll just have a club sandwich with some slices of tomato on the side."

Julie picked up both menus from the table. "Sure thing. You two sit tight and I'll bring your order as soon as it's ready."

Jorja watched Julie walk away, noticing she had a slight limp. She wondered if it was the job and the shoes or if she actually had a birth defect of some sort.

Taylor drew Jorja's attention away from Julie's walk.

"So, how did the visit go with your parents?"

Jorja took a sip of her tea before telling Taylor everything. Jorja stopped talking once Julie brought their order to the table. After making sure neither Jorja nor Taylor needed anything else, Julie left them to their meal.

Taylor took a large bite from her sandwich.

"Mmmm. Now that hits the spot."

Taylor swallowed with a loud gulp, took a sip from her glass and said, "So, wow, your aunt had twins? You could really have a cousin out there somewhere? A girl who is close to your age would be more like a sister. It's too bad they adopted her out. And you have no idea where to find her?"

Jorja slowly shook her head. "No, I don't know where to find her but I expect there's someplace I can start."

"What do you mean?"

"Well, there has to be a birth certificate for the twins, even the one who died, who would also have a death certificate. The doctor who my grandparents used has to remember something. I believe if I start with him, I might get somewhere. Maybe not, but it's worth a shot."

Jorja took a bite of her sandwich. She knew the sandwich was more than she could eat but she had already decided she would eat half for lunch and save the rest for dinner. She just didn't feel like worrying about dinner.

Jorja decided she better tell Taylor what she had done. "And there's something else."

Taylor looked at Jorja curiously. When Jorja didn't go on any further, Taylor finally asked, "Well, what? What else is there?"

"I did something before I left my parents' house that will probably really make Mom blow a gasket."

Taylor laughed. "I have *never* seen your mom blow a gasket. What the heck could you ever do to make her mad?"

Jorja hesitated and finally said, "Well, my mom went through the box without me and she found something she didn't want me to have. When I caught her with it, she told me it was a letter to her from Aunt Gloria but when I went back to look in the drawer where she hid the letter, it was actually an envelope addressed to me."

Taylor had been chewing her sandwich but at that news she suddenly stopped. She then attempted to force the food down before asking, "What was your mom hiding from you? Why would she take something that had been addressed to you? Was it from your aunt?"

Jorja shook her head. "I don't know yet."

"What do you mean you don't know yet? Haven't you read it yet?" Taylor's voice went up a notch as she asked the question and she lowered her voice when other customers looked her way.

"No, Taylor, I just found it this morning before I left their house and then I was fighting traffic to get back here for my appointment this morning. Since then I've done nothing but search through those files and now I'm here with you. I haven't had a chance to open it yet."

"So, what are you going to do? You want to open it, don't you? Do you have it with you now?"

Jorja looked at her purse. "Yes, it's in my purse."

"Well, do you want to open it?"

"Here? No. I think I'll wait until I get home."

Taylor could only envy Jorja's patience; she would not have been able to wait. "Why? Don't you want to know what it says?"

Jorja was secretly dying to open the letter. "Sure I do, Taylor. I just don't know that opening it here in a public place during lunch is really the best time and place. Plus, I have to leave soon to review the records at the sheriff's office. What if the letter is upsetting? I just don't want to read something upsetting and then try to concentrate while I go through more files."

"Well, if you open it at home tonight, just wait for me, okay? If it is upsetting, I want to be there for you." Jorja smiled at Taylor while Taylor finished off the first half of her sandwich. Jorja did her best to finish half of her meal but then finally asked the waitress for a to-go box. She just didn't have an appetite any longer.

CHAPTER 20

Jorja placed her lunch in the to-go box and said goodbye to Taylor before leaving for her appointment at the Sheriff's Office. She was glad the appointment wasn't until one-thirty, as she was able to avoid others who were trying to get back to work after lunch. She made it to the Sheriff's Office with plenty of time to find a parking spot, use the restroom on the way inside and enter the reception area with minutes to spare. An older male stood in the reception area as he was typing on his computer behind the bullet-proof glass. Jorja hadn't realized male receptionists were so common.

"May I help you?"

"Yes, I have a one-thirty appointment with Cheryl Dunham."

As he handed her a clipboard through an opening at the bottom of the glass he said, "I'll let Cheryl know you are here. I just need you to sign your name on this sign-in-sheet."

Jorja took the clipboard from him and signed her name on the last available space while the receptionist used his phone to call the clerk.

"She'll be with you in a moment," he told Jorja as she returned the clipboard to him.

Jorja waited a bit longer than a moment but was entertained by the number of individuals who entered the office either to ask about getting records, obtaining a gun permit, getting information on how to obtain a restraining order or make a complaint about a neighbor. Jorja thought a job with the Sheriff's Office might be very interesting.

"Ms. Matthews?" Jorja turned to find the clerk standing just behind her. "My name is Cheryl. I have the files ready for you to review. Care to follow me down the hallway?"

Cheryl then turned and walked down a long hallway while Jorja followed close behind. Cheryl soon turned left down another hallway and then shortly turned left again into a small office.

"You'll have to sit at this desk to review the files. We don't have access to an empty conference room at the moment but this office is unused so no one will bother you. I'll be just down the hall on the right and I'll leave my door open if you need me for any reason."

Jorja looked at the pile of files left on the desk. "Do I have a time limit?"

Cheryl shook her head. "No, you can have all the time you want. Like I said, no one is using this office. Just let me know when you are done or if you have any questions. I have provided all that I can for the twelve-year span you gave me. I hope you find what you're looking for."

With that Cheryl shut the door to leave Jorja to her task.

Jorja sat down at the desk and began to review each file. Like the city police records, the available records covered cases over the past twelve years as she had requested. All cases involved women who could not be identified either right after they passed away or when their bodies were discovered years later. There were a few more files than what she reviewed at the city police department but it was disheartening to discover that even a handful of women had families who weren't able to give them a proper burial. Jorja began with some of the oldest cases and worked her way towards the most recent. The cases involved similar stories or those she remembered reading about in the paper at some point: a teenage girl whose body was found alongside the highway, another young woman who jumped off a bridge over the freeway and was never identified, and the skeletal remains of a woman found at a logging site. Any cases involving just bones seemed difficult, especially when the medical examiner was only able to give an estimate on the age, ranging from twenty to thirty-five years old, and there was no physical evidence useful to an investigation. As Jorja reviewed the remaining cases, she felt overwhelmed as she realized she may not be able to review every case involving every "Jane Doe" in all neighboring counties. The odds were not only overwhelming but also stacked against her.

After reviewing all of the files, she was distressed not to find anything useful. She decided to look back through a few more, just in case she missed something and because she did not yet want to admit defeat. As Jorja was about to set aside one of the older case files, a notation caught her eye. This case was about a woman's remains found about ten years prior by a hiker who had actually gotten lost in the woods. By the time he found his way out of the woods, he had a difficult time directing the police back to the area where he found the remains. Eventually the police were able to find the remains using dogs because the hiker had removed an item from the shallow grave, which was used to help the dogs get a scent.

Jorja's attention was drawn to the item the hiker had removed from the shallow grave; a woman's red leather glove.

A chill ran up her spine.

She reviewed the report further and noted that when the remains were later removed from the grave, it was determined the body was that of a woman, age twenty to thirty and the probable year of death was one to three years before the remains had been discovered. Kat's mother had been twenty-nine when she disappeared. The timeframe of the year of death matched the timeframe for Kat's mother if the reason she disappeared was due to her immediate death. The real interest in this particular case was the red glove. Jorja recalled the statement in the police report about Vera's personal items when Vera had disappeared. Of course, Vera wasn't the only woman to own a pair of red leather gloves but as far as Jorja could tell at this point, Vera was the only woman with that type of glove who was also missing. The hairs on the back of Jorja's neck stood up as she realized it was actually possible she may have found Vera. She looked through the rest of the file to see if the police had included a composite sketch of the victim but she did not find anything. She finished her review of the reports where it was noted there were no obvious signs to indicate how the woman had died. The report classified her death as a homicide and made reference to the fact that the medical examiner determined possible death was likely due to strangulation for lack of obvious injuries.

Jorja stood up from the desk and stretched her back. She then walked around the desk, opened the door and peeked down the hallway. She could hear the records clerk talking and since she could hear no other voices, she assumed the clerk was on the phone. Jorja tentatively walked down the hall towards Cheryl's office and waited just outside the door frame. She could hear Cheryl as she finished her conversation.

"Yes, Sir, that's correct. I spoke to the witness myself and she is willing to remain cooperative and will give a taped statement this afternoon when she brings in the missing records. She will be coming by the office at three o'clock but if she doesn't show up, Detective Reynolds said he will go out looking for her himself. Yes, Sir, I will let you know the status as soon as Detective Reynolds has interviewed the witness and we know we have the actual records in our hands. I will call you back soon. Goodbye."

When Jorja heard Cheryl hang up the phone she waited a few seconds and then walked around the door frame into Cheryl's office as she also lightly tapped on the door.

"Ms. Dunham? I'm through with my review of the records."

"Please, call me Cheryl. So did the records help you any?"

Jorja nodded her head. "Actually, yes, I think I may have found a case that might possibly be the missing person I've been looking for. Can I show you the report and see whether or not there is more information I can review?"

Cheryl typed something quickly into the computer and then stood up. "Sure, show me what you found."

Cheryl followed Jorja back to the small office where Jorja gave her the file. Cheryl quickly glanced at the documents in the file and nodded her head.

"Yes, I remember this one. She may never have been found but whoever buried her picked a spot close to a tree, which was on a slope and it's assumed that after a very wet winter the tree fell over. When the tree toppled over the roots partially uprooted the body so that it was visible when the hiker walked by. It was sad that no one came forward to claim her when we attempted to identify her."

"Well, the husband had always thought his wife left him so any news of remains found might not have alarmed him."

Cheryl nodded in understanding. "So, what caught your attention to make you believe this is your missing person?"

Jorja pointed to an article about the hiker. "It was there. That article about the hiker and how the police used an item he took from the shallow grave so that the dogs had a scent. When I read the actual police report, the only items found were nondescript clothing but they were able to identify that the item the hiker took was a red leather glove. My missing person had a pair of red gloves. I need to ask more about the gloves but the husband apparently made a statement that both her Bible and the gloves were missing, so I assume those were both important items to her. Can you tell me if there was anything else found with the body that might help identify the person?"

Cheryl further reviewed the reports and other documents in the file.

"Well, there should be an evidence sheet here but I don't see it. I can try to find the items relating to this case but you'll have to give me a couple of days. You can come back to the office once I get authorization for you to review the items."

"I understand. I can wait. Will you call me when you have the items ready for me to review?"

"Yes, I'll call you. Here…" Cheryl reached down to grab a Post-It note. "Write your number on this note so I can keep it with the file."

Jorja wrote down her number and shook Cheryl's hand before leaving. She was optimistic but also terribly sad about her discovery. She wasn't sure what she should tell Kat but she knew she wasn't going to say just yet she thought Kat's mother was dead. What was worse? Believing a mother willingly abandoned a child to start a new life or discovering after all this time a mother had been forcibly taken away against her will?

Jorja didn't think either scenario was acceptable.

CHAPTER 21

The drive from the Sheriff's Office to the bookstore was a blur as Jorja's mind reeled at the possibility she may have located Kat's mother. She could not fathom having to tell Kat her mother had been killed and buried in a shallow grave in the woods. Jorja also could not imagine the horror Vera had gone through before her death. Now the real question wasn't what had happened to Vera but how it happened and who was responsible?

Jorja decided to stop by the bookstore before heading home, just to make sure there were no emergencies to take care of. While she did not regret the decision to keep the store closed on Sundays and Mondays, Jorja hoped to hire on additional help so that the store could remain open seven days a week. She had always disliked the fact that most businesses in town were closed on Sundays. In a small town where there wasn't much to do, it was even worse when none of the businesses offered their services on your days off.

As she neared the bookstore, she was happy to see her favorite parking spot was available. This was a benefit to small-town living; plenty of parking spots. She locked her jeep and entered the store using the back entrance as she noticed Taylor's vehicle was also parked in its regular spot. Upon entering the store, Jorja heard music blaring from the surround sound she had decided to have installed after first opening the store. She knew Taylor could not have heard her enter the store so she decided to make use of the opportunity to give Taylor a taste of her own medicine. As Jorja walked down the hall, she caught sight of Taylor sitting on the floor behind the front cash register. She then slowly snuck up behind Taylor before grabbing Taylor's shoulders with both hands and yelling, "Gotcha!"

Taylor dropped the books she'd been holding, threw her hands up and screamed a high-pitched squeal. She then looked up to see Jorja laughing at her. Taylor quickly stood up and with her hand over her chest, yelled at Jorja, "Oh, ha, ha, ha. Very funny Jorja! You could have given me a heart attack!"

Taylor reached over to turn the volume down on the stereo. Jorja did her best to stop laughing and held a hand over her mouth in her attempt but the look on Taylor's face made Jorja continue to giggle. Taylor's eyes narrowed and Jorja held up her hand in an attempt to ward off the verbal attack Taylor was about to give her. "Okay, okay, I'm sorry. I didn't mean to scare you that much! But you have to admit, I got you good. This makes up for you sneaking up behind me *and* for attempting to set me up with Brad at the café."

Taylor shook her head. "Oh no, this does not even compare! I will get you. Wait and see. Halloween is coming and there are many, many tricks up my sleeve!"

Jorja then realized she had opened a can of worms with Taylor. Taylor always had to have the last word, the last laugh and now, Jorja feared, Taylor would do anything to get the last scare. She would have to keep her guard up.

"Really, Taylor, I am sorry. I didn't mean to scare you that much. It was not an opportunity I could pass up and you have to admit, you would have done the same to me." Jorja raised an eyebrow at Taylor, tempting her to deny the statement.

Taylor opened her mouth in denial and then quickly closed her mouth and pursed her lips. "Ok, I'll admit, it was a great opportunity. But you scared the crap out of me!"

Jorja smiled and walked to the break room where they kept a small fridge and snacks. She grabbed two bottles of water and returned to the cash register where Taylor was still trying to catch her breath.

Jorja handed one bottle to Taylor and then opened her own bottle and took a drink. "Did all the books we order come in?"

Taylor opened her own bottle and took a drink as well. She took one more breath and then answered Jorja. "We got everything except for the newest Magic Tree House book that goes on sale this month. I'll have to call the distributer to find out when the books will arrive."

"Good, at least we received most of the shipment. The newest Tree House book is for the winter season anyway so as long as we receive it in time to put up a display before Thanksgiving that will be fine."

Taylor nodded in agreement. "By the way, Jorja, we need to decorate for Halloween. Do you have decorations or do we need to get some?"

Jorja hadn't thought of decorating, other than placement of the newest Halloween books for sale. She liked the holidays though and thought it was a good idea.

"No, we would need to buy decorations. Maybe while I'm catching up on paperwork tomorrow you can run into town to get some decorations? I'm sure you can find items that I'll like. We don't need a lot, just enough to decorate around the coffee stand, registers and the sitting areas."

Taylor was glad to go shopping, especially for holiday items. "Sure, Jorja, I don't mind going."

Jorja took another sip from her water. "Good, that would help me out."

Taylor decided it would be a good time to bring up another subject. "So, if you don't mind decorating, I have another idea I want to run by you. What if we have a small Halloween party here, an invitation only party, and we ask everyone to dress up as one of their favorite book characters? We could include adults and children and have prizes for age groups. What do you think?"

"I think that's a good idea, Taylor, and I think it would be a lot of fun. Halloween is only three weeks away. Do you think you can handle making a list of the items we'll need to purchase for the party and get the invitations put together? We should come up with a list of guests and get the invitations mailed this week."

Taylor was nodding as she clapped her hands together. "Oh, this will be tons of fun! Yes, I'll make a list of what we'll need and the invitations won't take much time at all. I hope you don't mind but I already hit Dylan up and asked if he'd help with catering the food. He loved the idea of putting together Halloween desserts and other treats. We have quite a few great ideas already."

Jorja loved Taylor's enthusiasm. "No, Taylor, I don't mind. I guess if he's willing to help, then we're in good hands with the food. Ask Kat if she wants to help you with preparations and then she and I can both help with the actual decorating right before the party."

"I'm sure Kat would love to help. I'll talk to her when she comes in tomorrow."

Jorja felt a sudden sadness at the mention of Kat's name. "Well, since I'll be here all day tomorrow, I'm going to head home now. I'm sure

Piper is dying to see me and go for a walk."

Taylor kneeled down to pick up the book she had dropped. "I'm almost done with this and then I'll head to the house myself. You still need to read that letter, don't you?"

Jorja paused before taking another drink. She looked at Taylor and said, "Boy, I almost forgot about that. Yeah, I still need to read it. I'll do that when I get home."

"Wait until I get home, okay? And why would you forget about it? I figured you would be thinking about it all day."

Jorja realized she hadn't filled Taylor in on the possibility of finding Kat's mom.

"Well, something else took priority this afternoon. I found some information that might be related to Kat's mom."

"You did? Did you find her? Where is she?"

Jorja shook her head. "I can't say for sure I found her. I may have found out what happened to her and it is not good."

Taylor frowned. "What do you mean? How do you know what happened to her if you didn't find her?"

Jorja did not respond, not willing yet to say the words out loud.

Taylor finally realized what Jorja meant. "Oh, you mean something bad as in she's no longer with us?"

Jorja gave a slight nod and said, "Yes and let's not get into it here. We can talk more at home, okay?"

Taylor walked up to Jorja and gave her a quick hug. "I'm sorry, Jorja. I know this must be hard when you think about having to tell Kat something like this. Okay, I'll see you at home."

Jorja told Taylor goodbye and then left the store. She appreciated the hug from Taylor but it just confirmed for her how difficult it was going to be when she finally had to discuss her findings with Kat.

CHAPTER 22

Jorja parked her jeep in front of the garage and before she was able to get to the front door, she could hear Piper excitedly 'talking' on the other side of the door. She unlocked the door and could barely open it before Piper rushed at her and rubbed against her legs. Piper then pushed her muzzle up against Jorja's free hand and forced the issue of a long overdue petting.

"Oh, I know, I missed you too." Jorja laid her purse on the hall table and bent down to give Piper a hug. Piper quickly caught a whiff of food and her nose was soon pressed up against the to-go box Jorja was holding.

"Oh, no. This is *my* dinner! You'll get your own food." She laughed and gave Piper another pat on the head before heading back to the kitchen. She placed the sandwich container in the fridge and checked the machine for messages. She then walked to the laundry room where she found a clean pair of socks, her baseball cap and her walking shoes. As soon as Piper saw Jorja pick up the shoes, she ran towards the door. Piper knew exactly what the shoes and hat meant. Jorja quickly put on her socks, laced up her shoes and placed the hat on her head before grabbing a light rain jacket.

Piper was patiently waiting by the front door with her butt planted against the door, her tail loudly thumping up and down.

"I know, you missed your walk with me. I'm excited too." Jorja grabbed the leash hanging just inside the coat closet and attached it to Piper's collar.

"Ok, girl, let's go walk off some calories."

Jorja was glad to get a walk in before Taylor arrived home. She needed to think about how she was going to approach Kat with the possibility that her mother might be dead. That her mother might have been *murdered*. She wasn't sure she should say anything until she knew for sure. And how was she to know for sure? Would they be able to perform some DNA tests? Were there dental records available to make a comparison? Jorja wasn't exactly sure how the process would work. She just hated the thought of the pain Kat would be going through.

After a good half hour walk, Jorja and Piper arrived back at the house. Taylor was already home and Jorja found her in the kitchen making a salad to go with their sandwiches.

"Whew, it's getting chilly out and it's getting darker earlier. It'll be more difficult soon to find a good time to walk, especially once we have steady rain."

Jorja shook off her coat and placed it in the laundry room with her shoes and hat. Piper was now patiently lying on the kitchen floor with the knowledge that dinner would soon be served.

Taylor finished placing the lettuce in bowls and then added sliced tomatoes and olives. Opening the fridge door to grab some shredded cheese for their salads she said, "I still have some of that raspberry dressing from Trader Joe's, would you like that on your salad?"

Jorja nodded as she said, "I love that dressing. Go ahead and give me extra cheese too."

Taylor added the shredded cheese and dressing to both salads before placing them on the table while Jorja fed Piper in the laundry room.

As Jorja and Taylor ate dinner, they discussed Jorja's visit the day before at the hospital and at her parents'. Jorja also filled Taylor in on what she discovered as she reviewed the case file at the Sheriff's Office.

"But just on the glove you think it is Kat's mother? Is there anything else?"

Jorja knew Taylor would play Devil's Advocate but Jorja already had her own doubts. "I really don't have anything else at this point other than that the timeframe seems to work, the area is close by and that type of glove was what Vera had apparently owned. I'll have to see what else they'll let me look at and then see if there's anything to help me identify whether or not it was Vera."

Taylor finished her salad and moved on to her leftover sandwich. "Yeah, maybe you should do that before you say anything to Kat. You don't want to give her any false information, whether it's good or bad news."

Jorja nodded. "Yes, I know. It's just that tomorrow when she comes to work she's going to ask me how the search is going. I don't want to lie to her. How can I tell her anything about what I have accomplished so far without telling her anything?"

Taylor shrugged. "I don't know. But I don't think you should tell her yet that her mom's body was found in a shallow grave ten years ago. That just sucks. Let her continue to hold out some hope that her mom's alive until you know for sure if this is her mom."

Jorja was torn. She knew Taylor was right in some respect but she did not wish to lie to Kat. She'd have to figure it out soon since she'd be seeing Kat tomorrow.

Taylor finished her sandwich and got up to place her dishes in the dishwasher as she said, "Don't worry about the dishes. I'll put them away. Why don't you grab that letter if you're ready to read it now?"

"I'm as ready as I can be. I'll be right back."

Jorja had put off opening the envelope long enough. She wasn't sure if it was because she felt guilty for taking it or because she was afraid of what the letter might contain. She was surprised her mother hadn't called her yet in a panic about the letter, which possibly meant she wasn't aware Jorja had sneaked the letter out of the house.

Jorja walked to the hallway where her purse still sat on the hall table. She took the letter out of her purse and stared at the handwriting scribbled on the front, *To Jorja and Jorja only*. The handwriting appeared to resemble the hand-writing on the letter she found in the tin box Piper had dug up. As she held the note, her hands began to shake and she realized she had a great fear of what the letter contained. Why else would her mother feel it necessary to hide the letter from her?

Taylor poked her head around the corner of the kitchen. "Are you coming?"

"Yeah, I'm coming." Jorja walked back into the kitchen where Taylor was now sitting at the bar. Jorja knew Taylor was curious but she had to admit her fear. "I'm actually afraid to open it now. What if there was a good reason Mom tried to keep me from reading this?"

Taylor was concerned for her friend and knew how difficult change was for Jorja. Just the recent turn of events was enough to put Jorja on edge. Now, with a new store and new purpose, Jorja was happy and Taylor knew Jorja was afraid of anything that might change the status quo.

"Well, you don't have to open it, Jorja. You can just give it right back to your mom...after you apologize for taking it behind her back in the first place. But then you'll always wonder, won't you? What is it that your aunt wanted you to know?

Either you believe what your parents tell you and call it good or you read for yourself what it is your aunt wanted you to know. Just make sure you can live with whatever decision you make."

Jorja was having some difficulty with that reasoning. "But what if I want to know but it turns out to be something I don't really want to know? I won't know that until I read it. I'm curious but what if knowing is not what I expect it to be?"

Taylor put her chin on the palm of her hand and looked squarely at Jorja. "That's the decision you have to make. Can you take whatever is in that letter? Can you deal with it no matter what? It might be nothing. Maybe just a love note from your aunt because she didn't get a normal relationship with you and is sorry. It might hold some family secret. But a secret your parents didn't want you to know? Either you talk to them about it and hope that they'll be honest with you or you just read the letter yourself and find out. I know it's hard for you, Jorja, but I'm here for you whatever decision you make."

Jorja looked down at the letter again. She wondered how long ago her aunt had written her name on the front of the envelope. She wondered why her aunt never gave her the letter before. She worried about whether this would shake the core of her beliefs or her being.

She finally turned the envelope around and opened the top flap. Her hands shook as she removed yet another envelope from inside the envelope. The second envelope also had the name

"Jorja" on the front in her aunt's handwriting. She then opened the second envelope to remove the stationary from inside. It appeared to be from an old stationary set. Taylor watched as Jorja carefully opened the stationary and began to read the letter. Jorja finished the first page and moved on to the second, where her hands trembled even more and her eyes soon flooded with tears. By the time Jorja finished the letter, she could not stop sobbing. She could not fully comprehend what she had just read and her chest felt heavy with what she'd just discovered. She did not *want* to believe what she had read.

"Jorja? What is it? What does it say?" Taylor stood up to approach Jorja, very concerned with her friend's response.

"Here. You can read it." Jorja could barely get the words out as she passed the letter to Taylor. Jorja then quickly left the kitchen, after which Taylor heard Jorja fiercely blow her nose in the bathroom.

Taylor looked down at the letter and began to read:

My dearest Jorja,

This will be the most difficult letter I have ever had to write. I don't know at what point you will see this letter but I hope there will come a day when you will forgive me. As I write, it is not with the intention to give it to you myself, as I don't believe I could ever deal with how you will respond to what I have to say. Please forgive me for being selfish and weak. If you are reading this, I will assume that something has happened to me and Nurse Willows has provided you with the box of items I left behind. Do not hold this against her, she was a good friend and is only doing as I asked. The reason for this letter is to ask you to forgive me for my sins. Whether this will help me now if I am already gone from this world, I do not know. Helen may hate me for this but I feel it is important for you to know where you came from and where your roots are bound.

When I was only 15, I became pregnant. I fell in love with a man who I thought loved me in return. Before I gave birth, however, he left me to deal with the stigma of being an unwed mother. My parents moved me away from town for some time in their attempt to hide my pregnancy but as my due date reared its ugly head, they decided to move me back home. I don't believe my parents ever intended to let me keep my babies but in the end it did not matter. It may be a shock to you to learn I was pregnant or that I had twins. You may wonder whatever happened to them and why you were never told what happened to them or to me. You see, I could not deal with the fact that the babies' father left me. My dreams were shattered. I was an unwed mother. My parents did not adjust well to my situation. In the end, I did not handle the strain well at all and the only thing I can say is that I literally lost my mind. I do not recall the day I gave birth. It wasn't until I gave birth that anyone knew I was even having twins. But what happened to the twins is something I can never remember while also something I will never forget. I was sent away to the institution because I did a terrible thing. A very terrible thing. From what I was later told by my parents, I harmed one of those sweet little babies while the other survived only because my parents were able to intervene. That is the reason I was sent away and why *you were not able to have a relationship with me. I cannot explain how terrible it is to live with the knowledge that I committed such a terrible act while not having a true memory of such act. My only hope is that I have somehow made it to Heaven where I can make amends with Jacob, my baby boy. Please believe me when I say I am truly, truly sorry for what I have done. I believe you have had a much better life than what I would have been able to provide for you. My sister has done a wonderful job raising you as her own. I truly hope you will forgive me. Your mother, Gloria*

Taylor felt numb. What the heck could she say to bring comfort to Jorja after reading this? Gloria was actually her mother? Gloria killed the other baby? She dropped the letter on the counter and went looking for Jorja. Taylor finally found Jorja lying on her bed staring up at the ceiling, tears streaming down the side of her face. Taylor's heart broke at the sight.

"Jorja? Are you okay? Of course, you're not okay. But really, are you going to be okay? Do you need anything?"

Taylor stood at the edge of the bed, looking down at Jorja. Jorja turned her head to answer Taylor but as she opened her mouth to reply, she began sobbing again. Jorja rolled on to her side and hid her face in a pillow as she cried. Taylor could only lie down beside Jorja and wrap her arm around her while she cried. The two of them lay that way for some time before Jorja cried herself to sleep. She woke with a sudden jolt when Piper nudged her foot at the edge of the bed. Taylor sat up to once again look down at Jorja and asked, "Are you okay Jorja? Do you need me to get you anything? A tissue? A drink?"

When Jorja did not immediately respond, Taylor got off the bed and grabbed a tissue from the bathroom. She handed it to Jorja who wiped at her nose and eyes and then slowly sat up.

"I can't even begin to imagine how you are feeling, Jorja. You can scream, cry, yell, whatever makes you feel better. I'm here for you."

Jorja attempted to smile at Taylor. She then took a breath and let out a long sigh. Her mind was reeling with the knowledge that the mother and father she grew up with were not her natural parents. She was also trying to accept the fact that her crazy aunt was actually her mother and she was lucky to be alive. What was worse was the knowledge that she'd had a brother who had been killed by their own mother. It was just impossible to think about and believe in.

Taylor waited but Jorja remained silent. Jorja feared an attempt to respond would open the flood gates again as she wiped at the tears beginning to form once again.

Taylor was very sad for her friend. She moved to sit beside Jorja to put her arm around her and give her a hug.

"Jorja, I know this is hard. Just take your time and let me know if you want to talk, okay?"

Jorja nodded her head as she continued to wipe at her eyes and cheeks. She then got up off the bed to walk into her bathroom.

The reflection she saw in the mirror gave her the ability to finally speak. "Oh, boy, I look awful. I need to wash my face and get this makeup cleaned up. Let me clean up and I'll meet you downstairs in a few minutes."

Taylor eyed Jorja for a few seconds before relenting. She then left the room and went back down to the kitchen.

Jorja cleaned her face with a warm washcloth and then wiped the mascara from her eyes. She wasn't too impressed with herself as she looked in the mirror but crying never brought out the best in anyone's looks. It was a great release but she decided she was done crying. She needed to figure things out. She would go downstairs to talk to Taylor and then eventually she would speak to her mother. Jorja was determined to have that conversation take place sooner rather than later.

CHAPTER 23

The following morning Jorja drove to work accepting the fact that she needed to keep busy and that she also had to take time to speak to Kat. She felt drained from the night before but decided she probably would have felt worse if she and Taylor hadn't stayed up late talking everything over. Without a friend like Taylor to talk to, Jorja wasn't sure how she would have handled her emotions after reading the note from Gloria.

After parking her jeep and entering the store, Jorja mindlessly went through her regular routine of turning on the lights, the heat, and unlocking the cash registers. As she finished opening the store, she heard Taylor enter through the back door.

"Good morning, Jorja," Taylor said as she moved towards the coffee stand to prepare herself for the first regular customers. "Do you want me to make you a cup of Chai tea?"

Jorja nodded her head and smiled. Taylor was still treating her like she might break down and cry again at a moment's notice. "Thanks Taylor that would be great."

"You rushed out this morning. I was a little worried about you. Okay, I lie. I am very worried about you. How are you doing?"

Jorja shrugged and thought for a moment before answering. "I'm doing okay, I guess. It's just a lot to take in, you know? I need to talk to Mom. Get all this out in the open. It'll be hard but really, she needs to know that I know."

Taylor finished Jorja's tea and handed it to her. "Well, I'm here for you. Plus, I make a mean cup of Chai tea, so at least that's something that'll make you feel better." Taylor offered a big grin.

Jorja smiled back. "Thanks Taylor. I'm going to go upstairs. I need to call Mom now."

"Go ahead, I'm sure our usual Tuesday morning rush won't be a bother." Taylor laughed at the thought, as their morning rush included a few students on their way to school and mothers with babies in strollers on their way to their morning baby gym day.

Jorja took her tea and went upstairs to the office. She knew she had to get the phone call to her mother out of the way or she'd never be able to focus on anything else. She didn't want to actually talk about this over the phone but she had to get the ball rolling.

Helen answered on the second ring. "Hello?"

"Hi Mom, how are you?"

"Oh, hi Jorja. I'm fine. How are you?"

Jorja couldn't help but sigh and she felt her heart flutter as she became hesitant to bring up the subject about Gloria.

"Uh, I'm okay. Actually, I need to speak to you about something but I was wondering when you were planning to come down here this week."

There was silence on the line as Jorja waited for her mother to answer. Helen finally said, "Well, I was thinking about coming down on Thursday. Why, do you need me to come down sooner than that?"

"Yes, actually. I was hoping you could come down tonight and stay over."

"Tonight? Why, what's wrong?" Jorja could hear the fear in her mother's voice. She felt like she was doing a terrible thing by making her mother face the past.

"I don't really want to get into it over the phone, Mom. I just really need to see you."

Helen was quiet but then finally said, "Okay, I can come down tonight but can you at least give me an idea of what you want to discuss? You're scaring me. Are you all right? Is everything okay?"

"I'm okay. It's…it's just that I…I need to talk to you about Aunt Gloria."

"Gloria? Again?" Helen was only able to whisper as she said, "What about her?"

Jorja took a deep breath and finally took the plunge. "Mom, I took that envelope you hid from me. It had my name on it so I took it. I read it last night and what it contained is what I need to speak to you about. Please, I don't want to discuss this over the phone. Can you come down later this afternoon so we can talk tonight?"

Jorja's heart sank when her mother's voice cracked as she said, "You took the envelope? Oh Jorja, why?"

"Because I had to, it was addressed to *me*."

Helen sighed. "Fine, Jorja, I'll be at the house this afternoon. I should be there around five-thirty. Is that okay?"

"Yes, that will be fine. Thank you. Drive safe on your way down, okay?"

"I will. I love you, honey. I'll see you tonight."

"I love you too, Mom. Bye."

Jorja hung up the phone with a heavy heart. She knew this would be difficult for her mother but it just could not be avoided. She felt tired although she hadn't yet been at the store for an hour. She rolled her shoulders back and rolled her head in circles to get out the kinks and ward off the stress headache that threatened to take over. She then took a long sip of her tea. Taylor made it perfectly, using soy milk as Jorja liked because the flavor blended well with the Chai tea.

She took a few minutes to enjoy her tea and attempt to calm her frayed nerves before deciding it would be best to work on being productive. At a time when she needed to be distracted from her personal life, she was thankful there was always plenty of paperwork to catch up on for the bookstore. When Taylor buzzed her on the phone a while later, Jorja realized just how well the distraction worked when a couple of hours had already passed.

"Jorja, you have a call on line one. A Cheryl Dunham. After this call, do you think you can take over down here while I run into town to get those Halloween decorations?"

"Sure Taylor. I'll finish the call and come downstairs. Thanks." Jorja picked up the phone. "Hello? Ms. Dunham? This is Jorja."

"Hello, Jorja. Well, I had a slow morning, believe it or not, so I thought I'd go ahead and track down the box of evidence you wanted to go through. I have authorization for you to review it while I'm present so if you'd like, we can set up a time to meet. Do you want to come in this afternoon?"

Jorja looked at the pile of paperwork on her desk and thought about the conversation she would soon be having with her mother. She wasn't sure she wanted to tackle anything else today.

"Can we meet tomorrow instead? I just have some things I need to take care of today. Would that work for you?"

"Sure, let me look at my calendar for tomorrow. Ah, I have some time in the morning around eleven or we could meet again after lunch, say, around two o'clock. Would either time work for you?"

"Actually, the morning would work best. Eleven o'clock then?"

"Yes, I will see you then."

"Thank you, Ms. Dunham. I will see you tomorrow."

Jorja hung up the phone and wondered what her inspection of that evidence box was going to lead to.

~ ~ ~

The rest of the day was fairly quiet, leaving Jorja time in the afternoon to finish working on paperwork after Taylor returned from her shopping spree. With the amount of work she'd been able to accomplish, Jorja felt free to go home at a decent time. But now that the time was drawing near, she was beginning to feel very nervous about the conversation she would soon have with her mother.

"Hi Jorja!" Kat said as she rushed up the stairs to the office, nearly causing Jorja to spit out the water she had just taken a sip of.

Jorja tried to hold back a cough as she swallowed the water. "Hello, Kat, how are you today?"

Kat sat down in the chair facing the desk. "I'm okay. School was...school. I had an English test today but I think I got a 'B' so I'm happy because it was a tough one. How are you?"

Jorja hesitated as she thought how to answer. "Well, I'm fine. I've got a few things on my mind right now. I'm trying to finish up here so I can head home soon. My mom is coming over tonight and I want to get dinner started early."

Kat tilted her head as she asked, "What kind of things? Things about my mom? Did you find anything out yet?"

Jorja felt like a heel because she did not want to lie to Kat. "Well, I'm still working on your mom's case. I may have a lead but I don't want to say anything until I speak to someone first."

"Oh? A lead? That's great!" Kat clapped her hands in excitement and smiled at Jorja.

"Wait a minute, Kat. Don't get too excited. I'm not sure yet what I'm going to find out. Don't expect too much just yet, okay?"

Kat held her hands together but continued to smile at Jorja. "I'm just glad you might find something out. That's all I want...to know where she went and why she left."

Jorja nodded at Kat. "I know, Kat, and I'll try to find what I can for you. In fact, do you think you could help me out?"

Kat dropped her hands to her sides and her demeanor became serious as she said, "Help you out? I'll help any way I can, Jorja, just name it."

"Well, I think I should have some photos of your mom. I have the one you already gave me but I think I should have a variety, showing how she wore her hair, what types of dresses or other clothes she wore, what type of jewelry she wore, that kind of thing. Can you see what you can find for me?"

Kat quickly nodded and said, "My dad had a photo album he gave me and there are a lot of photos you can have. Do you want me to just bring in the whole book?"

Jorja thought for a moment and then said, "You don't have to bring the whole book. Just bring me about a dozen showing your mom wearing different types of clothes but make sure most of them are within six months or so of when she disappeared."

"Sure, Jorja, I can do that. I'll bring the photos by tomorrow morning."

"Great. I'll let you know as soon as possible if I am able to come up with anything." Jorja was thankful Kat did not ask any further questions. To be safe, Jorja decided to change the subject. "Taylor has finished with the inventory of the new books we just received so I'd like you to put them out on the shelves for me. We have some Halloween books and you can help Taylor decorate a section for the holiday."

"Oh, fun! Okay, I'll get started on that. Anything else?" Kat stood up and waited for Jorja's answer.

Jorja shook her head. "No, that's all for now. It might take you some time to decorate with what Taylor picked up today. I think she went a little overboard because of how much she enjoys Halloween. You go have fun with that and if Taylor has anything else she needs help with she can let you know."

Kat then left the office and bounced down the stairs to help Taylor. As Jorja watched Kat leave, she became lost in thought at how difficult it would be to give Kat any sort of bad news relating to her mother. Kat was such a positive person, always kind and in good spirits. Jorja didn't want to bring Kat's mood to the low depths the news of her mother's death would surely bring her.

Jorja forced her attention back to her computer and finished what she could before she could no longer focus on the paperwork. Deciding she had done plenty for the day, she grabbed her jacket and headed downstairs. She found Taylor and Kat gleefully decorating a corner of the bookstore with Halloween books and decorations. Jorja had to admit their excitement was contagious.

"Okay, girls, I'm done with what needs to be done and I'm going to head home. Taylor, I'm making tacos for dinner so it's nothing special. I don't want to spend too much time in the kitchen when Mom and I have so much to talk about."

Taylor waved a hand at Jorja and said, "Don't worry about feeding me. Dylan called and said he wants to take me to dinner. I already told him I'm closing up tonight so he's going to work late and meet me here before I close up. I won't be home too late but I thought it would be good to give you and your mom some time to talk."

"Thanks, Taylor, I really appreciate it. I'll see you when you get home. Have fun. Bye Kat, see you tomorrow."

Jorja left Taylor and Kat to finish with decorating. As she climbed into her jeep, Jorja had a quick thought she tried to push away. No matter how much she disliked the idea, she reluctantly admitted to herself that she needed to speak to Lydia before her meeting at the Sheriff's Office tomorrow. As she drove to the salon where Lydia worked, Jorja thought about how she would start the conversation. There really was no easy way, as Lydia did not appreciate what Jorja was trying to do. Jorja decided all she could do was hope Lydia would be willing to speak to her.

CHAPTER 24

Jorja quickly found parking in the salon's parking lot but she took her time locking the jeep and walking towards the salon. She hesitated outside the door as she continued to think about how she would be able to obtain any information from someone who obviously did not like her. She quickly shook her head in an attempt to shake off her doubts and grabbed the door handle to open the door. Just as Jorja's hand landed on the handle, the door suddenly flung outward, hitting her and causing her to stumble over her feet.

"Oh, I'm sorry! Are you okay?" A dark-haired man in a police uniform was staring down at her with apologetic brown eyes.

Jorja again grabbed the door handle to regain her footing.

"I'm fine, no harm no foul."

"Well, still, I didn't mean to hit you with the door. I would have felt terrible if I'd hurt you. Please, forgive me." He held out his hand and tilted his head as he said, "I'm Officer Cooper. You look familiar, do I know you?"

Jorja held out her hand to shake his as she replied, "Officer Cooper? Are you any relation to Sandra?"

"I am. I'm her brother, Jim. Are you friends with Sandra?"

"Sort of, through my mom. I'm Jorja. She and my mom were friends in school. I'm not sure if you and I have met but I'm sure it's possible."

Jim smiled. "I remember now. My sister has been talking about you quite a bit recently. You opened the new book store. Sorry I haven't had time to check it out yet."

"Oh…that's okay. Just stop by whenever you can. We have coffee so you should make sure to stop by next time you head out for your shift. In fact, I would like to speak to you sometime if you have a few minutes to spare."

"Oh? About what?" Jim's gaze made him appear slightly interested.

"Well, I have been researching an old case and it appears you were the investigating officer."

Jim's gaze was now intently curious. "An old case? Which one?"

"It involved the disappearance of a woman named Vera Myers. I'm checking into a few things for her daughter, Kathleen, and I was just wondering if I could discuss the case with you."

Jim scratched his head as he looked down at his feet in thought. "Hmm, I do slightly recall the case but what I remember was that there was nothing to conclude other than that she ran away. Why are you looking into this case?"

"I agreed to do it for Kat, or Kathleen. I'm just trying to help her find some closure."

Jim grabbed the door handle and opened the door to the salon. "Well, I'll have to check on whether or not I'm allowed to speak to anyone outside of law enforcement about the case. It depends on whether the department views it as still open or closed. Let me get back to you on that, okay?"

Jorja was thankful he did not completely shoot down her request. "Thanks, Officer Cooper, I'd really appreciate that."

Jorja thought he would ask her to call him 'Jim' rather than 'Officer Cooper' but she quickly realized he preferred the formal title as he said, "Well, it was nice meeting you Jorja. Guess you should get inside before we let out all the heat." With a slight grin he waited until she entered the salon and then walked away towards his patrol car parked across the street.

"Jorja! What a nice surprise!" Sandra was already moving around the front desk towards Jorja to give her a hug. "What brings you here? Do you need a hair cut? A manicure? You name it."

"No Sandra, thanks. I was actually hoping Lydia had a few moments to speak to me."

Jorja could see Lydia standing near her work station with no client in sight. Lydia heard her name and looked up from the magazine she had been looking through with only mild interest.

"Sure Jorja. Lydia doesn't have another client scheduled for about twenty minutes. You two can use the break room if you need privacy."

Jorja was certain Lydia heard what Sandra said but she remained where she was standing, waiting for Jorja to approach her. Jorja saw Lydia raise a quick brow in question as to why Jorja wanted to speak to her.

"Hi Lydia."

"Hello." Lydia threw the magazine down on a nearby table and waited.

"Sandra said you had a few minutes to spare. Could I talk to you? Sandra said we could use the break room."

Jorja tried not to show her frustration as Lydia took her time in answering. Finally, Lydia said, "Okay, but I only have a few minutes. Follow me."

Jorja followed Lydia down the hall before turning right into a small break room containing a small table, four chairs, a small fridge and a counter area with a sink and microwave. It was a bit claustrophobic for Jorja, especially when Lydia's attitude took up most of the space.

Jorja thought Lydia would sit down at the table but instead she remained standing by the counter. Jorja finally decided she needed to take control.

"Lydia, can you please just sit down and talk to me for a few minutes? It's about Kat."

Lydia showed obvious concern as she said, "What about Kat? Is she okay?"

Jorja nodded and said, "Yes, she's okay. I just need to speak to you regarding my search for her mother."

Lydia frowned. "Oh. Well, you know how I feel about that. That woman gave up on the best thing in her life, a family, and I don't want any part of you tracking her down so Kat can have a relationship with her now."

Jorja sighed. This was going to be difficult. "Lydia, please sit down. There's more to it than that, I'm afraid. Please?" Jorja offered one final plea before Lydia finally relented and sat in a chair. She crossed her legs and then her arms in defiance of the whole conversation.

"Thank you. Now, I haven't found her mother yet. Or at least, I haven't found her alive."

Lydia's eyes widened at that comment. "Alive? You mean she might be dead?"

Jorja shrugged. "Well, either she's been very good at covering her tracks for the past twelve years or something happened to her and it is the reason she never returned to her family."

Lydia's forehead wrinkled as she thought about Jorja's statement. She remained silent and let Jorja continue.

"I have not told any of this to Kat yet. I don't want to alarm her and I don't want to provide her with information that might not be accurate. However, I've searched every way I know how for any records that might show where Vera could be living and what name she might be using. Nothing has come up. I'm beginning to believe she did not leave Kat like the police think she did."

Lydia jumped in. "Why? You didn't know her. How could you know what she would or would not have done?"

Jorja relented and said, "You're right. I didn't know her but she was a mother. I can understand if she wanted to leave her husband, for whatever reason there might have been, but to leave her child and never have contact again? I'm just having difficulty with that. Mother's do terrible things but it's difficult to believe Kat's mother just left her."

Jorja thought about what her birth mother had attempted to do to her after taking the life of her brother. Yes, mothers did terrible things. She just hoped Kat's mother wasn't one of them.

"Well, whatever you believe there's no changing it now, Jorja. She's gone. Why bring it all back for Kat to deal with now? Just let it be!"

Lydia stood in her frustration. Jorja knew she had to settle Lydia down. This was too important to let personality conflicts stop her from gaining additional information.

"I'm sorry, Lydia. I don't mean to upset you. Please, just hear me out, okay? I really want to help Kat and she has asked me to do this for her so I need to follow through with it. Can you please just give me a few more minutes?"

Lydia looked down at Jorja and glared at her before finally sitting back down in the chair. Again, she crossed her arms and waited.

Jorja took a deep breath before she continued. "Thank you. Okay, because I began to wonder whether Vera was still alive, I searched for records relating to 'Jane Does' in our area and within sixty miles of this area. I have been able to search through some old cases and yesterday I came across one that caught my attention. But I need to ask you something before I look into this any further. Okay?"

Lydia was showing more interest now. "You mean you think you found her?"

"I can't say yet, Lydia. I don't want to jump to that conclusion until I conduct some further research. And please, don't tell Kat what I've told you, okay?"

Lydia shrugged and said, "I don't talk to Kat about this. You know how our relationship is; frayed and strained, just as it has been ever since her father died."

"I'm sorry about that, Lydia. I hope that soon you and Kat can mend your relationship. Maybe once she finds out where her mother is, she can move on with her relationship with you."

Lydia didn't show much hope in that thought. "Yeah, maybe. Okay, what do you want?"

Jorja looked at the clock on the wall. She'd already spent ten minutes trying to get this far with Lydia and she didn't have much time left before her client would show up.

"Do you remember if there were any certain clothing items or personal items that Kat's mother usually wore or used? It's my understanding she had not taken much with her when she left, just a few items of clothing. But was there anything else she may have taken with her? Anything important to her?"

Lydia remained silent as she tried to remember anything that might be of relevance. Finally, she said, "Well, I'm not exactly sure if this helps but leading up to the time she disappeared, Vera wore her favorite jacket and gloves every day and I'm fairly certain she was probably wearing them when she disappeared. She also had a locket she always wore. I believe it was a simple heart locket, something my brother picked up for her when they were on a trip at the beach. Other than that, the only thing I can think of that would be important to her would be her Bible. She was always going to church. Tried to get my brother to go but he never wanted to. He didn't argue when she wanted to take Kat to church with her and Kat seemed happy going to Sunday school. If I remember right, the Bible was given to her by her father, who was a preacher back when she was a kid. There's really nothing else I can think of."

Jorja felt tingles as she asked, "What about the jacket and gloves? What were they like?"

Lydia didn't hesitate. "Well, the jacket was black but I'm not sure what material it was made from and she always wore a red pair of leather gloves during the cooler months. I thought red was too much but she wore them everywhere. Sometimes she'd wear another jacket, depending on her outfit but she would almost *always* wear those gloves. Why? What have you found out?"

Jorja was glad she had stopped to speak to Lydia but she wasn't sure she should divulge what she'd discovered before she got a chance to speak to Kat.

Jorja weighed in her mind what response she should give Lydia. She finally decided to have faith in Lydia and be honest about what she had discovered. "I haven't had a chance to speak to Kat about this and I don't want to until I learn more but I have discovered a case where a woman's body was found and there is a possibility it could be Kat's mother."

Lydia opened her mouth to speak but then closed her mouth and intently stared at Jorja. Jorja wasn't sure what Lydia was feeling, considering she didn't seem to harbor any real affection for Kat's mother.

"So...you really do think Vera is *dead*? How? In an accident or actually killed by someone?"

"Why do you think anyone would kill Vera?"

Lydia shrugged and said, "I don't know. She's been gone a long time and we don't know who she got messed up with when she left. Maybe she hooked up with the wrong type of guy. It happens, you know."

Jorja nodded and said, "Yes, it happens. And yes, this person was murdered and buried in the woods. There were certain details that made me take an interest in the case and I'm going to try to obtain more information to see whether or not it could be Kat's mother. If it is, it will explain a lot of things, I think, except for why someone would want to kill her. Do you know of anyone who would have wanted to harm her?"

Lydia had been looking at the clock to check the time but her head snapped back at the question. "What do you mean, do I know of anyone? Why would I know of anyone who might harm her? I didn't have a great relationship with her but I won't say she was a bad person. I really can't imagine why anyone would want to harm her. And it wasn't my brother, if that's what you're suggesting!"

Jorja held up her hands and said, "No, I certainly wasn't suggesting Kat's father had anything to do with it. I'm just curious about whether she did get herself involved with anyone who might have harmed her. Did she and your brother have a good relationship? Do you think she might have been having an affair?"

Lydia looked shocked at the thought. "My brother treated her like a queen. If she was seeing anyone else, well...I just don't see her as the type, really. She and my brother seemed happy and he never suggested anything to indicate otherwise. He was distraught when she left, or when he thought she left him. I just can't imagine Vera having an affair but of course, you don't always know what people are capable of, do you?"

Jorja had to agree with that. You just never knew what anyone was capable of.

Lydia continued, "Besides, the whole question about why Vera left was basically put on the back burner, I think, once that girl's body was found."

Jorja started at that bit of information. "What girl?"

Lydia casually waved a hand as she replied, "Oh, a young girl, just out of high school, was found dead near the railroad tracks. There were a lot of stories about what happened to her because of who she was but in the end the police determined she had been hit by the train."

"Why? Who was she? How soon after Vera disappeared was the girl's body found?"

Lydia thought for a moment and then said, "I think it was during that same week, actually. It was a big deal because she was the Mayor's stepdaughter so whether Vera ran away or not wasn't really the most important issue at that time."

There was a quick knock and Sandra poked her head in the doorway. "Lydia? Your appointment is here."

"Thanks, I'll be right out." Lydia stood up and Jorja followed suit.

"Lydia, I'm going to research this other case before I speak to Kat about it. Can you please make sure not to mention anything to Kat about what I've told you? I don't want to upset her prematurely. Can you do that for me?"

Lydia rolled her eyes and said, "I told you, Kat and I don't have the best relationship. It's not like we're having heart-to-hearts every night. I won't say anything. As fragile as our relationship is, I wouldn't want to be the one to give her the bad news about her mother. I'll let you do that."

Jorja gave Lydia a forced smiled. "Gee, thanks. Okay, well, I'll let you get to work. Thanks for speaking with me."

Lydia gave Jorja a quick wave of the hand to dismiss Jorja's appreciation. "Don't thank me. I'd prefer you just leave all this alone so Kat doesn't get hurt. You might dig up more information than you expect and it could be something that might hurt Kat if it in anyway makes either her mother or her father look bad."

Jorja had thought about that possibility but she believed Kat could deal with whatever she was able to uncover. She was actually more surprised at Lydia's statement and realized Lydia really cared for Kat. "Yes, I know that is a possibility but Kat needs to know the truth. She can't go on wondering if her mother left her for no reason."

"Well, don't say I didn't warn you. I have to go. You can see yourself out." Lydia then quickly left the room.

Jorja followed and said goodbye to Sandra as she left the salon, promising to tell her mother hello from Sandra. She then ventured home, desperately trying to ignore the butterflies in her stomach as she thought about the conversation she would soon have with her mother.

CHAPTER 25

Jorja opened the front door and was happily greeted by Piper, who was not only wagging her tail but also her whole butt.

"I know, I know. I've been neglecting you lately, haven't I?"

She bent down to give Piper some attention, at which point Piper playfully sprawled out on her back so that her belly was exposed for a much-needed scratching.

Piper was able to extract a few solid minutes of Jorja's time before she finally had to stand up. She then removed her jacket and shoes and placed them in the coat closet.

"Mom?" Jorja walked into the kitchen, expecting to see her mother cleaning or organizing, as she usually did when she was nervous or stressed. Based on how stressful the situation must be for her mother, Jorja expected it was possible her mother may have cleaned the whole house.

Finding the kitchen empty, Jorja finally spotted her mother outside sitting in a patio chair. It was getting dark and it was chilly but her mother seemed to be concerned about neither. She noticed her mother did not appear to hear the door open as she stepped outside.

"Mom? Are you okay?"

Helen appeared slightly startled after being torn from her thoughts.

"Oh, hello dear. Yes, I'm fine. Just enjoying some fresh air."

"Well, it's pretty cold out here and you don't have a coat on. Do you want to come inside? I'm going to start dinner. I hope you don't mind if we just have tacos."

Helen slowly stood up and wrapped her arms around herself as if she just noticed the chill in the air.

"Yes, tacos are fine. I really don't have much of an appetite so don't make too much."

Helen followed Jorja back inside the house with Piper right behind them.

"Just sit down, mom. I don't need any help."

Helen didn't argue as she sat on a stool at the bar. She picked up a nearby magazine and tried to get interested in the contents but Jorja knew nothing in the magazine would hold her mother's attention.

"Do you want some tea, Mom? I have some Chai tea or some orange tea. Do either of them sound good to you?"

Helen nodded and said, "Yes that does sound good. I'm really feeling the chill now and a hot cup of tea would be nice. I'll make it myself while you start dinner. Do you want some?"

"No, not now. I'll wait until after dinner."

Jorja began making dinner while her mother fixed herself a cup of tea, both of them quietly working on their tasks. Jorja had to admit it would appear neither of them was eager to get started with the conversation.

Once the taco meat was cooked and seasoned, they both fixed their plates and sat down at the table. They put off the inevitable by making small talk about the bookstore and Helen told Jorja how her father had agreed to run a golf tournament at a local golf course. Once dinner was over and the dirty dishes were put away, Jorja finally decided it was time to get on with it. She took the letter from Gloria out of her bag and sat back down at the table with her mother. She could not help but wonder if she was doing the right thing when she saw the look in her mother's eyes. Her mother looked more anxious than Jorja had ever seen her and that frightened her. Helen remained still as she waited for Jorja to say the first words.

"Mom, I know this is going to be difficult to talk about but I really need to know the truth. I need to know the truth about Aunt Gloria. I read this…" Jorja held up the letter in the envelope. "…and it's a letter from Aunt Gloria to me. The letter says some terrible things. Things I just do not wish to believe but that I do think I have the right to know."

Helen's eyes widened as she looked at the envelope in Jorja's hand and Jorja saw her mother visibly shrink away at the sight of it.

"Mom, you withheld this letter from me even though Aunt Gloria wanted me to have it. I understand you were trying to protect me but now I also understand you were trying to protect yourself."

Helen tried to respond but could not form any words before she began to cry. She covered her face with both her hands as she sobbed, her shoulders shaking uncontrollably. Jorja was barely able to hear her mother say, "Oh, Jorja, I'm so sorry."

Jorja wiped her eyes as her own tears began to form. She patiently waited for her mother to look up at her before she began again.

"Mom, here, read what Aunt Gloria wrote to me."

Jorja handed the envelope to her mother. Helen hesitantly took the envelope and she carefully removed the letter. As Helen began to read, Jorja watched her mother's face as the emotions openly changed from fear, to sadness to anger and back to fear again. When Helen finally finished the letter, she set it on the table and then made eye contact with Jorja.

"Mom, I've asked you twice now about the truth behind Gloria and each time you lied to me. Why didn't you ever tell me?"

"I know this must be difficult for you to understand, Jorja, but I really was looking out for your best interests. I just didn't see how the truth would help you and can't you see why? Look at the type of person my sister became! She killed your brother and she would have killed you too if my parents hadn't caught her in the act. It was a terrible thing to happen and when my parents asked me if I would take you in, I didn't even hesitate. Your father and I had been married for almost three years but we hadn't been able to get pregnant. I agreed to call you my own and I will always call you my own. Gloria gave you up the night she planned to kill you!"

Helen suddenly jumped up from her chair and left the room. Jorja then heard her slam the door to the bathroom. While she was stunned at her mother's outburst, Jorja thought it was certainly understandable. She thought about the fact that her own mother had planned to actually kill her. What type of mother would do that? Why? What would drive her to that? As the questions continued to run through her head, Jorja heard the bathroom door open before her mother returned to the dining room.

Helen cautiously walked towards the table as she said, "Jorja, I'm sorry. I didn't mean to get so upset. I'm upset with Gloria, not with you. I love you with all my heart and I only wish to protect you for the rest of my life. This was something that I truly hoped you would never know about. I hope you know your father and I have loved you as our own and even though you now know we are not your real parents, I hope you understand that to us you will always be our child. You were never Gloria's child. She may be trying to make it up to you now, even after she's dead, but she could never have been a good mother to you due to her condition. I think she knew that. Why she had to tell you this God-awful truth about what she did, I don't understand but maybe she felt it necessary to cleanse her soul. Whatever the reason, I'm here for you and I'll try to answer any questions you have. Just know that I love you, honey, and I don't want to see you hurt."

Helen bent over to give Jorja a hug and then she sat back down in her chair.

Jorja thought about what her mother said. She knew her mother loved her; she had no doubts about that. She had to admit to herself she was probably fortunate to have been brought up by her mother rather than Aunt Gloria or, God forbid, sent away to an orphanage.

"Mom, I understand. I just really wish you had told me because getting all this information now, after all this time, is just such a huge shock to me." Jorja held up her hand as her mother attempted to respond. "I get it. You were looking out for my best interests. It's just difficult to take all this in after all these years of being lied to about my past. That's all."

A look of sadness crossed over Helen's face. "I'm sorry you view it that way, Jorja. We just thought it was better to keep the truth from you so that you could live a normal life. I can't imagine what type of childhood you might have had if you'd known your real mother did not want you and had, in fact, planned to kill you. I actually did some research in order to consider our options and I finally decided it was better to bring you up as a happy, healthy child who believed she had two loving parents rather than an insecure child who doubted her self-worth because her own mother did not value her life. Honestly, I still stand by that decision. You have turned out to be a wonderful person and I believe that might not have happened if you had known the truth as a child. I'm sorry, Jorja. I truly hope you can forgive me but I cannot say that what we did was wrong."

Jorja's mind raced with thoughts and she now wasn't certain how she felt. She only knew for a fact that she truly loved her parents and they had given her nothing but the best when it came to their love and attention.

"It's all right, Mom. I forgive you. I am upset but I can understand what you and Dad did because you thought it was right."

Helen breathed a sign up relief. "Oh, thank you, honey. I am so glad."

Jorja decided to take advantage of the fact that her mother would now want to make it up to her for lying to her all these years.

"Mom, what happened to the other baby? Was it a boy named Jacob?"

Helen nodded and then looked away. "Yes, there was a boy and he was named Jacob. According to my parents, Gloria was suffocating him when they found her out in the garden. You were still lying on the ground in sheets. Daddy called the local doctor who came to the house. The doctor checked you over and declared you to be healthy but he said Jacob might have been without air for too long. Mother and Daddy let Dr. Hanson take Jacob so that the baby could be adequately cared for in a hospital. I never saw Jacob because by the time my parents called me to tell me what happened, I wasn't able to travel back home until the following day. It was then that my parents asked if I would take you in as my own. They told me that if Jacob survived but had health issues or brain damage, they were not going to ask me to take him but were going to give him up for adoption. I was truly sad about that but as a young woman, I'm not sure I could have handled two new babies much less one with health issues relating to brain damage."

Jorja felt great sorrow upon hearing that her grandparents planned to just give away her twin brother if the doctor said he wasn't healthy.

"So what happened? Did they give him up? You told me he died. What's really the truth?"

"Jorja, he did die. Dr. Hanson called my parents the next morning to tell them that the baby did not live through the night. He said the baby had been without oxygen for too long."

"So, where is he? Was he buried? Can I go see his grave site?"

Helen frowned. "I don't know where he is, Jorja. There was no service for him that I'm aware of. Your grandparents were so overwhelmed with the fact that Gloria had killed one of the babies, they were more focused on getting her the help she needed and were relieved when Dr. Hanson took care of the burial arrangements."

Jorja shook her head in disbelief. "They didn't care what happened to Jacob's body? What about Aunt Gloria? Were the police called? Was she charged with the crime?"

Helen's discomfort in the subject grew and she stood up to look at her reflection in the window. She answered without looking at Jorja. "It's not that they didn't care, Jorja. It's just that they wanted to protect Gloria. Calling the police would not have brought back the baby. They made a decision they thought was right at the time. Dr. Hanson told my parents he would take care of the arrangements necessary for Jacob's burial. With all the arrangements my parents had to make to get Gloria committed to the institution, I believe that alone was all they could deal with."

"Well, I think it's terribly sad that there is a baby buried somewhere, my twin brother, and we have no idea where. Do you think we could speak to Dr. Hanson about it?"

Helen finally turned to look at Jorja. "Oh, Jorja, he might have been able to tell us but he passed away about a month after Gloria did. He moved to another state after you were born but I saw an obituary for him in the local paper here, probably because he lived here for the first fifty years of his life and still had family here. It's my understanding he just died in his sleep. I'm sorry, but we probably won't be able to find out where Jacob is buried."

Jorja felt something brush her leg and she looked down to see Piper staring up at her. Piper then laid her muzzle on Jorja's knee. Jorja had no doubt Piper sensed the sadness she was feeling. Jorja reached out her hand and affectionately rubbed Piper's head as she looked back up at her mother.

"Well, I'm going to try to find the records, if I can. There has to be *some* record somewhere, either with the doctor or with the county. It doesn't hurt to try."

Helen shrugged. "No, it doesn't. I have to say I just wish you'd leave it alone but I know you won't."

Jorja grinned at her mother. "Yes, Mom, you can ask but no, I won't leave it alone."

CHAPTER 26

Jorja woke the following morning completely exhausted, knowing full well that her current state was due to all the emotions she was battling after the discussion with her mother. She took a long hot shower before getting ready and heading downstairs. Her mother had already made breakfast, which Jorja had no appetite for but did not want to admit to after her mother put in the effort. Even though coffee was all she really wanted, she obediently sat down at the table after her mother's insistence.

"Will you be going to the store before you head to your morning appointment?" Her mother asked as she refilled Jorja's cup with fresh coffee.

"Yes, I want to discuss a few things with Taylor about our calendar of events and maybe come up with some other ideas on how to bring more people into the store during the holidays."

"Well, if there's anything you need me to do before I leave to go home today, make sure you leave me some notes on the desk, okay?"

"Why, aren't you coming in this morning?"

Her mother shook her head. "No, I'm going to meet up with Sandra at the hair salon. She's going to touch up my roots and give my hair a trim. I'll be at the store later this morning so I should be there when you get back from your appointment."

"Well, I'm sure Sandra will be glad to see you, especially if she's getting paid to visit with you."

Her mother laughed and stood up to take her dishes to the sink. "Yes, she and I have some things to catch up on, I'm sure. She knows something about everyone so she'll catch me up on the gossip."

Jorja frowned. She didn't like gossip and she knew how much of it was flung around the salon by all of the ladies. Although Jorja knew her mother would not repeat any rumors, she did not like the gossipy atmosphere at the salon when the ladies did not consider if the rumors they were spreading were true.

Not wanting to leave on a disagreeable note, she decided to leave the issue alone. "Well, have a good time. I better get going. I'll see you at the store later."

Jorja grabbed one more cup of coffee, her jacket and her purse but before heading out the door, she grabbed a treat for Piper. Piper quickly took the dog bone from Jorja's hand and moved to the next room to eat in privacy.

Funny dog, Jorja thought to herself. Piper's habit had always been to eat her treats away from anyone else, person or animal.

"Bye Mom!" Jorja said as she headed out the door and to her jeep.

On the way to the bookstore, Jorja thought again about what her mother told her the night before. She decided she had to figure out how she was going to find records relating to her brother's death and where he might be buried. She couldn't explain why she had to know but she also couldn't understand why anyone wouldn't *want* to know.

Jorja parked her jeep outside the bookstore and ran inside to find Taylor. She hadn't had a chance to talk to Taylor to fill her in on the whole conversation with her mom so she wanted to do that before she had to leave for the Sherriff's Office.

"Hey, Taylor, you got home late. Where the heck did Dylan take you? Canada?"

Jorja placed her jacket and purse behind the counter.

Taylor couldn't stop grinning. "Oh, we just had a nice time and got to talking and lost track of time. It was one of the best dates I've ever been on Jorja!"

Jorja could see the look in Taylor's eyes and knew Taylor was in love. It was not a common sight, as most men did not meet Taylor's high standards.

"That's great, Taylor. I was getting worried about you though. Mom and I sat up late talking and when you still weren't home when we went to bed I couldn't get to sleep. If I'm tired later this afternoon I'll be blaming you for my lack of sleep."

Jorja gave Taylor a smile to let her know she was kidding, although she truly had been worried while she waited for Taylor to get home.

Taylor's look was apologetic. "I know, I'm sorry. We just didn't realize how late it was by the time I decided I should get home. So how did it go with your mom? Did she tell you everything?"

Jorja sat on one of the nearby chairs. "Oh yeah, she filled me in on exactly what happened and she verified what Aunt Gloria actually tried to do. Or, actually, what she did do to my brother. I just got lucky. I can't even imagine what brought Gloria to do such a terrible thing. It's awful and just so sad. I can't help wondering who my twin brother might have grown up to be. Mom doesn't know where he is buried and she told me the doctor who took care of his burial died shortly after Aunt Gloria did. Mom wants me to leave it alone but I want to know where he was buried so I'm going to see what I can find out."

Jorja finally took a breath as a customer walked into the store. She waited for Taylor as the customer ordered a latte. Once finished, Taylor walked over to sit beside Jorja.

"Wow, Jorja. I'm really sorry for everything you're going through now that you're finding this all out. I don't blame you for wanting to find out where your brother was buried. Is there anything I can do to help out?"

Jorja shrugged. "I'm not sure. I'll check into a few things and then see what I have to do to find the records. If there's anything I need help with, I'll let you know."

Taylor patted Jorja's hand. "Good, you know I'm here for you. By the way, Kat stopped by on her way to school. She said to give you this envelope."

Jorja took the envelope from Taylor and peeked inside. "Oh, good, it's the photos I asked her for." Jorja stood up. "Well, I better get on my way. I don't know how long it will take me to go through the evidence in this case but I'll try to be back as soon as I can."

"Okay, Jorja. Good luck...or whatever should be said at a time like this."

Jorja grabbed her jacket and purse and said goodbye as she walked out the front door of the store.

The drive to the Sherriff's Office gave Jorja some much needed quiet time as she mulled over various thoughts. The fact that her mother was actually her aunt, her aunt was actually her mother, and she had a twin brother who was murdered by their mother. Then there was the fact that Kat had a mother who disappeared and who everyone thought had run away when in fact she may have been murdered. Two mothers; one a murderer, the other murdered. One hiding in plain sight while the other was hidden three feet deep. Jorja could understand why some people never wished to know the truth, as the truth could sometimes hurt so much worse than any lie used to cover the truth.

After pulling into the parking lot at the Sheriff's Office, Jorja parked her jeep and walked into the reception area. The same receptionist was at the front desk and he asked her to wait. It was only a few minutes before Cheryl Dunham came through the door and asked Jorja to follow her. They took an elevator down to the evidence room and then walked down a short hallway before entering a large room where a box had been placed on the table.

Cheryl grabbed a pair of gloves and placed them on both her hands. She asked Jorja to do the same.

Cheryl then used a knife to cut the seal from around the box. Jorja could see a case number, dates and other information written on the outside of the box. After Cheryl cut the lid off the top, she removed the lid and placed it on the table. She then began to remove envelopes from the box, one at a time.

"Okay, Jorja. We have some items here, all of which have been placed in evidence bags and envelopes. Based on the notes here on the box, this is the first time this box has been inspected since it was sealed about ten years ago. I have the evidence sheet so we'll just go through the list one item at a time. We won't open the envelopes or the bags unless it's really necessary."

Jorja listened to Cheryl's speech and watched as she removed the remaining items from the box. She could tell some of the items were clothing. Others, she couldn't guess.

Cheryl continued, "The first couple of bags contain some clothing. Here we have what was a dress, these were her stockings, this was a belt which was still cinched around the waist of her dress and here we have one shoe. From reading through the reports again, it appears the second shoe was never located. We also have a bag containing her jacket. I'm not sure what condition these clothes are in but the report indicates the dress had a flower print, the belt was red leather and she was wearing a black jacket made with synthetic fibers. The envelopes here contain the gloves. The gloves were placed in separate bags because one was found still buried with her while the other was taken by the hiker and used so that the dogs could locate the grave."

Jorja continued to listen as Cheryl explained the items of evidence that had been placed in the box. She had a sense of foreboding that these items truly did belong to Kat's mother.

"So, which items hold the most interest for you?"

Jorja was pulled away from her intense thoughts of dread.

"Well, the jacket and gloves were the items I really wished to see. However, I was able to obtain some old photos of my client's mother and she is wearing a floral dress in some of them. Now

I think I better get a look at the dress to see if it matches anything she might be wearing in these photographs."

Jorja grabbed the envelope of photos from her purse.

Cheryl looked with interest at the envelope. "I'm glad you brought those. If this victim is your missing person, it would be nice to finally close this case. Let's see what you've got."

Cheryl quickly looked through the photos and found a few with Vera wearing various dresses, a black jacket and a few where Vera wore the jacket with red gloves. She chose those photos and placed them in a row in the middle of the table.

"Well, let's start with the jacket." Cheryl carefully cut the tape from the top of the evidence bag, placed a clean piece of brown paper torn from a nearby roll onto the table and then pulled out the jacket and placed it on the paper. The jacket was very dirty and from what Jorja could tell, it was in bad shape. Jorja had to remember that the jacket had been buried for a couple of years with the body before the grave had been found. Cheryl chose a couple of photos showing Vera in a black jacket. As Jorja looked at the photos and compared them to the jacket on the table, it was difficult for her to tell if it was *the* jacket. Jorja was dismayed to realize no characteristics of the jacket stuck out enough in the photos to easily compare it to the one held in evidence.

"Let's look at the dress." Cheryl said as she returned the jacket to its bag and then carefully opened the second evidence bag the same way she had done with the jacket.

Jorja was saddened at the condition of the dress. However, she was able to see the dress did have a print. She was also able to see white daises and could tell that the color of the dress appeared to have been a light blue color. Both Jorja and Cheryl carefully reviewed each photo showing Vera in a dress. Finally, as they examined the photo next to the last one, Jorja's breathe quickened. The photo was of Vera sitting on a porch swing wearing a blue summer dress with white daises.

Jorja and Cheryl both looked at each other and Cheryl quietly picked up the photo to look at it more closely. She then set the photograph to the side away from the others as she said, "Now, the gloves."

Cheryl removed the gloves from the evidence bags and placed them each on a clean sheet of paper. Both gloves appeared to be the same color and stitching. As they again examined each photo, it was apparent to Jorja that whenever Vera wore a jacket, she also wore her red gloves. While Jorja knew it wasn't concrete, she thought that the floral dress, along with the red gloves, were enough to make her believe she'd located Vera.

Cheryl finished her review of the photographs and then chose a couple with Vera wearing her black jacket and red gloves. She set the photographs alongside the photo with Vera in the dress.

"Okay. Well, I'm going to say I think we might be getting somewhere. I won't say it's a fact, but it is possible we might have your missing person here."

Jorja nodded. "What other items were found with her? I spoke to her sister-in-law who told me the only other item she knew was important to Vera was her Bible and that she always wore a locket her husband gave to her."

Cheryl looked at the evidence list. "Well, let's see..." As she ran her finger down the list, it stopped about half way down.

Cheryl looked at Jorja and said, "It does appear she was found with a book. They don't list what the book is though so I guess we'll have to open the bag to see."

Cheryl looked through the items before finally finding the right bag. She then carefully opened the bag, reached inside and removed the book. Cheryl turned it over to reveal that it was a Bible.

Jorja did not know what to say. She slowly sat down in a nearby chair.

Cheryl looked at the Bible and opened it in an attempt to view the first few pages. It was in no condition to read, as the pages had rotted together into one big clump while it had been buried with the body.

Cheryl placed the Bible back in the evidence bag. "It's too bad the body wasn't discovered sooner. I'm betting the victim's name was written inside the Bible and she would not have remained a 'Jane Doe' all these years."

When Jorja did not respond, Cheryl sat down beside her. "Look, I know this is a shock. You probably hoped this would turn out to be nothing. I'm just glad you were persistent with your requests to view this evidence. Now we can actually let the family lay this woman to rest. Think of it that way, okay?"

Jorja laid her head in her hands and said, "I know you're right but I hate to have to tell my client that her mother has been dead all this time."

"Well, we can tell her. After all, we're the police and it's our job. But we really can't say for a fact yet that this is her mother. We need to verify it so we'll also ask your client to submit to DNA testing so we can verify whether or not this is her mother."

Jorja nodded her head. "Yes, she'll want it verified so that she can make arrangements to have her mother buried next to her father."

Cheryl began to reseal the bags and return them to the evidence box.

Jorja then remembered something. "Wait, was any jewelry found on the victim? Vera had a locket she liked to wear and I don't believe that the necklace was ever found after she disappeared."

Cheryl again reviewed the evidence sheet. "It does appear she had some items of jewelry on her when they found her. Let's see...the list isn't specific enough so we'll have to open the bag. Let me reseal the rest of these bags first."

Cheryl resealed the bags and set them to the side. She then searched through the rest of the evidence and found a small envelope containing jewelry. After opening the bag, she carefully poured the items onto a sheet of paper.

"Hmm...looks like we have a pair of pearl earrings, a gold band and a necklace but no locket. Actually, it looks like the necklace was broken so if there was a locket, it may have fallen off."

Jorja looked carefully at the items and took note that they could have belonged to anyone. If there was a locket, it had not been buried with Vera.

"Well, thanks for looking. Even without the locket, I think there's enough here to make me believe this was Vera. I will tell my client, you don't have to. After I explain everything to her, I'll help her make arrangements to meet with whoever will be conducting the DNA testing."

Cheryl did not argue. "That's fine. Let me know when you've discussed this with her and then call me so we can make arrangements for the testing. I'll let my supervisor know the status of this case so that a supplemental report can be prepared. This case will be assigned to a detective so that we can move forward with a murder investigation once we are able to verify the victim's identification through DNA testing."

Jorja was humbled by the concept that she took part in reopening an unsolved murder case. "Would it be possible to get updates with regard to the investigation? I know you probably can't reveal any details to me but for my client's sake, is it possible to be included enough in the investigation so that she and I are aware of what your office is able to come up with?"

Cheryl shook her head and said, "No, I'm sorry. Any information obtained during a pending investigation will not be divulged. However, I will let you know which detective is assigned to the case so that you can make contact with him or her during the course of the investigation. They will tell you what they can and maybe it'll be enough to give your client some satisfaction. Plus, it's likely the detective may wish to speak to your client during the investigation. Any information she is able to offer may be of great assistance in the investigation."

Jorja was disappointed but understood the reasoning. "Her knowledge about the case will be limited but I'm sure she'll be more than willing to assist in any way if it'll help the detective determine why her mother was killed."

Cheryl gave Jorja a half smile. "Sometimes, even the smallest detail can make a difference."

Cheryl resealed the remaining envelopes and placed them back in the evidence box. "Okay, you call me when she's ready to come in for the test. For now, we're done. I just need you to sign this form for me."

Jorja signed the form with her signature and dated it. The act gave her a positive feeling...things were moving forward and although she was saddened by the knowledge of Vera's death, she was grateful something might be done to determine the cause.

"Thank you very much for all your help, Ms. Dunham, I really appreciate it."

"No, Jorja, I really appreciate what you have done. Cold cases are never-ending nightmares for victims' families and for the police who try to work the cases. It's always good to end that nightmare for everyone when we are finally able to close a case."

Jorja shook Cheryl's hand and told her she'd be in touch. She then left the Sherriff's Office with dread building in her chest as she thought about how she was going to explain to Kat what she had discovered.

CHAPTER 27

Jorja parked her jeep near the bookstore and remained in the vehicle while she thought about how she would approach Kat with the information about her mother. She really didn't know how to make the conversation any less difficult than she expected it to be. Reluctantly, she locked up her jeep and was able to walk into the bookstore unnoticed by both Taylor and Kat. Jorja quietly watched them as they chatted and laughed together while going through another box of books that had apparently just arrived. It suddenly struck her how important Kat had become to her. She felt the need to protect Kat and did not relish the thought of hurting her.

"Hey, Jorja, I didn't realize you were back." Taylor said, tearing Jorja away from her thoughts. "Look at the new shipment we just got. It's the most recent book in this vampire series and the movie from the first book will be playing in theaters Halloween weekend. We also received some items relating to the movie so we're putting together a table for all the books and the movie materials."

Taylor held up the book but Jorja could barely focus on the title. "That's great, Taylor. Where ever you can make room for the table will be fine."

Taylor slowly lowered the book as she looked at Jorja with concern. "Is everything okay?"

Jorja quickly nodded and glanced at Kat. "Uh, yeah, everything is fine. I just need to speak to Kat."

Kat had been busy removing the rest of the inventory from the box. She looked up as Jorja said her name. "Sure, Jorja, what's up?"

"Well, I need to speak to you but I think we should go up to the office."

Kat stood up as she keenly stared at Jorja. When Jorja didn't say anything else, Kat glanced at Taylor who quickly became interested in the remaining books still lying on the floor. Kat then met Jorja's eyes again and said, "Okay, sure. Do you want me to come up now?"

"Yes, if you can. Taylor, do you mind?"

Taylor adamantly shook her head. "No, I can finish here. You two go ahead."

Jorja began walking towards the stairs with Kat right behind her. Once they both climbed the stairs to the office, Jorja waited for Kat to sit down.

Kat looked nervously at Jorja as she said, "Has something happened? Have you found my mom?"

Jorja took her time hanging her jacket and her purse on the coat rack before turning to face Kat. She then moved around her desk and slowly sat in her chair. She took a deep breath, unsure of how to begin. "Kat, I, uh, I do believe I may have found your mom."

Kat jumped up and smiled as she said, "That's great! Where? Where did you find her? Is she close? Does she want to see me? Did you speak to her?"

Jorja held up her hand and motioned for Kat to sit down.

Kat did not sit down. Her smile of gratitude quickly turned into a frown of worry. Her eyes just as quickly filled with tears. "What's wrong, Jorja? She doesn't want to see me, does she?"

Jorja waited another heartbeat and finally said, "It's not that, Kat. It's just that she may have wanted to see you but she can't. I'm so, so sorry. I don't really know how to say this but I don't believe your mom left you and your dad by her own choice. Something happened to her. Someone hurt her and, I'm truly sorry to say this but..."

"What do you mean, 'someone hurt her?' What happened to her? Is she okay?"

Jorja shook her head. "No, Kat, she's not okay. She's dead. Someone killed her."

Kat's face became pale. "What? What do you mean she's dead? Someone murdered her? When? How? Where was she found?" Emotionally exhausted after her outburst, Kat could not fight the need to suddenly sit down. "Oh, Jorja...please tell me this isn't true." Kat barely finished the last sentence before she began to cry uncontrollably.

Jorja stood as she grabbed a tissue box and walked around the desk to crouch in front of Kat. She rubbed Kat's back with one hand and held the tissue box in front of Kat with the other. "Kat, I am so sorry to tell you this. I found a case involving a woman who was found murdered and I believe it was your mother."

Kat took a tissue which she used to wipe her eyes and blow her nose. Her eyes were glistening with tears but also with intensity as she asked, "You mean all this time she's been gone because someone *killed* her? Where did they find her?"

Jorja wasn't sure how much Kat could take at this point. "Are you sure you want to know, Kat? It might be difficult for you to hear."

Kat impatiently wiped away at the tears as they slid down her cheeks. "Yes, I want to know. Tell me."

Jorja stood up and leaned against the desk as she told Kat about her review of the police files, finding her mother's case and discovering the reference to the red glove before viewing the evidence at the Sheriff's Office. Kat silently listened as tears continued to spill down her cheeks faster than she could wipe them away.

"So are you sure it's my mom?"

"Well, I'm fairly certain it is probably your mom. But we need to run a DNA test to verify the results before the police can continue with their investigation. I'm just saying that based on what I've seen so far, I believe the test will verify this is your mom."

Jorja watched as Kat seemed to mull over the information she had just received. She waited until Kat looked up at her and seemed willing to talk more.

"Are you okay? I know this is hard to hear, Kat. I hate to have to tell you this and I know how much it must be hurting you right now."

Kat wiped her nose again. "I don't know how I feel, Jorja. All this time I thought my mom had left me and just didn't want to see me. Now you're telling me that all this time she was buried and then dug up and her things have been in an evidence box just waiting for someone to come forward to claim them. I just need some time to think. Is it okay if I leave? I just want to go home."

Kat stood up and Jorja moved away from the desk to give Kat room. "Of course you can leave if you want to. Are you sure you want to be alone? You can come to my house, if you want." She wanted to give Kat a hug but wasn't sure how Kat would respond.

Kat shook her head and said, "No, thanks, I'll just go home. I'll be fine, Jorja. I just need some time alone. I'll be in tomorrow after school."

Kat grabbed one more tissue before heading down the stairs with Jorja behind her. Jorja waited until Kat left the store before she moved towards Taylor, who was standing near the cash register patiently waiting.

"So, what the heck happened? What did you tell her? She tried not to look at me as she said goodbye but I can tell Kat has been crying. What did you find out?"

"Oh, Taylor, it's the worst news. I really believe that case file involving the body found by the hiker was Kat's mom. It's terrible. I hated telling her but she needs to know so we can set up DNA testing to verify whether it is her mom."

Taylor didn't respond but continued to stare at Jorja. Jorja thought the stare had lasted long enough when she finally said, "What? Why are you looking at me like that?"

Taylor grinned. "Why am I looking at you like this? Jorja, I'm just proud that you were able to do this for Kat. I know the news you gave her is terrible but at least now she knows what happened to her mom. Plus, even though it's an awful thing that her mom was murdered, at least Kat no longer believes her mom left her. This gives her *closure*, Jorja, and she needed that. I'm so proud of you for taking on her case. You were persistent and you found the answers for her."

Jorja felt embarrassed as Taylor expressed her admiration. Jorja did not feel all that great for giving Kat the worst news of her life. "Well, she can't have real closure until the police figure out who actually killed her mom."

Taylor rolled her eyes and said, "Jorja, whoever killed her mom is not the point here. It's the point that she now doesn't have to feel like she wasn't good enough or that she did something to make her mom leave her. Can you imagine what that girl has been dealing with all her life? How insecure that must have made her feel? Kat's own father wasn't able to help his child understand because he also thought she had left them. With this information, you will at least have helped Kat understand her mom would have never left her if someone hadn't physically taken her away."

Jorja thought for a moment. Taylor made a point. "I guess you're right. It's just hard, that's all."

Taylor put an arm around Jorja. "You're a softie, that's all. That girl has gotten to you, admit it."

Jorja could not deny the fact that she now thought of Kat like she would a younger sister. Taylor laughed lightly as she squeezed Jorja's shoulders just a bit tighter. "Yeah, Jorja, you're a softie and I have to admit, that's just one of the reasons you're my best friend."

CHAPTER 28

Jorja was pleased with the amount of work she had accomplished at the bookstore for the day so she decided to tackle another project. It had been a few days since her conversation with Kat and she had not yet been able to research articles relating to the dead girl Lydia had mentioned while they had discussed Vera's disappearance. Although Jorja could not assume there was any connection, the whole idea of two women from the same town dying within a short time frame of each other was a coincidence she could not ignore.

Grabbing her jacket and bag, she quickly made her way down the staircase to find Taylor on the phone. She patiently waited as Taylor finished her conversation.

"Yes, Ms. Bennett, we would love to have your class here for a book reading next month. Just let me know when you confirm the date with the school. I'll make sure we have plenty of cocoa on hand for the kids. Okay, then, I will wait to hear back from you."

Taylor hung up the phone with a smile on her face. She turned to Jorja and said, "Oh, this is going to be fun. Did you hear that? Ms. Bennett's second grade class will be coming here for a book reading. They are so cute at that age."

Jorja nodded in agreement as she said, "Let me know what date she chooses so we don't end up double booking." She then looked around the store. "Is Kat here yet?"

Nodding, Taylor said, "Yeah, she's in the back room going through some boxes for me. Why? Do you need her?"

"No, I just wanted to make sure you had help. I need to go to the library for a little while. Can you do without me for about an hour?"

"I think we can manage. What are you doing at the library?"

"I'm going to look at past news articles around the time Vera disappeared. I can't really explain why I'm looking up the information but I'm hoping to verify something Lydia told me. Don't tell Kat what I'm doing though because it's not about her mom."

Using her fingers to make an "x" over her heart, Taylor said, "I cross my heart and promise not to tell. Although how can I tell if you won't tell me what you're up to?"

Jorja gave Taylor a slight look of annoyance. "It's not that I don't want to tell you, Taylor. It's just that I'm not sure if there is anything to tell you. I'll fill you in more tonight, okay?"

Taylor shrugged and replied, "That's okay, Jorja. You'll tell me when you're ready, I understand. Don't worry about the store. We've got it covered."

Leaving the store, Jorja had a nagging feeling and she worried about whether she hurt Taylor's feelings. Taylor's feelings were not easily hurt but Jorja wondered if she wasn't confiding in Taylor enough with regard to her research.

Jorja walked to the library located three blocks from the bookstore. She was glad she had a scarf handy in her bag to wrap around her neck and lower jaw during the short walk because the cold wind made the air feel that much cooler.

Once Jorja reached the library and walked inside, she was thankful for the warmth when she closed the door and moved towards the microfilm machine. She opened the nearby drawers to find the film marked with dates surrounding Vera's disappearance and then sat down at the machine and got comfortable. Carefully she placed the film in the machine and waited until the film caught so she could easily work her way through the articles. She searched for the date Vera had disappeared and any articles relating to the police investigation.

Finally, she found an article dated two days after the disappearance:

```
Police   are   searching   for   any
information   relating   to   the
disappearance   of   Vera   Myers,
last   seen   Tuesday   afternoon.
```

Police say the vehicle she had
been driving is also missing.
According to her husband, Robert
Myers, she was running errands
and was last seen by an
acquaintance. The Myers' young
daughter had been left with a
babysitter and is safe at home
with her father. The police are
conducting an investigation into
the disappearance but have also
indicated to this reporter they
do not at this time suspect foul
play. Anyone with any information relating to the whereabouts of Vera Myers is asked to
call the local police department.

Jorja scanned articles published over the
next few days and found a small article titled,
"Body Found Near Tracks."

She read the short article which offered no
actual clues:

The body of an unidentified
female was found near the railroad tracks alongside Highway 99
early yesterday morning by
railroad personnel. The police
are currently investigating the
matter and have not yet
determined the cause of death.
The identity of the victim is
being withheld pending notifica-
tion to family members.

Scanning further, Jorja found another article
two days later about the young girl:

> The body of a young woman found near the railroad tracks along Hwy 99 on Friday morning has been identified as 19-year-old Samantha Tibbetts. Railroad personnel made the discovery while conducting routine checks along the tracks in the area. Although police have confirmed the victim's death is related to blunt force trauma, the actual cause of death still remains undetermined. Samantha's mother, Gina Jeffries, and her step-father, Mayor Benjamin Jeffries, both request that anyone with any information regarding this matter please contact the local police department.

Jorja found it difficult to imagine the grief the parents must have felt after being informed where and how their daughter had been found.

Searching for more articles, she found one relating to Vera the following day:

> The search for a missing wife and mother is no longer active, according to local authorities. While Robert Myers has reported his wife, Vera, as missing, the local police department issued a statement indicating that evidence obtained during the investigation has led to the conclusion that the dis-appearance of Mrs. Myers was not due to suspicious circumstances.

Jorja was dissatisfied with the information provided in the article. She reviewed the articles throughout the next few days and into the following week but found none relating to Vera and, more surprising, no articles relating to the young girl.

What had been the cause of death? She wondered why there was no follow-up article. Quickly jotting down the name of the reporter, she was hopeful she would be able to track him down to see what he remembered. Many papers or reporters were very good at their jobs while others did not do well following through with information.

She was determined to discover which label could be pinned on this reporter.

~ ~ ~

Jorja decided she needed some caffeine as she left the library and quickly made her way back to the bookstore. At her request for a pick-me-up, Taylor was more than happy to comply.

"You want to try a pumpkin spice latte? It's really good, if I do say so myself." Taylor said with a wink.

"That sounds great, Taylor." Jorja reviewed some paperwork Taylor had been working on as she waited for her drink.

"Here you go. Nice and hot. Are you going back upstairs?"

Jorja took a careful sip and enjoyed the first taste of the flavor before responding, "Yes, I need to make a few phone calls. Let me know if you need anything though, okay?"

Taylor waved a hand in dismissal. "I'm fine. You'll have to let me know later on what the heck you're up to."

Jorja promised to fill Taylor in later that evening as she headed up to her office. Once at her desk, she placed her first call to Betsy at the police station.

"Hi Betsy, my name is Jorja Matthews, do you remember me? You tracked down an old file for me to review."

"Oh yes, I remember you, dear. How are you?"

Jorja was thankful Betsy was so cordial, as she made up for the Chief's lack of it.

"Well, I'm fine, thank you. I was just wondering if you could do me another favor. I was wondering if I could review another case file. I still have a copy of the public records request form and I could fill it out and fax it to you. Would that be okay?"

"That would be fine. Why don't you go ahead and tell me what it's about and I'll look for the file. You can fax the form to me and pick up a copy of the file at your leisure or you can just bring the form in with you when you pick up the file."

Jorja then gave Betsy as much detail about Samantha Tibbett's case as she could and Betsy promised to find the file and have it ready for Jorja to pick up.

After hanging up the phone with Betsy, Jorja did some research in an attempt to locate the reporter who had written the articles about Samantha's death. She was thankful his name was not too common and that he had stuck with the same type of work. She finally found him listed as a reporter for a local paper near Seattle.

After dialing the number, she only had to wait one ring before a woman with a high-pitched voice answered the phone. "Sun Valley News, can I help you?"

"Uh, I was wondering if I could speak to Mr. Reinhold Grotsky. Is he available?"

"Let me check. Can you hold for a minute?"

"Yes, I…" Jorja was put on hold before she could finish her sentence. She waited for about a half minute before the line was finally picked up again.

"Hello? This is Reinhold. What can I do for you?"

Jorja immediately preferred Reinhold's voice much more than the receptionist's. It wasn't as grating on her ears.

"Hi, my name is Jorja Matthews and I was wondering if I could ask you a few questions about an article you wrote about twelve years ago when you worked for the Timely Independent. A young girl was found near the railroad tracks and her stepfather was the Mayor at the time."

"Oh, sure, I remember that one. Girl's name was…a boy's name. Let's see, wait! Don't tell me. I pride myself on my memory. Sam! That's it. Her name was Samantha but she went by Sam. Yeah, that was a sad case. Can I ask why you are calling about it?"

"Well, I was curious because Samantha was found just after another woman in town disappeared. I wondered if you remembered the details about Samantha's case because other than an article you wrote stating there was blunt force trauma, I didn't see any other article relating to what the cause of death was determined to be."

"Hmm, well, there weren't any other articles. You are right about that. Tell me again why you are asking?"

"It's just something I was looking into because of the other woman's disappearance."

"Why, are they related? I don't recall that ever being the case."

"Well, no. It's not that. It's just out of curiosity that I'm asking. Can you tell me why no additional articles were printed or what you remember about the cause of death?"

Jorja heard Reinhold sigh and then he was quiet for a moment. He finally said, "What I remember is that I wrote no additional articles because I was asked not to."

"By who? And why?"

"Well, by the Mayor, that's who. The police investigated the case, determined Sam was on the tracks when she was struck by the train and it was ruled a suicide. The Mayor did not want any negativity about Sam in the news if it was going to shout out to everyone that she had taken her own life. Because I had already printed the article of interest informing everyone of the body being found and then the second article identifying her, I decided to let it be at that."

Jorja marveled at the ways of small towns. "Do you remember who the investigating officer was at the time?"

Reinhold gave a small chuckle. "You are testing my memory, aren't you? Let's see...the investigating officer was...he was a young cop, or new anyway. I remember wondering at the time if he had enough experience. Uh, I remember he was tall, thin, reminded me of wire...copper, oh yes! Cooper! That was his name. Glad to see my name game still works after all this time." Reinhold laughed again.

"Jim Cooper?"

"Yes, I believe that was his first name."

Jorja decided to see what else Reinhold could recall. "Do you remember anything about this case that troubled you?"

"Troubled me? What do you mean?"

"Well, do you think she committed suicide? Is there anything about her death that you found suspicious?"

Reinhold took his time responding and Jorja was afraid she had somehow lost the call. "Sir? Are you still there?"

Reinhold answered gruffly, "Yes, I'm still here. I'm just not sure how to answer your question."

"Well, can you answer it? Was there something about the case that bothered you?"

"It's not that I can't answer it. It's whether or not I should. Look, I was a small town reporter, just doing my job. I don't know that anything I have to say can help you with whatever you are looking for now."

Jorja was confused. Why was he being defensive? Did he know something?

"I'm not trying to upset you. I was just wondering if you had any other information. Whatever you can share would be very helpful." Jorja hoped her diplomatic skills proved useful here.

"I really don't believe there's anything else I can tell you. The police investigated and it was ruled a suicide. Her parents believed it was a suicide based on what they were told. The coroner ruled it a suicide. I did not write about those facts because the Mayor asked me to leave it alone. If there was anything more to that girl's death, I'm sure the police would have found it."

Jorja was beginning to wonder. "Well, I'm sure you're right." It didn't appear she was going to get any further with the reporter so she decided to end the call. "I should let you go. I'm sorry to have bothered you but I do appreciate the time you've been able to give me."

"Oh, it's not a problem. I'm sorry I couldn't be of more help. You have a nice day." Reinhold then hung up the phone as Jorja continued to wonder whether he knew more than he was willing to say.

Jorja replaced the handset and was about to check her email when the phone rang. She answered after the first ring. "Jorja Matthews, Books 'N Brew, can I help you?"

"Jorja? Hi, it's me Betsy. Hey, I just went down to check on the file you asked about and I can't seem to find it."

This doesn't sound good, Jorja thought. "Has someone else checked it out?" Jorja asked.

"Well, there is nothing to indicate it was removed for any reason and there is no reason I can think of that it would be missing. I asked the Chief and he said he doesn't have a clue where it might be. He was a bit irritated though, when I asked him, and I'll give you a heads up he wasn't too happy with your request but I reminded him you made a public records request. I will look some more but I just wanted to let you know not to come by the office yet. I will call you when I'm able to find it."

Jorja hung up the phone with a heavy heart. The fact that the file was missing did not sit well with her. She felt fortunate she had been able to get a copy of the report relating to Vera's disappearance. She wondered at the reasons behind the Chief's irritation and the fact that Cooper had investigated both cases. For reasons she could not pinpoint, Jorja did not believe Betsy would be able to locate the missing file relating to Samantha's case. That fact made it so much more important for her to understand why it was missing in the first place.

CHAPTER 29

Jorja grabbed a bottle of water from the small fridge and sat down at the table in the break room. She just needed a break. *No*, she thought, *I need a vacation.* She was finding it difficult to focus on any one thing when she felt torn between so many different issues. Jorja's thoughts were constantly overwhelmed with bookstore business, worrying about Kat, the results of Kat's pending DNA test, eagerness for word from the Sheriff's Office on any news relating to Vera's murder and also with trying to adjust to the fact that her parents had been hiding the true identity of her real mother.

After filling out the appropriate form with the county to obtain her brother's death certificate, Jorja received a certified copy verifying Jacob had died the same day as their birth. The signature on the death certificate was that of Dr. Hansen and the cause of death was listed as respiratory distress. Jorja was saddened by the listed cause of death now that she knew the true meaning behind the distress her brother had suffered. She also requested a copy of Jacob's birth certificate, as well as her own. Those records only confirmed for her that she and Jacob had the same birth date, Gloria was their mother and their father's name was listed as "unknown." Jorja had not been able to obtain any answers with regard to where her brother had been buried. Without being able to speak to Dr. Hanson, she was worried she would never find the answer.

"Hey Jorja! You back here?" Taylor asked just before poking her head around the corner of the door frame. "Oh, good. Hey, I was just going through the mail and it looks like everyone we invited to our Halloween party has RSVP'd. We're going to have a great turnout!"

Jorja smiled and said, "That's great, Taylor. It'll be fun."

Taylor tilted her head and gave Jorja a curious look. "Well, you don't seem all that excited about it. What's wrong?"

Jorja took a drink of her water, stalling a moment before answering. "It's not that I'm not excited, Taylor. It's just that I have a lot on my mind, that's all."

Taylor nodded in understanding. "Hey, I know you have a lot to think about but you can look forward to having a good time, can't you? This will be good for business and besides, you need to take a break and do something fun."

Jorja knew Taylor was just trying to help. "I know, I know. I'll be fine. I know the party will be fun. I'm just glad you've taken on a lot of the work. I don't think I could focus on what needs to be done right now with everything else I've been doing."

Taylor laughed and said, "Well, you're right about that. You've got enough on your plate. Besides, I *love* putting on parties and this one is going to be the best one in town. So, other than finalizing the menu of goodies with Dylan and picking up other last minute food items, we're all set. We just need to set up a decorating party the morning of the party. Kat will be here, your mom said she and your dad will come down to help, Ruth will be here and Dylan will help out for awhile until he has to go back to the bakery to finish up with last minute preparations."

Jorja knew Taylor had put a lot of work into preparing for the party and she realized she should be more grateful and show her appreciation.

"Well, I plan to help out too. What time have you told everyone?"

Taylor gave Jorja an appreciative smile. "I told everyone to be here around ten o'clock. We should have everything done in a couple of hours so that we can all go home to change into our costumes before coming back here around four o'clock. The invitations say the party will begin at five-thirty but I'm betting people show up early so I want to be ready for them."

Taylor's excitement was beginning to win Jorja over. "Okay, sounds good. Do you have all the decorations we're going to need?"

"Almost. I'm going shopping tomorrow to pick up just a few more items and I think we'll be set."

They both heard the bell chime as someone entered the bookstore. Taylor turned to walk down the hall as she said, "Stay put. I'll go see who it is."

Jorja took a few more drinks from her water bottle as she thought about the upcoming party. She had no doubt the party was going to be a hit since Taylor was in charge. The idea of just having fun and using the time with friends and family to wind down and enjoy the holiday was probably just what she needed.

"Hey, Jorja? There's someone here to see you." Taylor said as she abruptly entered the break room.

Jorja raised her eye brows in question. "Who is it?"

Taylor's look showed confusion but also concern. "Uh, I'm not sure. He won't give me his name but he said it's important that he speak with you. He's acting a bit odd but not in a scary way. Do you want to come out?"

Jorja was curious. She tried to peek down the hall to catch a glimpse of the unknown guest. "Where is he?"

"You can't see him where he's sitting. He's on one of the couches waiting for you."

Jorja tentatively walked down the hallway and into the main floor of the bookstore. She then saw the man sitting on the couch but was only able to see the back of his head. She moved towards the sitting area and around the couch in order to face her visitor.

"Hello? I'm Jorja. You wished to speak to me?"

The man had been looking down at his hands and appeared to have been in deep thought. He jerked his head up as he heard her voice and he quickly stood up.

"Yes! Hello. You're Jorja?"

Jorja was struck by something when his eyes met hers but she would never have been able to put her feelings into words. There was something about him that caused her to feel something...a connection of some sort, like she had met him or known someone like him before.

He held out his hand to shake hers. "My name is Ryan."

Jorja took his hand and shook it. She felt her heart begin to race and she did not understand why.

"Hello...what can I do for you?"

Ryan looked around the bookstore. A few customers were sitting at the tables drinking coffee while others were sitting nearby reading books. "Is there a place where we could speak in private? There's something really important I need to speak with you about."

Jorja carefully looked at Ryan. She felt she had nothing to fear from him but she did fear what he might have to tell her. It was an unreasonable fear but one she could not shake. "Well, I guess we could go up to my office. Follow me."

She quickly informed Taylor that she was taking Ryan up to the office. Taylor could not conceal her interest or her concern as she said, "I'll be down here if you need me, Jorja."

As Jorja asked Ryan to follow her up the staircase, her mind raced with thoughts as to why he wished to speak to her. Once in the office, she asked Ryan to take a seat as she sat down in her chair.

"Okay, Ryan, what can I do for you? Do I know you? Have we met before?"

Ryan shook his head and hesitantly began to speak. "No...we haven't really met before but I think you know me."

Jorja raised an eyebrow. *What the heck? What was he talking about?* "What do you mean you think I know you? How do I know you?"

"Well, maybe you don't but I'd be surprised if you don't understand what I mean after what I have to tell you."

Jorja took a deep breath as she attempted to ward off her frustration with his inability to make his point. "Can you just tell me why you are here?"

Ryan stared at Jorja a moment and then took a deep breath himself. "We know each other because...you're my sister."

Jorja fixed a stare on Ryan that easily showed her disbelief and then her anger. She stood up, planting both her hands on her desk as she shouted, "My brother is dead! Who are you and why are you here? Talk fast, because I'm inclined to kick you out of my store!"

Ryan held up his hands in defense and moved to the edge of his seat as he intently looked at her and said, "No, Jorja, I *am* your brother. You were only told I was dead but it was to hide the fact that I was taken away from you and your family."

Jorja heard Taylor running up the stairs before Taylor entered the loft at a brisk walk and with a concerned expression. "Jorja? Is everything okay?"

Taylor narrowed her eyes as she glanced at Ryan with suspicion before turning to look at Jorja again.

Jorja tried to calm herself as she replied, "It's okay, Taylor. I'm fine."

Taylor stared at Jorja for a moment, not quite sure what to believe. Finally, Taylor gave Ryan one more quick glare as she turned to leave. "If you say so. But I'll be right downstairs if you need me."

As she listened to Taylor walk back down the staircase, Jorja felt like her chest had been slammed with a fist. She slowly sank back down into her chair and had some difficulty breathing as Ryan's words sunk in. Her voice cracked as she asked, "*What* are you *talking* about? What do you mean you were *taken* away from us?"

"I know this is a shock. Just hear me out. It took me a couple of months to get the confidence I needed to even find you so I could tell you what I have learned."

Jorja tried to speak but her mouth and throat felt dry. She picked up her water bottle to take a drink and realized her hands were shaking. She set the water bottle back down on the desk without taking a drink.

"And what did you learn? You're telling me my brother did not die and that you are him? How can that be? Who told you this?"

Ryan tried to hide a look of shame but he failed. "I found out from my father. He died recently and days before he passed away he told me something he had kept secret all my life."

Jorja crossed her arms to control her shaking hands as she leaned back in her chair. She wasn't sure she wanted to believe anything he was about to tell her but she said, "Go on, tell me what he told you."

Ryan's relief at Jorja's willingness to listen caused him to also lean back in his chair. "My father told me that when I was born, I should have died. In fact, he thought I was going to die. He said my true mother tried to cause me harm, for whatever reason he could not say but she would have succeeded if our grandparents had not found her in time. He said our grandparents told him they did not want the police involved and that they would willingly put her in a mental institution but they could not care for either of us.

He was apparently a long time friend and he agreed to help them by telling them he would take me to the hospital and if I died he would also make arrangements for the burial."

As Ryan continued to speak, Jorja's heart raced and she felt light-headed.

Ryan looked at her with concern. "Are you okay? Can I continue?"

She could barely nod in response as she finally said in a whisper, "Yes, please continue."

"Well, from what my father tells me, he did not take me to the hospital but instead he took me to his house where he cared for me himself and waited to see whether or not I was going to survive. His wife was out of town visiting with family so he was alone and able to care for me that evening and into the next day. Now, what he told me was this: he said he and my mother had been trying to have children for years but that as it turned out, she was not able to get pregnant. They had been married for twenty years but had no children of their own and attempts to adopt had failed. When my father realized I was going to survive, he made what many would say was an appalling decision. He decided to tell my real grandparents that I had died. He told me he made this decision because he knew my grandparents were going to give me up for adoption anyway and he thought this would take the burden off of them from having to place two babies in the system. I know, it's a little screwed up but he truly believed he was doing what he thought was best at the time. I believe my father wanted to make up for his wrongdoing when he decided to tell me the truth about my real family before he died. He gave me the address where I was born. I stopped by to speak to whoever lived there and one of your neighbors told me I could find you here."

Ryan paused and gazed at Jorja. She held Ryan's stare briefly but then looked away. She could not fight the tears and she quickly tried to wipe them away with her sleeve.

Jorja looked at Ryan again and wiped at another tear as it attempted to escape. "So, your father? His name was…?"

"My father's name was Clifford Hanson…Dr. Clifford Hanson."

"And your mother? Did she know what he did? What he was capable of doing? He lied about you dying, he took you from your true family and he kept that lie going all your life. Did she also take part in the lie?"

Ryan hung his head slightly at the question. He then took a deep breath and raised his head to look at Jorja again. "No, my mother never knew. She passed away about ten years ago and my father told me he never told her the truth. What he told her was that a young woman had gone into labor and had died in childbirth and he made arrangements to adopt the child because she had no other family. She believed him. Even if she had her doubts, I think she wanted a child so badly she didn't question him."

Jorja thought about what Ryan had told her. She thought her head might spin out of control as she began to believe it was possible she was staring at her twin brother. She could not deny the fact that their eyes were the same oval shape and shade of green, that their hair was the same warm auburn color and that they were even of similar build, although he had more muscle and was a few inches taller. But there were many people who probably looked like her. It did not mean they were related to her. Jorja decided to voice her doubts.

"So how do I know you're telling the truth? Or that your father was telling the truth? I mean, really, you can say you think you're my brother but how do we really know it's true? Are you willing to submit to a DNA test?"

Ryan did not seem surprised at her request. "Of course, I'll submit to a test. I do believe my father, honestly, but I can understand why you'd like to verify the truth with science. I'll pay for half. Do you want to set it up or would you like me to?"

"I'll go ahead and contact a company where we can schedule a date and time to meet and get the test done. Can you leave me your contact information so I can call you once I have a date set? Do you live around here?"

Ryan stood to remove his wallet from his back pocket and he took out a business card to hand to her. "I'm staying at a hotel nearby. The number on that card is my cell number and you can call it anytime."

She glanced at the business card he handed her. According to the card he was known as *Ryan C. Hanson, Book Editor.*

Ryan held out his hand to shake hers once again. "It was really nice meeting you, Jorja. I know what I've told you is very upsetting. Believe me, I was stunned when my father told me but I've had a few months to digest the whole idea. I'll understand if I don't hear back from you right away but I'd like to confirm the DNA test as soon as we can if that's possible. I look forward to getting to know you and I truly hope you will soon feel the same."

Jorja was hesitant to show any kind of commitment. "I'll be in touch, Ryan, as soon as I can set something up."

Ryan gave her a quick nod. "That's fine. I'll wait to hear from you." He then turned from her to walk down the staircase. Jorja remained in the loft, waiting for the bell to chime as Ryan opened the door to leave the store. Once Jorja was certain he had left, she headed down the stairs to find Taylor, who had been closely watching Ryan as he left the store. When the door shut completely, Taylor quickly set down the books she had been restocking and rushed to Jorja. A few customers were still in the store browsing, causing Taylor to whisper, "*So? Who was that? What did he want?*"

Jorja looked around the store. "Where's Kat? Is she here yet?"

Taylor shook her head. "No, it's only two o'clock, Jorja. Why?"

"I was hoping she was here so we could go speak in private, that's all."

Taylor leaned closer and asked, "Why, what's wrong? What did that guy want?"

Jorja turned so she could quietly whisper in Taylor's ear, "That *guy* says he is my brother."

Taylor pulled away with a startled look. "What? What do you mean he said he's your *brother*?!"

Both Taylor and Jorja quickly looked around to see if the customers heard Taylor's outburst. Other than one customer quickly glancing their way before looking back at the book she was holding, none appeared overly concerned.

"Hush, Taylor. I don't really want anyone to know about this yet."

Taylor grew frustrated. "Well, what do you *mean* he said he's your *brother*? How can that be when your brother is dead?"

They were interrupted when one of the customers walked towards them with a questioning look. "Miss? Can you help me?"

Taylor turned towards the customer and tried desperately not to show her displeasure at being interrupted. "Yes, what can I do for you?"

Taylor gave Jorja a piercing look which Jorja knew meant *we'll discuss this later*. Giving Taylor an obliging nod, Jorja walked to the break room to take a few moments to think. She wasn't sure if she should tell her parents now or if she should wait until the DNA test results were verified. If she had to be honest with herself, she knew there was no way to keep this secret from her parents. It was too big of a secret to keep, whether Ryan was telling the truth or not.

CHAPTER 30

Extremely nervous was all Jorja could feel as she waited for her parents to arrive at the house. It was the weekend before the Halloween party and she had asked her parents to stay overnight. The news about Ryan was something she knew she would have to tell them in person but it had been very difficult to express to her parents how important it was that she see them without divulging why. Jorja could not help a slight chuckle and then some guilt as she thought about her mother's attempts to get even the slightest detail from her. However, guilt at causing her mother distress was quickly suppressed by her feelings of betrayal after being lied to all these years.

Having some time before her parents arrived, Jorja called Ryan to tell him she had found a company where they could have their DNA tested. Although the company was in Seattle, they offered to take the samples at an office in Olympia so neither of them would have to travel far.

"We don't have to go to the clinic at the same time, Ryan, just call them and schedule a time that works for you and I'll do the same. Once they have both our samples, they'll send them to the lab for testing and they said they could have the results in about five days."

"Thanks, Jorja, for setting this up. I'll let you know when I'm scheduled to go in. Will you let me know once you receive the results?"

"They'll contact you when they contact me, since you're the other interested party. Once we both get the results, we can talk more, okay?"

Ryan was quiet for a moment before he replied. "Okay. That sounds good. We'll talk soon, then, huh?"

"Yes, we will. Well, I should get going. I'll talk to you later."

"Okay. Goodbye."

Jorja had a quick thought, dismissed it but then decided *what the heck?*

"Hey, Ryan?"

"Yes?"

"Are you doing anything next weekend?"

"Well, no. I don't know anyone here and I don't have any plans."

"Would you like to come to the Halloween party Taylor and I are holding at the bookstore next Saturday? We're asking everyone to dress up as their favorite book character. It'll be fun and a good way for you to get to know some people from around town." *Especially me,* she thought.

"Well, sure. That sounds like fun. Do you mind if I bring a guest?"

"A guest?" Jorja was instantly curious. *Who would he bring if he didn't know anyone in town?* "Of course, that's no problem. The party starts at five thirty. So I will see you there?"

"I will be there. Thanks for the invite, Jorja. I'll see you next Saturday."

As Jorja hung up the phone, she thought about her decision to invite Ryan to the party. She wasn't sure she should get to know him just yet but she was beginning to think of the possibilities that the test result would come back positive.

She glanced at the clock and realized her parents would be arriving any time. She put on a fresh pot of coffee, made sandwiches for lunch and was wiping down the countertops when she heard Piper give out a quick bark at the front door. Jorja then heard a knock just before her parents entered the house.

She heard her mother's voice first. "Jorja, we're here!"

Wiping her hands dry with a towel as she walked down the hall, she said, "Hi, Mom...Dad. How was the drive down?"

Helen shook off her coat with Rick's help as she said, "Oh, it was fine."

Rick had to add his two cents as he took off his own jacket and hung it in the coat closet. "There wasn't much traffic as we left Seattle but we ran into a traffic jam as we drove through Tacoma. There's something going on at the

Tacoma Dome and it sure was snaring up traffic. Other than that, it was smooth sailing."

Jorja gave both her parents a hug and then asked them to follow her into the kitchen. "Do you both want coffee? I made some sandwiches for lunch so we can sit down to eat."

"I'll just have tea. Don't worry, I'll make it myself." Helen grabbed a cup and looked through the pantry for the flavored teas she knew Jorja kept on hand for her.

"I'll just have a glass of water with my lunch and then I'll enjoy some coffee afterwards. Helen? Can you grab a glass for me?"

Jorja cut the sandwiches she had prepared in half and laid them on plates along with carrots and celery sticks. She placed the plates on the table and made herself a cup of coffee before sitting down. Her mother then sat down after placing her tea cup and a glass of water on the table.

"Thanks babe." Rick said as he gave his wife a loving look.

Helen smiled back at him before turning to Jorja. "I know you made us lunch but honestly, I haven't had much of an appetite since you said you needed to speak to us. The way things have gone lately, I'm worried that whatever you have to say will be upsetting."

Jorja noticed her father didn't have the same afflictions as her mother. He had already consumed almost half of his sandwich. She did understand what her mother was saying because she did not have much appetite herself.

"I know you must be worried, Mom. It's just not something I wanted to discuss over the phone because it's too important."

Her father gulped down a bite of sandwich and took a drink of water before asking, "Are you pregnant? Or are you sick?"

"No, Dad! I'm not pregnant! And I'm not sick."

"Well, good, if you're not pregnant and you're not ill, then there's nothing you can say that will cause me a bellyache."

If the subject weren't so serious, she might have laughed. She looked at her mother who was still frowning as she waited for Jorja to continue.

"I had a visitor earlier this week at the store and he had a very interesting story to tell me."

Both her parents remained silent as they waited for her to go on. She was beginning to feel herself sweat from anxiety as she realized she had no idea how they would take the news.

"He told me his name was Ryan and that his father's name was Clifford Hanson."

Her mother thought for a second before asking, "Dr. Hanson? The one who…"

"Yes, the one who helped grandma and grandpa after Aunt Gloria gave birth."

"Well, why is he making contact with you? What did he have to say?" Her mother's face remained impassive and Jorja was glad to realize her parents had not known about this secret and therefore were not keeping it from her.

"He told me...he said that, uh...well, he said he's my twin brother. He never died like Dr. Hanson led on. Dr. Hanson decided to keep him and raise him and he only just found out about me."

Jorja was glad the words were finally out. She waited as what she said slowly sank in and her parents attempted to process the information. Her father sat back and looked at her with concern. Her mother looked at her with disbelief.

Rick finally spoke, "How do you know he's telling the truth? What kind of bull is this kid trying to play?"

Helen took a deep breath and her voice trembled as she said, "That's right, how do you know he's telling the truth? I can't believe a doctor would take a baby and lie about it. Why would he do such a thing?"

Jorja wasn't sure if her answers would appease her parents. "Well, I don't know why he did it except from what Ryan told me. He said the doctor and his wife hadn't been able to have any children and the doctor was under the impression that our grandparents would give us up for adoption."

Both her parents were silent as they thought about the explanation. Helen finally asked, "Well, still, how do you know he's telling the truth? What if he's up to something? Dr. Hanson is dead so how will you know if what he said is true?"

Jorja nodded as she listened to her mother; she understood her mother's concerns. "I know it's possible he might not be Jacob, Mom. He and I have agreed to DNA testing. I've been in contact with a company up in Seattle who can conduct the test for us after taking samples from us at an office in Olympia. Once the samples are sent to the lab, it really doesn't take very long to find out the results. I'm trying to set up a time next week when he and I can submit to the testing and then we'll have an answer within a week or so after that."

Rick was the first to comment. "That seems pretty quick."

"Yes, it is. I really need to know if what he says is true. I hope you both can understand."

Helen's eyes began to tear as she said, "Oh, honey, of course we can understand. We just don't want anyone taking advantage of you, that's all. If this really is Jacob, of course we'd want to know that as well."

Rick leaned forward and grabbed Jorja's hand. "That's right, sweetheart, we just don't want you to get hurt. Even if this is your brother, you need to be careful. You don't really know how he was brought up or what kind of person he has turned out to be."

Helen vigorously nodded her head. "That's right. He was raised by someone who would steal a baby from someone else!"

Jorja frowned. "I don't think he's like that. I met him and I think he truly just wants to get to know me. I don't think he's a bad person or that he was brought up to be a bad person. Dr. Hanson did a bad thing but I think it was because he truly wanted a child of his own. I have to believe he raised that child with nothing other than love."

Both her parents were quiet as they quickly looked at each other. Jorja watched as they seemed to communicate silently before turning back to her. Her father said, "You're right, honey. We don't know him or what kind of person he is. We just want you to be careful. I'd also like to meet him for myself. Get a chance to see for myself what kind of person he is."

"Well, you're going to get your chance because I invited him to the Halloween party."

Helen's eyes widened as she said, "The party? Next weekend? Well, you don't even know if he's your brother. Do you think it's wise to form any type of relationship with him before you know for sure?"

"I've thought about it and I don't want to put off getting to know him. I believe what he's telling me and if it's the truth, the test results will prove it. I just don't see any reason why he would lie to me and I don't see any reason why Dr. Hanson would have told him this elaborate lie when it obviously does not paint a good picture of him. I thought the Halloween party would be a good idea because we can slowly get to know each other."

Her mother stood to place her uneaten sandwich on the kitchen counter. "Well, if that's what you want to do, there's nothing we can do about it."

Rick patted Jorja's hand and said, "We're here for you, honey. You let us know if you need anything."

"Thanks, I appreciate that you are both behind me on this. Just think if the test results come back positive, you'll have a nephew."

Helen's face went pale as she thought about the possibility. "Well, let's not move forward so fast. You find out what comes of the test and then we'll see."

Jorja knew this was going to be hard for her parents but she had already decided she wanted the tests to verify her brother was alive. She optimistically looked forward to what kind of relationship she would be able to form with him after all their time apart.

CHAPTER 31

"Aren't you excited, Jorja? This is going to be the best Halloween party this town has probably seen in years!" Taylor exclaimed as they were preparing for the arrival of their guests. Taylor was dressed as Scarlett O'Hara from *Gone with the Wind* and Jorja thought no one else could have pulled it off any better.

"Oh, I'm excited, Taylor." Jorja hefted a large box off the floor in the hallway to store it out of sight in the storage closet. She found it tricky to avoid catching the glasses hanging from the chain around her neck as part of her Rita Skeeter costume from the *Harry Potter* series. She had decided it would be amusing to dress up as the annoying reporter who enjoyed embellishing the facts in her news stories.

"Admit it, Jorja, you'll have fun. You need a break to just laugh and enjoy yourself. Oh! I bet that's Dylan...or, I mean, that must be Rhett Butler!" Jorja laughed as Taylor hefted her skirt and quickly ran down the hallway to see who had arrived first.

Jorja took her time following Taylor just in case it was Dylan. The two had been very affectionate lately and Jorja didn't want to intrude on their time together.

Dylan greeted her when she finally decided it was safe to join them. "Hello, Jorja. I've pulled my van up to the door so we can easily carry in the food I've made for the party. By the way, your outfit looks great."

"Thanks, Dylan, or should I say, Rhett. You don't look so bad yourself." She would have to tell Taylor later exactly how *good* Dylan looked in his outfit. The suit was an excellent fit and with the dark wig and fake mustache, Jorja was astonished by how much Dylan resembled Clark Gable when he portrayed Rhett Butler in the movie. "I can't wait to see the treats you've made. Taylor tells me you've been baking up a storm and that I'll be very impressed with what you've managed to pull together for the party."

Dylan blushed slightly as he grinned at Taylor in appreciation for passing on the compliment. "Well, I've done my best and Taylor helped quite a bit too. We came up with some great ideas and I think your guests are really going to enjoy them. Taylor? Do you want to help me bring in the food?"

Before Taylor could reply the bell chimed as the door opened and Kat walked in with Jorja's parents right behind her.

"Perfect timing. Can you all help us bring in the food from the van? Oh, Kat, I just love your outfit. You look adorable as Nancy Drew!" Taylor exclaimed. "Of course, Rick and Helen, you two also look great. Robin Hood and Maid Marian...how cute is that?"

Jorja had to agree Kat pulled off the Nancy Drew costume very well and while her parents did look great, she secretly thought she'd prefer never to see her father in tights again.

~ ~ ~

The Halloween party was in full swing and Jorja could not have been happier with the results. As Taylor had promised, just about everyone they had invited had agreed to attend so they had a full house. And it was a full house of characters, to be sure. Taking stock of the costumes, she could see quite an assortment from her vantage point as she sipped her hot apple cider. She spotted the Cat in the Hat, Frankenstein, Sherlock Holmes, the Mad Hatter from *Alice in Wonderland*, Gandalf and Aragorn from *Lord of the Rings* and Dracula. Brad was dressed as Hercules and Jorja wondered how long he worked out in the weight room before heading over to the party. She wouldn't admit it to him but she was impressed with how well he looked as Hercules. She had noticed Lydia was also impressed but unlike Jorja, Lydia made her appreciation known by brushing up against him whenever an opportunity arose. Jorja found it difficult to watch and couldn't help thinking Lydia's costume of Dorothy from the *Wizard of Oz* couldn't be further from her true character. *A more suitable character would have been the Wicked Witch of the West*, Jorja thought. She had to bite her tongue to keep her thoughts in check as she was trying her best to get along with Lydia under the circumstances. Jorja turned her attention to the children who had attended the party. She was able to spot Harry Potter, Tinker bell, Cinderella, Batman, Spiderman and even Winnie the Pooh. Taylor had put treat bags together for the children who attended and Jorja could see by their faces that the bags were a hit.

Kat caught Jorja's attention and walked over to stand next to her.

"Hi Kat, are you having a good time?"

Kat was holding a glass of punch in one hand and one of Dylan's cupcakes made to look like a witch in the other hand.

"I'm having a great time. This is a great party, Jorja. Um, I just wanted to let you know someone came in and was looking for you. He's over by the food tables dressed as some type of wizard. He also has a kid with him."

Jorja peeked around guests towards the tables but did not catch a glimpse of the wizard. "Do you know who he was?"

"No, he didn't say. He just asked if you were here and I told him you were around mingling with the guests."

Kat took a bite of her cupcake, severing the witch's head from her body. "Boy, these cupcakes sure are good. Dylan made so many different types; it's going to be difficult to try them all!"

Jorja smiled and said, "Well don't get sick trying. I'm going to see if I can find the wizard."

Jorja left Kat and moved towards the food tables, trying to spot the unknown guest. She finally spotted him standing next to Taylor and Dylan and Jorja could tell Taylor was attempting to make small talk. As she walked up to the group she realized Taylor and Dylan were speaking to Ryan.

"Hi, Ryan, I'm glad you could make it. Have you had a chance to see all the food there is to choose from?"

Ryan nodded as he replied, "That was the first place we checked out. Taylor was just telling me how Dylan made most of the desserts. It all looks great, Dylan. You did a wonderful job."

Dylan nodded slightly towards Ryan in acknowledgment and said, "Well, thanks Ryan. I aim to please and so far it sounds like I've done pretty well."

"Oh stop! You know you did great." Taylor said as she playfully hit his arm. She then leaned over and slightly hugged him as she continued, "This man is a genius with food. That's all I can say. I'm going to have to step up my exercise routine if I continue to date him. Well, Dylan, let's go see who else is here so Ryan and Jorja can talk."

"Nice to meet you, Ryan." Dylan said as he and Taylor moved away to welcome other guests.

Jorja looked more closely at Ryan and his costume and then she asked, "Are you Merlin from *The Sword in the Stone*?"

"Yup, good guess. Glad the costume actually looks like the character I intended."

"Daddy! Did you see the cupcakes and the cookies? How many can I have?"

Jorja was surprised to hear the small voice coming from behind Ryan while small hands pulled at Ryan's robe.

Ryan turned to look down at the small boy. "Yes, Nicholas, I saw all the treats. Now, you are interrupting and that's rude. Come here. I want to introduce you to someone."

Ryan slightly nudged the young boy so that he moved around Ryan to stand in front of Jorja.

"Jorja meet Nicholas. Nicholas, this is Jorja. Can you say hello?"

Nicholas shyly held up his hand and said, "Hello, my name is Arthur. Nice to meet you."

Jorja gave Ryan a questioning look as she held her hand out for Nicholas to shake it. "Arthur? I thought your name was Nicholas?"

Nicholas reached down to grab a toy sword hanging from his belt. He held the sword up for Jorja to see as he exclaimed, "My name is Arthur Pendragon and I'm in an awful pickle because I'm king!" Nicholas suddenly swung the sword and ran off, pretending to chase an unseen enemy.

Ryan chuckled and said, "Sorry about that. *The Sword in the Stone* is one of his favorite movies and tonight he is Arthur, which is why I'm dressed as Merlin."

Jorja watched Nicholas as he found his way to the children's corner where Taylor handed him a treat bag.

"He's cute. How old is he?"

"He's five and a handful." Ryan smiled as he watched Nicholas accept his treat bag from Taylor. From what she had seen in only a few short minutes, Jorja had no doubt how much Ryan loved his son.

"So you have a son? Where is your, uh, are you married?"

Ryan's smile faded a fraction as he replied, "I was. I'm a widower. My wife passed away two years ago."

"Oh, Ryan, I'm so sorry. Does Nicholas remember his mother?"

Ryan gave her a thoughtful look and said, "He remembers her just a little but mostly I think his memories are based on what I have told him the past two years. He might think he remembers her but I'm not really sure how much he recalls on his own. She was a wonderful mother and I have tried very hard to make him remember that."

Jorja wasn't sure what to say. She turned her attention back to Nicholas. "He is adorable and I'm sure he'll have a lot of fun here with the other children. Taylor has come up with some fun games for them to play and, oh, it looks like she's starting a game now. Why don't you go watch him while I check on the other guests?"

As Ryan left her to watch Nicholas take part in games, Jorja grabbed a few cookies from one of the tables and nibbled on them while she watched Taylor with the children. She hadn't realized how good Taylor was with kids and she began to think about how good a mother Taylor would make one day. If Taylor were to get married some day and have children, Jorja would be like an aunt to them. It struck her, suddenly, that she may already be an aunt. If Ryan was her brother, it would mean his cute handful of a son was her nephew. She warmed at the thought but decided it might be better not to think too far ahead.

"So who's the cutie? Is he new in town?" Jorja had been so deep in thought she hadn't noticed Lydia standing right next to her. She jumped a fraction and then moved slightly away from Lydia, who was standing just a tad too close.

Jorja was afraid she knew who Lydia was referring to but she asked anyway. "Who are you talking about?"

Lydia quickly pointed towards the children and Ryan, who was helping Taylor with the games. "That guy over there, dressed like a wizard."

"Oh. Yeah, he's kind of new in town but I'm not sure he's actually staying in town. He's just visiting."

Lydia turned to look at Jorja. "Who is he visiting?"

"He's visiting, uh, well, he's just visiting. His dad just passed away and his dad used to live here so he's catching up with old friends and family."

Lydia gave Jorja a hard stare before she said, "Uh-huh, okay. If you don't want to tell me, that's fine. I'll find out for myself."

Before Jorja could stop her, Lydia walked away and moved towards Ryan. Jorja anxiously watched as Lydia approached Ryan and she could feel her heart flutter as she wondered what Ryan would tell Lydia. Lydia stopped when she was standing right next to Ryan before starting a conversation. Jorja watched as Ryan hardly gave Lydia any attention while he focused on Nicholas and the other children. After a few short comments from Ryan, Jorja grinned as Lydia appeared to have had enough with being ignored before she curtly turned away from Ryan and walked away. Jorja was relieved Lydia did not return to question her further.

It occurred to Jorja that she hadn't yet introduced her parents to Ryan. She waited until the children were finished with the game and then asked Ryan and Nicholas to follow her to the sitting area where her parents had planted themselves on a couch to chat with Sandra and a few other guests.

"Mom, Dad, sorry to interrupt but I wanted to introduce you to someone. This is Ryan and right behind him is his son, Nicholas. Ryan, these are my parents, Helen and Rick."

Ryan held out his hand to shake both her parents' hands while Jorja caught her mother's questioning look at Nicholas. Rick said, "Hello, Ryan, it's very nice to meet you. I hope you and your son are enjoying yourselves."

"Oh, we are and I know Nicholas has very much enjoyed himself. Jorja and Taylor did a great job making this a kid-friendly party."

Sandra had been listening in on the introductions and she suddenly stood up. "Hello. My name is Sandra Bennett. I own the local beauty salon. I don't remember seeing you before. Do you live here or are you new to the area?"

Ryan glanced at Jorja quickly before responding to Sandra's question. "I'm new to the area but I haven't yet decided if I'm going to live here or not. I have a few matters I need to take care of first before I make that determination."

"Oh? Well, if you decide to live here, you'll love it. This is a nice quiet town we live in and your son will grow up in a nice environment."

"Well, thank you. I'll take that into consideration."

Jorja was thankful when Taylor motioned for Sandra to join her in a conversation across the room. Once Sandra left them, Jorja, Ryan and Nicholas sat down across from Jorja's parents.

Helen got right to the point. "So, you're Ryan, or more to the point, you believe you are Jacob."

Ryan looked surprised at Helen's question. He turned to Nicholas and said, "Son, why don't you go back and see what other games the children might be playing."

As Nicholas walked back to the children's area, Ryan turned to Helen and said, "Yes, I do believe I am Jorja's brother. I have no reason to believe my father was lying to me when he told me what he had done after my birth. If it's true, I would very much like to get to know Jorja. At this point, Nicholas is my only family and if Jorja is my sister I would like him to get to know her and also both of you, if you will let him. I have told Nicholas none of this because he very much would like more family and I don't want to get his hopes up."

Helen could not hide her embarrassment at Ryan's slight admonishment. "I'm sorry for questioning you in front of Nicholas. I appreciate your discretion with regard to sparing his feelings should the test results come back negative." Jorja listened to her mother's apology but knew it would not deter her mother away from her resistance to the whole idea. Helen continued, "I can understand not getting Nicholas' hopes up. As far as a relationship with us, I guess we'll have to work on that later depending on what happens."

Ryan did not question or argue with Helen and Jorja was glad for that. He just nodded and said, "Good enough. We'll wait and see what happens."

Before they could discuss the issue any further, Sandra returned and asked, "Jorja, you've met my brother, haven't you?"

Jorja looked up to see Sandra standing next to her brother, Jim, who was dressed in his police uniform. "Yes, I met him briefly when I stopped by your shop last time."

Sandra laughed and said, "Oh, that's right. Well, Jim, you know Rick and Helen but I bet you haven't met Ryan yet, have you? Ryan, this is my younger brother, Jim Cooper."

Ryan stood and held his hand out to shake Jim's as he said, "Nice to meet you."

Jim shook Ryan's hand and said, "You too. I'm sorry, I didn't catch your last name."

Ryan hesitated only slightly before responding. "My name is Hanson. Ryan Hanson." Jorja noticed Ryan's hesitation and she was certain Jim did as well.

"Hanson...hmm, we have a few Hanson's in the area. Any relation?"

Ryan quickly shook his head. "No, no relation as far as I know. I grew up in Wyoming."

Jim seemed to absorb and process Ryan's responses. Jorja was beginning to think Sandra purposely brought Jim over in order to grill Ryan. She was irritated by the thought that Sandra was just another small-town gossip, hoping her brother could get the scoop on their new visitor.

In an attempt to change the subject Jorja asked "So, Jim, is this your costume? What favorite book character do you represent?"

Jim turned to her and did his best to switch gears but Jorja could tell his mind was still focused on their new guest. "I'm sorry, Jorja. I would have come in costume but I had to work. Besides, if I had to pick, a policeman is my favorite hero so I'm sure there must be a book character out there I can represent." Jim then gave her a wink but he quickly turned his attention back to Ryan. "So, Ryan, how long do you plan on staying?"

"I'm not sure yet. Like I told your sister, I'm taking care of a few matters before I decide whether or not I'm going to settle down here." Ryan appeared willing to take on Jim's questions but he did not offer as much information as Jim might have hoped.

Jim eyed Ryan a moment before loudly slapping Ryan on the shoulder. "Well, I'm sure you'll love our little town if you do stay put."

The awkward introduction received a welcome interruption when Kat suddenly ran towards the group and exclaimed breathlessly, "Jorja! I just got a call from the detective and he's putting together some flyers about my mom. Can I have him fax them here so I can see what they look like?"

Jorja had to think about what Kat was asking. "Flyers? Are they going to distribute them before getting the test results back?"

Kat shook her head and said, "No, not yet. He said they want to put some flyers together with the photos we gave them and once the test results are verified, they will hand them out. He's just getting them ready because he's hoping they get the results back sooner than later. Can he fax them here to me?"

"Well, of course he can. The number is on the fax machine up in the office."

"Thanks!" Kat said as she turned and ran up the stairs towards the office.

Sandra was the first to ask, "Her mother? Test results? What is that all about? Has her mother reappeared after all these years?"

Jorja hadn't realized how well they had kept the secret about the discovery of Kat's mother. Jorja was certain the discovery had remained a secret because no one had yet told Sandra. Now, that was about to change.

She was hesitant to get into the subject but all eyes were on her as they waited for her response. "Well, in a way, yes, her mother has reappeared but we are still waiting for test results to verify that fact."

"What kind of test results?" Jim asked as his gaze followed Kat's path up to the office.

"Oh, you know, DNA tests. To make sure she is Kat's mother."

"Well?" Sandra said with some frustration. "Where was she all this time? Why did she come back now?"

Jorja wasn't sure what she should reveal to them. She was anxiously hoping someone would interrupt them. "She didn't come back, really. She was found."

Sandra crossed her arms and said impatiently, "Really, Jorja! Why are you being so evasive? What do you mean, she was found? Was she hiding? Where was she? She has a lot of explaining to do after leaving Kat when she was just a baby."

Jorja's parents and Ryan were eyeing her with mild curiosity, Sandra with annoyance and Jim was patiently but intently waiting for her response.

"Look, it's not that I'm being evasive. I'm just not sure how much I should say because it's a police matter now."

This bit of news interested Jim who asked, "Police matter? Why? When you said you wanted to discuss the case, you failed to mention the case had been reopened."

Jorja hesitated and Helen finally spoke up. "Honey, why can't you just tell them? Sandra and Jim won't go around telling everyone and Jim is with the police so you know he'll keep it confidential."

Jorja would have preferred telling her mother Sandra wasn't the best at keeping secrets but at this point she knew if she didn't give them something, Sandra would just have Jim dig for the information anyway.

"Well...because it is a police matter." Jorja looked at Jim, "When I ran into you, the case had not yet been reopened and I just wanted to ask you a few questions. Now the County has taken over the investigation so I'm not sure what I should divulge. What I will say is that it would appear Kat's mother may have been murdered. The County is running DNA testing to verify whether the body they found was Kat's mother."

Everyone remained silent. Jorja waited, not wanting to speak any further about the details. She finally heard her mother moan slightly before saying, "Oh, that poor girl...both of them. The mother for her death and Kat for just now finding out the truth."

Jim then asked, "When did all this come out?"

Jorja decided she had said enough. "I don't think I should say anything more about it. The police are looking into it and we're waiting to see what they come up with. I'm sure if you contact the County to speak to the detective in charge, he'll tell you what he can."

Sandra chimed in, "It is terrible news to hear Kat's mother was murdered but I suppose it is better she finds out the truth even after all this time."

Everyone nodded and murmured in agreement while Jim remained silent. Finally, he said, "Yes, it's always good when a cold case can be closed. Well, I need to get home. The party is great, Jorja, but I'm tired and I need to get a good night's sleep before I start my shift in the morning."

Jim said his goodbyes and everyone but Jorja and Ryan got up to get more food or visit with other guests.

"Well, what did you think of that?" Ryan asked her.

"What?" Jorja asked.

"I don't know. It just seemed to me that Jim wasn't too happy with the news about Kat's mother's case. He's a cop and you'd think he'd be more pleased that an unsolved murder might soon be solved."

Jorja thought about Ryan's comments. "Well, it could be an ego thing with him. He was the one who investigated her disappearance and he determined she had just run away. Maybe he's upset no one told him about the possibility her body may have been found. Or he's upset they didn't include him in on the current investigation. I think they first need to confirm with the DNA test that she was Kat's mother before they can actually conduct a thorough investigation so maybe they would have contacted him at that point. Who knows. He's probably miffed no one has included him in on the case yet even if he does work for another department."

Ryan shrugged. "Maybe. He sure seems to be a hard-ass though. I thought he was going to ask me for proof of identification and verification of where I'm staying. Is he always like that?"

Jorja laughed. "I'm not sure if he is or not. I barely know him. Just stay clear of him, I guess, until you are able to give straight answers next time he asks you anything. I don't know about you but I really don't want to be telling everyone why you're here until we figure out how we're going to explain where my long lost brother has been all this time and why."

Ryan nodded in agreement. "Yeah, it's not something I really want to explain either. Between what my father did and what our natural mother attempted to do, there are quite a few skeletons in our closet. That is, of course, if the test verifies we're related."

"Right, we'll just wait for the test results. Did you get into the office this week to give a sample?"

"Yes, I did. Did you?"

Jorja grabbed a few empty cups to throw them away as she replied, "Yes, I went in on Thursday. I'm really hoping they get the results back as soon as they can. Until then, I've been thinking that we should go ahead and spend some more time together. Would you like to come over to my house for lunch on Monday? You can bring Nicholas. I have a dog who would absolutely love to play catch with him."

Ryan smiled and his eyes sparkled with excitement as he said, "I would really like that, Jorja. I would love for you to get to know Nicholas."

"Good. Come by around noon. I should go mingle some more with the guests and you should make sure to eat some of the food before it's all gone."

With that they both awkwardly separated as Jorja took the empty cups to place them in the garbage. She then visited with guests as she moved around the store to see how everyone was doing. Not spying Kat, she decided to go to the office to check on her. She found Kat at the fax machine carefully reviewing flyers that had already been faxed from the detective. Jorja could tell Kat had been crying and she understood why Kat had not hurried back to the party.

"Kat? Are you okay?"

Kat turned away from Jorja as she attempted to wipe the tears from her face. She then said, "I'm okay. It's just so sad seeing all these photos of my mom. She looked so happy and beautiful. I'm sick about the thought that someone hurt her and she was all alone with some madman when she died."

Jorja put her arm around Kat to comfort her. "I know, Kat. It's hard and I'm really sorry you have to go through this. Your mom would be very proud of you and how you are helping with her case. We can only hope there is something the police can find to prove who killed your mother so that she can rest in peace."

Kat leaned in and accepted Jorja's hug. Kat then broke away from Jorja, folded the flyers and placed them in her back pocket. She wiped her face again with her hand and turned to Jorja. "Thanks, Jorja. You have been great through all this and I appreciate all you've done for me and for my mom."

Jorja smiled at Kat. "Just always remember I'm here for you. Now, why don't you go use the bathroom and clean your face before you go back downstairs. Do you plan to stick around or would you rather go home?"

Kat turned the light on in the half bath connected to Jorja's office. "Go home to what? Lydia's here and it's dark and dreary at the house. I'd rather stay here with you and everyone else so I don't have to be alone. I'll wait until the party is over so I can help clean up."

"I'm glad you want to stay, Kat. I wouldn't enjoy myself here if I had to worry about you being home alone right now."

Jorja waited as Kat washed her face and checked her mascara before they both returned to the party. Jorja mingled with the guests for awhile and then decided to get herself another glass of punch. As she took a sip, Taylor moved up alongside her.

"Hey Jorja. The party has gone pretty well, wouldn't you say?"

She responded after swallowing the sip of punch. "Yes, Taylor, the party has gone very well. I think everyone has had a terrific time and you did an amazing job with everything."

Taylor smirked at Jorja and said, "Oh, you think I was fishing for a compliment? Well...maybe I was. But you're wrong, it wasn't just me. I had a lot of help, including from you. You are right though that everyone is having a great time. Some of the guests have already asked me what party we plan to have next."

Jorja looked around at all the guests still in attendance. "Maybe we could plan something again soon. How about something in December for the holidays? That might be fun."

Taylor jumped at the opportunity. "I was hoping you'd say that! I would love to put together a Christmas party. I already asked Dylan and he said he would help out with the food again."

Raising an eyebrow in response, Jorja decided not to question Taylor's reason for asking Dylan before they even discussed it. Taylor had, after all, done most of the work for the Halloween party so Jorja knew she couldn't very well argue against a Christmas party if Taylor wanted to take on most of the work.

"Okay, Taylor, we'll talk about it soon. Looks like some of the guests are starting to leave so I think in the next half hour or so we can wrap this up."

Taylor quickly looked over her shoulder where Dylan was standing. Once Taylor caught his eye, Dylan walked over to stand next to her. Taylor then turned to Jorja and asked, "Do you have any plans tomorrow, Jorja?"

"No...why?"

"Well, Dylan and I were going to take a day trip tomorrow to see the underground city in Seattle. Would you like to come?"

Jorja didn't look forward to being a third wheel and Taylor immediately picked up on that. "We want you to come with us Jorja. You wouldn't be intruding. I just think it'll be fun and I'd like you to see it with us."

Jorja thought about how busy they'd been all week preparing for the party along with everything else. She thought maybe a day away would be a great idea. "Okay, that sounds like fun. I've never been there, have you?"

Taylor shook her head. "No, never been and Dylan said he hasn't seen it either so it will be a new experience for all of us. We thought we'd leave around eight in the morning. That way we can go to Pike's Place Market first to look around and then go to lunch before we take a tour of the underground city in the afternoon."

Jorja was nodding in agreement as Taylor spoke. It all sounded good to her. Brad caught her eye and he wandered over to the group. He gave Jorja a quick smile and then turned to Taylor. "So, are we all set for tomorrow then?"

Jorja quickly looked at Taylor in question with raised eyebrows. Taylor knew exactly what Jorja was thinking and tried to steer Jorja away from backing out of the trip. "We're all set, Brad. Jorja said she'd love to hang out with us tomorrow and we're going to leave the house around eight o'clock. Will that work for you?"

Brad nodded and said, "That sounds great. I look forward to it and I look forward to some real sight-seeing. I haven't been to Seattle in awhile and I've never been to the underground city. You sure you don't mind me tagging along?"

While she knew this was her opportunity to deter Brad from tagging along, Jorja decided it wouldn't be worth the effort. She knew what

Taylor was up to and she knew if she got out of this double date, Taylor would just set up another one the first chance she got.

Taylor gave Jorja just enough time to say something and when Jorja remained silent, Taylor knew she was in the clear. "We don't mind, Brad. We want you to come, right Jorja?

Jorja could have kicked Taylor but instead she turned to Brad and said, "Sure, it will be fun."

"Okay, good. Well, Jorja, looks like the evening is winding down and the guests are leaving. Do you want me to start putting some of the tables away for you?"

Before Jorja could respond, Dylan interrupted and said, "Actually, Brad, that would be great. You want to come help me take care of a few things now?"

When Brad and Dylan left the girls, Taylor cautiously peered at Jorja. She knew Jorja wasn't happy with the double-date blindside but she knew Jorja would get over it. "Are you okay with tomorrow? Don't be mad, okay? We'll have fun, I promise."

Jorja gave Taylor a stare that could have melted butter but then she suddenly smiled and said, "Don't worry, Taylor, I know I'll have a good time. But you can bet if I get the chance to pay you back, I will give you better than you gave me." Taylor knew Jorja was serious but at that point she didn't really care, especially if it meant pushing her friend towards a relationship that might actually make her happy.

CHAPTER 32

"Jorja? Do you think Piper can come home with me?" She turned at the question to look down at Nicholas. Nicholas was kneeling beside Piper with his arms around her neck.

She smiled at Nicholas and said, "Well, Nicholas, it's possible Piper might like that but I would be very sad without Piper. What would I do if you were to take her home?"

Nicholas thought seriously about Jorja's question as his brow furrowed and his lips pursed. He then snapped his small fingers and said, "I could send you pictures! My dad could take lots of them and we could send them to you every day!"

Jorja laughed and marveled at the mind of a five year old. He thought it would be that simple. "Well, Nicholas, I don't think a photograph could take the place of me being able to give her a hug when I need to and there are many days when I need her here so I can give her a hug. I'd be very sad if she wasn't here. Have you asked your dad if he could get you a puppy?"

"Oh no, you don't!" Ryan said as he suddenly rounded the corner and walked into the kitchen. "Nicholas and I have already had this discussion and we're not getting a dog right now. I've offered him a fish and that's as far as I will go."

Jorja was about to respond but Nicholas beat her to it. "I can't hold a fish! That's no fun! We need a dog, Dad. He can get your slippers for you and he can get the paper for you..."

"Yeah, and he'd dig and he'd chew and he'd need to be walked every day. No, Nicholas, forget it. We can't get a dog right now."

Nicholas hung his head but made no attempt to hide his pouting face. Jorja hadn't realized how well a child could work a parent when she saw Nicholas was attempting to develop some tears.

Ryan would have none of it. "That's enough, Nicholas. Subject is closed. Now, go play with Piper while I speak to Jorja, okay?"

Nicholas slowly stood and replied, "Okay," in a very small voice. "Come on, Piper."

Ryan watched Nicholas leave the room with Piper.

Jorja watched Ryan watch Nicholas. Again, she had no doubt about his love for his son.

"He's a cute kid, Ryan."

Ryan turned to look at her as he said, "I will admit, he can try my patience sometimes but I think he's the most adorable kid out there. I am, of course, prejudice but there you go."

"I haven't known you and Nicholas long but I say I'll have to agree that he is the most adorable kid out there. You want another cup of coffee?"

Ryan agreed to another cup and they both sat down at the table to chat while they ate lunch.

Ryan started, "So how was your trip up to Seattle yesterday?"

"Oh it was fun. We visited Pike Place Market where I found quite a few gift ideas for Christmas and then we had lunch at a local café before we met up with the tour guide for their underground Seattle tour."

Ryan tilted his head as he asked, "Is there really an underground city? Did you actually walk under the city of Seattle?"

"Yeah, it was really something. You know, I've lived in Washington all my life but until recently I didn't realize the story about the underground city in Seattle was actually true. Maybe you and I could go up there one day. Many of the buildings aren't in the best shape but if you use your imagination as you walk along the old sidewalks, it's really pretty awesome. I'm not sure if it's something Nicholas would enjoy because there are stories about the place being haunted and it might be difficult to keep that information from him."

Ryan nodded, "Yeah, we don't need him to have any nightmares. We'll just stick with the zoo."

Jorja smiled. "Sure, there are two great zoos we can take him to and there's also the Seattle Aquarium. And in Olympia we can take him to The Children's Museum. It's a great place for kids his age. He'll just love it."

Ryan again nodded but Jorja thought he appeared noncommittal when he then changed the subject. "So, what's the deal with you and Brad? Are you two a couple?"

She rolled her eyes before she could stop herself. "Uh, we're not a couple, not anymore anyway. We dated back in high school and now we're just friends."

"Hmm, I just thought there was more to it. I don't know, I think it was something Taylor said…"

"Oh, don't listen to Taylor. She would like for me to be in a relationship. You know, she's happy with her man and now she feels compelled to make me happy too. No, Brad and I are just friends."

Ryan gave her a sideways glance before taking a sip of his coffee. "Well, do you think Brad feels the same way?"

As she shrugged she had to admit, "I don't know. I think he's *comfortable* with me and he easily moves back into that role when we are together." Jorja did not feel comfortable with the topic so she decided to turn the subject back to Ryan and Nicholas. "Have you thought about what you're going to do? Where you and Nicholas are going to live?"

Ryan pondered her question for only a moment. "I haven't really decided, actually. I think I just want to take it one day at a time."

Jorja decided to probe further as she asked, "Well, what if the results are positive? What have you thought you might like to do?"

Ryan moved salad around with his fork and finally stabbed at a cherry tomato. "There are many things I would like to do, Jorja. I'd like to get to know you and your parents, I'd like you and your parents to get to know Nicholas and I'd like to show Nicholas he does have other family. That's what I would like."

Jorja was quiet as she thought about what Ryan said. She understood because she felt the same way. She had begun to enjoy the thought of having a brother and a nephew and she was secretly thrilled with the whole idea of getting to know them more. Even in the very short time she had known them she was feeling a connection with both of them. She did not want to think about how disappointed she would feel if the test results did not come back as she expected.

~ ~ ~

Jorja's thoughts kept returning back to her conversation with Ryan as she attempted to update her bookstore blog the following day. She tried to focus on what she was typing but it was difficult when Ryan, Nicholas and the looming DNA results dominated her thoughts. She inwardly forced her attention back to her blog. She had decided it would be a good idea to start the blog in order to keep her customers informed of upcoming book events, book club meetings, new releases and other events. As she typed the last paragraph of her blog post, the sound of someone running up the stairs drew her attention. Looking over her computer, Jorja saw Kat quickly reach the top step before approaching her desk. Kat was breathless but excited as she said, "Jorja, I got a phone call from the detective on my mom's case!"

Jorja felt tingles go up her spine as she asked, "You did? What did he say?"

Kat tried to calm her breathing as she sat down and then just as quickly stood back up. She paced in front of Jorja's desk as she said, "The detective said the lab results prove we're related! It's her! Now he'll add her name to the flyers and he said he'll distribute them beginning tomorrow. Can we put one here, at the bookstore? Is that okay?"

Jorja thought Kat was going to hyperventilate so she asked her to sit down and take a breath. Then she said, "Of course you can hang a flyer here. Someone from town may know something about your mom's disappearance they hadn't realized at the time was important. Maybe now we can find out what happened."

Kat stood up again. "Thanks, Jorja! I'll bring one in with me when I come to work tomorrow."

"You're welcome, Kat. Did he say anything else? Did he say where they are with the investigation?"

Kat shook her head. "No, he didn't tell me anything about the investigation. He just said that he'd be in touch when he had something to tell me."

"Well, that's all we can ask for at this point." Jorja stood and rounded the desk, stopping just in front of Kat. She lightly grabbed Kat's shoulders as she said, "I'm glad the test results came back so that you know for sure but I know it must also be difficult. Remember I'm here if you need to talk, okay?"

Kat nodded. "I know, Jorja. I appreciate it. Thanks for everything. I better get back downstairs. I didn't even say hello to Taylor!"

Kat then left the office and headed down the stairs to the main floor. Jorja thought about what Kat told her. Even though Kat's attitude was upbeat, Jorja knew how painful it must be for Kat to know her mother was a murder victim. The one consolation was that there could soon be some type of closure for Kat because it was much better than not knowing anything at all.

CHAPTER 33

Jorja felt slightly stunned as she hung up the phone. She had just confirmed with Ryan that he had received the same phone call she had just received from the lab. The test results verified she and Ryan were related. With the knowledge she would not be able to continue working after hearing the news, she had invited Ryan to her house to talk more about their situation.

After grabbing her jacket and purse she slowly walked down the stairs, still stunned by the news. Taylor was helping a customer so Jorja waited, only to discover she could no longer stand. She quickly found herself sitting on a couch, willing herself not to cry.

Taylor said goodbye to the customer and walked towards the couch. "Hey, Jorja, we're doing pretty well with sales today. The window display is drawing in some new customers too and I think…Jorja? Are you okay?"

When Jorja did not answer, or even look up, Taylor knelt down to grab both her hands, which were lying limp on her lap. "Jorja, what's wrong?"

She finally looked at Taylor. She felt like she might explode from the emotions she was feeling. "I...the lab called. The results prove Ryan and I are related." Jorja sighed heavily. "I'm just...I don't know. I didn't know I would feel like this once I found out. I'm happy but I'm also angry. I'm angry at what Aunt Gloria did and what Dr. Hanson did and for the fact that Ryan and I have been separated all this time."

"Oh, Jorja..." Taylor sat down on the couch to give her a hug. "I really can't imagine how you are feeling right now."

She hugged Taylor back and said, "Thanks Taylor. I really can't focus on work right now so I asked Ryan to meet me at the house so we could talk."

"That's good. Now that you know the results, you can actually talk more about the future. I'll see you tonight when I get home."

A customer entered the store and walked towards the espresso counter so Taylor got up to help them. Jorja took a moment and then finally stood up and left the store, waving a silent goodbye to Taylor as she walked out the door.

She arrived at the house only minutes before Ryan, who now sat at the kitchen table as she made a fresh pot of coffee. After turning the coffee pot on, she sat across the table from him.

Jorja spoke first, trying to hide her nervousness. "So...has it hit you yet about the lab results?"

Ryan chuckled. "Has it hit me? I honestly felt like I couldn't breathe when I got the phone call. I was afraid of what they were going to tell me. What if we were related? What if we weren't? All the scenarios were running through my head."

Nodding in agreement she said, "I know what you mean. I was nervous waiting for the call and then all these emotions ran through me when I got the results. I'm glad though. I'm thrilled to have you and Nicholas as part of the family."

Ryan's look turned serious. "I haven't told Nicholas yet. I thought we should talk first. It will be difficult to explain to him and I won't be telling him the whole truth. I don't plan to ever tell anyone what our mother was planning to do to us or what my father did when he essentially kidnapped me. I don't want anyone to know what her intentions were and I'd rather not speak ill of my father now that he's gone. What about you? Have you told anyone?"

Jorja shrugged and said, "Well, my parents know and so does Taylor but, I agree, there's no reason to tell anyone else. It's a family secret that can remain a family secret as far as I'm concerned."

"Good. I've decided to tell Nicholas that our mother could not keep us because she was too young and we were both adopted separately by different parents and only just now recently found out about each other. It's what I'd prefer to tell anyone who asks about our relationship and why we are just now meeting each other."

Frowning, she thought about Ryan's explanation. "Well, I'm not sure that will work for anyone other than Nicholas. Everyone who knows me and my parents think I am Rick and Helen's daughter. I don't know how I can explain where you came from without also admitting Aunt Gloria was my real mom. I'm not sure my parents want anyone to know they aren't my real parents. Even if they agreed to let the cat out of the bag about them adopting me, I'm not sure how we would explain why they did not also adopt you." Jorja shook her head as the dilemma seemed to grow while she spoke. "Boy, I guess I should speak to my parents. I need to figure out how to deal with this once the word does get out that you are my brother."

Ryan was silent as he thought about Jorja's comments. Finally, he said, "You don't have to tell anyone I'm your brother, if you don't want to."

Jorja adamantly shook her head. "No, Ryan. You and Nicholas are my family and there's no reason to keep that a secret. It's just all the other stuff I'm worried about."

Ryan looked relieved. "Okay. Talk to your parents and then we'll talk more about how Nicholas and I will be introduced at future get-togethers." Ryan gave her a grin and then stood to get a cup of coffee after noticing the coffee had finished perking. "Do you want me to get you a cup?"

Jorja wasn't sure her nerves could stand caffeine right now. She remained in her seat and said, "No, I'll pass on coffee for now. Have you decided what you want to do? Will you live here or are you going to stay in Wyoming?"

Ryan carefully carried a full cup of coffee to the table and sat down. "I have thought about it, yes. I could sell my parents' house, or rent it out if I can't sell it, and move here but I need to think more about it. Whether Nicholas and I move here or stay in Wyoming, I would like Nicholas to have a relationship with you. I'd also like your parents to fill in as grandparents more than the aunt and uncle they really are, if they are willing."

"I'm sure my parents would love to spoil Nicholas. It won't take long for them to grow fond of him, I'm sure."

Ryan sipped his coffee and sat the cup down on the table. "I know it's a lot for them to take in. I just hope they realize I want to try my best to make Nicholas' life as normal as possible. Having family is very important and I am grateful that you are so willing to accept us as we are. I just hope your parents are the same."

Jorja felt her emotions stir. She knew Ryan wasn't sure where he stood and he was fearful her parents would not accept the situation or accept Ryan and Nicholas as family. Jorja had faith her parents would not only accept them but would do so with open arms. She would be astonished if her parents did anything less than that.

Jorja could tell Ryan had something else on his mind but seemed reluctant to say anything more. She finally asked, "Ryan is there something bothering you?"

Ryan hesitated to respond at first but finally relented and said, "I do have something that is bothering me. I've thought about it ever since my father told me who my real mother was. Do you have any idea who our real father might be? My father told me he wasn't aware if Gloria ever named the father and of course, after he moved us away he didn't make contact with your family again. Do you know who he is?"

Jorja shook her head. "I have absolutely no idea, Ryan. I did find a letter Aunt Gloria wrote to the father but there is no name. My mom didn't know and I guess Aunt Gloria wouldn't tell my grandparents who the father was. I'm afraid it's one piece to our past we may never figure out."

Ryan was silent as he thought about what Jorja told him. He then said, "I figured as much. It's too bad. I'd really like to know who he was, what happened to him, if he even knew we existed. Guess we might never know."

~ ~ ~

After Ryan left the house to return to his hotel room, Jorja decided it was time to finish going through the box her aunt, or rather, her real mother, left for her. She wasn't used to calling Gloria anything other than her aunt. Now, though, after thinking more about the fact that the items in the box were from her biological mother, Jorja was determined to finish going through the box.

Piper followed her up the stairs as she headed to her bedroom. She removed the box from the floor of her closet where it had been sitting for the past few weeks and sat it on the bed. Piper plopped down on her dog pillow, seemingly tired after her afternoon with Nicholas.

"What's the matter, girl? You're not used to playing with someone so young, are you?"

Piper raised her head just slightly in response and then placed her muzzle back down on her paws. Jorja smiled and thought it would be a great idea to have Nicholas over every couple of days. It might help keep Piper fit.

Sitting on the bed with her legs crossed, she opened the box. She lifted the items out of the box one by one and set them on the bedspread. First she removed the scarf and the broach belonging to her grandmother and then the jewelry box with the hummingbird on top. She then gingerly removed all of the remaining items from the box and placed them on the bed.

Once all the items were neatly laid out, she carefully looked over each item. Jorja picked up one of three journals and opened it to reveal Gloria's handwriting. In quickly glancing over the dates, she noted that many of the entries were from the time Gloria had been in the mental hospital. She set the journal aside with the intention of reviewing it and the others further. A pile of reading books appeared to be well worn and Jorja guessed these books were Gloria's favorites. Looking at a few titles with some interest, she realized most of the books were written by English authors. She found books by Jane Austen, Charles Dickens, Agatha Christie and Mary Shelley. She found it curious that Gloria favored some of her own favorite authors but decided she did not want to think too much on whether reading preferences had anything to do with DNA.

She turned her attention to a pile of envelopes and flipped through them, quickly realizing they were all letters Gloria had received while in the hospital. A quick glance showed return address labels from Jorja's mother and also her grandparents. She set the letters aside with the journals. There were a few other items wrapped in cloth and Jorja opened the cloth to reveal hummingbirds made of blown glass. Her aunt liked birds, she had known this, but hummingbirds were obviously her favorite. Jorja herself had always enjoyed watching small birds but she especially appreciated the largest of birds; hawks, eagles, even ravens. Removing the cloth from each hummingbird, she quickly noted they were all in very good condition. She decided she would make room on one of the shelves in her den for the hummingbird collection.

Having separated the largest items from each other, Jorja turned her attention to the jewelry box. She opened it to look again at the items inside. She picked up the heart-shaped Yin Yang necklace with the saying: *Two Together, Two Apart, Two of a part of me, Forever.* Chills went down her spine as she realized the depth of what those words meant to Gloria. She could never understand what took over Gloria's mind to make her want to kill her own children. She wondered if the poem helped Gloria cope or if it was a sad reminder for what she had done. Setting the necklace aside, she carefully removed the remainder of the jewelry. There were various rings and necklaces; pearls, some plain chain necklaces, some costume jewelry, earrings and necklaces with diamonds or what may have been cubic zirconium, she wasn't sure which, and a few bracelets with various charms. A few of the chain necklaces had a single item attached, one included a "G" with what she could tell were fake diamonds, another was a locket with a yellow rose and yet another was shaped like a hummingbird.

As Jorja was placing the items back in the jewelry box, a thought struck her. *The locket.* It looked familiar to her. Why would it look familiar to her? It had been in the box since before Gloria left the hospital so she knew she could not have seen Gloria wearing it after she returned home for good. Jorja picked up the locket to look at it more closely.

Catching her breath she suddenly realized where she may have seen it before. She quickly jumped off the bed, causing Piper to yelp out of fright at the unexpected movement. Jorja then ran downstairs to the dining room to locate the expanding file she had stored all the documents relating to Kat's mother's case. She hurriedly dumped the items on the dining room table and riffled through the papers in search of the photos she kept after the sheriff's office picked through the ones they wanted for the flyers. Once Jorja found the envelope, she tore it open, spilling the photos onto the table. She was frantic as her mind began to wrap around the possibility of what she did not wish to believe. She finally found one and then another photograph showing Vera in a floral dress while wearing a necklace. A necklace with a locket she always wore, according to Lydia, but which had not been found with her body. Jorja ran to the den to find a magnifying glass and used it to look closely at the photos, where she saw a heart-shaped locket with a yellow rose on the front.

It has to be a coincidence. There must be more than a few necklaces that look like this! She thought to herself.

Jorja carefully reviewed her notes. She reviewed the time frame Kat's mother disappeared and when Gloria was released from the hospital. She then breathed a sigh of relief as she verified the dates: Vera disappeared when Jorja was around nineteen years old and Gloria had not been released from the hospital until Jorja had turned twenty-one years old. *Thank God!* She gladly accepted the fact that there was no way Gloria could have had any part in Vera's disappearance or death.

But was it a coincidence that the necklaces were similar or was this actually Vera's necklace? If this was Vera's necklace, how would Gloria have it in her possession?

Jorja wasn't sure she believed in coincidences. She had to figure out how Gloria could have gained possession of a necklace that was most likely the last item removed from Vera's neck before she had been killed.

CHAPTER 34

Expecting to hit a brick wall when she made a phone call to the hospital to speak with Nurse Willows, Jorja was pleasantly surprised when the nurse agreed to help. Having come to the conclusion that the only way Gloria could have gained access to the locket was if she received it from someone else, Jorja wanted to dig up past records relating to Gloria's visitors. Why anyone would give her such a thing was the question but if the list of visitors could be narrowed down, it would help her find some answers. It had not escaped Jorja's thoughts that the person who gave the item to Gloria might also have been involved with Vera's murder.

After arriving at the hospital fifteen minutes early, Jorja took the time to make a quick call to her parents to let them know she was nearby and would stop by for a visit.

"Why are you going back to the hospital?" Her mother asked once Jorja explained where she was.

"I need to speak to the nurse again, Mom. Aunt Gloria had an item in her box of belongings that I believe she should not have had and I want to figure out how she got it. I don't know how long I will be but I plan to stop by to visit on my way home."

"What kind of item could Gloria have possibly gotten ahold of?"

Jorja was hesitant to elaborate until she knew more herself. "Mom, I'll just talk to you about it when I stop by, okay? I need to go. I love you and I'll see you soon."

Jorja could hear her mother sigh over the phone. "Okay, honey, I'll see you when you get here."

After saying goodbye Jorja got out of her jeep. It was lightly raining so she jogged to the front entrance of the hospital. Once inside she asked for Nurse Willows and did not have to wait long for the nurse to appear.

"Hello, Jorja. It's nice to see you again. I have everything ready for you back in the office."

She followed Nurse Willows past the reception area into a large office area, where Nurse Willows sat behind a desk and motioned for Jorja to sit in a chair opposite her.

"Well, it took a little doing but I was able to obtain some information for you. What I have is a print out of the names of visitors who came to see your aunt during the time she resided here. I don't have the actual dates they came to visit each time because getting the sign in sheets for every day the twenty plus years Gloria resided here would not be approved or even feasible, really. However, I have a list of all the visitors who were allowed to visit with your aunt in a given year. Each visitor had to be approved by her doctor before they could be added to her visitor list. After they were approved they could visit her anytime during regular visiting hours but they had to be reapproved at the beginning of each year."

She listened to the nurse with anticipation and was impatient to look over the list. Nurse Willows reached her arm over the desk to hand Jorja the paper.

"Now, this is a list of names, Jorja, but that's it. We can't provide you with their address or other contact information unless there's a good reason to do so. My boss, Mr. Bailey, told me that the names are all we can provide to you at this time."

Jorja took the paper from Nurse Willows' hand. She was too eager to see the list to be disappointed by Nurse Willows' comments. She took her time as she looked over the list of names under each year her aunt resided at the hospital. The list was pretty much the same from the first year Gloria was institutionalized 1980 through 1988 when Gloria came home for a week and was quickly brought back to the hospital. The only visitors approved during those years included Gloria's parents and her sister, Helen. Again, from 1988 through 1997, she noted the same visitors were approved but when she glanced at the names under 1998, things changed. Her brow furrowed and she straightened up as she caught sight of a new name on the list of approved visitors...Mr. James Cooper.

What the heck? Jorja thought to herself. *James Cooper? Jim Cooper? As in Officer Cooper? Why would he visit with Aunt Gloria?*

She wondered if Jim visited with Gloria regarding a case. But what case? She then scanned the remaining years her aunt received visitors and saw Jim Cooper's name was also approved for 1999, 2000 and 2001, the year her aunt finally came home for good. If he had actually requested approval for all three years, there was no reason to believe he had visited Gloria to speak to her about a case. It had to be something more. But what?

Jorja looked up from the list and asked, "Do you know why this man was visiting with my aunt?"

Nurse Willows took the list from Jorja to look at the name on the list. She took a moment as she attempted to pull anything from her memory that might help answer the question.

"I really can't recall, Jorja. I know your aunt did not get many visitors but when she did, she didn't speak to me about them. Your aunt and I became friends but she still kept her past life outside the hospital pretty private. I'm not even sure I ever met the man, to be honest. I didn't usually take part with the visitations."

She was disappointed but not surprised by Nurse Willows' response. If the nurse had known, it would have just been too easy and Jorja had already accepted the fact that digging up the past was not an easy task.

"Well, that's fine. Can I ask you one more favor?"

Nurse Willows nodded and said with a grin, "Sure, if it's something I won't get in trouble for."

"Can you tell me when my aunt was sent home the first time? The time she was gone only a week or so before returning back here?"

"Well…sure, I can look that up for you. Let me see if it's in the system here…" Nurse Willows punched a few keys on the keyboard and looked at her computer screen. She typed in some more information and waited for the computer to catch up. Eyeing the screen results she looked up at Jorja and said, "Well, it's not noted here. I'll have to go find the hard copy of her file down in the storage room. Can you wait in the lobby for me while I go look? We have the espresso stand now so you can order yourself a coffee while you wait if you're in the mood for one."

"Thank you. I will do that." Jorja walked out to the lobby and ordered herself a latte while Nurse Willows took off for parts unknown. Jorja could only imagine a huge expanse in the basement of the large hospital where multiple files were being stored right along with creepy cobwebs and ghosts of past residents. She hoped the files were organized well enough so the act of finding the file would not be a chore for the nurse.

As she planted herself on the sofa with her latte, she grabbed a *Good Housekeeping* magazine from the side table. Full of Halloween ideas and upcoming Thanksgiving dinner ideas, Jorja realized she needed to think about Thanksgiving dinner. In the past she had always gone to her parents' for dinner but this year she hoped she could have dinner at her place. She would invite Ryan and Nicholas. It would be a bit awkward, she thought, as she and Ryan were only just now beginning to form a relationship but what better way was there if not for holiday gatherings?

She was mindlessly flipping through the magazine, daydreaming about holiday plans when she heard Nurse Willows call her name.

"Jorja? You want to follow me back to the office again?" Nurse Willows held a file in one hand as she motioned to Jorja with the other.

Jorja followed Nurse Willows back to the office where Nurse Willows sat down at the desk again and opened the file. She watched as the nurse carefully reviewed some notes that appeared to be nothing more than scribbles from Jorja's vantage point.

"Okay…I see here the doctor makes note of Gloria getting his approval to return home. She had been here for eight years, he thought she was doing well although she'd need to continue with treatment someplace close to home…let's see. Ah, here it is. She was released to return home on April eighth and she returned to the hospital on April thirteenth. She was not well when she came back but I can't go into any details that the doctor might have noted."

Nurse Willows looked up. "Is that what you needed? Anything else?"

Jorja had removed a pen and pad from her purse and she wrote down the dates of her aunt's release and return to the hospital.

"No, the dates are fine. I appreciate you taking the time to find the file for me."

Nurse Willows closed the file and set it to the side of her desk. She leaned back in her chair as she said, "It's no problem. I'd like to help you out more, if the need arises and so long as it doesn't jeopardize my job. Gloria was my friend and if giving you this information helps, it's the least I can do. By the way, what are you looking for?"

Jorja tilted her head and thought about Nurse Willows' question. She finally replied, "I'm not exactly sure what I'm looking for. I know my aunt received an item while she was here and I believe a visitor gave her the item but I can't understand why. Now that I have the name of the visitor, I just have more questions."

She shook her head in exasperation. "Honestly, Nurse Willows, I really wish my aunt hadn't died because I would so much like to speak to her right now. There are so many questions I have for her and I'm afraid I might never know all the answers."

Nurse Willows frowned at Jorja's frustration. "I'm sorry you lost your aunt and I'm sorry you have questions only your aunt may be able to answer. I wish there was more I could do for you."

Jorja thought about her next comment and began to speak but then had second thoughts. Nurse Willows quietly watched and waited. Finally, Jorja appeared to make a decision as she leaned forward and said in a low voice, "I think I should tell you something, since you were my aunt's friend."

"Yes? What is it?"

Jorja again hesitated for a moment before she said, "Well, you know about the fact that my aunt had babies, or she may have let on she had just one baby?"

"Yes?" Nurse Willows waited.

"I'm one of those babies. She was my mother and the other baby was taken away but I recently met him. I have a brother I never knew about and he has a son."

She wasn't quite sure why she wanted to tell Nurse Willows what she had discovered but she believed the nurse was probably the only friend Gloria had ever had. Why Gloria never told her secret, Jorja guessed it was because Gloria thought she had killed her baby boy and there was no way she would admit that to anyone, even her only friend.

Nurse Willows stared at Jorja for a moment without saying a word. Finally giving a quick nod, she said, "Well, that makes sense. Honestly, I had always thought there was more to the story, especially after I met you. I'm glad to hear you found your brother, even after all these years."

Jorja had to wonder how perceptive Nurse Willows was as she asked, "Did you know I was Gloria's daughter?"

"Well...I wasn't sure but I knew her sister had a child the same age as the child Gloria would have had and it made sense that Helen would have taken the child in when Gloria was brought here. But, it was never anything Gloria ever admitted to so, of course, I could not assume anything. I hope you understand why I did not say anything."

Jorja nodded as she said, "No, I understand you could not say anything. Well, thank you and thanks again for helping me. I should get going and let you get back to work."

Nurse Willows stood and huffed loudly as she replied, "Work around here is nothing like it used to be ever since the State took over the facility." She leaned over and whispered, "Honestly, I'm ready to retire and I'm looking forward to traveling more often."

Jorja said goodbye to Nurse Willows and left the hospital. She was glad the rain had let up for the drive to her parents' house. She did not recall much of the drive as her thoughts were so preoccupied with what she had discovered. She had to determine why Jim Cooper had visited Gloria and if he was the one who gave her the necklace. Even more important, if the necklace was Vera's, she had to determine *how* he came in possession of the necklace and *why* he gave it to Gloria. If the necklace belonged to Vera, it was a disturbing thought. It was further disturbing to Jorja that if Jim Cooper and her aunt had some type of relationship, was it also possible he might be the one who had gotten her pregnant? The idea did not sit well with her at all.

CHAPTER 35

It was late by the time Jorja arrived home after visiting with her parents. She had filled her parents in on what she had discovered but her mother was not able to offer anything concrete where it concerned Gloria's relationship with Jim Cooper. Helen said she was aware the two had attended high school together but that Jim was two years older than Gloria and she hadn't realized they ever formed any type of friendship. The fact that he had visited Gloria at the hospital was also news to Helen.

Jorja entered the house as quietly as she could, in case Taylor had already gone to bed. She shut the front door and relocked it before setting her bag down on the hall table. The house was fairly dark so she hit the switch for the hall light, not wanting to trip over any of Piper's toys. As the light came on, Jorja heard Piper running down the stairs to greet her.

"Hey, girl, how's it going?" She bent over to give Piper a good scratch on the head. "Come on, let's go upstairs," Jorja said as she headed up the stairs to her bedroom. She silently shut her bedroom door after Piper followed her inside. She then went to the closet, picked up the box containing Gloria's items and set it on the bed. Reaching into the box, Jorja rifled through the items until she found what she was looking for…Gloria's journals. She hoped the journals would give her the answers she was looking for.

Thumbing through each journal, Jorja found the one with dates near the time Gloria was first released for a week. She flipped through the pages and found an entry the day before Gloria was to go home:

April 7ᵗʰ

I get to go home tomorrow! The doctor said that I'm doing well enough and can finally go home. I've been here for so long…8 years, and I'm ready to go home. My parents came to see me the other day and I think they just wanted to see for themselves that I'm okay. They said they wanted me to know there would be rules and that I had to abide by them but really, what else can I do? I'm just so happy I get to go home!!

Jorja turned the page and found another entry more than two weeks later…

April 26ᵗʰ

What was I thinking? How could I even possibly think I could go home? I was so excited because I believed I could handle anything. I found out I'm not as brave or as strong as I thought. Being home with my parents should have been a good thing but they treated me like I was going to snap at any moment. I began to have terrible dreams. Dreams where I do something awful, horrible…dreams I do not ever want to have again. I had truly thought going home was the best thing possible but I'm glad to be back here where I am safe from

*doing harm to anyone and where I am around only those who I
wish to see.*

Jorja read the entries again and then set the
journal down on the bed. So many thoughts raced
through her head: Gloria was happy to go home
but based on her dreams and who she saw while
at home, it completely changed her attitude. What
were the dreams about? Was her subconscious
remembering what she had done after Jorja and
her brother were born?

Glancing at the time on her alarm clock she
saw it was already a quarter to midnight. She
wanted to call her mother but decided it was just
too late. Jorja had to admit her mother most likely
had no answers if Gloria never shared the identity
of the father or the reasons behind having to go
back to the hospital.

Jorja picked up the journal again as she
thought about whether Gloria might have
mentioned anything about the necklace. The first
journal included what appeared to be Gloria's first
ten years at the hospital. Reaching for the second
journal, she scanned through the pages and found
the year Kat's mother disappeared. The entries
were about once a week and usually fairly short
with regard to how Gloria was feeling. There were
longer entries whenever Gloria received a visit
from her parents or from Helen. Jorja flipped
through the pages and began to consider she
might not find anything helpful when she landed
on an entry about a year after Vera's
disappearance.

March 22nd

I had a new visitor today! I guess I should remember him but I don't. He said we used to be friends and that we have known each other for a long time. I tried to remember but I just couldn't. I felt terrible but he told me he understood because the doctor explained how my medication has affected my memory. I wish I could remember him. He was very nice, very handsome and he said he wanted to be friends again. I think he likes me and understands me. I don't know why he wants to be friends but it will be nice to visit with someone other than my parents and my sister.

Scanning through the remaining pages of the journal, she found a few more entries when the mystery man visited with Gloria. Jorja knew this had to be Jim Cooper. She finally found the entry she was looking for…

September 9th

I had such a nice visit today! I never have much to tell him when he asks me questions about myself but I enjoy hearing about how exciting his job is. He has such interesting stories! He also told me some sad stories, stories about bad things that happen to women. He told me I was lucky to be here, safe from all the bad people. He said if I ever do leave the hospital, he will always be there to protect me. I believe him. He also gave me a gift and it is so beautiful! It is a necklace, a locket, with my favorite color rose on the front. He said he didn't have a photo to give me but that maybe someday we could put photographs of each other inside the locket. I just love it and I will always treasure it.

Jorja quickly read through the remaining entries. Gloria received a few more visits from the mystery man over the course of a year before she was released but the information about their visits was limited. Gloria just seemed happy every time he came to visit. Jorja finally came upon an entry near the end of Gloria's stay at the hospital.

June 12th

I never thought I'd be writing this again but I am going home, again. The doctor said there is nothing more he can do for me here. He believes I am capable of living on my own outside the hospital. I won't deny I am petrified! I have decided to pack and take home what I need but there are some items I have decided to pack up and store away. I don't plan to take them with me. I will leave them with someone who will know what to do with them when the time comes. I have come to terms with the fact that I have a daughter who will never know me but when I die, I want her to at least have the items that were precious to me, for one reason or another. She might not want them, or understand why they are important to me, but I have decided it's all I can really give her. She will never know me as a mother but hopefully soon she will know me as a friend.

Jorja tried to avoid the tears that wanted to form. She did not want to mourn the mother-daughter relationship she never had with Gloria. Instead, she had to find the answers relating to Vera's murder and why Gloria had her necklace. Jorja knew she should not approach Jim Cooper right away with her questions. She had to be careful because she did not know if he had anything to do with Vera's disappearance. He had been the investigating officer at the time. Did he somehow come into possession of the locket while he was conducting his investigation? Did he take it as a piece of evidence? Did he remove it from Vera's home? Why would he have kept it for himself rather than place it in evidence at the police department?

Jorja rubbed her temples as she realized she would not be able to find answers to her questions before getting some much needed rest. She decided she would go to bed, get some sleep and figure out her next step in the morning.

CHAPTER 36

"Well good morning!" Jorja was just about to take a sip of her coffee when she heard Taylor's voice behind her. She did her best to keep the coffee in her cup and not in her lap so that the coffee landed on the table instead.

"Woops! Sorry about that. I didn't mean to scare you." Taylor quickly grabbed a paper towel and handed it to Jorja.

"That's okay. Good morning to you too. You sure are chipper this morning."

Jorja wiped down the table and attempted to take another sip of coffee. As she did, she watched Taylor sit at the table after grabbing her own cup of coffee. Taylor took a sip from her cup as she looked out the window but Jorja thought Taylor appeared to be staring off into space instead.

"Did you sleep okay? You were in bed already by the time I got home." Jorja said as she began to wonder about the glazed look in Taylor's eyes.

Taylor sat her cup on the table and said, "Uh, yeah, I slept great. After closing up the store, Dylan and I went out for dinner and then we came back here and had a nice long talk."

Jorja waited, expecting Taylor to offer more but when Taylor kept quiet Jorja finally said, "Thanks for holding down the fort. Did you and Kat do okay? Were there any problems?"

Taylor shook her head. "No, it was fine. A slow day, really. I'm hoping it'll pick up again once everyone realizes we're just over a month away from Christmas. So how did your day go? What did you learn from the nurse at the hospital?"

Jorja told Taylor what she found out about Jim Cooper and what Gloria's journals provided.

"Wow, what do you think all that means? Where did he get the necklace and why did he give it to her? What type of relationship did he have with Gloria?"

Jorja frowned and said, "I don't know, Taylor, and it's just killing me as I wonder and worry. I just don't know."

"What are you going to do? Do you think he had something to do with Vera's death? He's a cop; he can't be the suspect...can he? But if there's a chance, you can't just go to him and ask him, he could be dangerous!"

"I know, I know. Believe me, all those thoughts are running through my head. I'm not really sure what to do yet. I thought maybe I'd stop by the hair salon today to speak to Sandra.

See if I can get her to tell me a few things without letting her know why I'm asking. It's my only shot at this point, the safe one anyway."

Taylor wasn't sure she liked the idea as she asked, "Do you plan to go by there today?"

Jorja nodded and said, "Yeah, I can't wait. I need to get some answers. I'll go by the salon and then meet you at the bookstore. Do you mind opening up?"

"No, I don't mind."

"Thanks. Now, why don't you tell me about the 'nice long talk' you and Dylan had last night."

Taylor gave her a blank stare. "What do you mean?"

Jorja laughed and said, "Oh, come on, Taylor. Before we started in about what I found out at the hospital, you were in la-la land. What were you thinking about? Something you and Dylan talked about last night?"

Taylor grinned. She couldn't help it. "Yeah, we had a nice talk. *Really* nice. We just talked about what we both want in life and in the future, that's all."

Jorja gave Taylor a curious look and then her expression grew serious. "Wait a minute...what kind of future stuff are you talking about? What's going on?"

"Well...Jorja, I didn't want to get into this right now. You have a lot going on and I thought we should focus on what you need to do before you need to worry about me."

"Worry? Why would I need to worry?"

"I don't mean worry, really. I mean, I don't want you to focus on me."

Jorja was getting impatient. "Okay, Taylor, spill or I'm going to get upset. Is something going on? What the heck is wrong?"

Taylor waved a hand in dismissal at Jorja. "Nothing is wrong; quite the opposite. I'm elated, I'm happy and I've finally found someone who will always be there for me, other than you, of course."

Jorja waited. She knew there had to be more so she stared Taylor down until she finally gave in. "Okay, okay. Jorja, it's really something, I just wasn't expecting it so soon but Dylan asked me to marry him!"

Jorja sat back in surprise. "What? You've known him for…maybe five months now? Isn't it a bit sudden?"

Taylor tried to hide her look of disappointment. "Well, yeah, I know it's sudden but he and I have hit it off and I have fallen in love with him and he's fallen in love with me. It just feels right, Jorja. Please be happy for me."

Taylor was her best friend and Jorja wanted nothing more than to be happy for her. She just wasn't sure about such a quick union. "How soon do you plan to have the wedding?" Jorja tried to peek at Taylor's ring finger. "Did he give you a ring?"

Taylor offered her hand for Jorja to see there was no ring. "No, he said he would rather let me choose my own ring so we're going to pick a day next week to shop. And we'll wait on the wedding, to give ourselves more time. Don't worry, Jorja. We're not going to completely rush into things. We thought we would plan the wedding for next fall, around September when the weather should still be decent."

Taylor stopped talking to take a breath. She waited and hoped Jorja would see how happy she was. Taylor continued, "I didn't want to tell you yet, Jorja. I just thought you had way too much on your mind right now and once I ask you to be my maid of honor, well, that just means one more to-do list you'll have to make. You will be my maid of honor, won't you?"

Taylor could not conceal the look of fear that crossed her face as she anticipated the possibility Jorja might say no. Jorja saw the look and realized it was not even remotely possible for her to deny her friend anything as important as this. "Of course, Taylor, I would love to be your maid of honor."

Jorja stood to give Taylor a hug. "I am happy for you, Taylor. I'm here for you and I'll help you all the way."

Taylor stood to accept Jorja's hug. "Thanks, Jorja. You mean everything to me and I would never want to get married without you. I won't make the same mistakes my parents made, don't worry. This feels right and I know Dylan will make me happy."

Jorja stepped back and gazed in Taylor's eyes. What she saw was true happiness. "Well, if you say it feels right, then there's nothing for me to do but begin my to-do lists, right after I meet with Sandra, that is."

CHAPTER 37

Jorja arrived at the salon just minutes after the doors were opened for business. She spotted Sandra standing behind the reception desk speaking to one of the young hair stylists. When Sandra saw Jorja walk in, she smiled and held up her finger to indicate she'd just be a minute. Jorja took the time to look over the hair care products the salon showcased on the nearby shelves. She made a mental note about a few she thought might be what her hair could use but not until she was more serious about spending the money.

"Jorja, it's nice to see you. How are you this morning?" Sandra moved around the desk to stand next to Jorja. "Are you interested in some hair care products?"

Jorja shook her head and said, "No, not today, Sandra. I was hoping I could speak to you for a minute or two."

"Well, sure, do you want to sit here on the couch?" When Jorja hesitated, Sandra said, "Would you like someplace more private? Well, come on back to the break room. If anyone is in there, we'll just kick them out."

Jorja followed Sandra to the back of the salon where they found the break room was free for them to use.

Sandra sat down and motioned for Jorja to do the same. As Jorja took a seat, she thought carefully about how to approach the subject of Sandra's brother.

Sandra carefully folded her hands in front of her on the table and asked, "So, what can I do for you, Jorja?"

"Well, I was hoping I could talk to you about, or ask you a few questions maybe, about my Aunt Gloria."

Sandra gave her a quizzical look and replied, "Well, sure, what would you like to know? I didn't know her very well, you know. She was six years younger than your mother and I and we just didn't have anything in common with her when we were in school. She was still in middle school when we both graduated and moved on with our lives."

Jorja nodded politely and said, "Yes, I know you probably didn't get to know her very well because of the age difference. How about after she came home, did you get to know her very well then?"

Sandra shook her head and said, "No, she pretty much kept to herself. She stayed at that house and didn't seem to venture out much unless your mother came down to take her shopping or out to lunch. She never made an effort to make contact with me and because we really didn't have any history with each other, I didn't bother to make contact with her. Why do you ask?"

Jorja thought for a moment and then said, "I'm just curious about the friends my aunt might have had, whether in school or after she returned home from the hospital. Do you know who her friends were in school?"

Sandra's forehead creased as she listened to Jorja's question. "Well, no, I don't know who her friends were. Like I said, she was still in middle school when I graduated and left for college. I don't know who her friends might have been when she was in high school either. You should ask your mother that question; although she had also left for college I'm sure she must have had contact with Gloria about school and friends."

Jorja glanced towards the door as a hair stylist quickly walked down the hall. She then turned back to Sandra and said, "I did ask her and she didn't know. She said that she and Gloria really weren't that close. Mom said they never really discussed their personal lives before Gloria was sent away, while Gloria was at the hospital or when Gloria came back home."

"Hmm, well, I don't know what to tell you, Jorja. Why are you interested in the friends she had?"

"I'm just curious. Do you know if, well, whether or not Gloria and your brother were friends?" Jorja held her breath as she watched

Sandra's expression.

Sandra offered Jorja a raised brow before she spoke. "Jim? Gloria and Jim? Well, now, I don't know about that. Jim was four years younger than me and two years older than Gloria so I guess they were in high school for a couple of years together. Whether they were friends? I never got that impression."

"But you weren't here while Jim finished high school, correct? Do you think it is possible that they were friends? Did he ever mention her to you?"

Sandra accidentally snorted as she attempted to hold back a laugh. "Oh dear! Sorry about that. Did Jim tell me anything? No, I have to say my brother and I were not close enough to discuss friendships with each other. He was an arrogant sort during his high school years and I only saw him when I came home for the holidays or summer break. From what I heard from my parents, he kept them hopping with the trouble he seemed to get himself in to. That's why I was so surprised when they told me he was going into law enforcement. I was always worried that the money he knew the two of us would be inheriting from our grandparents' trust made him believe he had a free ride but I guess he finally grew up and realized he couldn't act juvenile all his life."

Jorja considered what Sandra told her. It was unfortunate that both her mother and Sandra did not have a close relationship with their siblings to offer her any useful information. She wasn't sure exactly how she could determine Jim's relationship with Gloria without asking him herself. She still did not think that option was a good one.

"Jorja, why do you need to know about Gloria's past friendships? Is there a reason?"

Jorja wasn't sure how much she should say. She finally decided she would have to trust Sandra. "Yes, there is a reason. It would appear he visited with my aunt while she was at the hospital. I don't know if they had a relationship while in school but it appears they did have some type of friendship while she was at the hospital. If they continued their friendship after she was released, it appears to me they somehow kept it a secret from you and from my mother."

Sandra gave her a bewildered look as she asked, "He visited her at the hospital? Was it often or just one time?"

"It was more than once and over the space of about two years just before she was released. He also gave her a gift while she was at the hospital. I would think they continued their friendship after she came home but I really don't know if they did. When did he stop working here for the city, do you remember?"

Sandra looked down at her hands as she tried to remember back. "Well, let's see...where was he when Gloria came home? Hmm, I'm not really sure, Jorja. I think he might have worked here for another year or two before he transferred to his current department but you'd have to ask him yourself."

Jorja tried to hide her look of reluctance but Sandra caught on. "What's the matter, dear? Is there a reason you don't want to speak to Jim about this?"

Jorja shut her eyes and again thought about how much she should confide in Sandra. She opened her eyes and looked at Sandra again before saying, "Honestly, no, I'm not sure I want to speak to Jim about this although it appears he is the only one who can answer the questions I have."

Sandra quickly glanced at the watch on her wrist and said, "Oh, Jorja, I'm sorry. It's about time for my first client to arrive and I have a few more things to do to prepare. I hate to cut you short but maybe you should speak to Jim if you really want to know about his relationship with Gloria."

Sandra stood up and waited for Jorja to get up from the chair. Sandra's eyes suddenly widened and she let out a quick breath as she said, "Oh! Jorja, you don't actually think Jim might be the *father* of the baby your aunt had been carrying, do you?"

Jorja forgot Sandra was one of the few people who knew her aunt had been pregnant. Her mother had told Sandra about the pregnancy but had let Sandra believe the baby had been adopted out.

"I'm not saying that, Sandra. Mom said Gloria never told her, or I guess anyone, who the father was. I have no reason to believe it is Jim."

"But you mentioned he gave her a gift? What kind of gift? Something a friend might give to another friend or a boyfriend would give to a girlfriend?"

Jorja decided not to tell Sandra about the locket. She just wasn't sure if Sandra could keep it to herself. "It was nothing, really. I just thought that because he visited her and gave her a gift that they may have been friends. It's really nothing, Sandra. I just wanted to understand my aunt better but it doesn't appear anyone really knew her that well. Can you keep this to yourself? There's really no reason to talk to Jim about it."

Sandra looked undecided. "Well...sure, I guess. But Jim might be able to tell you a few things about your aunt. It wouldn't hurt to ask, would it?"

Jorja quickly shook her head and said, "No, Sandra, really. It was too long ago and it's not really necessary. Just forget I asked, okay?"

"Well, all right dear, if you say so, I'll respect your wishes. I should get going so I can prepare for my client."

"Oh, sure, I didn't mean to hold you up." Jorja stood to leave the break room but as she walked through the doorway to enter the hall, she collided with Lydia.

"Jeez, Jorja! Watch where you're going!" Lydia gave her an angry look but as Jorja made eye contact with her, Lydia quickly looked away. Jorja had a terrible feeling Lydia had been standing outside the doorway listening in on her conversation with Sandra.

"Sorry, Lydia, I didn't expect you to be standing here."

Lydia attempted to give Jorja a look of indignation. "I wasn't just *standing* here. I was on my way to the bathroom! Now, excuse me. I need to get back to work."

Jorja remained silent as Lydia walked away. Sandra stood closer to Jorja and whispered, "Is there any reason the two of you don't get along?"

Jorja could only shake her head as she said, "It's just old history, Sandra. We really didn't get along in high school and I guess nothing has changed since then."

"Well, I'm sure the two of you can mend fences if you just try. She's a pistol but she's a good person and I think the two of you might make good friends if you just try."

As they walked down the hall Jorja replied, "Just try, huh? Well, Sandra, it would take both of us having to try and I don't get the impression Lydia is really up to the chore."

CHAPTER 38

Jorja had been working on the computer all afternoon and she was beginning to feel another headache come on. She looked at the time and realized there was no possible way she could finish out the day without fending off the worsening pain the headache would soon cause.

Digging through her purse she found the pill box where she kept extra Ibuprofen on hand. She selected two pills and swallowed them with a drink of water from her water bottle.

Ouch!

Pain shot through her head and Jorja realized the headache was much worse than she thought. Jorja knew the pills might not do any good at this point. She sat back in her chair and closed her eyes as she rested while waiting for the Ibuprofen to take effect. Soon she felt more sharp pains and then she groaned as she felt the first stirrings of nausea.

Oh, great! I'm either coming down with something or I'm working on a migraine!

She decided it was pointless to stay at the bookstore where she would be useless. It was time to go home.

After grabbing her purse and jacket, she slowly moved down the stairs to find Taylor speaking to a customer. Jorja waited until the customer left and then told Taylor she needed to go home.

"Are you sure you're okay to drive? I can take you home if you'd like. Kat can take care of the store until I get back."

Jorja shook her head. "No, I'm fine. I just need to go home and lay down for awhile. If I feel better after an hour or two, I'll come back to help you close up."

"Jorja, don't worry about coming back. Just go home and rest, okay?"

Jorja thanked Taylor and left the store. She soon regretted not taking Taylor up on the offer for a ride when she realized her eyes were very sensitive to the street and traffic lights. After driving home as carefully but as quickly as she could, she parked her jeep in the driveway. She then grabbed her purse and jacket, hurried out of the jeep and moved towards the front door. As she unlocked the front door and stepped inside the house, she envisioned climbing into bed and pulling the blankets over her head. Hitting the wall switch to turn on the hall light, Jorja immediately shielded her eyes from the brightness and reached over to turn on the hall lamp before turning off the overhead light. She then set her purse and jacket on the hall bench and kicked off her shoes.

"Piper?"

She waited but did not hear Piper's happy gait that usually accompanied her rush to greet Jorja.

"Piper…I'm home!"

Jorja walked down the hall into the kitchen. She decided to forego the kitchen light and turned on the overhead oven light instead. It wasn't as bright to her eyes but it still hurt. She knew she needed to lay down soon in order to sleep off the impending migraine.

She grabbed a glass and filled it with cold water from the fridge before heading to the sliding glass door in search of Piper. Opening the slider, Jorja turned on the patio light and again called out for Piper.

"Piper, here girl! Where the heck are you?"

She began to feel concerned. Piper was always so happy to have her home. Not even a new toy or a bone would keep her from saying hello. Since the patio light did not light up the whole yard, Jorja tried to focus on any movement. Seeing and hearing none, she decided she better get a flashlight and head outside to see what Piper might be up to. She hoped Piper hadn't figured out a way under the fence. She didn't like the thought of Piper running around the neighborhood where she could get lost, taken or, God forbid, struck by a car again.

Turning from the slider, she quickly opened a nearby drawer and reached inside for the flashlight. But as Jorja backed away from the drawer with the flashlight in her hand, she heard a noise.

"Piper?"

She waited but heard nothing more. The hairs on the back of her neck suddenly tingled as she began to feel a fear she could not quite understand. All her senses were on high alert as she felt something was not quite right.

She wanted to call out Piper's name again but was afraid due to the unexplained fear. Jorja tried to push down the fear by making another attempt but as she did, her voice cracked and she was only able to get out a whisper. Silently she closed the drawer, turned on the flashlight and took a few steps towards the kitchen table before hesitating. She wasn't sure where to go from here. As she began to wonder whether she really had heard a noise, she strained to listen, hearing nothing.

Maybe it was my imagination. Maybe it's Piper. Maybe it's Bella.

Well, shoot! That's it. It's the damn cat!

Jorja felt a rush of relief. Bella was supposed to stay in Taylor's room upstairs but she must have found a way out.

"Bella? Here kitty, kitty, kitty." Jorja called for the cat as she rounded the kitchen table to enter the family room. As she again wondered why Piper had not yet come to say hello, she bent over to turn on a side lamp but before she could turn on the lamp, she heard another noise.

Jorja froze.

This time it sounded like a piece of furniture scraping against the wood floor.

Holding the flashlight in one hand, she covered her mouth with the other in an attempt to stifle any sound she might make.

I need to get out of here!

She quickly thought about how she should attempt to call 911. Should she call from the house phone where the call could be traced to her address? Or should she grab her purse and run out the door where she could use her cell phone from a safe distance? Deciding to grab her cell phone and run outside, Jorja waited and listened again for any other noise. Not hearing anything, she tried to step quietly through the family room towards the hallway near the front door. Her steps sounded like firecrackers as the boards beneath her feet cracked and groaned beneath her weight. She held her breath as she continued to walk towards the hallway, trying her best to curb the urge to run for the front door at full speed. Reaching the entryway, Jorja was relieved she had decided to leave on the hall lamp as she slowly peeked around the door frame towards the stairs and the hall leading back towards the kitchen. Seeing nothing, she stepped into the hallway and bent over to reach for her purse on the bench.

As she grabbed the bag she straightened to turn towards the front door but after taking just one step she felt a presence behind her. She quickly turned, catching only a glimpse of a man before she felt something hit the side of her head and everything suddenly went black.

CHAPTER 39

Ryan made his decision. He wanted to stay in town and let Nicholas get to know Jorja and her family. He stopped by the bookstore to speak to her but Taylor informed him Jorja had gone home due to a headache. Ryan knew he should let her rest but he did not want to put off telling her now that he had made his decision.

As he parked his rental vehicle across the street from Jorja's house, he thought about how she would react to his decision. He opened the door and stepped out of the vehicle, watching the house for any signs of movement. Not seeing any as he walked slowly towards the house, Ryan also noticed most of the house was dark except for a light coming through the door window from the hallway. His gait slowed even more as he had second thoughts about bothering Jorja if she wasn't feeling well.

If I'm going to be her brother, I may as well act like it. He quickened his gait as he decided only a best friend and a sibling could get away with intruding on someone's space, even if they did not feel well.

Ryan walked up the stairs on to the porch and then to the front door but as he was about to knock, he heard an odd noise from inside the house.

What was that? He stood still, wondering about the noise. *It sounded like a thump.*

Ryan strained to listen and could hear something but it was not a noise he could immediately identify. Backing away from the door, he began to feel the stirrings of unease. He then moved silently from the front door to the family room window. Peering through a small slit between the window coverings, he could faintly see the family room furniture but nothing more. Moving the angle of his head in an attempt to look past the family room into the hallway, he still saw nothing but as he began to back away from the window, he suddenly caught sight of movement. He moved back into place and positioned himself so he could see towards the hallway again. Ryan's breath caught and he felt panic as he saw stocking feet slowly disappear behind the wall down the hall and towards the kitchen.

Thoughts about what he saw overwhelmed him as he quickly looked back at his car. He knew he should call the police but he had left his cell phone behind in the car. Ryan's fear for Jorja increased as he thought of what might happen to her if he took time to go back to his vehicle for his phone.

If she wasn't already dead, he reluctantly thought.

Ryan silently slipped down the steps off the porch and wound his way towards the back yard. As he slipped through the back fence gate, he wondered where Piper might be and worried she might bark at him, giving the alarm to whoever was inside the house. He was relieved when he was able to enter the back yard without Piper making his presence known.

Crouching low, he slowly crept towards the back door but after only a few steps, his foot brushed against something. Not able to clearly see what his foot struck, he knelt closer to the ground to feel for the item. Just as quickly, Ryan pulled his hand back as he felt soft fur. He warily reached his hand out again and was dismayed with the realization he had found Piper. As he laid his hand on Piper's side he discovered she was warm to the touch. Feeling hopeful, he kept his hand on her side as he placed his face near her muzzle, feeling relief as he heard her breathing, although faintly. Whispering in her ear, he said, "It's okay, Piper. I'm here. You're going to be okay."

Ryan moved around Piper towards the back door. He reached the door and as he grabbed the door knob, he spotted a crowbar on the ground. Not having any type of weapon on him, his only thought was that it would have to do. He grabbed the crowbar before silently opening the back door, quickly realizing the door had been forced open. As he crept into the laundry room and peered through the door frame into the dining room, he saw the shadow of what appeared to be a man.

He did not see Jorja. He could feel fear threaten to take over but he pushed the fear back, letting his need to help Jorja surpass his fear.

The man's shadow was distorted but once Ryan's eyes adjusted to the dim light, he realized it was because the man was bending over. He could only guess that the man was looking down at Jorja and he was struck with dread as he thought the man might mortally harm her. His fear for Jorja made him take action. He quickly sprinted towards the man with the crowbar raised above his head and before the man could turn to defend himself, Ryan struck him with the crowbar. The crowbar glanced against the back of the man's head and shoulder as Ryan heard a sickening thud. Ryan then heard the man grunt in pain as he placed a hand over the back of his head and turned towards Ryan. Ryan's fear turned to shock when he realized the man was the officer he had met at Jorja's Halloween party.

Ryan took a step back, confused about what had just happened.

"Officer...Cooper? What are you doing here?"

Officer Cooper kept his hand pressed to the back of his head. He took a few seconds before responding to Ryan's question. "I'm responding to a call from this residence because there was an intruder in the house."

Ryan thought back to what he saw…feet disappearing down the hall. Why would Officer Cooper move Jorja?

"Where is the intruder? Did you catch him?" Ryan glanced behind Officer Cooper and saw Jorja lying on the floor. "Is Jorja all right?"

Officer Cooper shook his head. "No, by the time I got here, I found her unconscious on the floor and the suspect had already fled the scene. She has a nasty bump on the head." He brought his hand down to look at it and saw blood on his palm. "Look, I need to call the medics, for her and for me. Do you mind?"

Ryan warily watched Officer Cooper and listened as the call for medical assistance was made.

"You can put down the crowbar now. I understand you didn't realize who I was and you were just defending Jorja. I'm not going to charge you with an assault."

Ryan slowly lowered the crowbar down to his side but he did not set it on the floor. He remained where he was as he stared silently at Officer Cooper.

"Did you hear me? I told you to set the crowbar down."

Officer Cooper reached over in an attempt to take the crowbar but Ryan took a step backwards and slightly raised the crowbar. Officer Cooper backed up as he laid his hand on top of the gun resting at his side.

"Put down the crowbar before I decide to take out this weapon and use it. Do you understand?"

Ryan's mind was in overdrive as he attempted to decipher all the thoughts running through his head. He could not release the urgent need to again strike at Cooper. He could not understand the need except that he believed he was staring at pure evil.

"Did you find her in here or did you move her in here?" Ryan asked.

"What the hell are you talking about? I *found* her here where the suspect left her. I'm not going to tell you again...but down the weapon, now!"

Officer Cooper released his gun from the holster, raised it and pointed it at Ryan. Officer Cooper spoke through clenched teeth as he said, "Put the crowbar down. This is your last warning."

Ryan feared for his safety regardless of whether he held on to the crowbar or released it as instructed. He finally realized he had no choice and slowly lowered the crowbar to the floor.

As Ryan straightened, Officer Cooper said, "That's a good boy. Now, tell me how you know Jorja? You were tight-lipped when I asked you questions at the Halloween party."

Ryan did not want to talk about the party. He wanted to understand what was happening.

"I saw Jorja being moved when I looked in the window. Are you telling me you weren't moving her?"

Officer Cooper lowered the gun as he listened to Ryan's question. He appeared to mull over his thoughts and then he said, "I already answered your question. I told you I found her here. However, you have not answered mine so I would appreciate it if you would tell me how you know her."

Ryan thought it was bizarre that Cooper felt the need to have this discussion now. "Well, if you must know, I'm her brother."

Officer Cooper frowned. "Her brother? I didn't know she had a brother."

"You wouldn't. It's not something we've made public yet."

Officer Cooper looked curiously at Ryan. "Where did you come from?"

Why are we having this conversation now? Ryan thought to himself as he tried to understand what was happening. "We only recently met not knowing the other existed until now. We were separated at birth."

Officer Cooper smiled but the smile along with the glint in Cooper's eyes only made Ryan's blood run cold. "You, my man, are a liar. Her brother is dead. So if you've come forward claiming to be her brother, you must have other intentions and you are also not who you say you are. What are you up to? Is there any reason you might want to hurt Jorja?"

Ryan was confused and dumbstruck by the question. "Hurt Jorja? Why would I want to hurt her?"

"Well, that's what the police will try to figure out when they attempt to solve why you used a crowbar to break into the house and then hit her over the head to kill her. I will merely be an unsuspecting witness as a concerned citizen and an off-duty officer on his way home after a long shift. As I drive by the house, I will notice something suspicious which then causes me to investigate."

Ryan felt his breath quicken as he realized Cooper seemed to be formulating a plan as he was speaking.

Officer Cooper continued, "Neither of you will be alive to answer the police department's most dire questions because it will, unfortunately, have become necessary for me to defend myself against the suspect as he came at me with the crowbar in an attempt to also kill me."

Ryan watched in a daze as Officer Cooper raised his weapon and fired the gun. He felt a burning sensation in his chest as he was thrown back from the force and then a burst of pain in his back as he landed squarely on the floor. As he lay on the floor, he began to feel numb as the shock quickly ran through his mind and through his body.

He tried to fight from going unconscious and through blurred eyes filled with tears he looked up to see Cooper standing over him. Ryan could hear contempt in Cooper's voice as he said, "You really thought you could just come in here and play the hero? Well, I'm sorry to say, you're going to be the villain instead."

Ryan had never felt more helpless as he watched Cooper again point the weapon at him. He wasn't sure if his body even moved as he attempted to brace himself for a second impact. As he waited for the sound of the gun to go off, he heard a slight shuffle and saw Cooper turn slightly to look behind him. Ryan then heard a loud impact as glass broke and a low grunt expelled from Cooper. Before Ryan could understand what was happening, Officer Cooper's body was suddenly falling towards him.

~ ~ ~

Jorja fought to work her way out of what felt like the deepest sleep she had ever experienced. As she did, she felt the pain in her head and thought she was still working against the migraine. She felt sick. She then realized she was not in her soft warm bed but instead on a cold hard surface. She lay still and waited for the nausea to pass. As she fought off the nausea, it dawned on her that she was in her kitchen...on the floor...and she heard a voice; no...two voices, both she felt she could recognize. *Who was in her house?* Her head felt fuzzy and she had a hard time making sense of what was going on. *Had she fallen and hit her head?* She felt nauseas once again and waited for it to pass as she listened to the words she could seem to only partly make sense of.

"Hurt Jorja? Why would I want to hurt her?"

Jorja closed her eyes as the pain again took over but she thought to herself, *Ryan, why is he here?*

She then heard the second voice and she felt as if her head might explode as she did her best to match the voice with a name.

"Well, that's what the police will try to figure out…"

Jorja desperately attempted to stop the darkness from taking over but she began to feel herself slip away. She struggled to resist and as she did, it felt like she was clawing her way out of a long, dark tunnel. *She had to get out! She had to get out of the darkness!* She heard the voices again and focused on them in her attempt to stay conscious as she attempted to move her body.

She then heard the second voice say, "As I drive by the house, I will notice something suspicious which then causes me to investigate. Neither of you will be alive to answer the police department's most dire questions because it will, unfortunately, have become necessary for me to defend myself against the suspect as he came at me with the crowbar in an attempt to also kill me."

Jorja felt a sudden shock run through her body as an explosion rocked the kitchen. She almost blacked out again but was able to remain conscious as she tried to make sense of what had just happened. She sat up. *Oh God help me!* Jorja felt the full force of her nausea as the pain in her head multiplied when she sat up. Again she had to use all her strength to stop herself from blacking out.

She slowly turned her head to look toward the source of the voices and as she focused she saw a man standing over the body of another man. *Where was Ryan? Which one was Ryan?* Jorja wanted to scream out her frustration but even with the pain, nausea and uncertainty of her circumstances, she felt in her bones the need to stay quiet out of self preservation.

Slowly she stood up, using the kitchen counter to help steady herself and to keep from falling. She knew someone was at risk, whether it was Ryan or not, she did not yet know, but she felt the need to help whoever was lying on the floor. She slowly and silently walked up behind the man standing with his back to her. She then heard him say, "You really thought you could just come in here and play the hero? Well, I'm sorry to say, you're going to be the villain instead."

Though her thoughts were hazy Jorja knew she had to do something. She grabbed the first item she could reach, the coffee carafe, and as she removed it from the coffee maker and moved towards the figure, he turned around to look at her. She instantly recognized Jim Cooper and had second thoughts about using the carafe until the look in his eyes told her all she needed to know. She quickly brought the carafe down against his head, causing him to grunt as he let out a breath and then his legs went out from under him as he fell with a thud on top of Ryan.

Jorja tried to move towards the men but in her attempt to do so, she swayed, felt the blackness take hold and was unconscious again before she hit the floor.

CHAPTER 40

Taylor noticed the house was fairly dark when she arrived home so she quickly assumed Jorja was laying down upstairs. She wondered if Ryan even bothered to stop by or just decided to wait until Jorja felt better

As Taylor entered the front door, she wasn't surprised when Piper did not greet her and demand attention because she knew Piper was probably upstairs with Jorja. Taylor moved through the hallway towards the kitchen but soon paused as she noticed the rug in the hallway. The rug was not in its original position and instead was rumpled close to the entry of the kitchen. Taylor knew how much of a neat freak Jorja was. Jorja would not have walked by the rug without returning it to its original location, regardless of how sick she might feel.

Taylor took off her jacket and laid it over Jorja's jacket on the bench. She then moved the rug back into place. As she made sure the rug was where Jorja would want it, Taylor heard what sounded like a moan.

"Jorja?" Taylor quickly looked up the staircase. She heard another moan and realized the sound wasn't coming from upstairs but from the kitchen. She moved towards the kitchen where the stove light offered her a dim view of an empty kitchen.

What the heck? Where is she?

Taylor heard the moan again and was startled as the noise came from the dining room to her left. Taylor could see dark objects on the floor and quickly realized they were bodies. As she attempted to push down the fear in her gut, Taylor reached towards the wall to flick on the overhead light.

"Jorja!" Taylor shrieked as she ran towards Jorja on the dining room floor. "Oh my God, Jorja, are you okay?"

Jorja moaned again but slowly raised her hand to her forehead. Taylor put her arm under Jorja's neck and carefully placed her knee under Jorja's head. Taylor felt something sticky and pulled her hand away from Jorja's head to reveal her palm covered in blood.

Taylor began to weep as she cried out, "Jorja! Please talk to me. Can you hear me?"

As she waited for Jorja to answer, Taylor quickly glanced over at what she now realized were two more bodies on the floor. One on top of the other so that she could not see the face of either but she could tell the male on top appeared to be wearing a police uniform.

What the hell happened here?

"Jorja! Answer me, please!"

Jorja moaned again, slightly opened her mouth as if to speak but made a whimpering noise instead.

"Okay, Jorja. Hold on. I'm going to lay your head back on the floor. I need to call the medics. Hang on!"

Taylor gently placed Jorja's head back on the floor and then swiftly got up. She grabbed the house phone from the charger and as she dialed 911 she raced around the corner into the family room where she grabbed a pillow off the couch.

"911 what is your emergency?"

"Help! Please send medics here as soon as possible! Something has happened to my friend and there are two other men here who also appear to be hurt...or dead, I'm not sure. It looks like one of them is a cop! Please send someone here quickly!"

Taylor held the phone against her shoulder as she moved back into the dining room and knelt down to place the pillow under Jorja's head. She verified the address with the dispatch operator and then was mildly concerned when she was not able to confirm for the operator whether or not a suspect was still in the residence.

"I don't know...I don't know what happened or if the suspect is gone or not. I can't leave my friend though. Can you please send someone right away?"

"Miss, I have already dispatched the call and police and medics are on their way. I would like you to stay on the line with me until they arrive. I would prefer you remove yourself from the scene for your own safety..."

Taylor was quick to reply, "No! I can't leave my friend."

The operator continued, "...but if you are not willing to leave, please stay on the line and let me know when you're sure the officers have arrived. The medics will not enter the house until the police can verify the scene is clear. Do you understand?"

Taylor told the operator she understood as she kept the phone wedged between her shoulder and ear while she slowly stroked Jorja's hair and quietly wept. Jorja was not responding to anything she did and it was scaring Taylor to death.

"Please, Jorja. Please be okay." Taylor whispered as she continued to stroke Jorja's hair.

After what seemed like a very long time but was probably only minutes, Taylor finally heard the faint sound of a siren. "Oh! I hear a siren. I think they are here!" Taylor told the operator.

"Stay·on the line with me until an officer is inside the house, okay?" Taylor agreed and it wasn't long before she heard an officer enter the house and begin shouting. "Police! Please respond so I can locate you!"

"In here! We're in the dining room!" Taylor shouted.

An officer came around the corner and Taylor had never felt more relieved. "Here, my friend is hurt! Can you help her?"

The officer looked around the kitchen and dining room, at Jorja and at the two men lying on the floor. "Do you know if anyone else is in the house?"

Taylor shook her head. "I don't. I just came home and found them in here. I haven't been anywhere else in the house."

The officer withdrew his weapon and sternly looked at her. "You stay here. Don't go anywhere. My partner and I are going to check the rest of the house and once it's clear we will let the medics inside."

Taylor could only nod her head as she watched the officer leave her. She felt distress at seeing Jorja's chance for help leaving the room but she waited and listened while the police searched the house. She heard them as they walked through the house and then upstairs, going through each room as they moved up to Taylor's bedroom on the third floor. She hadn't realized she was holding her breath until she let loose the air from her lungs when she heard the officers' footsteps coming back down the staircase.

The first officer returned to the kitchen and said, "Okay, miss, we've checked the house and it's clear. My partner has gone out to inform the medics they can enter."

Taylor heard some commotion at the front door as medics and the second officer hurried into the house and to the dining room.

"Miss? Can you get up and let the medics look at your friend?" The officer moved closer to Taylor and held down a hand to help her up. She looked up at him and then back down at Jorja. She bent her head down next to Jorja's and whispered into her ear. "It's okay, Jorja, I'll be right here while the medics take care of you." Taylor then sat up and hesitantly raised her hand to accept the officer's offer of help. As he pulled her up off the floor, she almost collapsed as her knees buckled in pain. Only then did Taylor realize her calves had fallen asleep from sitting on the floor for so long.

"Hey, it's okay, I've got you," the officer said as he grabbed her around the waist. He used his strength to hold Taylor up as he moved her away from where Jorja was lying. Taylor did not like feeling so helpless. Once she began to feel strength in her legs again, she quickly made it known she no longer needed the help.

"I'm okay. I can stand." Taylor looked over at the medics who seemed so frantic in their attempts to help Jorja and the other two men. The room wasn't large enough for all the confusion and chaos she was watching. A medic worked with Jorja while three others separated the two men and began working on them. Taylor could not tell if either of them was alive or dead.

"Miss? Can you tell me your name?" Taylor looked back at the officer, who was now holding a small notepad and pencil, waiting for her to respond.

"Uh, my name is Taylor...Taylor Bishop."

"And did you see what happened here? How did your friend get hurt? What about the two men over there, one of which is an officer...do you know who he is?"

Taylor felt tears slide down her cheeks. She felt helpless because she could not make sense of anything that had happened.

"No, I don't know what happened. When I got home I found them all like this." Taylor looked again at the medics who were now helping the two men. She edged closer to get a look and was shocked when she realized the officer was Jim Cooper and the other was Ryan. Her emotions played out on her face as the officer watched her.

"Do you recognize them?"

Taylor nodded and she tried to keep her composure as a knot of fear tightened her gut. "Yes. The officer is Jim Cooper and the other man is Ryan...uh, I can't remember his last name. He is Jorja's brother. Or, long lost brother, that is. They just recently met. He told me he was going to stop by to speak to Jorja when I told him she went home with a headache. I don't know why Jim would be here." *Did Jorja actually ask Jim here to talk about the necklace?* Taylor quickly ran various scenarios through her head as she wondered whether Jorja had accused him. She was hesitant to mention to the officer that Jorja believed Jim could have been involved in Vera's death. What cop would believe another cop would do anything like that?

The officer scribbled notes down in his notebook and then he called over to his partner. "Hey, Fritz, the officer is Jim Cooper. You want to call the county to assist us on this one?"

"I'm on it." Fritz said as he walked down the hall and out the front door.

"Okay, Ms. Bishop, I may need to speak to you again later but I'll contact you and let you know if that will be necessary. Here's my card. My name is Officer Reynolds. My number is here in case you think of anything that might be important. I'm going to check on a few more things right now. Can you stay out of the way while the medics get your friend and the others out to the ambulances?"

Taylor numbly nodded her head. She did not want to stay away but she would stay back an agreeable distance. Taylor watched as the officer walked away and then she turned her attention back to Jorja. The medics had placed a brace around Jorja's neck and had finished checking her vitals. She watched as they carefully placed Jorja on a gurney and maneuvered their way around the corners and furniture as they wheeled Jorja out of the house. Taylor was about to follow but moved just a bit closer to see what the medics were doing with Ryan and Jim. She was shocked at all the blood she saw on the floor. Jorja had bled quite a bit but it appeared Ryan had bled more than a human possibly could.

"I'm feeling fine! Let me up!" Taylor was shocked at the outburst and realized the words came from Jim Cooper, who had sat up and was attempting to stand. The medics were asking him to remain on the floor and to stay calm but Jim was listening to none of their advice.

"I will go to the hospital later. Just leave me be! Right now I need to make sure the suspect is under control." Jim was yelling at the medics as he stood and almost lost his balance. "Get away from me!"

Taylor was struck by what Jim said. The suspect? Was he talking about Ryan or Jorja? Was he setting Jorja up? Or Ryan? Taylor didn't know Ryan well enough yet but she had a hard time believing Ryan would have attacked Jorja.

As Jim was ranting at the medics, demanding that they let him speak to the officers on scene, Taylor decided to go outside to check on Jorja before she was taken by ambulance to the hospital. She rushed out of the house and ran down the steps, spotting the gurney with Jorja on it inside one of the ambulances. Taylor ran up to the open back door of the ambulance and spoke to the medic inside. "Is she going to be okay?"

The medic did not look at her as he responded, "She's taken a nasty hit to the head but we'll do our best for her. She was just mumbling a few words here a minute ago so she is finally coming around."

Taylor didn't hesitate. She jumped up into the ambulance without asking permission and looked down at Jorja on the gurney. The medic looked at Taylor in surprise as she asked, "She was talking? What did she say?"

"Well, it didn't make much sense, really. She's been hit pretty hard. She might have no idea what she's saying."

Taylor inched closer towards the medic and towards Jorja's head. Although the medic looked irritated, Taylor did not give him time to tell her to leave. "Can I just try to talk to her for a minute before you leave? Please?" Taylor pleaded when she saw the medic might refuse.

Finally, the medic gave in. "Okay, but just for a minute while I finish getting ready for transport. Stay out of my way if you can."

Taylor offered the medic a bright smile as she moved closer to Jorja and bent towards her head. Grabbing Jorja's hand, Taylor asked, "Jorja? Can you hear me? It's Taylor. Jorja? Can you tell me what happened?"

Taylor waited but Jorja did not respond. Taylor hung her head slightly as she gave a quick prayer, asking for her friend to be okay. Taylor suddenly felt very scared at the thought of what could have happened and how she might have lost Jorja tonight. Even worse was the thought of losing Jorja while having no idea why. Taylor gritted her teeth. *It would not end this way!*

"Jorja! Can you hear me? Please, *please* wake up and talk to me!"

Taylor could feel the medic's impatience and she quickly gave him a pleading look. Her eyes widened and she felt a slight shock as Jorja's hand suddenly squeezed her own. Taylor quickly turned her head to look at Jorja again and she was overwhelmingly relieved to see Jorja looking up at her.

"Oh my God! Jorja! Can you hear me? Can you talk?"

Jorja opened her mouth in an attempt to speak. Taylor lowered her head closer and waited. She finally heard Jorja say, "Jim...shot...Ryan."

Taylor leaned back to look at Jorja. "Jim shot Ryan? But why? What did he do?"

Taylor bent over again to hear Jorja's response. "Jim said...Ryan was the villain. He said...he had to defend himself because...Ryan tried to kill me."

Taylor sat back again. She was stunned. "What do you mean? *Did* Ryan try to kill you?"

A tear slipped down Jorja's cheek. Jorja gathered a bit more strength and was able to speak more clearly. "I don't know who...hit me. I don't know why Ryan was there or why...Jim was there. I had to hit Jim. He looked so crazy...he was going to shoot Ryan when he...was helpless on the floor." Jorja let out a moan as pain suddenly struck her. "Oh, it hurts!"

The medic quickly moved to stand next to Taylor and he forcibly said, "All right, that's enough. We are ready to transport her to the hospital. You need to leave so we can move out. You can follow in your own vehicle, okay?"

Taylor quickly bent over and gave Jorja a kiss on the forehead. "I'll see you at the hospital, Jorja." Jorja kept her eyes closed and only slightly nodded to show she heard Taylor's words.

Taylor climbed out and watched as the doors were closed and the ambulance disappeared down the street. She heard more commotion and turned to see Ryan on a gurney as he was being placed into a second ambulance. She desperately wished she could speak to him but the officers were standing around Ryan's ambulance as they listened to Jim explain what happened inside the house. Taylor tried to pretend she wasn't listening but she heard Jim as he said, "He attacked the resident and then he attacked me and I had to defend myself. Check out the crowbar inside the house. It has his fingerprints on it!"

Taylor hadn't noticed Officer Fritz until he jumped out of the ambulance. She was immediately curious about the look she saw on Fritz's face. She did her best to get closer without being noticed and could hear Fritz say to Jim, "Officer Cooper, can you tell us how you happened to come to this residence?"

Jim quieted down and turned towards Fritz. "I was on my way home after my shift and I saw something suspicious. I knew the resident and thought I should check it out. When I looked inside the window I saw Jorja on the floor and I knew I had to get in quickly to help her. I did not see the suspect as he approached me from behind while I was attempting to determine whether Jorja was all right. Then, as you can clearly see, I had to use my weapon in defense of myself and Jorja."

Fritz appeared to listen intently to what Jim had to say. "Okay, so how did you see Jorja on the floor? Through which window?"

Jim opened his mouth to answer. Then he closed it and narrowed his eyes at Fritz. "What the hell are you asking me questions for? Have you arrested the suspect? Is he in custody?"

Fritz held up a hand as Reynolds gave him a questioning look. Fritz then answered Jim's question. "He's not going anywhere, Cooper. That bullet is going to keep him down for awhile. So just help me out here. We need to prepare our reports, you know that. Just tell us what happened."

Jim eyed Fritz, then Reynolds and finally the two county deputies who had arrived as back up.

"Okay, okay. What was your question?"

Fritz waited a fraction of a second and asked again, "What window did you see the resident from? And where was she when you saw her?"

"Oh, well, I saw her from the front...no, I heard a commotion from the front. I then ran around the back and from the slider, uh, no it was from the kitchen window I saw her on the kitchen floor. I then made the decision to enter the house. I did not see the suspect and again, like I said, as I was checking Jorja he snuck up behind me and hit me. There, is that enough so you can fill out your damn report?"

Fritz turned towards Reynolds and motioned for Reynolds to follow him. Taylor watched as the two moved away from Jim and the other officers. She stood where she was, hoping they would not notice her so she could continue to listen to what they had to say. She held her breath as she strained to hear them. She then overheard Fritz as he said to Reynolds, "Look, the witness woke up. He told me that he came to see his sister but before knocking on the door he thought he heard an odd noise. When he looked through the front window he saw what appeared to be his sister's feet disappearing down the hall. He went to the back of the house, found a dog lying in the yard, located the crowbar and went inside the house where he saw Cooper. He said he hit Cooper before realizing who he was. Cooper shot him for no reason, he says, and then as he was on the floor Cooper would have shot him again but something happened. He doesn't know how Cooper ended up on top of him."

Taylor listened and thought about what Jorja had said. Who struck Jorja? Was it Jim? Taylor was terrified to think Jim would be so bold as to attack Jorja.

"Uh, I'm sorry to interrupt but...there may be something you should know." Taylor said to both of the officers, who turned to her first in irritation at her interruption and then in interest at her declaration.

"Yes? Do you know something that might be important?" The officer called Fritz asked her.

"Well, yes, I think I do. But you might not believe me." Taylor held Fritz's gaze as she made the statement.

He narrowed his eyes at her and asked, "Why wouldn't we believe you?"

"Because, I don't think you'll like hearing that one of your own could be capable of doing anything wrong."

Reynolds jumped into the conversation, showing some impatience as he said, "Miss Bishop, if you know something important, tell us what it is. Don't hesitate because you are concerned with what we might think."

Taylor shrugged and replied, "Okay. I think it is possible Ryan is telling the truth. I believe Jim may have harmed Jorja and Ryan was probably trying to help."

"What makes you say that?" Reynolds asked, as he crossed his arms and stood at attention.

Taylor took a breath and began to explain. "My friend, Jorja, has been looking into a case about a woman who disappeared twelve years ago. The woman's body was found in the woods some time ago but she was not identified until recently when Jorja did some research and discovered the body may belong to the missing woman she was trying to find. You'll have to ask Jorja more about that case but anyway, it turned out the woman had a necklace her husband gave to her that was never found when they discovered her body. Jorja believes she discovered the necklace with some items belonging to her aunt, or her mom, well…that's a long story. Anyway, her aunt should not have had the necklace but Jorja found out Jim Cooper visited her aunt while she was in the mental institution."

Both detectives were listening intently but as she finished Fritz raised his brows and Reynolds frowned. Taylor continued, "Really, Jorja can make sense of it but what I'm trying to say is that Jorja discovered Jim gave the necklace to her aunt. He should not have *had* the necklace. How did he get it unless he was the last person to see this woman before she was killed?"

Reynolds stared Taylor down as Fritz took a peek at Cooper, who was chit chatting with the county deputies.

Fritz looked back at Taylor. "Did Cooper know Jorja found the necklace with her aunt's things?"

Taylor shrugged and said, "I'm not sure. Jorja wasn't going to ask Jim about it but she did go speak to Jim's sister. I know she asked Sandra not to discuss it with Jim but I don't think Jorja should have trusted Sandra to keep the secret from Jim. I don't know. You'd have to ask Sandra but it is possible Jim found out from her."

Fritz looked at Reynolds as he said, "That bedroom was all tore up. Like someone was looking for something. What do you think?"

Reynolds turned to look at Cooper and then faced Fritz again as he replied, "All we can do is ask. Come on. Miss, you stay here."

Taylor watched Reynolds and Fritz as they moved towards Cooper and the deputies. Taylor couldn't quite hear well enough so she slowly edged closer to the group. She then heard Jim respond to a question posed by Fritz.

"What do you mean by that? Why does it matter if I went upstairs? I had to check the premises, didn't I?"

Taylor could see Fritz shaking his head. "No, Cooper. You said you looked in the window, saw the victim on the floor and went inside the house where you were attacked by the suspect as you were checking on the victim. You did not mention having any time to view the rest of the house. So, did you go upstairs or not? Will your prints be on any items on the second floor or did you remain downstairs the whole time?"

Although she could not clearly see Jim's face due to the darkness of the hour, Taylor could imagine his face reddening as he stared down the officers while he took his time to respond.

"Look, I don't know where this is going. I had a few minutes to run upstairs to check for the suspect. Seeing no one, I ran back down and was checking on the victim when I was attacked."

Fritz slowly nodded as he continued to keep eye contact with Cooper. "Okay. So did you get a chance to see the condition of the bedroom upstairs?"

Cooper sighed heavily as he replied, "Well, yeah, I saw it was a mess. Looks like someone went through it pretty good. If the suspect is her brother, he must have been looking for something important. Whatever it was, you will have to ask him!"

Taylor could see from Jim's stance and his clenched fists that he was getting even more upset and probably feeling cornered. *Good,* she thought. *If you had anything to do with Vera and for what happened to Jorja, you deserve it!*

Taylor waited to see what was going to happen. It was Reynolds who decided to add to the conversation as he asked, "Did you happen to take anything from the scene? Anything we should be aware of?"

"Why the hell would I take anything? Why are you asking me that?" Cooper's voice became louder as he said, "I've had enough and I'm leaving! You can call me if you have any more *relevant* questions relating to the investigation!"

Cooper attempted to walk away but Reynolds and Fritz both stepped in front of him. Cooper stopped before he slammed into them. He turned around in an attempt to leave only to discover the county deputies were also standing in his way.

"What right do you have to treat me like this? I'm leaving and you can't stop me!"

Fritz held up his hands as if he would surrender to Cooper's request but first he said, "You can leave, Cooper, but before you do just show us what items you have in your pockets."

Cooper straightened his back before turning to look at Fritz. "Why should I show you anything?"

Fritz calmly replied, "You can either show us and leave or you can wait while we get a warrant. It's your call, Cooper. If you have nothing to hide, we can just get this over with. If you need an attorney, we'll work on that for you while we work on the warrant."

Taylor held her breath as she waited for Jim's response. She was fearful he might just reach out and bust Fritz's lip but she couldn't believe he'd be that stupid. Finally, she heard Jim say, "You will not treat me like a common criminal. I want an attorney."

CHAPTER 41

Jorja felt like a whole new person after what she had dealt with the past two weeks. She had remained in the hospital for a week for tests as requested by the emergency room doctor who wanted to eliminate any worries of a brain injury from being struck on the head. During her stay in the hospital, Taylor visited daily to fill her in on the results of the investigation. Jim Cooper had requested an attorney and was taken in for questioning, during which time he was searched and the locket had been found in his possession. Cooper had no good explanation for why he had the locket so the police were trying to piece together exactly what happened with Vera so many years ago and how Cooper obtained the locket in the first place.

Jorja was lying in her own bed at home while Taylor kept busy picking up the room as they discussed the most recent developments.

"So how is it you know all this, Taylor? You have a new friend with the police department?"

Taylor smiled as she said, "I asked Officer Fritz to keep me in the loop if he could. He and I met for coffee a few times and he's been nice enough to fill me in on a few things. He called and said he might stop by today because he has some more information."

Jorja watched Taylor as she attempted to straighten and tidy up the room. "Well, don't clean the house on his account. I'm sure he doesn't care."

Taylor stopped what she was doing, looked at the cloth she'd been dusting with and then with some embarrassment put the cloth in the laundry basket.

"Well, I just figured you wouldn't want your room to be a mess when he got here, that's all. Do you want me to fix your hair for you?"

Jorja raised her hand to her head and felt the back of her head. Her hair did need a good wash but she certainly didn't care to do it now. "No, Taylor, don't worry about my hair. If Officer Fritz saw me that first night, he won't think any worse of me now."

They both started as the doorbell rang. Piper let out a quick bark and ran out of the room. Jorja smiled as she heard Piper flying down the stairs to the front door.

"I'll be right back, Jorja. Do you want me to bring him up here or would you rather try to come downstairs?"

Jorja thought for a moment and said, "You know, I'll just come downstairs. I need to get my energy back and lying in this bed for another week is not going to do it."

"Okay, I'll see you down there." Taylor left the room while Jorja gingerly moved her legs to the side of the bed and slowly stood up. She felt well enough but there were days still when the injury to her head caused her some pain and sudden headaches. The doctor said it would take time and that she just had to be patient.

Before heading downstairs Jorja quickly brushed her hair and pulled it back in a pony tail. She then grabbed her robe and slipped it on as she headed downstairs.

"Jorja! It's good to see you up and around." Officer Fritz exclaimed as she walked into the kitchen. "How are you feeling?"

Jorja grabbed a glass and moved to the fridge where she poured herself some apple juice. "I'm feeling okay, I guess. Still healing and the doc said it'll take some time before I feel one hundred percent again. Taylor has been a big help so I'm fortunate. So…how is your investigation going? Has Jim said anything more or is he going to take this to trial?"

Fritz was sitting at the dining table as he waited for Jorja to pour her juice and sit at the table with him. Taylor stood near the bar as she waited for Fritz to answer Jorja's question.

"Well, yes, Jim has offered more and we've been able to tie up a few things now. Your curiosity about the Mayor's stepdaughter was right on, Jorja. After we searched Jim and found the locket on him and the lab results verified your blood and hair were on his gun from when he struck you, he was ready to talk. Cooper might never have given up the information about the Mayor's step-daughter but I asked the prosecutor to include that case when he negotiated with Cooper. The prosecutor agreed not to request the death penalty as long as Cooper came clean about all three incidents, which he finally did."

Fritz stopped talking for a moment and looked out the sliding glass door where he watched Piper as she playfully chased after a ball. "So how is your dog doing? Is she back to her old self?"

Jorja looked out the window and smiled as she saw Piper playing with the ball. "Yes, she's doing great. The vet said that the poison Jim apparently tried to feed her would have most likely killed her if she hadn't thrown up the meat he gave her. She got enough in her system to knock her out but not completely take her out. I don't know what I'd do if I lost her…she's like a kid to me."

Fritz turned to look at Jorja again. "You know…the ex-Mayor and his wife had been told their daughter committed suicide, something which they never really believed to be true. This has been a blessing to them to finally discover what really happened to her. I called and spoke to them to explain what we discovered and they asked me to give you their thanks and appreciation. I myself appreciate the fact that you were able to help them find full closure and also put to rest their fears that their daughter hurt herself when she did not."

Jorja felt uncomfortable as Fritz continued to stare at her. She finally looked down at her glass and raised it to take a drink. After setting the glass back down she finally said, "It was nothing I did, really. It was just a lucky break but I'm glad they are now at peace in knowing what actually happened to their daughter."

Taylor watched both Jorja and Fritz as they spoke. She wondered if Jorja could sense what she believed to be true; Fritz had more than a passing interest in Jorja. Taylor had to smile as she thought about Brad. If the attention Jorja received from another man did not make him step up and take action, nothing would.

Taylor finally tired of waiting and asked, "So, what else did you find out? What's going to happen to Jim?"

Fritz looked at Taylor and then back to Jorja. "Well, he has agreed to take a plea bargain to avoid the death penalty. Cooper will plead to manslaughter regarding the death of Samantha Tibbetts, murder with regard to the death of Vera Myers, attempted murder of your brother and the assault on you. He got lucky on the charge involving you. I think they should have kept the charge at attempted murder as well. In exchange, he told us what happened and why he killed Vera. I've already discussed the matter with Kathleen so she fully understands why her mother's life ended the way it did."

Taylor moved around the table so she could sit down as Fritz continued to explain what Cooper admitted in order to take the plea bargain.

"So, the way Cooper explains it, Samantha was seeing another young man who her parents approved of but she was also secretly seeing Cooper without her parents' knowledge. Apparently, Cooper and the Mayor did not get along. On the day Samantha died, Cooper and Samantha were fighting when he struck her and the force caused her to fall and strike her head. The blow to her head when she fell was enough to kill her so out of self preservation Cooper came up with the idea of placing her on the tracks. Then, when her body was found, it was Cooper who conveniently ran the investigation and he concluded the case was a suicide. Even if it was an accident as he claims, Cooper has admitted to his part in Samantha's death."

Taylor and Jorja were leaning forward, hanging on his every word. Fritz took a quick sip from the glass of water Taylor had previously given to him.

"So, what about Vera, what did he say about her? What possible reason did he have for killing her?" Jorja asked.

Fritz pursed his lips and then said, "Well, that one was not an accident, I'm afraid. The way Cooper explained it he did not plan it but felt he had no other choice. Apparently the weekend before Samantha was killed, he had an argument with Samantha, it got physical and Cooper didn't realize until it was too late that Vera was delivering something to the neighbor's house next door. Cooper and Samantha had kept their relationship private and it might not have mattered except that within a week Samantha is dead and Cooper recalls the fact that Vera saw him and Samantha fighting. He knew Samantha's body would be found eventually but he wanted it to look like suicide, which it would not if Vera told the police what she saw. The day of Vera's disappearance, Cooper saw Vera when she was running errands and he followed her home. She trusted him enough to allow him into her home where he questioned her in a way that led him to believe she had seen too much. He made up a story about receiving a call that her daughter had been hurt so she would willingly leave the house with him. Sadly, she did not hesitate to leave with him, apparently after grabbing her Bible so she could pray during the drive. He then drove her to a location where he killed her after forcing her to write that note."

"Oh my God. That poor woman!" Taylor said as she held a hand over her mouth. "She did not deserve that! The only reason he killed her was because she had been in the wrong place at the wrong time?"

Fritz nodded. "Yeah, that's pretty much what happened. Many victims become prey for being in the wrong place at the wrong time. I guess we can be thankful her daughter wasn't with her because I honestly can't say for sure what Cooper would have done."

Jorja and Taylor both looked shocked at that thought. Neither could imagine what kind of monster would be capable of killing a child.

Jorja slowly rubbed the back of her head as she felt it begin to ache again. "What about the locket? Why did he take it and why did he give it to my aunt? How did he know I had it? Did his sister tell him?"

"Jorja, do you need something for your head?" Taylor asked as she looked at her friend in concern.

Jorja shook her head. "No, not now. I've had enough pills to last me a lifetime. Officer Fritz? What did Jim say about the locket?"

"Cooper said he didn't mean to keep the locket. He said it got caught on his clothing. He didn't realize it until he had left the location where he abandoned Vera's vehicle with the keys inside, which was someplace up north where he knew the car would be stolen and parted within hours. For whatever reason, he decided to keep the necklace and when I asked him why he gave it to your aunt, he just shrugged and said because they were friends and he wanted to give her a gift."

Jorja thought about her aunt and wondered why Gloria became friends with Jim Cooper. Jorja was also very curious about what the two of them discussed when Jim visited Gloria at the hospital. One thought still caused her anxiety and she hoped to alleviate that anxiety soon.

"But how did he know I had the necklace?" Jorja asked again.

"Oh, well it wasn't his sister. I guess when you were telling his sister about the necklace you didn't realize someone was listening in on your conversation."

Jorja gave him a quizzical look and then with some surprise asked, "Lydia? She was outside the room when we were done. She heard and told Jim?"

Fritz gave a quick nod. "Yep. I guess she thought the two of them were friends or maybe she hoped they were more than friends but she just *happened* to mention to him that you had stopped by to ask about him and a gift he gave to your aunt. That's what caused him to break into your house to find the necklace but when you came home early it changed his plans, leading to where we are now."

Jorja felt overwhelmed now that all the pieces were beginning to fit. Jim accidentally kills Samantha, he feels forced to kill Vera to hide the fact that he killed Samantha and then he attacks her and Ryan after realizing she has the one piece of evidence that could link him to Vera's death. She shook her head as she tried to wrap her brain around how Jim could have lived with the horrible acts he had taken part in. And to think that as an officer he was able to compel an investigation to conclude that a young girl committed suicide when she did not and another investigation to conclude a young mother ran away from her family when in fact she was murdered. Jorja shuddered to think what would have happened if Jim had been able to get away with his plan of trying to frame Ryan for her own death. She felt very grateful her life had been spared and that Ryan had been able to survive the gun shot to his chest and would also soon be released from the hospital.

"So, it's all over then? He'll be sentenced soon?"

Fritz nodded and pushed back his chair as he stood up. "It is almost over, Jorja. You can attend the sentencing, if you wish. You can make a statement to the judge, if you'd like to. Ryan can as well if he's feeling up to it. Just let me know and I'll make sure the prosecutor knows you'll be there."

Jorja lowered her head as she thought about how she would tell him what she really wanted. She could feel Taylor's eyes on her, waiting. Jorja looked at Taylor and caught her gaze. After Taylor gave her a slight nod of encouragement, Jorja said, "I might go to the sentencing but I was wondering if I could see Jim before the sentencing."

"Before? Why?" Fritz frowned at her as he waited for her to reply.

"Well, I just have a few questions for him, that's all. I can't ask him during the sentencing so I was hoping I could go visit him in the jail before he is sentenced. Could you set that up for me?"

"Why do you want to see him, Jorja? What on earth could you possibly need to know from him?"

Jorja turned to Taylor for support and then back to Fritz. "It's just something I need to ask him about my family. Something he and my aunt may have discussed. Please, I can't really explain but I do need to speak to him. Can you agree to set up a meeting for me? Just tell me when and where and I'll be there."

Fritz narrowed his eyes and did not answer her immediately. He saw the pleading in her eyes and appeared to understand he would not be able to force her to explain.

"Okay, I'll see what I can do. You'll have to wait until after he actually signs the plea agreement so we know it's a go and then I'll make the arrangements. I'll have to check with the prosecutor on how he wants to handle this because the State will be asking for a lifetime restraining order between the two of you. I'll contact you as soon as I know when and how it can happen."

Jorja felt relieved. She was also very tired. "Thank you, Officer Fritz. I very much appreciate your help through all this. Now, if you don't mind, I think I need to go back to bed. I'll wait for your call."

As Jorja walked away to head back to her room, she was already thinking ahead to how she would start the conversation with Jim Cooper when they finally met again.

CHAPTER 42

Jorja was more nervous than she thought was possible. She breathed deeply in an attempt to calm her nerves as she rode along with Officer Fritz on their way to the county jail where Jim Cooper was being held. She had waited for this moment but now only two blocks from the jail, she was losing her confidence.

She glanced at Fritz as she asked, "So will I be sitting at a table with him? Or will I be talking to him on a phone with glass between us?"

Fritz watched pedestrians cross in front of them at the crosswalk as he said, "We have both options available to us but the prosecutor wants you to use the booth with glass and the phone. I tend to agree with him. There is no reason for you to be alone in a room with Cooper."

Jorja nodded as she let out a breath. She truly thought she could look Cooper in the eye as they sat at a table together but now that her option had been limited to the booth with glass, she realized it was the option which gave her the most relief.

"Okay, I understand. How much time will I have?"

"You can have up to a half hour. You could probably have more time if you really wanted it but do you really think you'll need more than that?"

Jorja thought for a moment as she wondered whether she would even need ten minutes with Cooper. "No, a half hour should be good. I doubt our conversation will take longer than that."

"Well, I don't understand what it is you think he has to tell you. Why is it so important for you to speak to him?"

Jorja sighed heavily as she stared out the passenger side window. "I just need to ask him something. I really can't explain without going into a lot of detail and right now I'd rather not do that."

Fritz glanced at Jorja, who continued to stare out the window. He finally looked back at the road as he inadvertently shrugged in an attempt to appear indifferent. "Hey, that's okay; you don't have to tell me anything you don't want to."

Jorja turned to give him an appreciative smile before turning back to stare out the window again. They rode in silence as Fritz continued to drive and found a parking spot a short distance from the jail entrance.

Jorja had been inside a jail before but only on the rare occasion she had to deliver or pick something up from the front post reception on behalf of her attorney's clients. This would be her first visit inside the actual jail.

Following Fritz's lead, she entered the lobby area to check in with the front post reception. After receiving badges in order to enter, Jorja locked her purse in a nearby locker before following Fritz to the door leading into the actual jail. Her nerves were on edge as she waited; not knowing exactly what they were waiting for. Finally, Jorja heard a loud buzzing noise before the lock on the door unlatched. Fritz grabbed the large handle, hefted the large metal door open and motioned for Jorja to enter before him.

Jorja and Fritz entered a small room with four doors, one of which was now closing behind them. As the door slammed shut, Fritz pointed at the door directly across from the first as he said, "We're going to enter through this door here. Then we will move down the hall to a door that will open into a small booth."

Jorja nodded but did not respond. She wasn't sure if she could speak without showing the fear bubbling inside her.

"Jorja? Are you okay? Do you still want to do this?"

Jorja looked up at Fritz and saw his concern. She nodded again and finally said, "Yes, I'm fine. I still want to see him."

Fritz gazed at her uncertainly as his hand rested on the door handle. He was about to say something else when they heard the buzzing noise and the loud click as the lock unlatched. Fritz pulled the door open and let Jorja enter the hallway before them. As the door slammed shut behind them, he gently guided her forward until they reached the door to the booth.

Fritz turned the knob and opened the door, revealing a small room with a counter, a phone and one metal stool. Jorja gazed at the stool and then at the glass divider, noting a similar room with a phone and stool on the opposite side.

"You sit on the stool and I'll stand here behind you. They'll be bringing Cooper here in a few minutes."

Jorja sat on the stool and waited while Fritz stood against the wall beside her. Jorja ran thoughts through her mind as to how she would start the conversation with Cooper. Fritz watched her as he wondered if this was a good idea.

Jorja jumped, startled by the noise as the door on the opposite side opened. She looked up to see Cooper as he was directed by a guard to enter the room and sit down. As they made eye contact Jorja tried to hold his gaze but she could not help looking behind him at the guard instead. She could hear the guard speaking to Cooper but she could not make out what was said before he backed out and shut the door, leaving Cooper alone in his half of the booth. She took a deep breath as she again brought her gaze to Cooper.

Jorja felt cold as her thoughts turned to how this man could have killed her after already killing others. He continued to stare at her, making no move to speak.

Glancing at the phone, Jorja reached over to pick up the receiver. She hesitantly placed it against her ear as she again looked Cooper in the eye. Seeing no remorse or fear in his eyes, she began to feel anger at his apparent lack of shame for all the terrible deeds he had committed.

Jorja waited as she stared at Cooper, the anger in her eyes more apparent as he stared back at her. Finally, Cooper reached over, grabbed the receiver and placed it to his ear.

"Hello, Jorja. To what do I owe the pleasure?" Cooper grinned at her and then gave a small laugh.

Her anger rose even further. "You think this is funny? How in God's name can you think this is remotely humorous?"

Cooper's grin faded but Jorja still did not sense any guilt from him. "No, Jorja, this is not funny. This whole situation is all a bit surreal and as dire as it may be, I can either cry or I can laugh. I do not cry, therefore I laugh."

Jorja gripped the receiver tighter. "You have no cause to cry. You are exactly where you need to be after the things you've done."

Cooper nodded slightly. "Of course, you're right. I've done some terrible things and this is where I belong. Is that why you are here to see me? Do you want to talk about my past wrongs?"

Hesitating slightly, Jorja glanced at Fritz who tried to pretend he was not keenly listening to the conversation. She finally replied, "I'm here because I want to talk to you about my aunt."

Cooper's eyes widened and he sat back slightly as he smiled. "Oh, you want to talk about Gloria? Don't you mean 'your mother?' What do you want to talk about?"

Jorja swallowed hard. She was afraid of what she might learn from Cooper but she knew she had to ask. "I need to know what Gloria might have told you. What she told you about her past and why she was in the mental institution."

"Hmm, well, what she told me was in confidence, don't you think? That's how it works when friends tell each other their secrets."

"Gloria is gone and I can't ask her these questions but I think she might have told you some things I need to know. You have to tell me. It's the right thing to do." Jorja held her breath, waiting for Cooper's response.

Cooper pretended to mull over Jorja's statement, irritating her even further. As she began to wonder what she thought she was doing, she lowered the receiver and slowly stood up from the stool. Cooper finally spoke loudly enough for Jorja to hear him through the glass. "Okay, okay. What is it you want to know?"

Jorja lowered herself back down on the stool and placed the receiver back against her ear. "I want to know what Gloria told you about why she was in the institution."

Cooper tilted his head. "And how do you know she might have told me anything?"

"Because she wrote about you in her journals. You visited her in the hospital and that's when you gave her the necklace."

"Well, if you know all that, you also know the answer to your question, don't you? It's because she killed one of her babies."

"She told you that? She told you what happened?"

"Yeah, she told me. We talked about a lot of things. I knew about the baby, I knew you were her daughter and that's why I knew that pretender was lying when he said he was your long lost brother."

Jorja remained silent, unsure if she should tell Cooper the truth. She finally decided to tell him. "He is my brother. Gloria did not kill him."

Cooper was visibly struck by that statement. He narrowed his eyes at her as he said, "What do you mean she didn't kill him? That's why she was in the hospital. If she didn't kill him, why would she be there?"

"Because everyone thought she killed him. It's a long story and one I don't wish to share unless you answer a question." She could feel her hand slip on the receiver as she began to sweat.

"What question?"

Jorja spit out the words as fast as she could. "I want to know why you gave Gloria the necklace and if she ever told you who the father was?"

Cooper did not say anything. Instead, he stared at Jorja and remained silent. She could not tell what he was thinking but it unnerved her as she waited for his response. Cooper leaned forward and rested his elbows on the counter. He grinned again as he said, "Why do you think I gave her the necklace?"

"I don't know. That's why I'm asking you." Jorja did not want to play his games.

When he realized Jorja was not going to offer a guess, Cooper winked at her. "Why do most men give women jewelry? It's because we liked each other. We were good friends and I wanted to give her a gift."

Jorja took a deep breath before replying, "But were you more than friends? What type of relationship did you have?"

Cooper suddenly sat up, eyes widening as he said, "Oh...you are wondering something else entirely, aren't you? You want to know if there's any chance I'm your *father*, isn't that right?"

Jorja heard a slight cough behind her as Fritz sucked in his breath. Jorja grimaced as she realized he now knew her reason for visiting Cooper.

As she held Cooper's gaze, Jorja said, "Yes, I need to know if you were the one who got Gloria pregnant. Was it you?"

"Would you be disappointed if I was your father?"

Jorja was beginning to feel sick. She needed to know the truth but the possibility that this man was her father was making her feel nothing but nausea. "I would be sad to know my own father tried to kill me."

Cooper gave a quick nod in understanding as he said, "Jorja, you will be more than pleased to hear that I am not your father."

She let out the breath she'd been holding as she asked, "Do you know who is? Did Gloria ever tell you?" Jorja heard her voice crack as she asked the question. She was relieved at his answer but now more anxious than ever to know if he knew the true identity of her father.

She watched him as he hesitated and then was dismayed when Cooper shook his head. "No, she did not tell me."

"Are you sure? Isn't there something she said that would have given you a clue?" Jorja saw Cooper again hesitate and she thought he might be willing to tell her the truth if he knew it.

But again he shook his head. "Nope. She didn't tell me."

Jorja took a deep breath. Shaken, she hung her head slightly as she thought about the questions still left unanswered about her father. Jorja felt a tap on her shoulder and looked up to see Fritz pointing at his wrist, indicating time was almost up. She nodded in understanding and turned to look at Cooper again. He sat immobile and waiting.

"Fine, Cooper, don't tell me. I think you know but for whatever reason you aren't telling me. I hope you have a nice long life in prison."

Jorja quickly hung up the receiver and stood up, almost colliding with Fritz as he turned to open the door. Fritz pushed the door open and Jorja scrambled out of the room, feeling claustrophobic as waves of nausea again began to assault her. She quickly walked down the hall towards the exit where she waited for Fritz to catch up with her.

"Are you okay?" Fritz looked down at her but Jorja looked away from him. She did not want him to see the tears in her eyes.

"I'm fine. Can we just get out of here?"

"Sure thing." Fritz pressed a button, waited for the door to unlock and then pushed the door open for Jorja so she could re-enter the small room with four doors. Fritz again pushed another button, waited for the door to unlock and escorted Jorja back to the front post reception where she retrieved her purse and returned the badge. When they finally opened the last door and walked outside, Jorja could not get outside fast enough. She was glad to be outside in the fresh, clean, open air.

As Jorja followed Fritz back to the patrol car, she ran the conversation with Cooper through her head. She would bet he knew who her father was but she could not understand why he would not tell her.

Whether he finally told her or she discovered the truth on her own, Jorja hoped the day would come when she would finally learn the truth behind Gloria's pregnancy and what caused the father to leave Gloria and his children behind.

CHAPTER 43

Jorja leaned over to grab the coffee cup on the side table next to the overstuffed recliner. The aroma of hazelnut tickled her senses as she carefully took a sip and then leaned back into the chair to enjoy the flavor. Holding the large coffee mug with both hands, she felt comfort in the warmth and she closed her eyes as she listened to the chatter around her.

"Ryan? How have you been feeling? You've only been out of the hospital for a few days now, haven't you?" Ruth asked while sitting in a nearby chair with her baby asleep in her arms.

Ryan was on the nearby couch where he had been resting for the past three days since his release from the hospital. "Oh, I'm doing pretty well. The doctor said the wound is healing nicely now and I'll be back to my old self in a few more weeks. I'm feeling very lucky the bullet did not cause more damage."

Ruth's husband, Pastor Pete, chimed in as he said, "It was more than luck, Ryan, it just wasn't your time. God has plans for you and I have faith you will live your life moving towards what you were meant to do."

Ruth murmured in agreement as she carefully moved the baby to her other shoulder. "Even though you were injured, Ryan, I believe one of the reasons you were brought here was to save Jorja from greater harm. Of that I will always be thankful."

Ruth stopped talking for a moment as she felt herself choke up at the thought of Jorja coming to harm. She finally found her words in order to change the subject. "So I hear you and Nicholas will be living here with Jorja and Taylor?"

"Yes, Jorja has graciously offered Nicholas and I a room here in the house. After the holiday, I'll make arrangements to have our items shipped here from Wyoming."

Jorja opened her eyes to catch Ryan staring at her. She was grateful for the fact that he had saved her life. He was grateful for her willingness to take him in and care for him. With the knowledge that the house would be full of company for Thanksgiving dinner, the two had spent the prior evening discussing what the future held for them. Jorja had asked Ryan and Nicholas to move in with her, not wanting to waste any more time in getting to know either of them. The events of the past few weeks had shown her how short life could be and she wanted to spend as much time with her family as she could.

Ryan tore his gaze from hers at the sound of Taylor's voice as she moved from the kitchen into the living area. "Did Jorja tell you her plans, Ruth?"

"Plans? About what?" Ruth asked with curiosity.

Taylor turned towards Jorja, giving her the floor. Jorja would have let Taylor fill Ruth in on her plans, but it became apparent Taylor was waiting for her to fill in the blanks. Jorja finally replied, "It's no big deal, really. I've just decided that in addition to running the bookstore, I am going to get a private investigator license on the side. There are cases I can get involved with where I can help others like I helped Kat."

Pastor Pete's brows furrowed. "Yeah but, that case almost cost you your life. Are you prepared to put yourself in harm's way like that again?"

Jorja shook her head. "What happened is not typical. I really don't believe I'll be putting myself in danger by helping others like Kat who just need to find someone. I've decided it's something I want to do but I need to get my license so that I can work legitimately and also have more access to some of the records I may need as I conduct investigations." *Not to mention my own investigation into who Ryan's and my father might be*, she thought.

Pastor Pete only frowned. Ruth patted him on his shoulder as she said, "It will be okay, honey. Jorja knows what she is doing." Ruth's words would have been more believable if she had not also given Jorja a look of concern at the same time. Ruth then changed the subject as she said, "So it must be something knowing you have a brother you did not know existed. It is so amazing after all this time that you found each other."

Jorja and Ryan quickly exchanged glances. Helen and Rick had finally relented to telling the truth to those close to them about adopting Jorja after she was born. Not wanting to tell anyone the truth about Gloria's attempt to smother Ryan as a baby nor the truth about Dr. Hanson's kidnapping of Ryan afterwards, they had finally come up with a story with Helen and Rick's agreement. Jorja and Ryan would tell others they were twins but had been separated at birth due to circumstances only Helen's and Gloria's parents would have been able to explain. Why Ryan's existence had been kept secret from Helen when her parents decided to put him up for adoption rather than ask Helen to raise both children would remain a made-up mystery.

Before anything else could be said, they heard Helen's voice from the kitchen. "Dinner's ready everyone. Let's all move to the dining room and eat." Jorja could smell the aroma coming from the kitchen and her appetite suddenly grew as she thought about digging into a nice turkey dinner.

Ruth stood to place the baby in a nearby playpen as she said, "Thanks so much, Jorja, for inviting us to dinner. I sure didn't expect my parents to fly off to Florida this time of year but I can understand my mother's wish to spend the holiday with her sister. Even though they invited us, I just did not want to fly with the baby."

Helen overheard Ruth's comment and she could not help replying before Jorja had a chance. "Ruth, you know you are always welcome. You are like part of the family and always will be." Jorja smiled at Ruth as she nodded in agreement with her mother's statement.

Jorja was grateful her mother and Taylor had agreed to prepare Thanksgiving dinner. She still did not have the energy to take on very much at any given time. She helped when she could but it was never for long because she was quickly shooed away with instructions to 'go rest.'

Nicholas ran from the kitchen into the living area and stopped short just before Jorja's chair. "Aunt Jorja, do you want to sit beside me at the table?" Nicholas held his little hand out for Jorja, wanting to help her out of her chair.

Jorja smiled at Nicholas, enjoying the dimples he displayed to her as he grinned. "I would love to sit next to you, Nicholas." Jorja placed her coffee mug on the nearby table before holding her hand out to Nicholas. She then pretended to let him help her off the chair as he pulled with all his might and made a few grunting noises in the process.

Nicholas continued to hold her hand as they walked through the kitchen into the large formal dining room at the other end of the house.

"Here, Aunt Jorja, you sit here." Nicholas pointed to a chair before he scrambled onto his own chair.

"Here, honey, sit down." Rick said as he pulled the chair out for her.

Jorja looked up at her father and smiled before sitting at the table. "Thanks, Dad."

Once Jorja was seated, Rick moved to the head of the table where the turkey had been placed. Rick grabbed the electric knife and began to cut the turkey, handing slices over as plates were passed his way. As everyone spooned food on to their plates, Jorja looked around the table and felt peace at having those she loved most around her. While the past few months had more than their share of highs and lows, Jorja was grateful for her life, her family and her friends. As Pastor Pete said a prayer for them before they began to eat, Jorja said her own little prayer of thanks as she realized there was no place else she would rather be.

THE END

ABOUT THE AUTHOR

P.J. Howell grew up in a small town in Washington State and has always called the Evergreen State her home. She continues to reside in the Pacific Northwest with her husband and two sons, as well as three spoiled dogs and two cats. While writing has always been a passion, P.J.'s desire to write books transpired after years of working in a law firm as a legal assistant and then as a criminal defense investigator when she opened her own private investigative agency. P.J.'s interests in criminal law, investigations and mysteries, combined with her desire to bring characters and stories to life, inspired her to put the stories on paper and share them with others. *No Mother of Mine* is the first in a series and will introduce you to life in a small town, characters you can relate to and what it takes to unravel the mysteries of life and crime. While P.J. chose to use her nickname for this book series, she also uses her given name in other forums. To learn more about her, be sure to visit her blog at www.paulajhowell.blogspot.com.